THE FATHER OF RAIN

Also by Martin Leslie West

Cretecea & Other Stories of the Badlands
Long Ride Yellow (novel)

THE FATHER OF RAIN

MARTIN LESLIE WEST

A NOVEL

Anvil Press // Vancouver 2023

Copyright © 2023 by Martin West

All rights reserved. No part of this book may be reproduced by any means without the prior written permission of the publisher, with the exception of brief passages in reviews. Any request for photocopying or other reprographic copying of any part of this book must be directed in writing to Access Copyright: The Canadian Copyright Licensing Agency, Sixty-Nine Yonge Street, Suite 1100, Toronto, Ontario, Canada, M5E 1E5.

Library and Archives Canada Cataloguing in Publication

Title: The father of rain : a novel / Martin West.
Names: West, Martin, 1959- author.
Identifiers: Canadiana 2023044993X | ISBN 9781772142105 (softcover)
Subjects: LCGFT: Novels.
Classification: LCC PS8645.E75 F38 2023 | DDC C813/.6—dc23

Cover design: Derek von Essen
Cover photograph: Greg Girard
Interior layout: Vancouver Desktop Publishing Centre (www.self-publish.ca)
Represented in Canada by Publishers Group Canada
Distributed by Raincoast Books

The publisher gratefully acknowledges the financial assistance of the Canada Council for the Arts, the Canada Book Fund, and the Province of British Columbia through the B.C. Arts Council and the Book Publishing Tax Credit.

Anvil Press Publishers Inc.
P.O. Box 3008, Station Terminal
Vancouver, B.C. V6B 3X5
www.anvilpress.com

Printed and bound in Canada.

"For the one who has lost everything, there is nothing but the passion of the absurd."
— Emil Cioran

ONE

MY FATHER DISAPPEARED on June 21, 1975. I was sixteen at the time. The last snapshot I have of his existence is a fur-lined hunting jacket vanishing between the folds of elm branches by our barn. He walked down the bicycle path that was still covered with summer dew, beneath some brambles and out of our lives forever. We never saw him again. I think he might have been wearing gumboots and carrying a Lee Enfield rifle, but I'm not sure. Those kinds of details escape you on a Friday morning when you're sixteen. Your mind is occupied with who will be getting beer for the weekend, what girls will be available and if the Vietnam War really had any relevance to our lives.

All in all, I believe that I could have survived my father's eclipse wounded but intact — many families do — had not my mother done exactly the same thing a year later. People liked to say it was a year to the day after my father vanished that my mother went missing, as if that provided a symmetry that made everything right, but that wasn't so. My mother left our Abbotsford hobby farm on November 11, sixteen months later, and I didn't even see her walk out the door.

In fact, I didn't see her at all that day. The last memory I have of my mother is of laundry hanging over her face the previous afternoon. She was wearing a billowing dress and stood on a square bench with blue slats. The clothes flapped back and forth in the hazy autumn sun and spat soap seeds on the sidewalk. Hanging up clothes was a back-to-the-land thing that country parents did in the seventies to persuade themselves that they hadn't fallen victim to the same kind of excesses that people in the city were folly to — cocaine, pornography and a string of Liberal governments that had changed the way the nation thought. But my mother was as modern as the best of them. She wore a postiche, drove a TR6 and had evening soirees so her guests could listen to the new quadraphonic stereo that had cost her six hundred dollars.

On that Thursday night, when she stayed out the entire dusk, evening and next morning, her party was cancelled. My brother and I were left sitting alone in the furnished basement watching the dryer go round. We listened to Fleetwood Mac and wondered what kind of demon had possessed our home.

The first search, the one for my father, was a massive event. Not quite like a country fair, but a well-intentioned grotesque public gathering. There were a squad of constables, a team of volunteers with yellow traffic vests, sniffer dogs and even a helicopter. It was a panicked and robust carnival that went on all day and all night. The RCMP set up a command post under a white tent where a stern-looking sergeant took reports on the radio and wrote everything down in a log book. The 4-H Club organized free coffee and hot dogs for the seekers, and the police conducted over two hundred neighbourhood inquiries. They even set up a roadblock off the Trans-Canada Highway and arrested a thief from Winnipeg on warrants. When it got dark, the neighbours used flashlights, and our gully was filled with fireflies stumbling between the summer yarrow stalks.

My parents were middle-class people. They were well off. My father was a Scout leader and veteran of the Second World War. My mother did volunteer work, and her children had hair that was only long enough to be considered fashionable. This all scared people, because if it could happen to us, it could happen to anybody. They wanted to help, but mostly they wanted a resolution. Late into the night they worked with infrared goggles that the Science Shop had supplied free of charge, but it didn't matter. My father was never found; there were no clues, there was no body, no resolution, only a layer of mist that hung about our property that pointed to nothing in particular.

There was always mist on our property. We lived in the Fraser Valley, outside of Vancouver, and the summer mornings were never quite crisp. It had something to do with a temperature inversion over the river and the first inklings of urban smog that would turn the air a faint yellow two decades later. By the third day, I hated the stuff. Through the morning mist, I could see the strewn coffee cups and map printouts that meant the tactical effort was over. My father's Massey Ferguson tractor emerged unmoved in the potato field, slick with condensation on the hood, and far down the gully, the RCMP were going through the grimmer, final stages of a search; they were dredging the lily pool with a tool that looked like an oversized rake.

Then the constables left and the detectives showed up. This wasn't good news and my brother was crying. One of them went into the study with my mother, and the other spoke to me in the living room. He was a nice enough man, although like most adults he underestimated the acuity of teenagers and undershot me by about a dozen years.

"Son, have your parents been arguing?" he said.

"No." I didn't like being called son, but he had a job to do.

"When was the last time they argued?"

"They don't."

"They must have once."

"If they did, I can't even remember."

"It's important. You must be able to recall one time."

"Years ago." Whatever I came up with was going to be half fiction.

"Tell me."

"The rock wall at the summer cabin. He wanted it finished, she didn't. There was nothing more."

My parents didn't fight, but that was outside of his consciousness. He wore a fedora, probably one of the last men on the planet to do so, and shuffled the rim between his thick fingers.

"Do you know what cannabis is?" he said.

This was 1975. Did he know what *Playboy* was?

"Weed," I said.

"Yes," he said. "Weed."

"What about it?"

"It's fashionable for people, adults even, to use it at parties, and then they do illogical things."

"My parents don't go to parties and they're not illogical."

"Did they have parties here?"

"My father is an engineer. My mother runs a hobby farm."

He nodded. In his postwar mind, that was all the explanation he needed.

"Was he a happy man?" he said.

Happy? Not a clue. Couldn't answer. He didn't look unhappy. He sang the Coca-Cola commercial, "Lili Marlene" and "Rudolph the Red-Nosed Reindeer" ad nauseam while we shopped at the Hudson's Bay in July, which made me embarrassed and him perhaps crazy, but I had no idea if he was happy or not.

"I guess."

"Mm," he said. "Well, no one has touched his bank accounts."

After my father vanished, I spent months wandering the house, the yard, the neighbourhood and forests looking for clues, under stones, in wasp nests, behind the woodshed that smelled of hickory. Somehow, I would uncover a pocket watch, a wallet, a comb or key chain that all of the police, volunteers, experts and canines had missed, leading me directly to him.

At first these epitaphs would lead me to my living father. They would also have to rationalize his disappearance with a charitable explanation. He was kidnapped by Quebec separatists (he was opposed to bilingualism) and was being held near Agassiz where a group of Francophone herbalists lived. Or, he had fallen and struck his head, which gave him amnesia. Bad amnesia. For the past year he had been living with an eccentric miner up the Fraser Canyon near Boston Bar who had not read a newspaper since Diefenbaker was PM, and I would walk in the ramshackle cabin shouting, "Dad!"

My searches through the country roads became imbued with ritual. Before I went looking for my father I would have to ensure the laces in my shoes were tied with the bows aligned. If I looked in one grain silo, I would have to seek out six more, because victims were always found in the seventh silo. If the trunk of a conifer was unearthed, then I would have to check the trunk of a deciduous tree, then a tamarack because I could not show prejudice to any living creature great or small. And at each intersection I had to check both ditches three times, for God was watching me, in threes, waiting for me to slacken, to be unfaithful, unjust only once so I would suffer the ultimate penalty of never having my father return. The nightmares came by the autumn and they were always the same. My father was locked in a drainage trap below the murky water of those deep country ditches. He had fallen in after pursuing a rare form of bird, a blackpoll warbler or Eurasian wigeon and had survived for five months by breathing through a reed and eating milfoil. But the water was rising and his air running out. I would be checking all the drain traps behind the Vedder Canal, and my father could see me coming through a crack in the cedar slats. He would cry out to me, but I would not answer. I had already turned and was walking away, slovenly in the orange autumn haze. He would sob, then drown in rancid slough because I was too lazy to check the seventh trap.

By October, the rituals had grown into a neurosis. The 303 casings on our back patio had to be organized into piles of prime numbers, the shoes at the end of my bed facing to within one degree of magnetic north and the elastic strap of my underwear wound sadistically around my scrotum. I could not defecate until I had finished the daily search grid, nor think of the blonde who played basketball on the new shiny gym floor. Twenty pine needles had to be ingested whole per day, and each and every skid mark that blackened our hot country road had to be both sniffed and licked to ensure they contained no trace of my missing parent. That sort of thing was possible. The essence of a person could be transferred to a distasteful receptacle. He always wore Aqua Velva and this was a scent that would stick.

An East Indian farmer, one of the first to work the area, rounded the corner of our winding highway to find a confused and crying teenager sprawled on the centre line, caressing a rubber burn. He drove me home. I remember his dark face and worried smile, his antiquated tractor and black seat with holes in the crotch, but I cannot remember his name. I remember my mouth tasting of tar.

The subconscious mind moves light years quicker than the conscious, and as the autumn turned from orange to grey I was eventually looking for clues that would lead me to my dead father — a gold wedding ring glistening out of the damp November soil, his plaid hunting cap crushed under a boulder in a blasting pit and eventually, the macabre: his ankle bone complete with pieces of shrapnel collected in Holland on D-Day plus One Thirty-Three.

By the winter, when the first snow fell on the row of untended corn I wanted merely a hint of his resurrected body, a war medal no one knew about, a great speech he had written or a turbine he had designed. Perhaps even a note from the Russian embassy who had purchased the machinery: "He was a brilliant man, though hardly a Communist."

Whatever attention my father's disappearance had garnered, the disappearance of my mother multiplied it by tenfold. The newspapers came. The television stations. The social workers and the police. Many, many police. Also came a trickle of curious onlookers with large-framed glasses who carried white Bibles and magazines pondering the Apocalypse. One of them asked us if we knew what we were doing for the rest of eternity, and the other asked if we would like to visit Jerusalem or Salt Lake City, Utah. The police shooed such interlopers away because they were less patient and more deliberate than the first time around. They were not looking for a body, they were looking for a motive. The television stations wanted not a tragedy, but a scandal. "And the mist settled over this small hobby farm, where two parents, pillars of the community, have gone missing in identical circumstances less than a year apart, leaving no clues, only questions in the sheets of white mist." No, really, they said that. It was the first and only time I heard my parents referred to as pillars. People love that kind of stuff because anybody can be an expert, and no one will ever likely prove their theories wrong.

Think about it for a moment. Your parents go missing. What do your neighbours say? Over the sink with carrot sheaths, listening to AM radio cursing free love. They must say something. One vagrancy can be attributed to an act of God — a drowning, a psychotic lapse, an errant locomotive — but for two, for two there must be a more sinister explanation that God cannot be held liable for. The most popular theory circulating when I was seventeen was that my parents were involved in an organized crime ring and were taken out systematically by the Mafia. That was the most tantalizing, I think, simply because it was the most ridiculous. Terrorists and drug cartels weren't on the radar screen yet, but the Mafia were still a tangible shadowy force that could explain a lot of disappearances.

The second was that they were involved in a suicide pact, hence the anniversary detail even if it wasn't accurate. The third was that my father never really died but had an affair with the postal clerk and came back to kill my mother, and this logic naturally produced the inverse theory that my mother had an affair, killed my father, then ran off to Acapulco after a safe time had passed.

There were also aliens, time travel and underground religious cults. These were the most cruel because they implied that my parents might someday stroll back alive, hand in hand, through the garden gate. "Why is everybody looking at us so strange and where the hell is the cat?"

The police, however, did not accept the extraterrestrial theories and would not concede that there was no trace. This apparently was a law of evidence. Every impacted surface leaves a scuff, every scuff a scow. The search lasted only four hours, then the detectives were inside the house. First, they went through my mother's drawers and cupboards, then through all her clothes. Her underwear, her nylons, her boots, they seemed especially interested in her boots. The high Italian kind that Sophia Loren might wear except they had spurs on the heels. They took an inventory of the books she read, the kind of tampons she used, her friends, her notes, her letters, her bills, and when they ripped the spine off her Gideon's Bible, I objected. But I was seventeen at the time, confused and not especially knowledgeable in the law, so the detective told me to mind my own business and shut the door to my mother's bedroom while they finished their disinterment.

Then they went into my bedroom and pulled up the rug. They slit my mattress and thought the cork grease for my alto saxophone was hash oil but strangely missed the joint that had been rolled up beneath the windowsill.

I didn't realize it then, but I was a suspect too, along with everyone else in the valley. There were no innocents. Round two had come back to bite them in the ass, so collateral damage was a sport, not a consequence. They made my brother cry again and convinced me that this was the work of evil, desperate men, and then they started the interview. These were pre-Charter days, and I don't know if locking a young person in an interview room for five hours without counsel was legal or common practice then, but it happened to me.

"Who was your mother seeing?" He had the sad eyes of one who wanted to be a dentist but ended up a detective and wore a herringbone jacket from the 1960s.

"No one," I said. The inside of the interview room was white, and I wanted to go home.

"Did she ever go out for the evening and leave the two of you?"

"Never."

"Did she drink?"

"She'd have a glass of wine when my grandmother came over but that was all."

"Just one?"

"Ask her."

"What's this?" He held up a chrome horseshoe with a hook on one end and diamonds embedded in the fullering.

"It's a horseshoe."

"Was she interested in the occult?"

"The what?"

"How about" — he paused — "women. Did she have any female friends?"

"Engineers' wives. Bowling. 4-H friends."

"No, I mean intimate friends."

"I don't know what you mean."

"Sure you do."

"Why don't you ask my dad, if you're able to at least find him?" and this angered the policeman greatly.

"Tell me," he said. "What type of parents do you think would leave their children? I mean, get up and walk out. Abandon them. What kind of people would do that? Tell me what you're thinking about your mom and dad right now."

I told him. I stood up and hit him as hard as I could in the face. Or tried to, at least. He was a cop, and this was his business, so within a second there were five of them in the room, and I was reduced to eating skid marks again. Nothing more came of it. Perhaps it was the norm. I never understood the direction nor intention of the questions that day. What I do know for sure is that after a year of searching, the police were zero for two, and I was alone.

When my mother went missing, my tactics shifted as well. I didn't waste any time looking for dead relics in the wasted earth. The thought of them sickened me. Worse than the Shroud of Turin or pieces of the Cross, they were lies, like the Ogopogo or the Easter Bunny. They were for stupid children, dumber than dogs and easier to dislike too. There are times in your life when you realize you understand a word, the deepness of the word that smells of marrow, and when my mother went missing, I understood the word "relic." It had been invented for me.

Instead, I started taking the evidence directly off people. Stealing them actually: *die Diebstahl, sans autorité, corripio non-Charter*. The butcher, the grocer, the pharmacist, the neighbours, anyone was fair game. These people had all basically said the same thing about my mother, and I didn't believe a word. They'd seen her the week before, the Tuesday previous, the usual afternoon date for bowling. She had been picking up a steak, aspirins, a letter, and she seemed fine. As fine as a woman could be whose husband of twenty years had gone missing the previous summer, but the facts were false. Made up. Bavardage. They were hiding something. A deep scar-ridden gristle of truth that they were unwilling to share. So, pay they would, and with interest.

Interest for emotion's sake is a cruel thing. You get overtly particular and particularly underpaid. The item I stole had to be personal and it had to hurt. From the potato bagger, I swiped a handkerchief with a heart sewn in the liner, to ensure sentimental injury. From the school bus driver, the button that had come off her tight jeans, exacting public humiliation, and from the kindergarten teacher, a gold-plated cigarette lighter that she had left on the jungle gym while stealing a lunchtime smoke, to induce shame.

For every object found I fabricated two narratives about my parents. For example, the ballet shoes liberated from the Letterman's place were actually not his, but a gift from my father to my mother that had been misplaced by a courier service. She had always been fond of *Swan Lake* and fantasized about living in Paris. In September she would lean against the plum trees with her automatic auger and perform pirouettes instead of drilling holes and, I'm sure, dream of things that could not be.

At the Dennison's country estate, I snuck into the lady's bedroom while she dozed (they slept separately) and absconded with a tube of lipstick. Half-naked and mostly unconscious, she sprawled on her oak frame bed with the window open, night gown askew and a tube of Valium spiralled on the dresser. There had been a song on the radio about housewives and tranquilizers, so I formulated the notion that my mother had lent Mrs. Dennison the makeup to improve her self-image and keep her from overdosing. Well, I was wrong. Perhaps I should have talked to her, or at least tried to wake her up, but that wasn't in my mandate then and was also a long time ago.

The loot was stored in my mother's study where everything remained still and untouched despite the chaos that surrounded our lives. She had become a neat freak in that sallow year, and the house was always in immaculate condition, or at least had been until the police got to it. An ugly insect bumped against the double pane of glass above her desk. Long as a string bean and wicked, the pinchers left a poisonous juice on the sill, so I crushed it with my mother's fat dictionary and watched the broken exoskeleton bake in the sun.

When, finally, the bank accounts were examined, the fingerprints taken and the polygraphs finished (I did three), my grandparents came to live with us. They were nice if not distant people. They had white hair. My grandfather served at Vimy Ridge and my grandmother bred parakeets. As far as I was concerned, they were doing their duty but really had no desire to solve the mystery that pervaded my life.

"Your mother was a handful," my grandmother said once. She sat on the front porch, nodding and gazing out across the field of corn stubble that had been dormant for two seasons.

"When?" I said.

"When she was growing up."

"What did she do?"

"You name it."

The day before, while I was storing appropriated items in my mother's drawer, I had come across a ball of leather string. Tightly wound and hidden under blue garters, this was the smoking gun. Who uses leather string and for what? Sewing canvas tents, fixing gash wounds on Yorkshire hogs or perhaps repairing sails on a schooner? But my parents didn't own a boat. We had no pigs. My mother didn't wear nylons. I unravelled the ball and in the centre was a gold needle with a heart-shaped head. Perhaps it could have served an engineering purpose, a tuning fork for concrete, a taxidermy device for birds, but my mind was drifting towards the obscure. It's only natural. All seventeen-year-olds cherish the perverse.

"What's this for?" I said to my grandmother.

"I have no idea," she said. She was peeling potatoes.

"I think it serves a deviant purpose."

"Where did you learn that word?"

"I read it in one of my mother's books."

"You've got to stop doing this," she said.

"I can't," I said.

And would not. Once you start seeing a pattern, the proof shows up everywhere. Like searching for the final digit of pi or the root cause of Rome's fall, the clues roll in undeniably and like a tsunami. In a stack of telephone bills dating back to 1967 lay a Polaroid of my mother. The sun had washed it yellow and moisture bubbled the film, but there was no doubt here, she was naked. Nude, stripped and in the buff. Tanned without bikini lines, her skin was an unbroken carmine sea of guile. On a strange couch, in a strange room, she lounged exposed save a pair of black stilettos. She smoked from a silver cigarette holder like Ava Gardner might use and gazed at an object of desire outside the camera's view.

The more I stared at the picture the fuzzier it got. This couldn't be my mother. The cheeks were too high, her waist too small and the pout on her face sent lemon juice down my jowls. After an hour of staring into the blistering photo, the face looked like that of a monkey, then a crater on the moon and then nothing at all.

But I kept the Polaroid. Like I kept the needle and also a copy of *Tropic of Capricorn,* covered with grease, found in the trunk of my father's 1971 Gran Torino station wagon. Parents weren't supposed to read Henry Miller. They just weren't. That was the regimen of rebellious university students, of which I was about to become a member, and this was not what you wanted to unearth beneath the spare tire of your family shuttle. Found also was a Canadian Armed Forces bottle of morphine dated from 1945 and a Miles Davis LP. My father had once referred to jazz musicians as a bunch of people who were "fond of Fidel Castro and couldn't tune their instruments." The inconsistencies were starting to add up.

The photo bothered me the most. Who was she waiting for? What were they going to do? They obviously hadn't done it yet. Then worse, who was she with? Was it my father on the other end of the lens, his fingers twitching with lust or bored silly while he contemplated the number of kilowatt-hours coming out of a sluice gate? Or perhaps the detectives had been right. Maybe my mother was sneaking out at night to meet longshoremen on the Vancouver docks or Asian landlords in Tangzhuang suits beneath the opium dens of East Cordova Street. Yen pox, yellowed teeth, sullen eyes and deep undersea fishlike sex, my mother sliding into a wreckage of exploitive passion to satisfy her hunger for the poppy. No, this wasn't her. She grew up on farm and was a secretary for a trucking firm when she met my father. She sang opera as a hobby and was particularly fond of Wagner but disliked his politics. They probably both voted Conservative, but as far as I was concerned everybody over thirty voted Conservative and besides, Pierre Trudeau was my hero.

My parents did entertain two distinct sets of friends, and that didn't sit right. My brother wasn't old enough to make the distinction, but I could. The first were engineers and their wives and these were dull affairs. The men played charades, talked turbines, and the women congregated in the kitchen and gossiped about vacations. Maui was popular. The other set was a little more difficult to get a handle on. They didn't come to the house. They had only first names. My parents stayed out late with them. My mother dressed oddly. With black mascara and a shawl that drooped down to her ankles, covering her tanned summer legs. It's possible I can recall the term "key party" once, but after you have been interviewed by two dozen social workers, an army of detectives and a flood of private journalists it's hard to tell what was real from what was suggested.

During the course of the investigation, I learned there were three basic kinds of missing persons, four varieties of B&E artists and a single solitude of sexual perversion. As far as MIAs went, there were those want to be saved, the kind that do not know they are lost and the subculture who wish to remain hidden. Hikers and their ilk form the first group. They will gravitate towards likely points of discovery and recognition. Mountain tops, timber clearings, bus depots or political parties that cling to the middle path. And they will leave signs. SOS patterns, engravings, bark scratches and smoke signals. The second group constitutes crazy or unconscious people, children and overdue honeymooners. Also ranked here are people undergoing a psychological metamorphosis. This lot leaves traces, but they are tangential and inadvertent. A bank statement, a lost shoe. The last unlucky collective are the underclass. Prostitutes, criminals evading debts or persons hiding secrets. Their clues are usually non-existent, but when they do surface, they are often ambiguous, sticky, even misleading or malicious.

"Which kind are your parents?" the detective said to me as he put his foot up on our front step and flicked a gold lighter between his fingers. The flint wouldn't catch on account of the mist. "I wonder which group you think your parents fall into now?"

Certain words came to fascinate me while I assembled the evidence of their resuscitation. Bereft, besieged, obsessed. Exhumed, engaged, autoerotic. Suppose it was another woman focusing the camera and the detective was right. I wasn't quite sure how women would do it or why, but all of our neighbours became complicit and high school teachers formed favourite profiles. I assembled a large collection of black and white photographs by Irving Claw that could be bought down on Granville Street for ten dollars each, no provincial sales tax included, to try and work the geometry out, with Miss Burke, Mrs. Shorpe and Ms. Downs playing lead roles. All right, I broke into their houses as well. I found secrets. We all have secrets, and those trying to seduce my parents would have plenty.

In Miss Burke's house I stood in the den by her grandfather clock that she insisted was given to her great-uncle by Sir Charles Tupper, but with the aluminum sealing was obviously not. Miss Burke would lock her cats up at night without water. Early into the morning she lounged against her rusting kitchen sink drinking Okanagan

Chardonnay with the glass sunk deep into her chin, fabricating yarns about how the instrument came into her care. Perhaps taken on the railway during the Métis Rebellion. Possibly rescued from the Fraser River at Fort Langley by a Messianic cult. Sent by Empire Loyalists to her mother, who remained a staunch Acadian. Inevitably, the narratives concluded with Sir John A. becoming Miss Burke's lover. The cats mewed on. So intense was her fascination that she never noticed my presence. I could come and go, eat cheese from her fridge or slip into her lingerie chest without her knowing. The blue garters, the only agents of association with my mother, were stacked unused and unnoticed beside tins of protein-supplemented cat chow.

Mr. Shorpe and his wife argued incessantly. About his salary, the state of the lawn furniture, her indifference towards her students (me being one of them). I played checkers on a board they no longer used and watched television in their den while they slept. Often Mr. Shorpe would retire to the toilet to read a copy of *Venus in Furs* while his wife cooked broccoli until it dissolved into a tasteless stew. For hours I sat silently in their loft while she sobbed over the vegetables and let the steam roll over her blue chiffon dress.

My talent for clandestine entry grew as time passed. The more entwined you become in an obsession, the less others notice you as a person. Like a washing machine, blue lichen, or a parliamentary backbencher, you come with the scenery. Ms. Downs kept a Lee Enfield rifle mounted above her fireplace, so I was convinced this was a prima facie clue.

"Sit, sit," she would say to no one in particular and talked often to a dog that had died years ago. She held her right hand in an OK sign as she consumed the details of the sterile room, the crystal hutch, the Lemon Pledge scent, the Ming vase with nude courtesans etched into the rim.

Each day at noon, she gazed out the window and pulled a package of brown cigarettes, Virginia Slims, from her vest pocket and lit up. I knew

Virginia Slims because the advertisements for them were in all the magazines, and they meant smoke, but they also meant other things. The green exhaust dampened the air between us. She spoke at length to the radio and to a cactus that floundered in ill health on her hutch.

On Sunday she did her laundry, so I waited in position behind her furnace duct for the right moment to get at the Enfield. But as I did, the heavy step of boots thumped along her porch. With them came the jangle of keys and the crinkle of a leather belt. In a flash of khaki, a constable with strawberry blonde hair passed between a potted elephant plant and chrome wind chime. The woman opened the door and greeted the police as if they were old friends.

"Come on out," the constable said, and stared in my no-longer-clandestine direction.

"Don't be too hard on him," Ms. Downs said.

We walked out to her squad car with the constable slapping the keys against her palm. "You've got to stop doing this," she said. "There's a limit to how much people will overlook."

We drove towards our farm in silence. Occasionally, the radio cackled about vehicle rollovers or flash floods along the Fraser River. The places I had been with my father — the Dolly Varden hatchery, the bicycle repair shop, the bird sanctuary — flashed by in the window as if they no longer mattered.

"I've got an exhibit for you," she said. She stared down at a plastic bag on the passenger seat. A wrinkle of impatience moved across her lips as if she had been sent to perform an ignoble act in a Shakespearean tragedy. Inside were my mother's high black boots. "We won't be needing them anymore."

"What did you need them for in the first place?"

"Fingerprints," she said. "Drug residue, pawn cards."

"Why even look for that kind of stuff?"

"There's a new kind of test the lab can do that can identify humans by their genes."

"And did they?"

"They didn't."

"Was the same thing true with the books and diaries?"

"We checked hundreds of phone numbers and addresses," she said. "Plane tickets, hotel reservations, credit cards, passport applications, visas and photographs. It was the most exhaustive investigation this detachment has ever undertaken."

"What became of it all?"

Her back stiffened and she adjusted the mirror. She searched my face over and over again, looking for a thread she apparently could not find. "Not much," she said. "And I have to tell you now, unless something new comes up, the investigation is considered inactive."

"Like finished?"

"Inactive is a better word. The investigation will never be considered finished until we have conclusive proof of where your parents are."

"What do you think the chances of that are?"

"I'll be honest with you," she said. "You're an adult now. At this point there is little."

"I don't want a point. I want an answer."

"I don't have one."

"You must have a theory."

"I don't."

"Well," I said. "I have my own. I'm gathering evidence."

"Your neighbours don't see it that way," she said and thought for a moment, maybe of a boyfriend or her annual leave or the green salal on the roadside, then said, "Digging too deep in any one place isn't going to bring you closer to the truth, and in the long run it's just going to bring around a lot of trouble."

The constable slowed the car down outside of our driveway. The gravel crunched under the weight of the tires. She put the car in park and then turned around and leaned over the seat. I remember the freckles around her cheeks and her thin eyebrows that were beautiful even without plucking.

"There's something I have to tell you," I said.

"Go ahead."

"I believe that my mother was a deviant."

"A what?"

"You know. She had desires."

"Most people do. Why are you onto this?"

"I found photos."

She nodded. She rolled one hand over the other and stared out across the first sheets of mist that were forming in the cottonwood groves by the creek.

"And I believe my father used morphine. They were probably in contact with Castro too. I've got the notes. If you want I'll give them to you."

She took out her notebook and tapped it on the steering wheel. Far down the valley potted geese fell from the sky. Was it an Enfield, a fallow field, a fixation?

"You keep them," she said.

"You don't think they're relevant to the investigation?"

"I think your parents left you a lot, and you should hold on to what you can."

"They left me," was all I said.

"I have to get you inside," she said. She undid her seatbelt. Nobody wore seatbelts then and I mistrusted anyone who did. "Your grandparents have been looking all over for you."

"Why?" I said.

"They think you've gone missing."

And then she walked me up to my house, turned the brass knob to my home and let in the known and the unknown, the living and the dead.

TWO

THE WEEKEND BEFORE I left my home, my grandparents hired a spiritualist. Of course, they didn't call her that. They had another name, a dark ochre noun that sounded Teutonic and of roots that might grow beneath a podzolic forest. The name they used was a euphemism. There had been a lot of those buzzing around our house for that last month or so. Nothing spoken could be taken at face value, so a great tension hung about the farm, like a wasp diving too close to the back of your head.

Moving to the city wasn't the issue. I wanted to go to the city. Movies, Camaros, college girls and cheap pot. The rumour was twelve dollars a lid and available at most public libraries. Also, pornography. I had become especially interested in Betty Page since I had found a stack of photographs in my mother's cupboard, and I knew there would be plenty of porn shops in downtown Vancouver.

Leaving was the only choice. Although this was the place I grew up in, went to school at, drank beer beside, smoked weed beneath and had my first sexual encounter within the resin of a seeping birch tree, there were too many memories and all of them morbid. A dead robin rotting in hay under the soffit. A jar full of crickets found in the blender hung over a ceiling hook on Saturday morning. Unopened funeral cards. All the talismen pointed in the same direction. Get out. My parents were gone and would never return, and their ghosts were everywhere. From beneath the trellis came the sound of my father clipping ivy vines with a pair of hand shears. In my mother's bedroom hung the scent of perfume that had lingered for over a year. Heavy and sweet, the odour clung to the linen like prunes no matter how many times my grandmother washed the sheets.

The neighbourhood was sullen with memory as well. Voices on the radio sounded like our ritual call for dinner. Farmhands in the rain looked as if they wore my father's hunting cap. Neighbours carrying rakes started to look like they were carrying Lee Enfield rifles. My grandmother often referred to the "vortex" and was afraid I would fall non-returnably into whatever that was. My grandparents spoke in hushed tones by the hayloft of the existential and the suppositional or the relative good versus the absolute good, then drew odd diagrams on yellow sheets of paper that stacked up by the radio. Finally, on the Sunday afternoon before the first moving truck came, my grandfather wandered into the kitchen with his hands stuffed in his coverall pockets. He was the kind of man that couldn't do any work without getting dirty, and sawdust chips always embedded in his hair. My grandmother was playing solitaire, and they were exchanging glances that meant a conversation they had started earlier had yet to be finished.

"Well?" he said.

"I have doubts," she said.

"There will always be doubts."

"We have a standard of stewardship to keep in mind."

"Exactly."

She placed the cards down on the table with a thin slapping sound, did up her collar button and gazed at the basement stairwell as if a wet possum might rise from the cellar at any moment. He nodded and went to the liquor cupboard. Caution was advised. His hand shopped around the dusty bottles and when it came to rest on a twenty-sixer of Johnnie Walker Black, he paused, thinking a long way back, perhaps back into his childhood.

"Scotch?" he said.

"Me?"

"Don't see anyone else here."

"How about Stan?"

"Stan is too young," my grandmother said.

"What's up?" Something had to be up. When was the last time your grandparents offered you Black Label without mix?

"We are worried about you," she said.

Who hadn't been? Social workers, doctors, relatives, psychologists, there weren't many exceptions. For the past year and a half, I had acquired the ability to be in the wrong place at the wrong time, and when anyone said they were worried it usually meant I had screwed up again. Gone where I should not have, smoked something I was not supposed to, taken liberties that were unlawful. The worry list encompassed about a dozen summary incidents and at least three indictable offences. I was particularly nervous about my nocturnal efforts that were leaving an incriminating pile of soggy socks clogging our washing machine. The fungal odour was becoming unbearable.

"We are especially concerned about the time you spend poking about," she said.

"Don't all seventeen-year-olds poke about?"

"Not in the same way you do."

"What way?"

"In a lonely, desperate way."

"This is a lonely, desperate situation," I said.

"Not anymore." She reached across the table and wrapped her paper-thin hands around my wrist. "You must accept that they are gone."

"How do you know they are gone for sure?"

She sat up, considered the point of logic and Granddad jumped in. "Don't you think it's time you went out and met people of your own age? Have friends. In a few days we'll be in a new neighbourhood, and you'll have to meet new people then."

"Then there's not any point in starting now, is there?"

"Look at it as a warm-up run," he said. "When we get to Vancouver, you're going to be swarmed by people. Girls. City girls. Dates. Action. You know, girlfriends. Or boyfriends if you're so in—"

"Shh," my grandmother said.

"I don't have time for that," I said.

"You are seventeen. That is what your time is for."

"Is that what you did when you were seventeen?"

"I plowed a field and was sorry for that." My grandfather stuck his finger into the Scotch.

"Exactly."

"Cirrus," she said. "You must listen to us now. That season is over. The hive is husked. You must move on."

"What's a husked?"

"It's just a saying." She brushed a mayfly off her arm with two fingers.

My grandfather drank his Scotch and stared at his pale reflection in the hutch. He had tawny hair and sunken jowls. He didn't pour me anything as promised. Instead, he simply rubbed his hands together, admitting the half-truth of Versailles or the October Crisis or maybe an affair he wasn't going to come clean about.

"Tenacity is one of your greatest strengths," he said. "That's why we'd like you to meet with someone today."

I had already met with a hundred people who came, pontificated and left without any solutions. A collection of professional cards was building up in my drawer. Everybody was getting them in the seventies. Plumbers, vacuum salesmen, priests, drug dealers. I kept one that a good-looking journalist from the CBC had tucked in my vest pocket with her manicured fingernails in case something "came up." Late at night I ran my tongue over the sharp edge and imagined this formed the onset of an erotic relationship.

"Not another shrink," I said.

"No. No psychiatrists. No social workers. No police or journalists. That's done too. There was too much of that and we're sorry."

"What's his name?"

"Her name is Gwendolyn. Gwendolyn Sharpe."

"Don't know her."

"She's a friend of ours."

"What kind of friend?"

"An old friend."

"So, she's old."

"Younger than us."

"Where do you know her from, then?"

My grandparents exchanged a complicated glance. They hadn't developed a cover story for that angle.

"India?" they suggested.

"What does she do?"

"She is a transcriber of sorts," Granddad said.

"A trans-what?"

"She can give you perspective on things."

"Can she find my mother and father?"

He curled his fingers around the Scotch and swallowed another mouthful. He liked the stuff. You could see it in his eyes, the kind of burn that people get when a deed is both pleasurable and nettled; my God it burns, but it tastes so damn good.

"No," he said.

"Then what is the point?"

"The point is she will provide a reference for your place in this world. A world in which your mother and father are still a part of.

But don't get the wrong idea. She's not searching for a body. She simply might make you feel better."

A hooker? I was hoping for a hooker. I didn't think my grandparents were that liberated but I would take what I could get. Hopefully a kinky hooker with a black leather catsuit. Like Emma Peel in *The Avengers*. This was really the least they could do.

"When is she coming over?"

The doorbell rang.

"Nowish?" he said.

My grandmother shrugged. The dice were cast.

I can't remember who answered the door. I don't think anybody did. I think Gwendolyn Sharpe came into the room with a bluster of white teeth and a stream of dried birch leaves that followed her around like servants. She was the generation between my parents and grandparents and wore yellow slacks and a white frilled blouse that said "swinger" in neon bold. Her hair was done up tower tight and her narrow face was both beautiful and crustacean. Basically, you knew she was going to talk too much.

Gwendolyn wandered between the furniture twirling a pair of glasses on a pearl strap, humming show tunes ("Don't Rain on My Parade" and "Wouldn't It Be Loverly"; I mean, good God). All this while she studied each object as if it were a museum piece. The grizzly bear my father had carved out of Brazilian ironwood, the watercolour of flowers my mother had published in Good Housekeeping. The Klimt by the potted manzanita tree especially kept her attention.

"You must be Cirrus." She held out her hand.

When you're brought up in a certain way, you do certain things. When an adult offers you their hand, you shake in a particular fashion. Firm, but not buddy-buddy and by no means sexual. But when Gwendolyn touched me that day, the old order fell away. Instead of the usual distant single shake, I got hot pulsing skin around my wrist, a finger in my palm searching for an unknown crevasse, waiting for an unseen want, and then her hand running up my sleeve to tighten my elbow. She stared at me for an uncomfortably long time, a dreadfully long time, then a French Resistance kiss, and her perfume was methane garrulous. Three flies bumped the kitchen window in their frenzy of autumn death and on the television, Spitfires fended off the invading Hun.

She bit her bifocals. "Yes, I can see the resemblance."

My grandparents stood.

"Scotch?" Granddad said.

"Double," Gwendolyn said.

"Ice?"

"Darling."

Gwendolyn's embrace had left a splinter of carmine lipstick on the shoulder of my bomber jacket. In an organ that was not yet discovered, an insect passion rose, breaking through the muskeg swamp and hatching from its larval state.

"That's a nice jacket," she said. "Sort of the Gregory Peck *Twelve O'Clock High* look."

"Who?"

"I'm dating myself."

She held out her palm and Granddad slipped the tumbler of Scotch into place. They clinked glasses, the ice rattled, so they had done this all before.

"Do you need time?" he asked.

"If you don't mind."

"We can transplant nasturtiums."

My grandparents evaporated. The room was still. My breath smelled. I had eaten three raw onions out of my parents' garden searching for yet another subterranean clue.

"If you don't mind me asking," I said.

"Who exactly am I?"

"Yes."

"I am a friend of your grandparents."

"Old friend? New friend? Dead friend?"

"I've known them for thirty years," she said. "We first met in Paris."

"I thought it was India."

"Paris briefly, darling, Paris. Before the war. The Left Bank. Your granddad's memory falters after a Scotch or two. True enough, the City of Light was where we first met, but Bombay was where we got to know each other. India in 1957 was chaotic, so Westerners stayed tight. My parents were in the diplomatic corps and your grandparents were merchants. The match was symbiotic."

"What's symbiotic?"

"We looked after each other. In the evening we'd pass the time in clubs and stay up late listening to jazz that filtered down through the colonial tube. English rule, a curse and a carpet. I had Charlie Parker records and your grandparents had gin. We stayed up all night drinking Bombay and a tincture of paregoric. Of course, you wouldn't know what that was. I was a lot younger then. We all were."

"What is it exactly you want to do here?"

"I want to understand what is happening."

"How about what has already happened?"

The issue was tangential for her. "Depends on how we get on."

"Do you do this for a living?"

"I collect antiques for a living. This is not a business relationship between us. I also want to point out that I'm not doing this because I feel sorry for you. I don't believe in self-pity. You don't want me to pity you, do you?"

"Uh, no," I said.

"Good, because I'm not a nursemaid. You're too old for that. Given what's happened, I only want to make sure you are pointed in the right direction."

"What are your, like, credentials?"

Gwendolyn had seen this coming. She extracted a package of Virginia Slims from her purse and then drew one of the brown tubes from the tin foil in a ritualistic way. Slims were popular amongst older women then. Sort of halfway between smoking cigarettes in public and saying "screw you" out loud.

"The decline of deference is an article I applaud in young people. If young people had asked 'What are your credentials' during the thirties or forties, we wouldn't have fought such a horrible war. If they'd asked the same questions during the fifties, we wouldn't all be so repressed today. But since you asked, I finished my undergraduate degree in physics from the University of Bombay and my graduate degree in anthropology from Guelph. That is in Ontario. Do you understand the difference between mythos and logos?"

"Sure," I said. Naturally. Who didn't?

Gwendolyn had a strange smell about her. Like dust, so your nose drifted closer to get a better whiff. Soon my head drifted towards her cleavage, where two marble globes plunged not so subtly beneath her blouse. Placing her exact age was impossible.

"Then I won't bore you by saying I work primarily with myth."

"You're not a medium, are you?"

She sipped the Scotch, then cleaned the rim with a Kleenex. "I'm not going to mediate anything between you and a composite."

"What the hell is a composite?"

"It's an idea of a person that is not a living person."

"Sounds like a medium to me."

"Would you like to give me a tour?" she said.

A tiny red flake of lipstick still clung to my jaw from where she had kissed me. We went into my mother's bathroom. She went through my mother's eyeliner and rouge. A bottle of muriatic acid kept in a crystal vase caught her eye.

"What's this for?" she said.

"It's girl stuff."

"There's lettering on the side."

"It's Arabic."

She turned the bottle over in her hand. "Etruscan, actually."

She put the bottle back, then checked her face in the mirror. My parents had a new kind of light with a concave glass that made faces huge. My mother loved it, my father hated it. What was the point in searching for microscopically imperfect pimples? he'd say. Gwendolyn's face had no imperfections, her flesh copper smooth with a thin film of oil on top.

"She used that mirror before they went out," I said.

"Where did they go?"

"Never asked."

"Not curious?"

"I stayed home and smoked weed."

"For sexual enhancement?" She closed the medicine cabinet and then ran her finger along the frame of the door as if she were looking for dust.

The two of us stood in the hallway and the oak clock ticked over every other second on the mantle.

"Take me to their room," she said.

We went down the hall to a door that had stayed locked for a long while. Granddad had put a bolt on the outside to keep me from obsessing. Obsessing is the polite term. The institutional phrase is manic psychosis in its acute form, leading to trances, muscular psychosis and even phagocytosis. That is like a grotesque case of shingles. Very nineteenth century. Bits of flesh fall from the body as in the moulting process. The victim rocks back and forth for hours, clutching the object of desire. Transfixed and immobilized, he sheds large patches of skin at an alarming rate that eventually changes the muscle composition of his body. The epidural layer becomes hard and crusted, like the back of a beetle, and the joints rigid, capable of withstanding hundreds of pounds of stress. After extracting me from a bedpost during a fit, a fireman once commented I had the strength of a 175-pound red ant. The next day the locks went up on the door.

Gwendolyn sat on the baroque chair that had been sent in from Italy for my mother's thirtieth birthday. She lit up another Slim. Those were the days when nobody asked if they could smoke. Everybody did it without asking. Asking was parochial.

"Sit," she said.

I sat on the edge of the bed and the air became sticky. Her eyes were brilliant green, and the irises penetrated each flinch my body made. As she smoked, her jaw moved back and forth, grinding out a plan of which I was now a part.

"Did you ever hear your parents at night?" she said.

"Like, screwing?" An onion seed was stuck under my tongue.

"If you like."

"What kind of question is that?"

"It's just a question."

"Well, stop it."

"Why?" She let the smoke seep out between her teeth.

"It makes me creepy."

She pointed her cigarette at the chandelier. The glass had belonged to a great-uncle and was shipped over from South Africa during the Boer War. Their side lost. "Have you ever wondered why?"

"Because it's normal. This was a normal family, and they were normal people."

"What do you mean, normal?" she said.

"They had jobs. They weren't criminals. We ate dinner together."

She got up off the chair and walked to the window. The translucent drapes moved against the glass, and across the driveway a truck carrying fennel seeds left its spray on the road.

"So, they were like other parents? Like the Dennisons or the Lettermans?"

"Mom and Dad were different than them."

"In what way?"

Briar patch, viscous oil and white teeth gnashing. Cocoons popping while I walked down the hall towards my parent's room at midnight listening to those noises, pushing open the door to a twister of yellow and black husks swirling above their bed. Gwendolyn was three times my age. My peers would have referred to her as a cougar plus, and right about this time I was becoming acutely aware my collar was damp and a thicket of thorns grew between my legs, so the words sprouted forth. "There were swarming noises at night."

"And?"

"And I had to go to the doctor."

"What did he say?"

"He gave me Ativan."

"Did it help?"

"They made the noises swarm in slow motion."

Gwendolyn sat down on the bed beside me. The muscle in my right cheek flinched, then flinched again and wouldn't stop. Her knee touched mine. Her teeth were perfectly rectangular. She reached down to my mother's Sophia Loren boots.

"There are two basic human emotions that are good," she said. "Melancholy and desire. Don't exorcise either of them. There is nothing wrong with you. You are not sick. You do not need to be psychoanalyzed. You do not need to be medicated or institutionalized. That is not what the situation requires."

"What does it require?"

Gwendolyn blew a column of green smoke across my face then turned the amethyst on her finger. "When your father disappeared, where was the last place you saw him?"

"The trellis, by his work shed."

The shed was a converted garage, but there was no road fit for a car, just a lean tractor path that cut a swath through tall grass. The cedar shakes were going green with algae, and the tar shingles on the roof were covered with seagull dirt. Inside, the floor was layered with spiral chips of fir, mahogany and pine from my father's lathe, and the walls were packed with shelves of screws, jars and tools. For a man who was fastidious, the workspace was a rat's nest. The shed had windows, but the inside was dark, never noon and always the in-between.

Here was the archaic. Stone grinders, chisels, hand-held magnifying glasses and a collection of sextants that stopped us all from getting permanently expunged from the corporal world. Here also were balls of twine, pin-stabbed insects stuck into bottles, manuals on water irrigation, arc welding and taxidermy for temperate climates. Yes, there was a photograph of Miss September 1974 stuck to the wall with a thumbtack, but also a photo of the first *Canadian Geographic* Issue, along with a full nude of Burt Reynolds autographed on the bottom in black felt: To Marjorie, from Bert. Probably a charity event. The air smelled of peanuts.

Gwendolyn spent a long time with the door handle. Then she moved to the shelves and reviewed a bottle of wheat husks, a Cretaceous shark tooth and a baseball-sized quartzite chip from Prince George that had been arranged in order of lustre from left to right. Her touch was non-effusive, the way in a foreign market you might handle silk that you were not interested in buying.

"Was suicide an option?"

She asked this off-handedly like asking if my father preferred jam over marmalade. I found it strange that social workers spoke in roundabout, obscene tones with regard to suicide over and over again but when I finally said, "No, it wasn't fucking suicide," they said, "Don't use the word 'fuck.'"

"If he had killed himself, they would have found him by now. He was the type of man who made statements in life."

She ran her hand over the grinder and then along the drafting board where he had been designing a new kind of fibreglass boat that could be used to plant cranberry bushes. On pencils and paintbrushes or cans of nails she would linger, then shake her head, no, not this, not that, not here, passing by the empty vessels.

"Bring me your investigative finds," she said.

Beneath the workbench there was a tool kit. Not very original but it kept casual marauders at bay. Inside waited a collection of brass rings and barbed couplets, shanks and tongs. A silver question mark two feet long with a sharp edge, a platinum clamp with marble tweezers, a tuning fork carved out of gypsum. The practical purpose of the objects was impossible to calculate. They were gynecological instruments for aliens, transmitting devices for Cro-Magnon cave dwellers or what a novice serial killer might have built during his industrial ed class.

She drifted off, maybe calculating the difference between mythos and logos, altruism and nihilism or even passion and perversion, but eventually she just pointed at me with her cigarette. "Put an artifact on the table."

I picked a tungsten centipede with a hundred tiny hooks spiralling out from its spine, waiting to catch an inattentive piece of flesh. Gwendolyn approached the bench, and her hand crept over the instrument luxuriously, as if the surface contained pornographic Braille. Then her fingers closed around the ring and her eyes fluttered. She spoke for a short spate to herself, or to someone else in the room whom I could not see. Her teeth ground and her lips quivered, and for a moment she was quite ugly. Then she fell silent and sad and gazed out the soaped window to the cornfield.

"My parents are dead, aren't they?"

Gwendolyn pursed her lips. Didn't say no, she didn't say yes.

"It's either one or the other," I said.

"Not quite."

"How can it be not quite?"

"Do you recall the McGautrie family?"

I did. In the ditch with his debt-ridden car. Saturday night. On the lam. Took months to find his body.

"They police came to me," she said.

"They do that?"

"With stealth. It's not something our national constabulary is going to confess to the tabloids. I went to their house. Mrs. McGautrie pleaded with me. She said even the worst news was better than not knowing at all. I said to her, plainly and professionally, 'I'm not getting any living resonance from your husband, so I must tell you, I believe that he is dead.' She collapsed beside the fridge. Then the police came and asked me a lot of silly questions. I told them what I knew. A day later they found him exactly where I described. The car turned upside down, soaked with skank water and stuffed with newspapers. They were obsessed with the newspaper detail, but there wasn't much they could do. They had come to me with their pockets empty, and the agreement was utter silence on both sides. So, you see, even in dire cases, I have no problem divulging the truth. But your case is not dire. It is distinct and may take you a long time to understand what is going on with the swarming noises, but so be it."

The shed mixed sawdust and 10–30 weight oil all by itself. I wanted to vanish into the trellis, have its green leaves fall about my shoulders and never be seen again. Gwendolyn's face got closer; I could see the blue lines in her iris, smell her breath with a taste of Scotch and for a brief second, I thought there was a cicada trapped in her blouse.

"I heard them everywhere," I said. "Down the bedroom vent, out in the meadow. Even in the halls at school. Cackling, wing-rubbing static. But turn around and they are gone. Follow their noise and you are tricked. They were closing in. There was mucus suffocation and I liked it."

The air was damp with river breeze. Gwendolyn adjusted the wrist buckle of her glove and leaned towards me. The dried grass crushed beneath her boots. Perhaps there were rats running around in the shed. She put her hand on my shoulder to console me, which I thought was odd because she was wearing gloves. Then I realized that she wasn't wearing gloves at all; her hands were hard as leather, and the buckles were shiny calluses of skin. Grasshopper chirping rose through the shed and grew from a drum roll to a jet airplane, and Gwendolyn's eyes sparkled emerald and cut into a thousand angles, I'd never seen a woman like this before, where it was impossible to look straight into her pupils because there were millions. There was the smell of burnt rubber and the fluttering of wings, and I foamed at the mouth and the nose and ears and then all over. Champagne bubbles exploded in my skull. I fell to my knees and my fingers slid down her boot. My grandparents ran across the lawn. Dirt filled my mouth and Gwendolyn stood above me, her chest rising and falling and the heavy stench of tar weighed the room.

"Is everything all right in there?" my granddad called from outside.

"Dn't get up." Gwendolyn said. She smoothed out her blouse and straightened her collar.

Then she smiled and lit up a third Virginia Slim, went to the door, greeted my grandparents out of view, leaving me to still ask today, Was what she did so wrong?

THREE

THERE IS AN evil I have seen under the sun. Common amongst most men and, above all else, banal. Garrulous and fraudulent, the evil waits with predictable lethargy in the suburbs of excess for someone else to do the work. Not where you might think. Not in dilapidated opium dens disguised as stuccoed grocery stores or industrial warehouses where stolen property lurked at midnight. Not even in the basements of pedophiles with Super 8 films running in black and white loops, but in the bored alleys of the nation, smelling of summer tar, where young men believed there was not a virtue pure enough worth sacrificing for. The economic crash had come. Good surf was over, and jobs were running out. Conservatives were taking power all over the world, so indolence was an accepted misdemeanour, like mildew. The good fight just wasn't worth fighting anymore. The year was 1981.

"Do you want to buy some weed?" Russell Hobbes said to me.

Russell had parked his 1972, rusted Dodge pickup, which we all assumed was stolen but was probably not, under the mountain ash beside the Irmin Street cannery. The month was September, and the berries were ripened. Crimson and bloated, they would fall to the ground in red splotches and be consumed by liquor-starved robins who would finish their days flying into windows, windshields and ventilation shafts. Then the autumn would come, and the yawning melancholy of Vancouver would pale the sky into a cream vale, cool and lonely.

Russell was a bully turned loser by natural selection. He wasn't going to make it as a real criminal in the city grid, so he was relegated to the fringe of suburban opportunism. In a younger life we had gone to school together in Abbotsford and in those days, he was just belligerent. He had beaten my head against the porcelain urinal in the washroom of our elementary school and pissed on my lunchbox. Everybody was afraid of him. He was big, bulky, wore a jean jacket and smoked American cigarettes. One of those children who grew mean and large at an early age, he got what he wanted which was usually what other people had. Basically, he had nothing to lose. His parents were separated. His academic prospects were slim. In Grade 7 he was diagnosed with a learning disorder and threatened the school nurse with a sharpened clam shell. People were frightened of him the same way they were frightened of the Rottweiler that lived down the street near the mailbox. Ten years on, Russell had floated down the Fraser River with the rest of the dead chum salmon to haunt the delta of Vancouver.

"Weed," I said.

"Sure, you know what weed is, don't you?"

"I know."

"Twenty bucks a lid. I think you should buy some."

"Twenty is too much," I said.

"It's not."

"I can get it from Hopper for fifteen. And he doesn't cut his with basil."

"No, I think you misunderstand me," Russell said. He was philosophic. "You should buy some from me here and now."

"I don't want weed. I want MDA. 'DA is in. Weed is out."

"What do you know about 'DA?"

"I know it doesn't give you lung cancer and it's only four dollars a hit."

"Big deal."

"That's all I've got. We're in a recession. Sorry."

Russell was a businessman. He wanted to say entrepreneur but couldn't pronounce it as he had developed the slightest of lisps in adolescence. So, he thought for a moment, balanced an equation, then ran his finger up the front of my sweatshirt. The new fleece was embossed with the gold embroidery of my boxing club's logo, and his fingernails were dirty.

"Give me this," he said.

"Not a chance."

"You going to wrastle me for it?" He pushed his thumb into the gloves sewn onto the chest pocket.

Times had changed since junior high school, but Russell Hobbes had not. A decade ago he had been a mean son of a bitch ahead of the curve, but the curve had moved on. His blonde fuzzy hair was still uncombed, sort of a derelict Scottish Afro and he was still stocky. Yet the advantage had faded. He wheezed from too many cigarettes and had lost the absolute belligerency that was his principal winning characteristic in youth.

The boxing logo had given him pause. My grandfather had forced me into the Kingsway Club. I wasn't very good. I got hit a lot. In the past year I had suffered three concussions, four broken digits, a chipped tooth and a fractured nose. This had hurt me aesthetically more than physically. We all wanted to look like Peter Frampton and getting your nose bent wasn't going to put you on the cover of GQ. There was discussion about whether suffering such injuries increased your chances at becoming a successful novelist. I thought yes, my friends said no because Hemingway no longer counted for anything.

Our coach was a Jamaican immigrant with a shiny face and broad shoulders who had grand dreams about raising an Olympic team for his newfound country and winning some unspecified sports medal from the Governor General.

"No," I said. "But I'll box a round if you've got the collateral."

Russell thought. "Tough guy," he said.

"Just a proposition."

He leaned over the slatted wood fence that separated the car lot stuffed with Ford Ramblers and Datsuns from the world of suburban back alleys and bird houses to survey the state of his nation.

"You'd be a good candidate for the NWO," he said.

"The what?"

"The New World Order. Know what that is?"

"No."

Russell smiled. "You go to college, you should."

"Enlighten me."

"It's in all the newspapers," he said. "You read newspapers, don't you?"

"*Globe and Mail, Economist,* the *Times*." Like he would know.

"I don't see how you've missed it then. It's on all the radio stations too. Fascism, man. Fascism is coming back."

This appealed to him. He pulled out a package of du Mauriers and lit one up. His eyes drifted from the open garages smelling of transmission fluid and inviting thievable television sets to the high school students wandering away on their lunch hour with flared pants and moon-shaped asses. This was his kingdom in twilight.

"What station do you listen to?" I said.

"Shortwave."

"You don't have a shortwave."

"Picked a set up at one of my jobs. I've got a ham licence. But I suppose you're more of the CBC kind, aren't you? What do they teach you in school, anyway, Woody?"

"Entomology."

"What?"

"I'm learning about insects."

"What for?"

"Because they interest me."

"And what are you going to do with that?" He stared down at the ember of his burning cigarette as if it might forecast the weather.

"Get a job in a museum or lab."

"Jesus, why?"

"Fifty thousand a year," I said. "Plus tax incentives. The feds pay well."

He nodded. That was a figure that made sense to him.

"Good coin if you can stand the goo."

"They give you gloves," I said.

"Not me. I'm a businessman and that's what I intend to stay."

"Do you really think you'd fit into a fascist world?"

"Woody," he said, and blew a column of smoke over the knuckles of his bizarre private ritual. "I know it will fit me like a glove."

He was probably right. I could see him on the lowest level of brown-shirted bureaucracy, one step off the pallets, carrying out the simple daily tasks of totalitarian life, getting paid in beer coupons and loving every second.

"You'd have to take orders," I said.

"Nobody tells me what to do. In the New World Order, the strong survive. The weak perish. You need the proper friends. We have a mailing list. Give me a cancelled cheque and they'll send you the newsletter."

"No chance."

"Fascists need businessmen, not bug collectors. Read *Mein Kampf*."

"It's eight hundred pages long."

"I did it in a day."

"Where do you get this shit from?" I said.

Someone in Russell's red Dodge leaned on the horn.

"Your mom?" I said.

"Screw you. How about that weed?"

Then, through the lacing of cracks on Russell's ancient windshield, a blonde head rolled back, hair tussled over, and I knew this was no mom. This was a thirty-something China doll with an Aryan set of cheeks, and the algebra wasn't adding up.

"Who's that?" I said.

"That's Addy."

"Who's Addy?"

"Friend."

"She's no friend of yours."

Russell modified his position.

"Business associate, actually," he said.

"Hot."

His voice was cold. "She's out of your league, man."

More than blonde, and not bleached white, the bangs were platinum. Her jaw was angular and she smoked disdainfully, as if time had cheated her. In Russell's story of a New Reich the pieces managed to become barely believable, far too alluring and not close enough.

"What kind of business?" I said.

"That, Woody, is something your middle-class college mind does not want to know."

"Introduce me."

"She doesn't take casual introductions."

"What kind does she take?"

He straightened his pants.

"Formal ones."

"Then give me a formal one."

"Can't."

"Is she like your Reichmaster?"

His nose screwed up in confusion.

"Boss," I said.

"Nobody is my boss."

"Well then, I'll come back to the truck with you. You sell me the weed, you say 'Addy, this is Cirrus.' Don't call me Woody, okay. I say hello and that's it. You did want a business proposition, didn't you?"

Russell ground his cigarette out on the worn pavement. The aluminum gutters on the dirty garages were creaking in the heat.

"All right," he said. "But twenty."

"Twenty."

We walked across the dried grass together and arbutus leaves crunched beneath our feet. Vancouver owns a washed-out light when it gets hot, wet and suffocating, as if there would be no air left but for bored people on the brink of death. She was wearing a suit with no shirt, a collar with chrome studs, and she was devastatingly, inhumanly beautiful. Down in my primordial mind, a scrotum told me this was going to be a fleeting, perhaps final encounter. The last boat was leaving the island and any act of lunacy was worth a ticket.

"What is that around her neck?"

"Just shut up."

We got to the back of the truck and Russell did a surreptitious shoulder check. He did it for affect, not tactics. Russell did not strike me as the type of person who would be heat conscious, or careful about his environment or, for that matter, his basic fundamental freedoms. It struck me, also, that being out in a known drug exchange lot was an exceptionally stupid place to be. A lot of people south of the border were taking the War on Drugs very seriously and Vancouver seemed a fine place to start.

Beneath his right rear bumper there was a crevice in the iron. Without bending over, his hand fluttered inside. He smoked, pretended to watch a magpie, then slid out a bag of dirty, stalk-ridden weed. He tossed the plastic into an empty paint tin.

"You'll like that," he said.

"There's no bud."

"Put your money in the tool kit."

Not that it mattered one bit, but I stuffed the twenty under a crescent wrench.

"And put the weed in your sock," he said.

"I'm not putting weed in my sock."

I let my eyes drift up to the cab.

"Come on," he said.

The two of us went to the passenger window. Cautiously, he folded his hands in front of his belt buckle.

"Addy, this is a business associate of mine, Cirrus."

She said nothing. She opened her mouth into an O and a pot of smoke seeped out. Her face was marble, cold and impersonal, and in the cocoon of my mind a larval form flinched.

"I like your collar," I said.

"Thank you."

"It's very Sadeian."

She stopped smoking and sized me up. She was looking for something that wasn't in my inventory so I couldn't capitalize, but she was clearly impressed by my vocabulary.

"Sadeian?"

"Like de Sade. The marquis. Him."

"Cirrus is at university," Russell said. "He studies bugs."

"Really?"

"All exoskeletal creatures actually."

"Why?"

"Exactly," Russell said.

"For their brutality." I had no idea where that came from. The words just popped out. Russell rolled his eyes.

There is too, a time in Vancouver's autumn when the afternoon is bleak and white. A torpid part of the day when thoughts come slowly and conversations lag. The static in the air ruffled, a leaf snapped and I had nothing more to entertain her with, not even a single word.

"Russell," she said. "Grab me a Coke from your cooler."

Russell wandered back to the rear of the truck and dug through his midden of urban collectibles.

"Russell's told me about you," she said.

"He has?"

"Here's my card." She reached into her purse and held out the card between two fingers. "Call if you have the inclination."

Russell came back with her Coke.

"Open it," she said.

Foam shot over the wheel well and Russell handed her the tin.

"We got to go, buddy," he said. "We're running a little behind and there's miles to go before we sleep. Nice doing business with you, and I trust you will take my counsel on the political circumstances of the day."

Russell smiled a strange, wan smile. He was, as all bullies are, insensitive to any kind of defeat. On a conscious level, anyway. Down at the reptilian level, some small red light registered that while physical force was no longer an option with this account, he had conducted a successful business deal through guile, facilitated a noble social introduction and unearthed a deeper, brutal truth: your old schoolmate may be stronger and smarter, but he's also lonely, and of all weaknesses that is the most exploitable.

The Dodge disappeared in a torrent of dust, and I was left holding a bag of weed that I would probably never use. Later, in my white-walled bedroom at my adopted house on Clinton Street, I drank Johnnie Walker Red through a straw and thought about how I could recoup my lost twenty dollars. I could sell it to a hood, but I knew none. I could give it to a woman but knew fewer. At midnight, the buses rumbled by. They made a sound like a 747, except much less romantic and more urbane. As the engine noise settled into the background I tried to sleep and pictured the woman in Russell's car. Her wide red lips, her poisonous eyes. I didn't believe for a moment her name was Addy.

Sleep never came to me at night, especially in the summer. I had tried everything the doctors could throw at me: Valium, Elavil, trazodone, Estazolam (Valium and Scotch, Elavil and gin, trazodone and rye, et cetera). Nothing worked. I would never slip into that fuzzy, warm blackout of youth and wake up the next day bright-eyed and bushy-tailed, as the times dictated young people should. I flicked Addy's card across my hand. There was nothing but seven gold numbers on the face. The conclusions were simple. She was either a con, a prostitute, a drug dealer or a fanatic. Probably all four. My mind drifted to sex with her and then it drifted to insects. And then insect sex. Seditious creatures with porous sleek skin and wings buzzing interminably in a cluster of hive arousal. Coarse hair and acrylic flesh. A vile sheath of exoskeleton juice and then pincers exploding from a beautiful carmine jaw.

I was about to slide my hands down my pants and release the earthworm of lust when my grandmother knocked. She had caught me with my pants down on more than one occasion before so she always knocked and waited, but this time she had a sad worn look on her face.

"Cirrus," she said. "The police are on the line."

The police. Retribution was swift and swifter for the stupid. They were probably on their way over with a search warrant. The scenarios played quickly. Russell had ratted me out. His truck *was* stolen and my prints were there. Addy was a hooker and I'd be on the midnight edition of Shame the John. Russell had killed Addy and I was a witness. Better yet, Addy had killed Russell and I was an accomplice.

Grandma polished her hands on her apron as she always did when nervous, and her cheeks supported a small tremor.

"What do they want?" I said.

"They've found something. They think it could be your mother's."

I got up and stumbled. The Scotch churned in my stomach and the Valium reduced my thoughts to buttermilk.

By the time I picked up the phone only a cold metallic hum waited for me.

FOUR

MY BROTHER WAS two years my junior. He was taller than me, had a more balanced view of the world and was well on his way to being a social worker. In the last few years, he had eclipsed me at university, kept steady jobs and had a real girlfriend. He was the brother who won track and field awards while I debated Faust with drunk colleagues in the basement. He had moved to the north to do volunteer work in a mental clinic for the summer, and the long-distance connection wasn't all that good.

"When did they call?" he said.

"At midnight."

"I wouldn't get too excited."

"They've found something."

"It's probably nothing."

"Suppose it is?"

He wasn't going to get too perturbed about this, and what annoyed me was how calm he could remain a thousand miles away when the police might be digging up our parent's ribcages.

"It's probably not," he said. "And so what if it is, what will it prove? What is it exactly they think they have found?"

"The bastards called when I was dozing off and left a message with the GM. By the time I got to the phone, they were gone. I called them right back and the person who called wasn't in. I got the duty sergeant, and he said the constable had gone home and they wouldn't give me his home phone number."

"No," Stan said. "They wouldn't do that."

"Why not, if it's all that important?"

"It's probably not."

"Then why did they call at midnight?"

"You've got to understand how bureaucracies work," Stan said. There was a television going in the background, and I could hear his girlfriend, Mandy, playing with her dog. "The cop was probably given this menial bit of information to pass on, and he had a ton of other more important things to do so he called before he went home, to clean his slate."

"Grandmom is on the file," I said. "Why didn't they give the facts to her?"

He sighed. Then he puffed his cheeks and blew. Mandy's dog barked. His name was Filbert, and he was the sort of poodle crossbreed that deserved to be injected with cough syrup or run over by a truck. I hated the animal and had once personally tried to poison it with Roundup.

"Maybe they did tell her," he said. "Maybe it slipped her mind. She's eighty now and she forgets. Or maybe she just didn't want to."

"How could she not want to?"

"She might not want to because of the pain involved for us to go through this over and over and she gets weary. Don't get pissed off at her."

It's hard to like someone who is patient, kind and right, especially when you are not.

"I'm not pissed off at her," I said. "I'm pissed off at the cops."

"There's no point in getting pissed off at them, either."

"He hung up."

"Why did he hang up before you got to the phone?"

"It took me a few minutes. I was disoriented."

"Disoriented. Yeah."

That was the polite way of us both acknowledging I was chemically incapacitated.

"We can't ignore this."

"Cirrus," he said. "How long has it been?"

I hated that question.

"Five years," I said.

"What does that tell you?"

"I don't know, what does that tell you?"

"It tells me that after half a decade, there's not going to be anything left worth finding. What is going to be out there of value in the dirt? A comb, a shoe, maybe if you're lucky, a wallet. And what is that going to do? At worst it's going to lead us to another dead end. Another ghost, a nothing trail. Another hotel where the guest's name turned out to be Wist and not Wood. Or a licence plate that was a digit off in Prince George, or a mix-up with another missing person case from Panama City where there were a pair of Czechs, not Canadians, remember that one? At best it's going to lead us to a body, right. We are looking for a body, aren't we Cirrus?"

That was about as moody as Stan got. My throat went dry. Maynard Ferguson played a triple high F on his horn, which was still the rage those days, sort of. I drifted off. Where was that business card Addy had given me?

"Cirrus," he said. "Talk to me."

"Yes. We are looking for a body, Stan. Two of them actually, if that makes you feel any better."

"It doesn't make me feel any better. It makes me feel shitty. But we have to make sure we stay on the right track, otherwise we'll all go crazy. Our parents are gone forever. They are dead and we will never know why or how. They will never be found, okay? We have to look forward. We must accept the past. We've been through this."

"You're starting to sound like Dr. Neufeld."

Dr. Neufeld was our psychiatrist. Assigned to us through the provincial services, he wore a green suit and had a strange nose. My brother liked him, I did not. He once barred me from the meeting because I had tripled my dose of antidepressants without leave and wouldn't stop talking about millipedes.

"I'm sounding like your brother," Stan said. "I can't stand to watch you do to yourself what you did all last year. We are not going to do that again, are we?"

"No."

There was a long silence. Stan relented.

"Did you talk to the primary investigator?" he said.

"Not yet."

"What was his name? You said he might have been Swedish."

"The primary is Fielding. The Brit. The one who thumped me in the interview room. They put all the old guys on cold cases because they're senile. He has a speech impediment and rambles about the Magna Carta. I think he suffered a brain injury in the line of duty."

"He did not," Stan said.

"He doesn't care. He's on annual leave. I called him this morning and they said he was gone until the fifteenth. Jesus, what a nightmare. These old guys are just putting in time."

"Gods and politicians come and go, but the bureaucracy is forever."

My brother had a saying for everything, revolutions, natural disasters, car crashes, tsunamis, *coup d'etats*, religious conflicts and plumbing mishaps. You've got to break a few eggs to make an omelette; the more we study religion the more we realize man never worshipped anything but himself; what goes down must come up. He was proud of them because they weren't Shakespearean and didn't rhyme. When I pointed out that they were often in iambic pentameter, he'd break up the end or change the syllables around, which to my horror made them sound better.

"Suppose," I said, "the bureaucracy has our parents' remains locked up in a morgue, where they will sit for two weeks. That's cruel and inhumane. It's also against the Charter."

"The Charter isn't law yet and they wouldn't be remains. They were clear about that. If they found a body, they would call us the same day and have us come down to do an identification. They were also clear about what they would say. If they had remains, they would say, 'We have found human remains that we believe could be those of your parents, and we need you to come and assist with an identification.' They don't have that now."

The dog on the far end of the phone yelped, and I imagined the creature strangling painfully to death on the belt of an exercise bicycle.

"How's the summer job?" Stan said.

"Over."

My job was a ten-week limited-term position at a lab filing pine beetle excrement for the Department of the Environment. Not even the actual excrement itself, but computer printouts of their excrement that were to be mailed to forestry agencies. The term was supposed to give aspiring scientists a chance to get field experience, but I wasn't in the field, and most of us knew it could have easily been done by an office clerk.

"Can you get an extension?" he said.

"No."

"Why not?"

"For two reasons. First, there simply is no more beetle shit to be classified and second, I have to start classes."

This, of course, was a lie. The department was offering extensions. In fact, they had offered me one not three days before, but I had declined. Owing to my calculations, I had enough cash to stave off the academic year, pay tuition, buy seven cheeseburgers and one twenty-six-ounce bottle of Canadian Club per week. Sundry expenses would be extra, but I would worry about that later. My grandmother charged a modest fifty dollars a month rent, which she looked at as ideological rather than financial compensation, but working was not something I wanted to do. Besides, the forestry companies were exploiting my labour for their own capitalistic advantage, so the system owed me heaps.

"I think you should ask again," he said.

"Why?"

"Have you been watching oil prices? We're in a second depression. It's going to be as bad as '29."

"Are you on glue?"

"The Americans are lining up at the pumps, our federal government is nationalizing the rigs and people are losing their houses. This is not good news."

"I have a house."

"Grandma's house," he said. This was a round peg in a square hole. "A job that pays a regular salary is a stupid thing to throw away."

"The multinationals are using me. Do you honestly think pine beetles are going to eat the nation's forests?"

"You're the expert."

"I need some time."

"Mm," Stan said. "Seeing anyone?"

There is nothing so painful as having a benefactor ask you if you are seeing someone when you are not. Especially when they are. The repeating horror show of chastity in suburban Vancouver remained unchanged. In the spring one hoped that the summer job would yield fertile fields. When it did not, hopes were set on autumn classes, which proved as parochial as Victorian lawn bowling parties. All this at an age when we were supposed to be in our prime and the trophies dangled before us proved our prime wasn't good enough: Cynthia, the sophomore who always strode aloofly past Sedgewick Library in a knitted sweater-mini-dress combination; Denise, the redhead with high black boots, who sat in the Buchanan reading hall with a Do Not Disturb sign taped to the study carrel. And Sandy, a brunette who wore open shirts showing her freckled, full chest as she walked braless every Monday, Wednesday and Friday at precisely twelve-fifteen past the clock tower, leaving a thousand broken hearts. A young lady whom I studied calculus with enlightened me on the topic: "You don't get it, Cirrus. Undergrads don't date undergrads. Undergrads date TAs. TAs date grad students and grad students do profs. That's the way of the world. Welcome to the 1980s."

Younger brother awaited my response.

"There is no anyone," I said.

"Someone will come along."

"No one comes along."

"Knock off the negativity and don't be so pejorative."

"Pejorative?"

"Women hate romantic despair," he said.

"I don't."

Romantic despair was one thing. Sexual despair, quite another.

"How about the cranberry farm gal?"

"Functionally illiterate, a socialist and she hated me."

"Only after you told her those first two things."

"She smelled like soup."

"The one from the bio-club. What was her name, Rhonda?"

"Randa?"

"Lives in Kamloops."

"Drive up there before gas hits a buck a gallon."

"She's Catholic," I said. "She doesn't drink, she doesn't have sex and thinks Faulkner is risqué."

"He is. Listen, I hate to break this to you, but most women want sensible, loving, rich men. If you're fishing outside that pool, you're going to have a long life at sea. I'm not saying that you have to aspire to that, but at least put on the facade like you do."

"Are you really my brother?"

"Sometimes I wonder too."

"I don't want someone watching me do chin-ups."

"Since you've not got much to do," he said, and I knew the victory couldn't last. There was a list on the way. "GM needs the back of the house painted."

"Yep."

"The paint is in the shed. You don't have to buy a thing."

"Okay."

"The brushes are cleaned and stuffed in the paint trough."

"Ten-four."

Somehow, taking one morning to paint two sides of a house was going to spoil any chance I had left of scoring illegal narcotics and following up on the latest clue to my parent's retrieval.

"And the cemetery. Can you take her to the cemetery?"

"Thursday," I said. "We go on Thursdays."

So now that was a Wednesday morning and a Thursday afternoon gone. My chances of sexual success were fast approaching zero.

"She needs you, Cirrus."

"I have taken her all summer. Every Thursday. I'll take her all autumn. I'll take her as long as she lives."

"You need each other," he said. "I know that doesn't sound cool but it's true. I am worried about you."

"Why?"

"What are you taking in the fall session?" he said.

"Biochem, invertebrates, calc three and one on Kafka."

"Kafka?"

"German lit."

"Whatever the fudge for?"

"There's nothing wrong with mixing a bit of good literature in with science. What are you worried about now?"

"I'm worried about the autumn, big brother. I know you go through cycles. Dangerous cycles. It's like there's a typhoon coming or a predator stalking in the tall grass, rustle, rustle. Maybe see the good doc about medication, lest we end up by picking you up at the hospital or yarding you out of the police station again."

"Name one time that happened."

"Last October," he said. "You smoked too much weed and spray-painted your penis red. With industrial rust remover, unfortunately. It's a good thing we have socialized medicine. Then the time you thought a clue had been deposited in the neighbour's chimney. The fire department took all day to bail you out. Then the time you tried to surf in the sewer outfall."

"Name another time."

"I don't want to see you become another statistic," he said. "If you're having problems, call me."

"All right."

"And Cir, please don't leave your books around the house where Grandma can find them."

"What's wrong with my books?"

"*Naked Lunch*, *Venus in Furs* and *The 120 Days of Sodom* are not what she needs to find while she's picking up your laundry. She might get the wrong idea."

I hung up the wall phone. Three books lay on the dining room table: the 1965 *Professional Engineering Handbook* (with appendices), *Life during The Permian Age* and *Harem Slave*. *Harem Slave*? *Harem Slave* was a lurid trade paperback from 1953. On the tarnished cover a trashy blonde American woman was forced into purdah by a stern Arabic male. The spine smelled of glue. Dozens of mites were crushed between the pages, tiny black splotches with hairy legs. What a life. Born in a larval state, never getting airborne, then forced to eat pulp and squashed into a comma. Did mites truly eat pulp or was that a myth? Somewhere in the house there was a

61

tick and mite catalogue. I had to check. I had to know. The skin on my neck itched. Humans infected with the carcasses of dead paper mites often manifested a wide array of symptoms: scratching, wheezing, blistered lips and sneezing. Perhaps I had been infected. I pictured my mother wearing a red and white apron and brushing dead bugs off our kitchen counter with a whisk. The flesh on the back of my elbow broke out in purple splotches. Tick infection, for sure. Lyme's disease was making the headlines. I wasn't allergic to anything that I knew of, so mite infection had to be it. Certainly, I would die. My bloated body would serve as a medical cadaver for a first-year epidemiology class, the lecture entitled "The Dangers of Dead Mites in Temperate Rainforests."

Mite powder was the only solution. The medicine came in small white bottles with Courier typeface, like foot powder. This was the eighties, but my grandmother wasn't quite there yet. I went to the kitchen drawer, pulled out a set of forks and a ball of string. A paper clip fell to the floor.

The woman on the cover of the paperback suddenly looked a lot like Russell's friend, Izzy. *Ilsa, She Wolf of the SS*, or the bitch heroine from the book of *Baal*. I yarded out a bottle of silver polish, a tube of camphor, and the room was filled with the smell of kerosene lamps. There had to be mite powder somewhere. I went through the fridge and jettisoned every container of cheese, macaroni, plums, milk, juice, chicken and butter. The hutch was my next victim, emptied of Royal Doulton dolls, sterling silver pie plates and over twenty-four varieties of imported dinner forks. Mite spray was the only thing that would save me, but deep down I knew what was truly happening. The doctor told me I was a textbook case; it was an obsessive-compulsive attack. A closed loop of the cognitive process. A Looking Fit. Good for me. It's always good to be the best at something. Dr. Neufeld had said there were always non-destructive choices to be made when these instances came on. The proper medication, yoga and good counselling. I disagreed. The only workable options were basically four-fold: getting loaded, jerking off, going for a marathon run or reducing yourself to a maudlin puddle of salty tears, but my preference was to just go with it. Reptilian ransacking, the repeating of useless but all-consuming tasks, can be an infinitely satisfying pastime. I ripped open the shoe polish box. I pulled the spine of my grandmother's cookbook into strips. On my grandfather's workbench sat oil tins, glue tubes and grease spouts. I unscrewed them all, but still no mite powder. Under the stairs, below the band saw. Boxes, tubs, cotton streams. My flesh became scorched and so off came the shirt. Then my pants. The muscles in my chest were wiry and filigreed, like the scales of a fish. Benzol, WD-40, hydrogen peroxide, I rubbed them everywhere. My socks came off too, as did my shoes and underwear. Musk mingled with the intense sexual pleasure of a dank basement immersed with cow parsnip, linseed oil, and then I was out in the backyard, the tool shed, the lawn mower cupboard, the greenhouse and boat trailer with the 4.5 Seagull motor wrapped in canvas all ripped to shreds, chewed, digested and spewed. At the top of the cherry tree was a blue jay house, and this was as good as any place for a feral tin of mite spray to be. Besides, I could climb, jump or fly. On the way up, the knotted bark cut into my shins. Orange sap stuck to my ear. The tree trunk was warm and the neighbour's roof was speckled with leaves. Far down the block, my grandmother looked up with her shopping cart, only mildly surprised that a naked young man was perched at the top of her Queen Anne cherry tree covered in citrus pitch and devouring the seeds out of her blue jay feeder.

FIVE

ALL ARTHROPODS HAVE refined the same distasteful but extremely successful strategies for survival. They have developed a dorsal anterior brain and a ventral nerve cord. They have segmented their bodies to increase axial flexibility and, of course, they evolved a hard outer shell known as an exoskeleton. They have been with us since the great Cambrian radiative flux over 550 million years ago, and they will be here on our planet long after we have gone or cared.

The arthropods survive fires and droughts, disease and floods. They don't notice tsunamis or earthquakes. Sunspots, even of epic proportions, aren't on their radar screen. Wars, stock markets, plagues and urban sprawl matter not a wit. They are never lonely. They can survive years in solitude, decades of isolation and epochs of entropy. They know not sadness, nor loss, melancholy nor desire, and despite how ugly or malicious other species may find them, their character is a fetish of success.

I picked a sleek spider wasp off the sunbaked wall of the RCMP detachment. The creature had an hourglass splotch on its abdomen. I admired its purity, the way it struggled against the odds and maintained complete indifference to suffering. I punched the insect inside my mouth, bit down and swallowed.

The Burnaby station was situated at the bottom of a reclaimed swamp below the provincial prison. Property owners in the area liked to call it a wetland, but that was only because they were rich. This was a swamp. Brown water percolated through the ferns, and when traces of cadmium showed up in soil samples, elementary school plans were ditched for a cop shop. Here, the new urban planning frenzy rose to a fevered pitch in an attempt to make everything appear like it was imported from Sweden.

But once you were inside this monstrosity, there was no mistaking where you were. The smell of disinfectant and dishevelled people crowded the halls. Loners mumbled to themselves. An underclass of civilian workers called commissionaires took fingerprints, gave out equipment and wished they were elsewhere.

If you didn't have a uniform on, you were suspect. Only two kinds of people came into police stations: those with uniforms and those with warrants.

Fielding stuck his head out of a doorway. Hadn't changed much, really. He was sixty, square face and brush cut. The SAS type before coming to Canada and finding too much colonial rye.

"Cirrus," he said. "Come on in, lad."

Lad, it was either lad or son. We'd known each other for five years and he'd never called me by my first name without tacking on one of the two. Sometimes, it was Big Guy but that was when there was bad news. His accent was appealing in moderation, but anything more than a nine-minute conversation was unendurable. Pictures of the Queen were posted in awkward places. Fielding punched a code into metal buttons on the door.

"I didn't want to get your hopes up too much," he said.

"You didn't."

"How is your brother?"

"He's mediocre."

He flicked his pencil between his fingers, weighing my mood.

"I know every time I call, you think there's a new clue," he said.

"You mean there isn't?"

"Not really."

"Why did the cops call me at midnight?"

"Gods and politicians come and go, but the bureaucracy is forever."

"Super."

"I'd like you to peruse a few objects. If you have time."

"I've got it."

"Excellent," he said under his moustache. "Excellent."

We waited for the elevator to take us downstairs. A plastic ivy pot hung in the doorway. Fielding had new cuff links.

"What kind of new non-clue is this?"

"Hard to describe."

"Rock, mineral or vegetable?"

"It's better if I show you," he said.

"Where did they find it?"

"Fish hatchery, near your old home."

"Who found it?"

"Neighbours."

"Did you interview them?"

"They're good Samaritans, lad, not suspects."

"What's the difference?" I was going to say what's the diff, because that's what we all said then, but that would have got me nowhere.

"You'd make a good copper," he said.

"Good God. Why?"

"This is our lab room." He opened the door.

The inside of the lab room was disappointing. Basically, I wanted a morgue. A filthy dungeon with chrome tables and smelly cubbyholes secured with toe tags. Test tubes, maybe boiling sulphate, and lots of protoplasm on microscope slides. What I got was an extended maple table that looked like it had been lifted from the nearest elementary school. The detective ran his finger along a wall of filing cabinets. A film of sweat collected beneath my rayon, yes, rayon shirt. Far down the runway, something dreadful was landing and my body got ready to absorb the pain.

"I think this is the one." Fielding held up a plastic bag to the light and tried to read the label. "Well, anyway, let's give it a shot."

"You seem certain."

"Our filing system is archaic."

Every sealed package had a number and signature attached so not even a civil servant could get it wrong.

"There's a particular way to do this," he said. "So, bear with me. I'll put the items down and you look at them from your side of the table. Tell me if they belong to your parents, but more importantly, tell me if they have any identifying characteristics. Details that could prove ownership conclusively."

Fielding's eyes flickered over the bag and his eyebrows twitched a millimetre. A trout jumped in the early morning mist of a distant lake making an almost imperceptible splash. The detective placed a tie clip on the table. Expensive fare: serrated gold edging and a garnet mounted in the centre.

"That's not his," I said.

"Are you sure?"

"I'm sure."

"Why?"

"That tie clip didn't belong to my father, or my mother, or brother or me, for that matter."

"How did you know so quickly?"

"Because I have a good memory."

"Mm," he nodded.

Maybe Fielding was an asshole, maybe he wasn't. I'd like to give him the benefit of the doubt and say he was doing his job, but nobody ever does that. He fished around in the bag as if drawing the winning ticket from a lottery barrel.

"Maybe I had the wrong bag," he said. "How about this one?"

A silver clip with ragged teeth tumbled to the table. On first take, I would have said roach clip for the rich. Rich kids collected that kind of paraphernalia for toking, but that's not what this was. This clip was studded with peridot and snapped tight enough to crush a reefer beyond suckability. Twelve inches of chain were welded to one of the arms and whatever had been on the far end was now missing, worn away into the memory of the earth.

"That's hers," I said.

"Whose?"

"My mother's"

He pushed the clip around trying to make sense of its purpose.

"Your mother had a tie clip?"

"Her initials are inside."

This was a detail he had missed. He donned reading glasses. "Where do you recall seeing this?"

"On my mother's dresser. Beside the jewellery box. Sunday morning."

"You do have a good memory."

"Some things stick with you. They'd been at a party the night before. The sun came through the drapes and made the stone sparkle. There were other things there. My dad's first pair of glasses, letters from Russia. Sunday mornings at our place always had a lonely feel that I never liked."

"Do you have any idea what it's used for?" he asked.

"You're the expert."

"I think it is probably for smoking marijuana."

"No chance."

"What makes you think it's not?"

"The clamp is too tight. Nothing would get through the tube."

"Experience?"

"Observation," I said. "I grew up on this planet."

He let the clip swing back and forth in a long pendulum. He really had no clue.

"How did it get here?"

"Like I said, lad, an old neighbour of yours, can't tell you who, can't say why. She liked to watch the salmon."

"What kind?"

"You Canadians are too particular about your fish."

"So, she picked a pair of rusted clamps out of a roe trail?"

"She found a box. Her memory twigged. She called us."

"What else was in this box?"

Fielding paused. "Not anything else relating to our issue."

"Now what?"

"I give it back to you."

"And?"

"And then I write it down in my notebook and attach the facts to the investigative details as part of the case."

"Then what?"

"Then that's basically it."

Fielding sat on the desk corner. Owing to his middle-age girth, he couldn't quite get his hand into his pocket. "I've got to tell you that the links could be completely tangential. These things could have been lumped together in a pawn shop and sold. They could have been dropped by a moving truck when you left the house. Your mother could have misplaced it at the Eaton Centre a decade ago. Taking anything from here is like asking the friend of a friend of a friend to comment on your memory. There are too many breaks in continuity."

The crustacean armour on my face broke down. My jaw trembled.

"I'm sorry," he said. "My main goal here today was to give this property back to you."

I didn't want to say thank you to a half-dead dick, but my eyes welled, so I found a quick distraction.

"Why do you work on these cases?"

"Cold cases?" Fielding straightened his back. "For many reasons. I like solving puzzles that no one else could. I think outside the box. I also like working on one or two projects at a time. A regular detective has a caseload of dozens. Too distracting. Also, I'm getting on now and there's no midnight call-out in this unit."

"Must be fascinating." It came out the wrong way.

"Has its moments." He leaned against the cubbyholes and the cogs in his mind kept turning, turning. "The field requires patience. Look at how long it's been for you and I."

"Ninety-six months."

"Seems like yesterday."

"I remember the police dredging the lily pond. I remember them tearing up my mother's room. I remember my brother crying and someone bouncing my head off the interview room floor. Oh God, sorry. That was you."

Fielding sucked air that sounded like a zipper going down. "Letters from Russia?"

"My father sold turbines to the Russians."

"Still have them?"

"I thought the Cold War was over."

"If you should come across them by chance." He was offhanded, but his eyes darted to the first clip, the drawers and finally to the ring on his finger.

"Isn't there anyone else we could talk to?"

"Not many people who we haven't."

"I mean experts."

"Whom?"

"Do you ever use private investigators?"

"No."

"Why not?"

"They have neither the experience, the resources, nor the dedication. They have their uses in specialized cases, like ferreting out unfaithful spouses or cheaters on injury claims, but on a project such as this, no. Their motive is profit. Not worth it."

"What about mediums?"

"Who?"

"Spiritualists."

"Never."

"Are you sure?"

"Positive."

"I thought you guys did that when you were desperate."

"We're not desperate."

"I am."

"No, lad. You're sensible. There's a difference."

He held out the jewelled clamp, signalling the interview was over. "Mediums. Only in the movies, lad. Only in the movies."

Enough dust had settled on the tachometer of my Buick to render the needle undetectable. I tossed the clamp into the box where I kept all relics: jewelled pins, unicorns' bridles, vacuum tubes and pulsating filaments. While Fielding discarded real evidence, I'd recycle the exhibits through true experts: fortune tellers, machinists, UFO enthusiasts and anyone else who might offer a more enlightened opinion. All I got in return was counterfeit money, thieves selling property in Florida and herbal cures for insomnia.

Through the grove of aspens lay a bird sanctuary and a museum where people dressed up as nineteenth-century characters and wandered around like they were either pioneers or prisoners. Not the kind of place that a man of twenty-one years should go near unless they were in a wheelchair. But inside the museum the city had financed a small insect exhibit. There were a few native bugs and exotics stuck there because no real insect museum would have them. The woman managing the exhibit was named Sal, which could have been short for Salim, Solange or Soliloquy, but probably just Sally. She cleaned the cages with an indolence that suggested she didn't want to be there either but had not the expertise nor the courage to go anywhere else.

Sal was a strange woman. Fragile and distracted, she had eyes that darted about like a small bird waiting to be eaten, or a minor civil servant about to be dismissed. Her front teeth were buckled, and I imagined her being sexed by huge grasshoppers as she climaxed.

"Hey," I said.

She glanced up with one hand on the glass counter. Her eyes took a long time to focus behind thick lenses. The argon lights hummed above us, and the room smelled of Pine Sol.

"Hey," she said.

"What's up?"

"I'm working."

Over at Terrarium B, a glass cube was filled with African dirt and burnt logs. A mound of red termites climbed lethargically out of a gaping hole as if they truly possessed the knowledge there was nowhere left to go.

"You mentioned you were getting *Clitarchus*," I said.

"What?"

"Stick insects."

"When was that?"

"In June, maybe," I said. Not that I cared.

She stood up and pushed a set of glasses up on her nose. "I can't recall."

"You got new glasses."

"Yes."

"They look good."

She rearranged the goggles on her nose, attempting to make them less homely. They were cheap, with red frames. The kind basic health insurance would provide if you ticked the special needs box.

"I think the stick insects got put in the end bowl," she said.

Fabulous. The end bowl. Stick insects were the dullest of creatures. *Clitarchus hookeri* were a family of bug that originated in New Zealand, and their sole claim to fame was that they grew very large and looked like a stick. They are the most commonly kept insects by collectors with scant imagination and they have a long lifespan.

Sal took her cloth to the collection of ladybugs that lived their lives behind glass walls. Her movements were awkward, and she didn't seem to care if anyone cared or not.

"Are you going back to school?" I asked.

"I think I'll stay here."

"You like it here?"

"It's kind of solitary."

I stared at the stick bug. The bottom line was more than likely she was not smart enough to go back to school. "Just you and your Clitty, then?"

She didn't get it.

"We might be getting Moroccan ones in October."

"Why October?"

"They're cheaper then."

"Ever been to Morocco?"

"No."

"I was there two years ago."

That much was true. I had spent a miserable week in Tangiers trying to get to Tunis on a visa that would never be processed. My wallet was stolen, I scored hemp instead of hash, was spat upon by an Islamic cleric and ingested water that caused my bowels to mimic the Bay of Fundy.

"Any good?"

"Fabulous." My right eye flickered, I hoped not a migraine coming on.

"Why?"

"Sensuous people, the Moroccans. Sensuous architecture, sensuous food. They love sensuous colours."

"What's the television like?" she said.

"I was trying to meet the people."

"Anybody interesting?"

Wallet thieves, disoriented tour guides and a legion of carpet salesmen who plied their victims with raki.

"I met a whirling dervish."

Silence passed between us. Sal counted out change and rolled the coins into brown cardboard tubes. As far as esoteric conversation went, this was a loss.

"What do you do for excitement, Sal?"

"Not much."

"You travel?"

"I went to Kelowna once."

"How was it?"

"My aunt got married," she said.

"Do you go to, let's say, parties?"

She thought for a long time. A frighteningly long time. A glacially long time. Surely, I should be allowed to dodge the draft and be exempt from military service for enduring the hardship of this woman's company.

"Big groups don't excite me much," she said. "I like to have a few friends over."

"And do what?"

She paused.

"Costumes, you know. Read."

"You read?"

"Yes," she said.

"What do you like?"

"*Chatelaine. Reader's Digest.*"

Jesus, Christ. *The Quick and the Dead* and I was descending rapidly into the latter. If I had anywhere else in the world to go, I should have gone and been there soon.

"*Reader's Digest* is good," I said.

"I like the anecdotes."

"Anecdotes?"

"Small stories of how people get by in life."

Sal, naked. With a lot of makeup on. In high boots. Her face, for once, tightened into abject need.

"I was just over at the cop shop," I said.

"Why?"

"The detective found my parents' artifacts."

She stopped and rolled the cleaning rag into her palm.

"That's right. Your parents went missing a long time ago."

"Six years."

"So, did they find them?"

"No."

"What did they find?"

"Jewellery."

"Well," she said. "That's something."

Sal opened the cash register. They sold bird seed mostly, but also strange ornaments that people could stick in their gardens to attract swallows. A spatter of freckles disappeared beneath the fabric of her blouse.

"Listen, have you had lunch?"

She exhaled.

"Lunch break is at eleven. I bring sandwiches."

On the counter beside her purse were a stack of letters. I wondered if they were from real people or were subscription reminders from *Chatelaine*. I got letters from people. From Jerome, whom I knew in high school. Jerome had flunked first semester, then joined the military. He had been shipped to Cyprus and was keeping the Turks and the Greeks from killing each other. Every few months, I got a form letter that kept myself (and others) updated on his situation, extolling the virtues of sacrifice and suggesting that we all sign up too and join the Princess Pats where he was soon to assume command.

"I was in the neighbourhood," I said. "So, I dropped by to see what you were up to."

Inside the cupboard, a variety of swabs, brushes and aerosols awaited Sal. Head buried in a cleaning bucket, she placed her wrist bracelet on the counter. Hieroglyphs were embedded into the silver.

"Okay," she said.

"I'll call you on the business line next week if I'm back."

"Whatever."

I slipped the bracelet in my pocket and walked out. Let a QB court work out the costs. Maybe she would weep over her misfortune. Perhaps she would kill herself. I would not go to the funeral.

Those seeking gratification while spurned, beware, and those seeking arthropodal company while lonely, note the following: there are basically three strolls for prostitutes in Vancouver. The A stroll in the West End, on Denman and Davie Streets where the highrises meet the forests of Stanley Park. Here, players stand on corners half-hidden by hawthorn trees and smoke, the long string of hedges producing a country estate feel. Next comes the B walk, off Richards. All Saturday Night stuff. Pink boots, Cosmo haircuts. A lot of cocaine, rip-offs and cops. Of course, a true voyageur might head off to Hastings Street, but one got what one paid for, and no one without immediate penicillin access would tread that path.

Red leaves above Cardero Street formed a canopy and the pavement was orange with sun. Three figures clustered in the shade of a yew smoking listlessly. Then the branches chattered, dandelion spores twisted and two of the silhouettes vanished. The remaining figure ran a Marlene Dietrich ploy. Plated cigarette holder, black fedora and a veil that covered her face.

I stopped the car twenty yards astern and rolled the passenger window down. She examined the end of her cigarette and watched the smoke curl out. Then she ground the cigarette beneath her shoe and started down the sidewalk. At the last minute, she turned abruptly and leaned into the window. She may as well have been speaking to the sky.

"You parked too faraway, fella."

"Sorry."

"What are you looking for?"

"I don't know."

"You don't know? Oh, super."

"It has to hurt," I said.

"I don't do that."

"Not you."

She dropped her elbows to the doorframe. An odour of mothballs wafted into the car. The veil meant determining her eye colour was impossible.

"How much do you want to spend?"

"Just the regular."

Great job, Plato, but that was all I could come up with. I popped a tin of Cola and foam spewed over the seat.

"Don't waste my time." She touched the black netting with her finger. There was a Band-Aid around the knuckle.

"Okay."

"Name a figure."

"Ninety?"

"It's one fifty for half an hour."

I should have showed more confidence. I should have negotiated more skillfully. Actually, I should have driven away and completed a *Penthouse* session at home, but instead I said, "Get in."

She was older than I thought and thinner too. The clothes didn't fit her well and the sunken pallor of her face was exciting.

"So, you like having the shit beat out of you?" she said.

"I wouldn't have put it exactly like that."

"How would you put it?"

"In more Sadeian terms."

"A lay costs extra."

"I don't want that."

She crossed her legs and scratched her face. "Whatever, skip-dip, drive."

"Where?"

"You don't have a room?"

"No."

"That's cheap," she said.

"So, now what?"

"I have a place on Thurlow."

I pulled the car away from the curb and spun down the alley.

"Show me the money," she said.

"Here?"

"You wouldn't believe the assholes out today."

I waved a roll of twenties over the dash.

"Keep it down." She stuffed a cigarette into her holder.

"Good prop."

"Joeys like it."

A column of smoke erupted against the window. Her lip was cracked. "What's your name?"

I lied.

"And you were born in what month? Turn left."

"August."

"Knew it. Leos. Strong men on the outside but when it comes to women they want to be abused."

"What's your name?"

"Call me Wendy. Wendy G. Lon, actually."

"Is that Asian?"

"I'm not."

"Where are we going, Wendy?"

"Stop at Delaney's first. Get me a bottle of Schloss Laderheim."

"Schloss?"

"Big bottle. I need a drink before I get heavy. Hard right."

Delaney's was one of the first wine shops privatized in the province. Bureaucrats figured privatizing liquor would spiral the city into a pit of iniquity, so they chalked the process full of puritanical snags. Rules on shop size. Regulations on advertising. Delaney's was an old convenience mart off Davie. Grey, stuccoed and drab, a tiny neon was the only indicator of economic life.

For one stupid moment I expected my companion was going to pay for the wine.

"Leave the radio on punk," she said.

Inside, the walls had been redone with Mediterranean tiles and the shelves were cluttered with import brands. There wasn't much under twenty dollars.

The clerk behind the counter wore a green apron. He looked like a graduate student and clearly didn't want to be working in a liquor store anywhere near a stroll.

"Do you have any Schloss?" I said.

"Schloss what?"

"Laderheim."

He examined the passenger in my car with distaste.

"Why?" he said.

"It's for my grandmother."

"Yeah, buddy."

"Dude, do you have any or not?"

"Beneath the Budweiser."

"Imperialist," I said.

The Schloss bottles had a horrid German pastoral design with Gothic writing plastered all over the label. My grandmother actually did drink Schloss before she converted to port, and I couldn't recall if I was supposed to be taking her to the cemetery that day. Back at the counter, the clerk adjusted his glasses.

"That's not the big one," he said.

"I don't want the big one."

"Are you sure?"

"Positive."

He cast another glance out into the parking lot. "I think you probably do."

"How much?"

"Eight ninety-nine," he said.

"You won't stay in business with an attitude like that."

"Buddy," he said. "People will do anything to get their booze."

Back in the car I handed Wendy G. the bottle. Her hat tipped sideways.

"That's not the big one," she said.

"The clerk was a prick."

"Drive down the alley."

In the West End, all the apartment buildings had underground lots with entrances off back alleys. This one had painted concrete columns and large signs warning of the penalties for improper parking.

"Park in the delivery stall."

"Why?"

"The landlord is too cheap to give everyone a spot."

"What happens if the delivery truck comes?"

"It won't."

The air smelled of halibut. An organ deep in my gut told me to make a run for it. Wendy was out the door quickly. She flicked her cigarette across the hood of a Dodge Dart. I slipped my wallet under the seat and locked the car. "Later, darling," she said.

I headed for the elevator but she pulled me in the other direction.

"Up the stairs," she said.

"Why?"

"I'm an exercise freak, okay?"

The stairwell was stained with urine and a stuffed koala was ditched under the steps. On the third floor, she pushed a master key into number 312 and the suite was barren. A table, a sofa and burned-out incense jars.

"I share it with a friend," she said.

"What does she do?"

Wendy moved through the cupboards, pushing a toaster and Mixmaster out of the way.

"I know there's wine glasses in here somewhere."

She found one and poured herself a glass. I didn't get any. Then she leaned against the counter and stared out the window across a field of television antennas to the pale waters of English Bay.

"I'm thinking of going to Toronto." The glass went to her mouth again. The veil never came off.

"What for?"

"The bedroom's down the hallway. Put your money on the dishwasher."

Strangely, the dishwasher was new, with a peephole installed so consumers could watch their cutlery get clean. Inside the empty bedroom a mattress had been stripped down to its metal frame and secured to the wall with wing nuts. A set of leather handcuffs had been fastened to each corner. There was also a pine dresser stacked with a row of dildos, satin gloves and horsewhips.

Wendy closed the door. She had already finished the wine.

"Let's get this dungeon on the road," she said.

I undid my shirt, but my fingers kept slipping around the buttons.

"Faster, whore," she said.

There went motor coordination and most of my common sense.

"I said faster, slut."

The more she talked the better things got. Bitch, whore, cocksucker, wench. My mouth dried out, my pants came off and Wendy gazed down with indifference.

"Fold your clothes up and give them to me."

She placed the clothing outside the room and when she came back, her wine glass was full again. Her eyes darted around the dungeon searching for an item that could not be located.

"Get down," she said.

There was a moment of silence between us, and then she picked up a leather ring from the bedpost.

"I'm knotting your balls, so the show won't end too fast."

As she anchored my torso to the springs, I realized her clothes had been in storage for a very long time, and in this peculiar geometry, there was simply no escape.

"Let me get my kink boots." She put on the satin gloves and pressed one finger to my cheek. Then she turned and left the room. The door closed. A toilet flushed, keys jangled and a radio went on. I pictured her ancient face towering above me, telling me she loved me or at least could use me for a little bit.

An onion smelling breeze came down the hallway and opened the door with a subtle click. I called out Wendy G.'s name, but no answer. Another minute passed and I sagged ten degrees. When the crack in the door widened, I saw the hallway and kitchen was empty. The front door to the apartment was open too, and out in the foyer a frumpy man with baggy cords walked past carrying a satchel of newspapers.

Advice to paratroopers, marooned sailors and those lost in snowstorms: stay calm. There is always a way out. Panic is your enemy. Logic is your friend. In ten years' time, none of this will matter, one way or the other. So, stay goal-oriented. Think victory. I twisted my arms until my shoulder blades threatened to pop from their sockets, but that didn't work. Bitch Wendy had secured the cuffs to the frame with incredible acuity. More advice to the lost. Do not become angry. Not at yourself, nor anyone else. Anger leads to irrationality. Self-loathing to failure. We all make mistakes. We all get lost. Given enough time, each one of us will lose our way.

From the adjacent suite, a television echoed through the plaster. The soap operas were over. The sit-coms had started. That horrible viewing slot before the dinner hour. I tried pulling one cuff over the frame with no success. There was simply no slack. Out the window, the shadows of chimneys grew long across the rooftop.

For a long while I waited. Perhaps this was part of the game. Maybe she had gone to get another bottle of Schloss. Or was putting on makeup. There was an off chance she was bringing over an associate, or a new glacial period might start. Perhaps if I crawled backwards up the mattress I would flip bug-wise behind the springs and gnaw the straps. If there was any circulation left. If my testes were not ripped off. Slim, but worth a try. Failure meant imprisonment behind the springs where I would have to scream for the fire department. Success meant I would get to kill Wendy G. Lon, slowly.

By the time a loud hum filled the room, my wrists were unrecognizably black, and a chunk of wall plaster was ripped away. The news hour rehashed weekly sport events. My gums bled, my pants had been turned inside out and the last of my cash looted. The bottle of Schloss was gone. So were my keys and Sal's stolen bracelet.

The lock on the Buick had been scratched beyond recognition. Each house key on the chain had been rammed into the tumbler, then bent sideways. The port window was cracked and the tail light kicked out. I went to the front bumper and reached into the sewer grate. All in all, I was out three hundred dollars, and in the rear-view mirror of my dusty Buick sat the reflection of a puzzled young man with his Polo shirt done up wrong and his mouth horribly bloodied.

My grandmother waited patiently in the living room. She had dozed off and her shortwave radio had slid into static. She listened to shortwave broadcasts from all over the world and doubted them all. Radio Free Europe was a creature of the CIA and *The Daily Worker* was a communist plot. She'd stay up until midnight to absorb the hogwash, then I'd get a rehash the next morning.

"Cirrus," she said.

"Sorry, I'm late."

"You should have called."

"I'm fine."

Her grandmother senses told her not all was fine; in fact, they told her something was badly screwed up. Her eyes scoured for familiar injuries and when she found them, there was no surprise.

"You had a spell."

This, of course, was GM's prime concern. Not that I was involved in an armed robbery, had been taken hostage by Middle Eastern terrorists or even that I had voted for the New Democratic Party, but that I had turned off, tripped out and boiled over on a psychosomatic rage looking for my vanished parents again.

"I went on a date that didn't work out."

"A nice girl, I hope."

Grandmom went to bed, and I stayed up. I had four shots of Johnnie Walker, then stole two of her experimental Percodan pills. Humiliated, I ventured to the backyard and smoked a yazoo of Russell's Panama Red/Burmese Bronze/Acapulco Gold until my fingernails went brown. In this agitated state of arousal, the world became a sinister place. A grey Orpheus of shadows spread tangles of guilt across the road. Time slowed to a panic; perhaps the police had put a radio transponder in one of the seeds. Or, the weed had been sprayed with Agent Orange and yellow blisters would bubble out my nose. The choices were slim. In fact, there were only two. Either fess up to my indulgences, call an ambulance and get my stomach pumped or be found a bloated mess in the morning. I kept choosing the latter. I turned on the basement television. A rerun of *The Avengers*, Mrs. Peel in her black skin suit. Mrs. Peel doing the nasty to her captured villain. The gerbil of want ran on. I perched myself naked on the bedroom sill, saw how turgid the human condition truly was and promptly sent a ruptured load of scalding effluent across the hedge until a voice lilted back up the alley. I ran down the list of possibilities: a neighbour sickened by my indecent act, an undercover bylaw enforcement officer, an alley cat in heat. Worse, my grandmother had lost her mind and was standing in the garden running her fingers through my cold excretion. *Cirrus*, the voice said. *Cirrus, we know you're there. You know who this is.* On the wall below my bedroom window, a six-legged creature with a bristled face clung vertically to the stucco and licked my discharge from the wall with its probing proboscis. The animal crept upward, and I slammed the window shut for all the good it would have done.

SIX

IN THE AUTUMN, my grandmother lost her sanity. We have different words for it now, but then we just called it going crazy. Bit by bit, piece by piece, her faculties fell away like flecks of rust on an aging ship. Caramel, Cameroon. Gandhi, gadflies. She got confused. Pizza, punctuation. Try explaining that to the delivery boy who had no Pericles sauce. From time to time, I took advantage of the malady. Not in cruel, obvious ways. I didn't steal her trust fund or use her car to transport weapons. But I told her things that weren't exactly true and doled out her prescriptions too generously. All for the sake of getting anywhere closer to the truth.

Truth out of my mother's mother was a furtive endeavour at best. Small threads of narrative came and went like cobwebs: where my mother went on that critical weekend before her disappearance, what kind of covert engineering venture my father was planning in that last summer of 1975 or a party that involved centipedes mating at the parental home.

Then in an instant, we'd be back to putting linen in the freezer, filling the dishwasher with blueberry stalks or waiting for a bus that never came. She spoke to people who weren't there. Traded inside jokes with tiger moths on the sill. When the house finally settled into midnight comfort with the furnace creaking and the smell of rhubarb wafting through windows, the sobbing started. Little gasps of air before the tsunami of grief hit the walls. Although I could tell her things were all right, they clearly weren't. Her husband was gone, her daughter was disappeared, and no one remembered who Lester B. Pearson was, let alone why Vimy Ridge was fought. "Pearson, I didn't care for his politics, but he was a nice man."

The summer departed Vancouver on the third Monday of September. The aspen leaves lost their crispness, the faint smell of smoke invaded the air and on every block, homes were being foreclosed. Excesses of the solstice hung around as charred buildings in a burned city, and I walked through the front door at midnight wearing my green hummingbird jacket and wide-belted jeans.

My grandmother played solitaire at the dining room table. For certain there had been voices, instantly faint, then foxgloved and quickly forgotten. There were also two decks of cards out, one facing her and the other set up for a second player at the empty chair across the table. The air smelled of camphor.

"Who are you talking to?" I tossed the key onto the hutch.

"No one."

"I heard voices."

"There's no one."

"Have you got two card games going at once?"

"How is your scrotum, dear?"

"Pardon?"

"You mentioned your injured privates, but no details."

No, the Absorbine Jr. hadn't helped one bit.

"Rugby game gone bad."

"You should really try and find a nice girl."

My grandmother tucked a handkerchief into her cuff.

"Did my mother want a nice man when she was twenty-one?"

"Your mother was a special case."

"Must run in the family," I said.

"I don't want to talk about it, Cirrus."

"How about a game?"

Grandmother stared over at the vacant chair and turned the wedding band around her finger.

"Gin?"

Cribbage would take longer so I pulled the board out on the table. "Tea?"

"I shouldn't this late."

"Salal Spice?"

Salal Spice was a hideous indigenous concoction of herbs, black Indian Nabob and honey. The ericaceous nightmare was enough to put anybody into a diabetic coma, and my grandmother couldn't get enough.

"One cup," she said.

Done. The other excellent, yet insidious, quality of Salal Spice was that the horrible taste could mask the flavour of anything. Like opium. I fetched a wad of Indochine's finest yellow paste, fired up the kettle and put on an LP of Chopin's nocturnes. When Mikhail Voskresensky reached a fevered pitch in C-Sharp Minor, I dumped the stash into the pot and hummed along. I had no idea what Grandmom's tolerance would be, so I doubled the dosage. GM took one approving sip, and her fingers trembled as she balanced the cup on the saucer.

"Deal," she said.

The cribbage board was made of caragana and came with ivory pegs from an elephant that Grandad had shot while touring Kenya during the Depression.

"Were they poached?"

"Big game hunting was fashionable then. But your granddad said he only shot the beast to impress an American novelist on his way to the Spanish Civil War. Then he showed him his machine gun wounds and gas scars."

"Gas?"

We played the first few hands reliving the horrors of mustard vapour, trench foot and the arrogance of the British officer corps while I lost the first game badly. The second one not so badly, so perhaps there was hope for me yet, and part way into the third, her hands stopped trembling.

"Do you find it warm in here?"

"They say the world is getting warmer."

"Who says?"

"Scientists."

"What do they know?"

"Was it warmer when you were young?"

"We sat on the porch and played cards."

Kubla Khan delivering on time, anyway.

"With mom?"

"Of course, with your mother."

"Was she any good?"

"Hopeless."

Right down to a sunless sea. My grandmother set the cards down and folded her hands. A bead of perspiration formed on her forehead and her pupils wandered.

"Marjorie was distracted by the strange," she said. "By the odd and the horrific. As a child, she expressed an interest in the occult. We tried to get her moved to astronomy. I read her Kepler, and she became obsessed with ghost life on other planets. I recited Shakespeare and she was only interested in the suicides. Not the kind of curriculum that wins entrance exams, and at puberty the real troubles started. I shouldn't talk about this."

"More tea, Grandmom?"

She stared down into the cup. A few opium flakes hadn't dissolved, and the brown dots fizzled in circles on the black tea.

"The bitter taste of India," GM said and swallowed.

Inquiries had to stay on track. The opiated mind needs guidance.
"You were mentioning mom's teenage years."
"Was I?"
"With interest."
"The fifties," she said. "They were repressive. Everything was black and white. You had to sign to buy a bottle of vodka. Some got on fine with that regimentation. For others, it's not in their nature."

My grandmother conceded how my grandfather and she were more liberal than most. My grandfather too much so. He let my mother do whatever she pleased, apparently. Spending hours in the garden with slater bugs. Having funerals for the dead ones. Using matchboxes for coffins and wearing veils as if in mourning. Many young people had morbid preoccupations, the doctor had said. Cemeteries, the dead, funerals: a phobia that started in adolescence when children realized they were mortal but were not yet old enough to understand reproduction. My grandmother bought her dolls as a distraction. Marjorie asked if she could put on a doll theatre for the neighbourhood children. The play was going to be *Troilus and Cressida*. What harm could it do? Shakespeare, at last, she thought. The play was scheduled for three o'clock on Sunday afternoon. My mother staged it at two o'clock, stripped all the dolls naked and hanged them from makeshift gallows. Then she ordered two audience members to undress and choke each other into near unconsciousness. When asked why she had conducted such a horrible performance, she stated simply, "Because the victims gleaned so much pleasure from their weaknesses," which might have been a line from the play but did little to console the neighbours.

My grandparents encouraged novels, as well, but Marjorie's tastes quickly turned to Edgar Allen Poe, Bram Stoker and Mary Shelley. Then the *True Detective* magazines arrived, as did the boys. Better real people than memorizing "The Masque of the Red Death." But they were older boys. Delinquent boys. Ones with money and cars.

And when sixteen-year-old girls start getting rides home in Cadillac convertibles, something is awry. She should have counted her blessings. The girls came next. She languished over her piano teacher and struck up a friendship with a woman from the World Socialist League. One night my grandparents came home late. The keys jangled in the lock and when the jangling finally stopped, they heard guttural sounds from my mother's room. My grandparents made noise, turned on the television, then politely knocked on her door. When a cry of pain erupted from inside, my granddad kicked the door open and shouted, "Marjorie? Are you all right?" Marjorie was fine. The hapless fifteen-year-old boy laying naked and hogtied on the floor not so much. His testicles had been sewn to his nipples with fishing line. My mother sat smoking on the bed with her heels dug into the boy's face. Apparently, the handsome lad had been wearing shorts all summer. There was a strip of white around his waist, and the rest of him was tanned and slicked with sweat. "Sorry about the cigarette," was all Marjorie said. "Marjorie," my granddad said. "That poor young man is clearly in some degree of discomfort, so I suggest you untie him and get everybody dressed immediately." That was all he said. The young man left quickly, and they never saw him again, never knew who he was or where he came from. Marjorie was seventeen and this young boy was two years her junior. The legal age then was twenty-one. Neither the parents nor police ever showed up. Nothing more came of it. A year later my mother met my father, and a year after that they were married. My grandmother concluded by saying that besides the end of the Second World War, that was the happiest day of her life.

"What happened after they were married?"

Grandmother finished her tea. Her eyes glazed over, and her face slackened completely.

"Oh, I don't know."

"You must know some."

"It simply wasn't our problem anymore."

"The police mentioned a chrome needle set."

"Let it go," she said.

"One more cup?"

Grandmom put the saucer down and a single splash of water appeared on the table.

"I'm an old woman who is alone now, and I don't have anyone except for you and Stan and a sister who lives at a care home in Montreal. All I want is for you to be happy, and now the hive must rest."

"Can I have some money?"

"How much?"

I did a quick calculation and came up with seven hundred fifty dollars.

"Tch, tch."

That was an out of the question no.

"How about one hundred and fifty?"

She raised one eyebrow and dabbed tea spice from her lip. Run-of-the-mill, no.

"Whatever for?"

"For a girl," I said.

"What kind of girl?"

"The kind I just met."

"The anthropology museum doesn't cost any money."

"She's an expensive girl."

"We have an arrangement."

"The cash would come in handy."

"I fear often you would spend it foolishly."

She stood up. Her knee, which always bothered her late at night, didn't seem to hurt so much then. She steadied herself on the hutch, contemplated the Ming vase, then hummed "Lili Marlene" and Chopin's Nocturne #9, but kept getting the tunes mixed up.

We all do things that we know are wrong yet summary in nature. Condomless sex. Choking on our own vomit. Voting Marxist-Leninist in a campus by-election. Other times, we do things that are unburnable, unrecyclable and unrealistic to turf into someone else's trash, and that is precisely what I had done, so I got the dream I deserved. The dream I had all my life. Ever since I was a boy and usually when I had committed an indiscretion. Every time, it went like this: I am in a park playing with other children. We are playing baseball. The leaves are green, the sprinklers on. Mid-summer. Everyone is safe, the way children like to feel in summer. I am in the outfield. The ball is hit, like a meteor across the sky, over my head and well past the fence, plunging into a ravine. A deep ravine. All ravines are cut deep into the damp earth by years of rain, the cliffs steep and tangled with fir, ivy and smelling of skunk cabbage. But I chase the ball down the slope, through the thicket of brambles and across a stream. The trees shroud out the light and the sun has gone. Then there is no longer a baseball, no longer a baseball diamond and no longer any other children. Nothing is safe, but I walk somnambulantly towards a clearing in the brush. There is an iron gate and a collection of stone slabs. A mausoleum and wilted flowers. I know what is going to happen and I keep on walking. The graves will open. The dead will come out. I will be eaten by the decrepit. I read the names off the tombstones, but there are only two I am looking for. The rocks smell. The soil bubbles forth. The corpses rise from their caskets and the white faces swarm around me. With one last effort, I crawl to the tombstones of my parents. The earth ruptures and their coffins are exposed. And then I see the horrible truth, that in my parent's caskets lie the exoskeleton remains of two great grasshoppers, husked and gazing skyward.

SEVEN

DAY OF THE jackal, night of the dog, the beast of Wendy G. Lon would not give me any peace. Every mistake, each stupidity and all miscalculations were replayed with masterful clarity like an old-fashioned movie reel. The commentary was merciless. (A hooker? Did you really think that someone coated with mothball juice and gulping Schloss Laderheim would have your best interests at heart? Or, that part about parking in the delivery stall. Little dodgy there, don't you think, Woody? Why? Hmm? Because really, she didn't have a stall of her own, did she? Why not? Because she did not live there. Had not ever. Non-habitant. *Persona non grata. Sans rien.* Also did it not bother you for one single second that she never showed her face to you? A veil for Chrissakes, Skip-dip. A goddamn veil. Did she have leprosy? Or perhaps she was Muslim? You were ignorant and flaunted it in pink neon. Better call little brother and fess up.)

Around rerun number one hundred fifty-seven the details of Wendy's departure turned into more generic abandonment images: my mother driving away in her first blue Pontiac, wearing gloves and an Easter hat. My father's shirt fading into the cornfield, the red stripes on his sleeves becoming more obscured with each step he took into the tall stalks.

An inescapable fact closed around me. The distance between me and my parents was growing larger. It would always grow larger. It would never get smaller. They would always be more distant and farther away than they had been the previous day. Nothing could change that. On the radio news an eleven-year-old girl had been found hacked to pieces in Burns Bog. Arms and legs surgically amputated, her bloodied torso neatly wrapped in silk pillowcases and preserved in fertilizer.

For me, the day — archeologically — had been less successful. The search was going poorly. A woman at Castor Chrome had balked at my suggestion of conducting a forensic audit of the silver clamp returned by Fielding, and while researching a possible address for Gwendolyn Sharpe at the Delta Library, I had been lured into the women's washroom by a red-haired transsexual posing as a straight librarian.

This couldn't go on. My search was like October. Every time I turned a corner another leaf fell from the tree. Soon there would be nothing left but husks and embarrassing memories. Bridges I had burned, places I could no longer go, people who were tired of my presence. At home, I leafed through my crumpled search diary. The pages contained all the places I had looked for my parents. All the leads I had pursued: paperweight similarities, laxative concentrations, sodium vapour levels. The Abbotsford locations were crossed off long ago, but since coming to the city, I'd started a new section entitled Urban Leads. Places where my mother or father could have been: Di Longs Deli on Fraser Street, where she bought specialized meats for the downtown party she attended. The Red Cross where she'd made donations to flood relief in Nigeria. Concrete suppliers for the summer cabin rock wall. Many had one tick, others two. Castor Chrome and the Delta Public

Library had none, but I fixed those with a set of double XXs. (Do not return. Ever. Resident hostile.) And at the bottom of the page was a sketch of a fishnet burka. Wendy G. Long's veiled face issued one last salacious sneer as I labelled her character as vespid with red ink.

"What are you doing?"

My grandmother stood behind me. She had been baking bread.

"Looking."

"For what?"

"Ice skates."

A lie so bad it didn't count even as a lie. Her apron had flour on the frills. With a weary flick, she brushed the powder aside.

"Sit down and have a scotch with me."

"You don't drink scotch."

"We can talk."

"About what?"

"Changing solar flares," she suggested.

"How about the task at hand?"

"How about we talk about you?"

"Sorry, not interested."

"Why not?"

Because I had just escaped an embarrassing encounter with the witless clerk at the chrome shop. That's why. Here are the facts: Castor Chrome, a.k.a Bert's Broken Bumper, a.k.a Cliff's Clandestine Auto, was renowned for midnight fixes on fender benders without the legality of accident reports, and as a cover did other assorted plating jobs. My parents had taken one of Fielding's cast of exhibits there for repair on March 21, 1973, and the receipts proved it. The clerk denied all authenticity.

"It wouldn't mean anything if they did, Cirrus."

"She wouldn't come clean."

"Did you get thrown out, Cirrus?"

"We had a disagreement about evidentiary value," I said.

"Where else did you get thrown out of today?"

"The library. I needed a number. You know. The psychic, Gwendolyn."

"She knows nothing."

"You thought she was a bastion of wisdom five years ago."

"That was your grandfather."

"I need her number," I said.

"I don't have it."

GM's temples pitched to a rogue wavelength, and I knew she was lying too, but this was one I couldn't win. For sure, Gwendolyn's number could be found deep in the earth where the soil smelled of wet leaves. I dug through garden tools, rakes, mowers, shovels, Rototillers and spades. Nothing. A termite extermination manual, a *Playboy* from 1976. I smoked an Old Port, opened a Heidelberg and concocted a dozen phone numbers that might have been Gwendolyn's, then wasted seven dollars in change calling unknown combinations in Glasgow, Peking and Chicoutimi. Then, with my last remaining dime, I dialled the number embossed on Addy's white business card. The past twenty-four hours had taught me precisely nothing.

"Addy?" I said.

"There is no Addy here."

The numbers on the card were blurred with sweat, so there was no way to check.

"There is a Mistress Azy here."

Russell, figures. Bully, loser and dyslexic scribe.

"Can I speak to her?"

"You are."

"It's Cirrus."

"Cirrus who?"

"The Cirrus at Russell's truck."

She thought a long way back to an obviously insignificant event.

"Can't recall."

"You gave me your card."

Inside the phone line, a clatter of barbed wire scurried closer.

"I need to talk to you," I said.

"I don't do talk."

Another long painful silence in the electronic medium and then she said, "But if you wish, we can arrange a consultation. The standard tuition still applies."

Tuition.

"When?"

"Two."

I checked my watch.

"That long?"

"Do you understand my services?"

"I think so."

"Know so. I do not offer sex for money. Can you find the Sikh Temple on Marine Drive?"

Architect Arthur Erickson might have got away with building left-wing universities up on mountaintops during the sixties, but sticking a Punjabi Picasso in the centre of working-class Marine Drive was front-page socialism.

"Turn north and attend the phone call booth at the corner store. You will call again and tell me the number of that phone booth. Call right at two o'clock. Not quarter to. Not five after. Two o'clock. Do not show up drunk or stoned. Mistress despises intoxicants. Do not show up with company. You will be polite and courteous. Shower before you arrive. Do not wear colognes or perfumes, Mistress is allergic. Do not try and top from the bottom and do not think for a second you are running this show because you are not, got it?"

I got it. Standard tuition still applied. The Sikh temple was still there and so were the corner store and phone booth. I stood outside the box and gave the future one last *Upper Chamber* review. As a child, once, I had watched a science fiction movie about a race of grasshoppers that escaped their dying planet and travelled to earth in a time capsule. The craft was submerged beneath the urban landscape for nine million years until an unlucky group of engineers conducting a survey unearthed the mechanical hive. Now, this hive had been buried beneath fifty feet of mud and sealed with five tungsten calipers, so the obvious message was *don't do that, stay away, don't open that hatch*. Do not open that hatch. But within moments, the obsessed scientists were probing and drilling the lock with carbon drills and laser guns to peel back the insignia of the horrible ant skull that should have been the equivalent of an extraterrestrial No Trespassing sign. Without a worry, they popped locks using magnetically charged diamond bits, opened the craft and the world was overrun by bugs. Huge, awful, hideous bugs that looked like they were giant escapees from a Raid commercial. So, I closed the door to the telephone booth, picked up the receiver and dropped in my dime.

My orders were clear, concise and non-negotiable. Do not park in the alley. Go around to the back of the house. Use the gate. Reach through the round hole, pull the string. Do not loiter. Go to the basement door and knock. Make no noise. Wait.

The alleys of South Vancouver in September were a deep and humic affair. Black coffee dirt percolated through layers of lichen, compost and grates. Fences were overgrown with ivy that cascaded down into drains plugged with Pixy-Stix. Everything reeked of decomposing grass except when punctuated by a riff of Acapulco Gold. Azy's house was supposed to be the seventh one from the corner, but I kept losing count. The back lots had all grown together in one continuous centipede of laurel. A hemlock gate with a hand hole made itself known, and so I tucked the pathetic relic of my parents' demise into a paper bag and pulled the string. The yard was maudlin: a wheelbarrow overturned, a flooded fish pool. Strips of moss peeled off the door and a tea towel hung over the glass for a curtain. *Don't open that hatch.* Do not open the hatch. I knocked crisply five times.

The towel was ripped aside, and a dark face glared through the glass from a cold kitchenette. She made a single downwards swipe with her fuck you finger. This was how people ended up on police blotters, had their organs harvested or got themselves entombed in the Burn's Bog of Shame. The basement door beneath the porch was in worse shape than the upstairs one. A slick of algae ran around the door rim. Dog hair stuck to the mat. It's always bad luck to say, How much worse can this get? But then Azy answered the door.

"I told you to come to the basement." Her voice was cold and there was no face, only a dark entity standing in a dark cave.

"Sorry."

"Don't be sorry, be smart. My roommate becomes unsettled when people knock at her residence."

"Sorry," I said again.

She stepped back and leaned against a timber. Stylized jockey suit, white pants, and knee-high boots.

"Close the door and turn the bolt."

Azy looked much taller than she had in Russell's truck. Meaner, too. This high-flying member of the sexual aristocracy appeared the type who had lost everything in the new decade, and her mouth was permanently turned down in a monument of disdain. I held up the bag containing my chrome relic.

"What is in the bag?" she said.

"Can you have a look?"

"Very well. But the regular tuition still applies. Go to the parlour."

The downstairs parlour was done up to look like a Shanghai living room circa 1920. Orange light, Asian fan chair, Ming curtains and shag carpet that smelled of sandalwood. Azy perched herself on a high brass stool that towered in the corner.

"What was your name again?" she said.

"Cirrus."

"And the first time I met you was where?"

"At Russell's truck."

She nodded. The equation at least half-balanced. She smoked Arabic cigarettes, which were then making the rounds in Vancouver. They cost twelve dollars a package and smelled like camel dung.

"Sit," she said.

My options were the sofa or a rattan chair.

"Not on the chair," she said. "On the floor. Chairs and sofas are for guests. You are not a guest. You are a slut. You will plant your cheap ass on the floor, bow your head and answer all the questions I ask you. If you don't answer them quickly and truthfully you will be leaving. If you don't impress Mistress during the first five seconds you will be leaving. If you have broken any of Mistress's previous arrangements, you will be leaving. If you are allowed to stay but fail to keep Mistress amused, she won't feel empathy for you. And believe me, there will come a time shortly when you will want her to feel great empathy. Where did you park?"

"On Clarke."

"How long have you known Russell for?"

"Since elementary school."

"Are you two close?"

"Associates."

That seemed to suffice. She stuffed her cigarette down into the brass bucket of an ashtray that teetered on an alabaster stand. "We need to take care of the business end of this first. Put the envelope with the agreed tuition in that slot on the wall."

In the middle of the cement wall there was a letter slot, Canada Post style, that had MAIL embossed on the iron. I dropped my envelope inside and waited for an explanation. There wasn't one.

"I know why you have come here," she said.

"You do?"

"You have suffered trauma. You feel less than human. That is because you are. You long, you hurt, you suffer. I can fix that, but first I need to know who else have you served."

"Served?"

"What other mistresses have you been with? You can say none if that's the case. But tell me so I know what level of idiocy I'm working with."

She pulled a pair of blue-sequinned gloves over her hands. A small light went on above the mailbox.

"Your tuition has been approved," she said.

"It has?"

"My house girl is also my accountant. Now, is there anything you need to discuss? Speak or forever hold your tongue because it's the last time you'll get a chance. Tell Mistress if you have any medical conditions. If you are allergic. If in your past, besides the one I already know about, if you have had any psychological disorders, psychiatric lapses, or schizophrenia diagnosis. What's that you've brought with you in your bag?"

I laid the device on the table. My new friend gazed down as if she was examining a laboratory specimen.

"Where did you get this?"

"From my parents."

Her eyes flitted far off, calculated a complex problem and solution. "Things are falling into place now." She picked the instrument up and walked across the room. Her heels made an exquisite clatter on the floor.

"You should have told me you were into this," she said.

"What exactly is *this*?"

"No need to be coy. You know exactly what this is. You also know it was never intended for human beings. That it was intended for that vile class of slut below human that exists only in arousal. Alien, ugly and utterly expendable. These are dangerous games, my little fool. People who play them go missing all the time. Now, take off every shred of your miserable clothing and crumple down on your knees. If you do that much right, perhaps I'll give you a try."

There was a long silence between us. This woman had it backwards. I was giving her a try. I was the consumer. She was the supplier. Free market rules applied. I had the money. I had the capital. The cards were stacked with me. She only smiled. Speak in imperfect tongues, you beast, was her favourite line.

Mistress A's dungeon also served as her pantry. The air still smelled of preserves. Pears, cold damp air with a hint of embalming fluid. One coloured light was fixed to the ceiling, perhaps cautioning against an air raid or incoming biohazard, and the one tiny window was boarded over. In the middle of the room there was a bench with stirrups, a suspended cage in the corner, and the far wall was a rack of shiny implements that could have been fishing gear, medical equipment or instruments used to revive cardio patients.

Only one civilized piece of furniture occupied the room, a tall mahogany stool and I didn't get it. After she wrapped a thistle clamp around my scrotum she sat on the stool, had another smoke and prepared for a lengthy interrogation.

"When we are in this room," she said, "you are nothing. You are meaningless. What you want is irrelevant. Unless I ask you, for technical reasons you will not speak. Then you will have to be forthright and complete. Never lie. If I ask what your limits are, you will explain. Never say that you'll do anything. A slave who'll say they'll do anything ends up by getting nothing. Never, ever, be coy. Coyness is a sickness and an evil. Look at Mussolini. He was coy. See what happened to him? You will never complain but neither shall you be bullish. If you are aroused and you are foolish enough to ask for more, you may say green and I will increase the tempo, but I can assure you, you will only ever ask for that once. If things are too difficult for your virgin white ass, you may say yellow, and I will slow down. I get that a lot, and many of my clients develop a fetish for the word itself. One of my slaves legally changed his middle name to Jaune, which is French for yellow. He was from Montreal. Screaming, yelling, begging is applauded. I don't consider it a sign of weakness or an insult. You may scream all you want, and no one outside will hear you. The room is soundproofed. If you say red, the session will stop. Terminate. End. *Finis*, no more. Do you understand that? Say red and we leave the dungeon. We may talk about it after, but there will be no more play. There are no refunds. Any questions?"

"How do I come?"

It sounded like a fair enough question. The only question, really. In the end isn't that what everyone wants? My Mistress exhaled once the way my grade three grammar teacher had when I had spelled the word "restaurant" wrong for the fiftieth time.

"Orgasm is not a slave activity," she said. "If you want a hooker, try Davie Street. Ask again for gratification and the session will be terminated. The only orgasm you experience is through me. You experience nothing for your own sake. I enjoy myself and you suffer. That is the natural order of things."

Super. She got up. Her boots creaked. The polished spurs on the heels slipped behind me and I thought she'd left the room.

"Get down," she said.

I was going to. Honest. I was getting around to that. I was trying to extinguish my male ego in the arctic water of her cruelty, but before I had the chance, a burst of white blew the filaments of my head out. Azy had electrocuted me with a cattle prod. In grade school I had stuck a fork into the television socket, but I was eleven then and didn't get aroused. This time, a supernova of light blew open my cranium, I smelled her perfume and hit the floor.

Strange sounds came then, alien sounds. The clicking of claws on the concrete. Feet with many heels, metal toes, perhaps centipedes with spikes or possibly mandibles tapping out a code on tin cans. In either case, there wasn't much I could do. My arms were bound in shackles and Azy's Persian carpet tasted of dirt.

There were a lot of places I could have been then, in the gym, playing volleyball, drinking Guinness in my pub or sitting at the poolside watching normal girls in normal bikinis. There were places I should have been also: painting my grandmother's shed, phoning my brother, studying Heimlen's *Biochemistry*, chapter eleven, and all of them would have been safer than this. This was a cold, dirty, disease-ridden and humiliating place. My captor ground the spur of her boot into my spine the way fat travellers force cigars into jars of mescal. I had the rank urge to hit her, but that was not possible. Nothing was possible. If there was any future for me, I had no hand in it. I could be beaten for my cash. I could have photos taken of my submission and sent to *Maclean's* or be blackmailed for more money than my trust fund would ever have. Or my captor could have walked out, taken my car and left. That was my most-feared scenario. That I be left alone forever, buried in a pit of solitary confinement and forgotten.

"You thought this was going to be light entertainment, didn't you?" she said. She examined her fingernail. "You thought this was going to be a little frat party where I'd dress up with pink balloons over my tits, giggle and then give you a blow job."

She kicked me in the gut, and I coiled up ditch-pig style. I tried to negotiate or to at least apologize, but she wasn't listening. She turned abruptly and walked over to the wall that housed a hundred inhuman instruments. There was a lot for her to choose from and none of the choices looked painless. Leather straps and wooden paddles with holes in the centre, chrome spurs and shackles with iron thorns. When I started to squirm, she hooked my shackles up to a D-ring that was suspended from the ceiling, hit a winch button, and I dangled there like a beef carcass. She selected a drab strap with copper burrs and struck my ass until the skin welted up in a lattice of white, and then she used a waffle rack that put blood dots between the squares. Aesthetic, but by then I wanted the hour to be over. Azy thought otherwise. She tested out a set of clamps to puncture my nipple and then a strip of adhesive tape to yard the hair from my chest. I screamed and she slapped me.

"Don't turn away from me," she said. "Don't ever turn away from me. Do you hear? I had too many people turn away from me when I was in the hospital. Hospital, you're asking? What hospital? You forgot to ask about that, didn't you? That angle wasn't covered, was it? All you were thinking about was your pathetic little cock. Well, I'll tell you now, I've spent a fair bit of my life in a hospital. Guess what for? Do you know what two years in a psychiatric ward can do to you? Never turn away from me. I had people turn away from me in prison as well, and I swore that would never happen again. You didn't know about that either, did you? Oversight number two. Forgot to run your security checks. Rather stupid, don't you think? All those years in college and you didn't realize that natural selection happens in the dungeon. Didn't you read in any of your textbooks that dominatrixes actually hate men? Why do you think we get into this business? Let me see. What should we play? I know. Let's pretend that you are a filthy common criminal, say, a rapist, which probably isn't too far from the truth, and you're going to have your balls cut off. Probably at one of your stupid frat parties where you porked a pre-teen on the billiard table with a hockey jersey stuffed in her mouth. You college dicks are all the same. I can't get all of you, but now I've got you so I'm making up for lost time. I'll tell you what's going to happen. I'm going to castrate you, kill you and let one of my boys dump you in the river. He'll probably screw you in the ass before he's done. Nobody cares if a slave lives or dies. Nobody misses them. Nobody will miss you. I bet nobody even knows where you are. I bet you didn't tell anybody. I bet you didn't call anybody, leave a note or flight plan. Maybe you were going to leave a message for your grandmother on her new pink stationery, but in the end, you got embarrassed and didn't bother. I bet you parked your car miles from here and walked in thinking that would make you safer. In fact, that made your situation worse. That's what I really like, you know, is killing the stupid ones. That's what turns me on. It's like they have it coming. They're easy. They're free. The ones who have no family. They're pathetic. What do you think about that, bitch? My little vanilla, middle-class slut who wanted a thrill and ended up with his throat slit open on his first visit to a whack-job whore. You think I'm a whore, don't you? Don't you?"

I didn't really, but she still spat in my face. The saliva tasted of tobacco. Her mascara ran. Then a titanium scarab on the rack caught her eye. The implement had wings, a metal spur and a thin wire between its antennae that would no doubt slice through my dick and I was right. The wire went around my scrotum. The spur curled into my balls. My testicles bled.

About this time, a childhood image of a red-haired, crazy woman flashed through my head. She had lived in the ditches outside Abbotsford and often beat cats to death. I knew at once that Azy was utterly insane, and my life was going from bad to worse. Her red lips touched my ear, and she whispered to me in garbled iambic pentameters. What was that magic "no" word, the one that made everything stop: rinse, relegate, radish, riddance?

The scarab wheel rolled over and my nuts gushed. Tiny little dots of blood that made the first outbreak of measles look easy. Then she took off her sequined gloves and put on a pair of rubber ones.

"This is so I won't leave any traceable oils," she said. "The medical examiner always looks for traceable oils when they find the body."

She went to the table and picked up the leather sheath. Then she stood behind me and wrapped the strap around my neck. Down deep in the recesses of my soul a switch flipped to half-life.

"At long fucking last," she said. She twisted the knot sideways and my throat closed off. My face went red and champagne bubbles burst in my head; all the insects from the spacecraft flooded onto their new home. Then there were people scurrying around, scribbling notes and a voice that sounded like an old grade-school teacher commenting on my lack of self-control.

My eyebrow was split. My temple was bruised. What might have once been a scrotum was cratered with spur marks. I knew this because Azy had set a mirror against the wall as we sat back in the parlour and drank green tea. She leaned back on her stool, sized me up and smoked.

"How was that?" she said.

Her voice was a long way off, coming through a thin metal tube. I was holding a glass of tonic water and all I could do was nod.

"I take it that means fabulous."

"What happened?"

She gazed at the embers at the end of her cigarette.

"You screamed in a strange language. You came. You passed out."

"I can't recall."

"Not surprising."

A streak of red came off in my palm. Between my legs was a blood-smeared remainder of shrivelled testicles that I no longer owned.

"You can use the washroom in a minute," she said. "Don't worry, I took the spur out. But sit tight for a moment because your brain is short on oxygen. If the bruises come up in conversation, tell your friends you hit your head while you were working on a car. That's always a good excuse. As far as your dick goes, well, don't attend any nude hot tub parties for a while. The swelling usually goes down in about a week."

"A week?"

"We did get interesting leads for next time."

"Naturally."

"I know what you're thinking." She showed some degree of pride. "That you'll never come back. That this all was a sick mistake and perhaps life in a monastery doesn't sound so bad. But I know a player when I see one. You'll be back. You just haven't decoded it yet. In a day or so the real impact will sink in. Stand up if you can. Turn around."

She motioned me up with her lighter. I did as I was told, a veritable vegetable on display in the produce aisle.

"Small on the cock bit," she said. "But you're in good shape. If I had to put you in a category, I'd say you are the college slut sort. A highly prized body type as far as the sexual underworld goes. You can obviously take a lot of pain, so I think you might be a fine investment with a little training."

Azy did some math in her head.

"I like to work with people on a long-term basis," she said. "Basically, the more you do of this, the better it gets. Also the more cost-effective. Soon normal sex won't appeal to you anymore. Normal people will bore you too. So will a normal life. That will scare you at first, but leave the fear behind. It's useless. Soon this will be the only worthwhile place to be. Getting to know me takes time. And money. You'll have to accept that. I don't take people on as associates or pets until I've established a solid relationship with them. I'm telling you the rules now because I think you have potential. Most of the people who come here, come once. They've fulfilled their single lifetime fantasy and they're gone. Others stay as clients. That's what you are now. A client. My protocol is strict. We do it the same way every time for now until you get the act down right. Then we move on to another act. Then we move on to other people. Sessions will always be booked in advance. I don't want you getting any wrong ideas. You will never be my lover. You will never be a pal. You have only one pro-mistress and that is me. Any deviation and you're banned. Any slipping up or lapse of manners and you're banned. Any showing up unannounced and I call the police or worse. Well, we don't need to go into that, do we?"

The amber light flipped on above the mirror.

"Our time is pretty much up," she said.

"Where do you buy the implements from?"

"Mistress doesn't buy anything. They are given to me. As offerings. There's some from France and Tunisia, even Moscow. I have a slave in town who owns a metal shop, and he builds them to my specs. I have another acquaintance who trades in the Middle East, and she imports them for me. They are ancient. When I was younger, I thought as a child, I acted a child. But now, I am what I am, and I have put away childish things. I'll keep the one you gave me as I gift. The house girl already has it filed. Get dressed now. It's after four and I have a five-thirty."

The back alley smelled of autumn trash, and the inside of my underwear stuck to my cock in a million pulpits of blood. The two surfaces would probably never be separated. The onset of mosquito season might be a good cover story, better yet, a rare disease that had no researchable symptoms. A mugging, beating or extortion plot was not beyond reason, but only to those who did not know me well. Hot tub parties and locker rooms I could avoid, but the overriding stare of my grandmother would be harder: "Cirrus, why is your cock perforated like the lunar surface and how did it happen?"

EIGHT

RUSSELL WAS CONFIDENT. The Jubilee Pool Hall was the most mythic place on earth, and he occupied its parking lot. Time had stopped. He would not grow old, and his teeth would never rot. From half a block off, he looked the romantic poet, his jean jacket riddled with holes, his T-shirt faded, and his gaze transfixed on the desert of gravel alleys and telephone wires that was his muse.

"Do you know I almost OD'd once?"

"Once?" I said.

"I had a dozen hits of White Blotter. I could get them at bulk for fifty cents and sell them for three bucks. Man, that is margin. Some constable who wanted to be a corporal disagreed. They had been trying to bean me for months, and he had a real boner for me. They have a network, you know, cops, like ants. You can't just move from one jurisdiction to another because they communicate. They rub antennae and the filthy cop juice gets carried from skull to skull. Doesn't even matter what language they speak. Cops have their own language so cops in Bolivia can talk to cops in Washington. That's how they got Che Guevara. Anyway, I had these hits of Blotter, and they cornered me at the end of an alley just like this one. The alley was not supposed to be a dead end, but they were putting in a condominium. Can you believe it, a condo? They jumped me like I was Jack the Ripper and bounced me to the ground, but I stuffed the Blotter in my mouth. I took it down with this huge gob of spit that I had been saving up. One of them screamed, "Don't let him swallow! Don't let him swallow!" They were frantic. He grabbed me by the throat and started choking me out. Man, like he was trying to hump me. But down the Blotter went. Into the old gut-ola of freedom. So, they drove me to the hospital in handcuffs and had the doctor pump my stomach. All they could think about was their evidence. They kept on asking the doctor, "Can't you do this, can't you do that?" And the old doc shook his head. I guess it was too late and the acid absorbed into my brain.

"At first it was like a regular trip and things were good. But then a few minutes later, not so good. I tripped bad, went black and the nurse stuck this needle in me. They tried a new kind of rehabilitation drug and then I thought I was dead. I've never been so terrified and, worse, it seemed like it was never going to end, which is the way it is if you're dead. Finally, after three days I realized I was not dead. The doc came into the room, and he said, 'You are a lucky young man.' And I said, 'Damn right. I almost didn't get that acid down my throat.' He shook his head again and walked out. Never saw those cops, either. I guess their evidence was destroyed."

"What did your parents say?"

"My parents?"

"In the hospital."

"God knows."

The Jubilee Pool Hall was supposed to be a place where bad things happened to bad people. Every month, when there was not much else on the police blotter, the community newspaper would report another drug bust, fist fight, arrest or imaginary adult swing club that supposedly met upstairs after hours. In fact, not a lot happened at the Jubilee except for billiards. That was the way of the suburbs, and the whole decade. Bad things never came from where you thought. There were twelve tables, and the best slate had a sign above it that read For Senior Players Only. There were all kinds of rules in the pool hall, signs that read No Obscene Language, and No Spitting, in Old Western curlicues, as if the sheriff might appear. I once bought a lid there for twelve dollars, but the contents had been primarily oregano.

"Anyway," Russell tossed his cigarette. "Let's get down to the business at hand. You need money, correct?"

Correct, Russell, correct.

"And what, may I be so bold to inquire, do you need the money for?"

Vices drive economies. Economies produce governments. Governments outlaw vices. This was public service.

"I thought," he said, "you had a million dollars coming to you."

"In a trust."

"What's a trust?"

"Where the bank doles out cash conditionally."

"Why?"

"Because I was technically a minor when my parents died." I stressed the word "technically." The legal age in British Columbia was nineteen. Not twenty-one or eighteen as in other provinces or in most US states. Nineteen. Prime number. Not good for much else except to be odd. The year 1919, the National Socialists formed a farmer's political party, the year Wilfred Laurier died in office and the year Mount Kelud blew a huge hole in the Indonesian sea floor for no apparent reason, but the litigious part of the will stated I couldn't collect my cash until the end of my twenty-fifth year.

"So come on," he said. "What do you need the money for?"

"Personal stuff."

"Personal, right."

"It is."

"It's for Azy, isn't it?"

"Who?"

"You know who."

"Your boss?" I said.

"She's not my boss."

"Seen her recently?"

"Occasionally, I see her."

"How is she?"

"It's for her, isn't it?" he said.

"I'm trying to accumulate wealth during a recession."

"Nobody collects cash, dude. Guys only want cash for three things: cars, dope and women. You strike me as the door number three kind. I can't tell you how to run your life, but there is one screwed-up lady."

"So, you hang out with her?"

"Strictly business," he said. "No huggy-huggy. If you're looking for tail, you are wasting your time. She doesn't do that. I pass on the intel since we're going to be associates."

"Just tell me how I acquire said funds."

"You have to be willing."

"No weapons, no robbery."

"No, none of that." His eyes scoured the horizon for spies, infiltrators or electronic detection equipment. "There's rarely any money in that, anyway. This one is easy. There are these people. Rich people. Capitalists. They own a drilling company. That's oil. They are not even from here. They are from Alberta, hitherto Texas, hitherto Commie Russia. Anyway, these people took something from us. We want it back. You help me get said thing back and I will give you the agreed sum. Two hundred dollars."

"Three hundred."

"Three then."

Russell rubbed his hands. Easy. I recalled the premise from *Bridge on the River Kwai*: easy, we'll get the prisoners to do it.

"What is it exactly that we are retrieving?"

"The less you know, the better."

I calculated. "Is it drugs?"

"No."

"Plutonium?"

"Are you freaking in or not?"

There were four plum neighbourhoods in town to do repo because they were old money and unguarded: Southeast Marine Drive, for the industrialists who lent their mansions out as movie sets; Shaughnessy, with rich partiers who lent their houses out to coke dealers; and the British Properties, whose owners lent their houses out to anybody but Jews; then, old Kerrisdale, where retirees lent their exotic orchards out to wasps after they died. In the summer of 1956, the city formed a wasp eradication program to deal with the red-jacketed threat growing fat on rotting peaches. Years later, the tangle of Clingstones remained, tinged with pyrethrum.

Russell's gearbox was a 3-on-the-tree, and after he pushed the arm into high, he punched CKLG, "Vancouver's Hottest Rock Station" to full volume.

"How often do you go boxing?" he asked.

"Two, maybe three times a week."

He nodded.

"Who's the coach?"

"Kimball. Kim Kimball."

"Get the shit kicked out of you?"

"Often."

He nodded again. These were the right answers. There was no point bringing up the past, and the inside of Russell's truck smelled as bad as a change room before a fight: nervous sweat, old running shoes and talcum powder all coated with a thick layer of Bengay.

"Isn't this cool?" he said.

"What?"

"Living the dream."

"Can we turn that down?"

"Sure. I get it. You need to concentrate. Me too."

He whispered a rehearsed set of instructions to the windshield because the grand design of the operation was so complicated it had to be sounded out phonetically.

By Oak Street, the bramble had shifted to laurel. By Granville, the trees were shaped into hourglasses, and past Arbutus, the yards were loaded with fan palms. That was the rage. Plant enough tropicals and winter would go away. We ended up at the end of the alley under a Norfolk pine.

"The target house," he said, pointing his cigarette. "It's the yellow split-level with the faggy garage."

"Faggy is gauche, Russell."

"The getaway vehicle has to remain covert, so this is as close as my truck gets."

"You mean we're not going in together?"

"Of course not, dude. You are the one getting the bucks. There's an Oriental flower painted on the door."

"What species?"

"It doesn't freaking matter what kind. How many houses do you know that have a huge monocot painted on the door? The door may be unlocked, it may not. If not, the windows are usually open. Failing that, well, you'll have to find a way. If you play it cool, like you belong, no one will know the difference. Take a tin of paint and a roller from the back of the truck. Pull a painter's cap over your eyes. Go inside. Go to the bedroom. You will find a box, a Chinese box. More like Polynesian. Well, to tell you the truth, it might look like a coconut husk. It's about the size of a football, bigger maybe. It's red with gold trim. Gay gold filigrees in a Second World War–

hand grenade kind of shape. Do you know what a filigree is? Think Ukraine. Take said box and vamoose. Don't take anything else. Don't touch anything. Don't breathe on anything. And for God's sake, don't jerk off. If you run into trouble, go for the cross street and I'll bail you out."

"Trouble?"

"You won't have any."

"Where in the bedroom is the box?"

"In a place a man would hide something, where a woman wouldn't find it."

"Give me the money," I said.

"That's not the way business is done."

"Give me half now and half when I get back."

Russell's eyes were neither brown nor blue. They only reminded me of October.

"Just go," he said.

The target house, as Russell put it, was exactly as he said. A beautiful split-level with a golf course front lawn and trees trimmed right out of the eighteenth century. One couldn't miss the flowers painted on the door, either. Black Lotus buds wandered around the doorknob and then up towards the eaves. So, I had the right house. I had my cans of paint. I thought briefly of how I should have been painting my grandmother's shed, knocked twice on the door and, when no one answered, I went inside.

This was a home not lived in. The hardwood floor had a waxy sheen. The living room was sparse with colonial furniture, a dark banyan wood table with a Libyan vase. A flask of velvet fruit. On the wall hung an oil painting of a man with an elephant in imperial Bombay. Sterile and beautiful, the residence was a collection of museum pieces that had been assembled by a group of curators who never met. Most incredible were the aromas, nectar blue and floral; the humidifier was laced with either pollen or cough syrup. It occurred to me then, this was a flower untouched. No one had ever broken into this place before. I was the first. A set of numbers and letters flashed across my mind: 264(A), CCC, but they soon fluttered away. The actual wording of the section is break and enter *with intent*, and my intent was to retrieve an object owed, not to steal it. So, no problem. Say you had to rescue a valuable piece of art from a burning museum. Same thing. *Sans intent* and out of jail free.

Upstairs, there were two master bedrooms, so whoever lived here slept separately. Unruffled silk comforters gilded in gold and black. All the clothes in the drawers were still wrapped, yellow pants, frilled white blouses. Here, nothing moved, nobody laughed, cried or wept over a lost cat. In the bottom drawer of the dresser, beneath a coil of string pearls and toiletries, lay the box with the filigreed orb. Antique for sure and not that covert. Russell could have done this on his own, but Russell was being smart. I was being stupid. I was taking the chances. Russell was smoking Players.

The orb was sealed with a gold lock, but no doubt Russell would have a hammer for that. I wrapped the prize in a tarp and a photograph caught my eye. The five by eight had been slipped under the corner of the mirror. The photo was nondescript and hazy, two distant people standing on a beach with an unrecognizable shoreline and unknowable faces. I'd seen faces like this in nightmares after my parents left. The scene played repeatedly whether I was asleep or awake or on the bus: my mother and my father were at our summer cabin. She lounged on the pebble beach in a lawn chair. He mixed concrete. The sun was bright on the water and the stone beach smelled like seaweed. I asked my mother a question. She answered, but there was no voice. Her lips moved, but no sound. My father still mixed concrete, but there was no clinking of gears or slapping of mortar. Like an old Super 8 movie, the motions slowed. Waves on the rocks, yet no lapping noise, a boat in the bay, no motor. And then my mother and my father dissolved into the glare of the beach.

I ambled down the rocks looking for them, but they were gone. Then I couldn't remember what their faces looked like. Maybe they never had faces, only dresses and work shirts. Seagulls circled piers, driftwood lodged between lobster traps, but my mother and father were gone. Far down the beach, I met a couple who said they were my parents. They looked a little like my parents. The woman had the same hair as my mother. The man had the same hands as my father, rough and weathered, but deep down, I knew this wasn't them, so I kept going. Later, I met another couple. They looked even less like my parents. There were one or two things that were like my parents, the same eyeglasses as my mother, or the same set of tools as my father, but that wasn't them either. Every successive couple I met on the beach after that looked less and less like the people I loved, and there was no sound.

"Where the hell were you?" Russell said. The inside of the cab was filled with smoke.

"Did you know most insects have no sense of hearing?"

"What?"

"Just drive," I said.

He shoved the truck into gear. I put the prize on the seat.

"Under the seat," he said. "For Chrissakes, put the loot under the seat."

We pulled off McMullen, then down onto Forty-First.

"What took so long?" he said.

"It's a small box in a big house."

"Did you have a nap or what?"

"Done, already."

"You put everything back in place?"

"Exactly in place," I said.

"No one saw you?"

"The place was empty," I said.

"Completely?" He gave his crotch a good yank as if the fact surprised him.

"For years."

Forty-First was crammed with buses, women in shorts walking dogs, ethnic food stores and hardware delivery trucks, so in a moment we were digested into the immense design of things. Russell had one hand on the steering wheel and used the other to pop a Molson. The beer was warm, the foam was warm and most of it ended up on the dash. "You okay, guy?"

"Where's my money?"

He did his standard shoulder check.

"In the glovebox, dude."

Two one-hundreds, four twenties, a ten and two fives. That made over two hours with the woman who loved to hurt me most. Russell stared down at my hands.

"You said you didn't touch anything," he said.

"I didn't."

"What's that shit all over your hands?"

Not shit exactly, but it sure wasn't soap suds. The fluid had the consistency of glue, smelled septic and was smeared up to my elbows.

"I have no clue."

"Where did it come from?"

"What is it, Russell?"

"They're your hands," he said.

"It's your target house."

"Did you lick the garden hose too?"

In the rear-view mirror, my lips were white and flaked.

"It's probably just slug trail."

"So, you sucked your fingers?"

"What's in the egg?"

"Never mind," he said.

"What if it's a biohazard?"

"You've got your money."

I stuffed the money into my pant pocket and drank the Molson.

"Spend it wisely," he said.

NINE

BY THE TIME my parents began leaving me clues I could understand, there was no latitude left to decipher them. I had a Buick Skyhawk, a September tan, a lot of cheap liquor and a new confidante with criminality for charm. Also, I had just committed my first *professional* B&E. Peter Gzowski was a star. You could surf at Tofino for free and cocaine was eighty dollars a gram. I was twenty-one.

No worthwhile clue ever comes the way anybody wants them. No notes on papyrus reeds, no cryptic patterns left in mirror condensation or prophetic old men with bony fingers. Simply an autumn garden free of snails. A lost car key showing up glued to the ceiling. Six houseflies entombed beneath a pillow. That last one should have been a red flag, half-digested bottlenoses in the bedding. Problem was, of course, twenty-one-year-old minds don't see real clues. The habit is to derail reality in twenty-four hours or by the last hangover reprieve, whichever comes last.

Take that lost car key I peeled off the ceiling Tuesday morning. The sugary lump of glue that secured the metal to the stipple tasted vaguely of taxidermy fluid and not ignition lube. Instead of analyzing the facts, I used my grandmother's ladder, retrieved the key and headed back to the liquor store. One bottle of sugar-drenched Red Berry Jack and a handful of GM's codeine phosphate later, I pondered the different scenarios my loot could purchase with the illustrious Mistress Azy: Azy et clamps, Azy avec whips, Azy sans mercy. By midnight, the Berry Jack was gone, but not to worry, a few local mushrooms and some Johnnie Walker overproof later, the fantasies flourished exponentially: Azy with a ball gag, Azy with a blowtorch, Azy's body hardening into a potassium blue shell and her delicate jaw erupting into mandibles until the shingled roof of my grandparents' house appeared only as a smudge of light in the suburban sprawl.

Wednesday morning, the keys were stuck to the ceiling again. Starting to see a pattern? My room was littered with things that didn't belong to me: a wooden toucan bird, a pearl tie clip and an unsigned letter from someone in the Seaforth Highlanders. Also, the inside of my mouth tasted bad. Too much like the common banana slug that frequented coastal compost piles in the fall (if you've ever had the pleasure).

The October light that filtered through my bedroom window was septic grey and horrible to be hungover in. The physical symptoms of a Scotch hangover were bad enough, but Vancouver hangovers were the worst. Maudlin, damp and smelling of pulp, a place that showed no mercy to the lonely, shuffling them off past the ivy on the Sylvia Hotel into the Pacific Ocean, to be eaten by fiddler crabs.

At that point, the details of my offence came back with disgusting clarity. Here were the facts. I had broken into a stranger's house for profit. I had taken their possessions for self-gain. I would use the cash to go to a sex trade worker. Prostitute. Dominatrix. Sexual care therapist, whatever. There was no way I could write this off as a misguided search for my parents. I had pillaged an innocent home like Hannibal crossed the Alps — over the stranger's kitchen, through their hallways and into the sanctity of their master bedroom, where I dissected their underwear, jewellery and journals. I may as well have shot my load in their toilet. I was now the exact kind of person my father would have talked about "shooting dead in the den" with his Friday night rummy pals while they mulled the stupidity of Dieppe.

I picked up the phone and called Russell.

"Dude, it is six o'clock in the morning."

Russell was confused. A female yawn surfaced from the sheets in the background.

"I'm worried about yesterday," I said.

"Who is this?"

"Who do you think?"

"I don't know you, man."

The line went dead.

Loneliness hits hardest on the ventral striatum of the brain announcing social failure. It's a nasty tool of human evolution that should have been exorcised eons ago. No surprise that Arachnidia, especially Araneae don't need friends and are such brutal hunters. They don't possess a ventral striatum. Van Gogh apparently had his damaged in a studio accident. Maybe I should have got Azy to cut my ear off. The phone rang back.

"You shouldn't have done that," the voice said.

"Who is this?"

"There is a limit to how much people will put up with."

"I'm coming by."

"It's just going to bring about a lot of trouble."

"What are you afraid of?" I said.

"Fingerprints. Drug residue, pawn cards."

"What?"

"I think your parents left you a lot, and you should hold onto what you've got."

Why people scream into a phone when they don't get an answer is beyond me. All it forces the other person to do is hold the phone farther away from their ear, which lessens the chances of getting a reply, but scream was exactly what I did. Then I smashed the receiver on the kitchen counter, the sink, the stove and finally split the earpiece by striking it on the fridge. I recalled the smell of old linoleum in my parents' house and the crunching of uniform boots on their gravel driveway, so I went to the extension phone and dialled a familiar number.

"Fielding," the voice said.

"It's me."

There was long pause. Obviously, I wasn't as high on the menu as I imagined.

"Cirrus, lad," he said. "How are you?"

"I'm fine."

I could see Fielding sitting back at his desk with his feet up on a copy of Humphrey's *Investigative Techniques*, his brown oxfords scuffed around the toes, his tartan sweater folded around his midriff, and a rubber squeeze ball being crushed between his fingers.

"Are you in trouble, sport?" he said.

Fielding's voice was always serene, the type of serene that would get you past your next examination if you played by his rules.

"Me, trouble?"

"I may be able to help," he said.

"Why are you on to that?"

"Policeman's intuition. It's also six in the morning."

"And you're at work?"

"Always, lad. Always."

"Someone phoned about my mother's exhibits."

A castor squealed from his side of the phone. Sliding back in his leather chair, he would extract a manila file from an oak bureau, then select a toothpick from the dispenser in his drawer.

"What did they want?"

"Fingerprints, pawn cards, bank records. It was the constable who returned my mother's boots."

"Boots?" he said.

"I recognized her voice."

Paper shuffled across the desk, the snapping of staples. "And which copper was this?"

"She drove me home from Ms. Downs's."

"What was her name?"

Name, name, I knew there was a name under Neanderthal. "Halocene, Holocene?"

"Like the headlights?"

"Like the geologic period."

"Hang on," he said.

The cardboard divider flipped between Fielding's thick fingers and he hummed "Für Elise" while making his way through the folio.

"Lad, we did take such effects, but there is no Holocene down as transporting property."

"She did so."

"Negative, lad. I keep entries of all seized items with a Report to Justice. I've got notes that go back to the initial search date on June 22, 1975. What did she look like?"

"You Brits would say a real cracker."

"And the boots?"

"High Italian ones."

"It worries me that a person posing as an official would phone and be so elusive. We don't work that way. She'd identify herself with a regimental number and state her inquiry. Somebody is having you on."

"She gave me a ride. We parked in the driveway. She was the only person who made me feel halfway decent."

"What blurs memory makes us feel better."

"Do you still have the boots?"

"There's no point in pulling random exhibits, sport."

"This needs work," I said.

"Let us do the work."

"I'll find out where the call came from."

"If you tamper with the environment, the trail becomes contaminated. I've seen this before. Family members introducing artifacts and soon you're investigating the disturbance and not the evidence. Then there's no fact from fiction."

Fielding gave me the standard rundown. The search for missing persons was an arduous affair. The area checked, the routes combed, the perimeter secured. Hazard areas. Exit paths. Hospitals, jails, mental wards, morgues. Vehicles, buses, cabs. All of that was done years ago. After that the avenues grow exponentially. Especially when a "Meditated Class Two Loss" (MC2) occurs and after my mother went AWOL, that's what we had. "Meditated" assumes that the people involved don't want to be found, and "Class Two" means those involved might be tampering with their trail. For this event, post offices, court documents, telephone records, voter registrations and family interviews are analyzed. So are fraternal associations. Go figure. More than ten percent of all missing persons categorized as MC2 belonged to a fraternal organization and contact them somehow after they disappear. Everyone who wants to slip silently into that good night wants a new name, and what you need for that is a birth certificate, social insurance card or, in Quebec, a baptismal record. Stolen will suffice. Then everybody wants a driver's licence. A favourite tactic of the morally impoverished is to find the birth certificate of a recently deceased matching the client, forget the body, then apply for a DL to put a face to the name. Easier in transient circles where no one misses a bottle collector, but in middle-class life, that's a tall order to fill. Most of the time, MC2s forge ahead with a stolen birth certificate and that's when they're caught. For example, when John Doe Missing and John Doe Found both apply for a new driver's licence, a ping goes off in the system and Fielding has his man. "An exhaustive Class Two search can consume three hundred man-hours easily," Fielding said. "And none of it romantic." If a "Type Three" case arises, where foul play is suspected but not quite enough to consider it a homicide investigation, then the hours can run into the thousands. This usually only happens with VIPs or cases that baffle the investigator's staff sergeant. Wiretaps, surreptitious searches, polygraphs and other methods, referred to as outside the box, are employed. Yes, lad, we tapped your phone. Sylvia Astor never loved you. Sorry."

In my grandmother's basement there was a fruit cellar that was unlocked easily. Tins of plums, apricots and apple pepper jam sat in rows and behind them, a chest of relics I kept hidden. Braids of hair, war memorials, an oar lock from the first rowboat my father constructed. Even a company wristwatch. Most things I didn't hide, my grandmother destroyed.

Entombed in plastic wrap still, taped by the good constable's hand, were my mother's boots. They were exactly as I remembered them: knee height with a glassy finish and tall stilettos. Tin spurs, thick laces and elaborate stitching. Thousands of knots embroidered in delicate bundles. Sewn to the cuff there was a small tag, Major's Fine Fashion Leather, and then the light faded into the deep well of the boot.

I slid my hand down to the ankle and discovered it was no thicker than a pipe. Then to the heel, where there was not a soft pad but a cruel divot. Finally, to the toes, where not five but six slots were cut into the cowhide.

"What are you doing?" Grandmom towered above me with a dishtowel furrowed in a broiler pot.

"Looking at boots," I said.

"What for?"

"The detective was asking about them."

"What did he want this time?"

"To know if they matched an exhibit."

"We had an agreement," she said.

"What agreement?"

"That you would not break through locked doors."

"It's just this once."

"It never ends at once." She rubbed my temple with the towel. "You look green as a garden slug."

"Long night."

"I heard."

"You did?"

"You became garrulous."

Garrulous wasn't good. Garrulous was humiliating. Be contrite when nighttime garrulity is detected.

"I'm sorry I kept you up," I said.

"You weren't in your room, either."

"I wasn't?"

"The window was open."

Fireflies, werewolves, alcoholic blackouts. I recalled the fluttering of red wings around the silhouette of a cherry tree.

"I needed to get out," I said.

"Through the window?"

"I'd been drinking."

"Find friends for talking and drinking," she said.

"This is a tough city to make friends in."

"Vancouverites are cliquey, I know, but please do try, and clean up after yourself."

My grandmother gazed down at me with an expression of deep pity, and then she turned and went back to the depths of carrot stew.

Major's Fine Fashion Leather had not been in the phone book for over seven years, and their number went through to the YMCA. The last address of the institution was 1440 Commercial Drive. This was a part of town that had gone from immigrant-working class of the 1940s to industrial to slum, then experienced a slight resurrection with the invention of the espresso machine. Most of the businesses were destined for obscurity.

Only a grey facade with whitewashed windows occupied the front entrance. On one side, a butcher shop had been reduced to selling kebabs and on the other, a dull furniture store lay empty. But Major's Fine Leather had faded into history. Some of the original letters were still legible on the marquee but that was layers before. A notary public had survived a short stint, and then Ted's Taxidermy Shop had a go but that too was the distant past. The brass handle wasn't going to turn, and the hours were slender. Ten a.m. until three, closed for lunch.

Around back, the alley dropped down to a rear entrance that had been renovated into a bohemian café. White tables, sun umbrellas and a few copies of the *Daily Worker*.

Sal sat with an older, refined-looking gentleman. He wore a blazer with war medals racked to his chest and drank blueberry tea.

"It would probably be better if you steered clear of her altogether," he said.

"She's hard to give up," Sal said.

Poor stupid Sal. She looked less interesting and far dowdier in a pullover sweater and jeans.

"Sorry," she said at last. "I didn't recognize you."

"What's up, Sal?"

"Not much."

"Not working today?"

"I don't work on Saturdays."

This would be a rerun of every single monologue I had performed in the museum for the past year and a half. I waited for an introduction but obviously I wasn't going to get one. Her partner rubbed his moustache and pressed a wrinkle in his jacket. A warbler lighted on the table and picked off a crust of biscotti. None of us spoke.

"I came down to check out the leather shop," I said.

"Why?" For the smallest second, her voice quickened.
"Check on a pair of boots."
"Boots?"
"My mother's."
"I think it's a taxidermy shop now," she said.
"You know it?"
"Of it."
"Have you seen the owner?"
"He comes and goes."
"When?"
"Cirrus's parents disappeared five years ago," she said to her tablemate, a man more interested in the tip of his tie than in either of us. The old veteran nodded gravely as if the whole affair was too tragic to consider, then went back to his tea.
"Is there a back door?"
"I don't think there is."
People like Sal just oozed optimism.
"How about meeting when I'm done?" I said stupidly.
Sal fondled the beads around her neck and consulted a distant calendar.
"Go ahead," the man said. "I've got to be off anyway."
"Are you sure?" Sal said.
"No, really, go."
"Dorios is down the block. But no later than two."
Right away you know you've made a mistake. Accepting dinner at a crazy aunt's place or giving a cheque to the Save the Donkeys of Peru. Right away you know it's not fixable. Sal's life was a knot of pathetic encounters with geriatric Korean War veterans and handicapped museum-goers and somehow, I had just bought in.
There wasn't anyone at the café counter, so I walked up the stairwell and rehashed the list of cover stories: my budgie needed stuffing, my antiques gilded or boots refitted.

But if anyone had kept shop upstairs that was another lifetime ago. The ceiling rafters were exposed, spliced with electrical wires, and mice faeces filled the cracks. On both sides of the narrow room stood rows of taxidermy animals affixed on stands. Falcons, badgers, raccoons and a wolverine all contorted in threatening poses with timeless eyes and yellow gums. At the end of the last row, encased in a glass booth, stood a six-foot grasshopper that might have been lifted off a movie set or out of a circus. Compound green eyes. Atrophied skull. The wings were translucent sheaths, and the beast held up a single hand in a Baal greeting. Physical contact became an immediate need. The creature's hind legs had also been fitted with leather boots, so locating a sledgehammer to break the glass was also essential. I took one step forward, spotted an open cash register filled with bundled drivers' licences, and then the floor caved beneath me, and gravity was no longer a friend.

I remember the plaster crumbling about my hair. I remember my arm catching in a loop of electrical wire, which was probably what stopped me from going right through to the basement, and then I remember the alarm going off. A conservative estimate would put me pinned upside down between the girders for between fifteen and twenty minutes, but that part was cloudy because a chunk of brass tubing had imbedded itself in my ribs. I heard voices above me, also, sharp heels striking the floor, clattering back and forth, then scraping in circles a dozen steps a second, but whoever was practising their cha-cha moves didn't bother to help me, so after another space of grey time, I counted to three, reached up, bent the rebar and crawled out.

TEN

RUSSELL MET ME in the parking lot of the Astor Hotel. The lot was shrouded with plumes of astringent fog that came from the Scott towels factory. Vapour that was supposed to be only water but smelled a lot like ammonia condensed on single-pane windows and left trails of white residue.

"What happened to you?" he said.

"I fell through a roof."

"Don't ever call me at home for business."

"I needed information."

"This is not a history tutorial," he said.

Russell asleep during history class. Russell unconscious during English Lit. Russell a no-show for everything else and if there was anything the man did not fear, that was failure itself.

"What are you afraid of now?"

"I'm not afraid of anything. I am cognizant of police techniques. I am unconvinced that the values of the Charter as espoused by what's his flick, François, mean shit for tits, and I am fully aware that female company does not need to hear certain conversations."

A wad of tobacco-infested phlegm hit the curb.

"What's your issue?" he said.
"Security concerns." Sort of the truth.
"There aren't any."
"My prints are on that box."
"Woody, I'm a pro. That's fixed."
"We need a system to transfer corporate information safely."

Russell pondered the suggestion. In a crevasse of his soul, a workable corporate agreement was being forged.

"From now on," he said, "if you call my place, ask if I want a beer. We'll meet here. If it's urgent, ask for Scotch. We'll meet at the corner. Don't, repeat, do not come to the house. The cops know this is their last free season, and they'll want to make quota for the rest of forever."

The Astor Hotel was Burnaby's greatest monument to banality. Embedded in the blue and white brick stood two entrances left over from the 1950s, which read Ladies and Escorts in pink neon above one door and Gentlemen on the other. Inside, the chalk line across the floor, which once separated male from female patrons, had faded, and the new era held Prohibition morals in contempt. Liquor was served until after midnight, or until customers passed out, and the desk staff couldn't keep C-stroll girls out of the second-floor rooms.

"A cop phoned me," I said.
"A what?"
"She called right after you did."
"Why didn't you say so?"
"I'm telling you now."
"What did she want?"
"My mother's boots."

A crow swooped through the fog to pick a worm off the asphalt.
"Your dead mother's boots?" he said.
"Missing mother's boots."

"Sorry dude, yeah, missing, but one more reason never to ding me at six a.m."

"She told me to be happy with what I had," I said.

"Who was she?"

"Didn't say."

"She didn't say, like, this is Sergeant Sister-clit or whatever?"

"No."

"No badge number?"

"Nothing."

"Someone is wanking you over." He brushed his hair back in a swath, relieved. "Don't freak me out like that. There's a million creeps probing the obits for people just like you. Don't give them your Mastercard number. Get your phone number changed. In fact, that's an excellent idea. Call B.C. Tel today. Jesus, what a relief. Let's get loaded."

The inside of the Astor Pub was not really a pub at all. It was a beer parlour, a turn-of-the-century, lumberjacking, peanut-pitching, hop-stained beer parlour large enough to run a light cavalry division through. Hundreds of small round tables with red terrycloth covers were scattered in absolutely no order over the concrete floor that was flaked in sawdust and always stunk of draught. They served the beer in small six-ounce glasses, limit five per call per customer, and on stage, the suburban circuit girls stripped down with a kind of hostility that many men found attractive. The ratio of males to females, not including the performers, was precisely fifty to one.

We took a table in the corner, beneath a gaudy eight- by ten-foot reproduction of *The Death of General Wolfe*.

"We're good here," he said. "Fabulous view of the ladies, and the washroom fire exit is unlocked so we can scram if need be."

"Why would we need to do that?"

"In case there's a fire," he said, but didn't mean it.

Russell ordered a full five-glass round, and up on stage, Vicki from Victoria went through her undulations while firing a cap gun at the front row.

"Do you like that?" Russell said.

"I'm in."

Russell watched the hostess toss her auburn mane around with casual indifference. He may as well have been watching a monster truck show.

"I knew a guy once," he said. "Dale Peters. Ever meet him? He was a fat fuck with a weird chin and sharp teeth. He ate beer glasses while he got loaded watching the girls. After a dozen beer he'd use his canine teeth to chomp off the rims and then grind the glass with his molars. The bar staff hated him, but he was good for a laugh. Said the glass aided his digestion."

"What happened to him?"

"Died."

The more I watched Vicki, the less she looked like Azy and the more normality became ancient history. Instant Azy scenario: the gentle Mistress drowning me in the Astor toilet wearing nothing but aluminum spray. Very working class, sucking off a urinal puck. Malcolm Lowry, Arthur Erickson and the Marquis de Sade on a date would have loved this place.

"So, these, uh, boots," Russell said.

"Major's Fine Leathers. It's a taxidermy now. There were stuffed animals in the attic."

"Makes sense."

"One of them wore the exact same pair of boots."

"Dude, that is creepy."

"Then I fell through the false ceiling."

I exposed the gash that had gone green below the ribs.

"Ouch, Jesus. Put that away. That's gross. I wasn't going to say anything on account of your pretty-boy complex, but man, you're a mess."

That I had hung upside down, Russell found intriguing, and that the owners had walked directly above me was far too entertaining.

"I guess you were their fall guy."

"I bent the rebar back and climbed out."

Russell picked up his beer glass and stared into the tawny centre where a line of dirty bubbles streamed to the surface.

"You were doing good until the rebar bit," he said. "I almost believed you, but industrial rebar has a test strength of two thousand pounds, so you can't bend it."

Vicki finished her set by shooting a ping-pong ball into low orbit, and I worked out another Azy scenario involving giant centipedes.

"The chicks here look like bugs," I said.

"They're not paid for their brains. Did you get your boots or what?"

I pictured Sal, standing stupid-eyed in front of Dorios restaurant with a daisy clenched in her lonely fist and tears streaming down her face.

"I missed a date."

"Well, easy come, easy go. Let's have a snortola." Russell scanned the room again and produced two medical pipettes. The centre of each tube was indented.

"Break it, stuff it, snort it."

I wasn't gauche enough to ask what it was, though with Russell it was a pretty safe bet. Methylenedioxyamphetamine had been around since the early 1960s recreationally but was invented by the German pharmaceutical company Merck in 1913. An evil mixture of central nervous stimulants and frontal lobe inhibitors, MDA was popularized by the Nazis looking for cheap ways to keep soldiers awake and make them think they were enjoying the privilege. The Third Reich vanished into history, but the chief supplier of the drug was still West Germany. Working on the adrenergic receptors, MDA overstimulates the production of epinephrine and dopamine, causing exuberance, increased strength and in some cases, mine at least, intense sexual arousal.

"Where does it come from?"

"Baden-Baden." The name amused him.

He dropped one of the vials into my hand and kept his eyes trained on anyone who might infringe our territory. Vicki paraded off the stage and the barman escorted her through the drooling throng of longshoremen, mill workers and drunken plumbers.

"Go," he said.

The syrette popped open, and I stuffed the left half to my nostrils. Like blowing your nose, but in reverse. Serious players use a handkerchief in public and can even get away with it during Catholic mass. Russell was less sectarian. He had the tube up his nose and inhaled with a sleight of hand.

MDA hits the central nervous system first and produces an intense elation similar to cocaine. More dirty than cocaine, at least more industrial and definitely more German. The lift is more through a monoxide fog than a fluffy white cloud, and the user is filled with violent, dystopic energy.

"How's that?" Russell said.

I sat back in the chair and watched the next woman, Marianne, a tanned blonde from Montreal do a horseshoe around the chrome pole. The amphetamine locomotive started far down the tracks of my gut, then rushed closer until I trembled beneath its black motor.

"Fabulous," I said.

"Baden-Baden," he said again.

Russell let his head sink back against the wainscotting, and his eye bounced up and down in time to the canned music. His nose twitched repeatedly.

"God, I love this place," he said.

"Why?"

A Goodyear Blimp hung from an exposed water main. The blimp had breasts. The nipples lit up.

"It's purity."

The DA tightened a nasty spring and Marianne existed solely to torment me. Fellation, fecund, feline, ferocious, her flesh liquidized into a neoprene membrane that sweated green bile. Were those gills in her neck?

"So how was it?" Russell paused a dramatic three seconds. "The other day?"

"What other day?"

"Down south."

"You mean midterms?"

"You know what I mean."

I figured I'd stay noncommittal. As noncommittal as you could when your spleen approaches terminal velocity.

"Just another day," I said.

"That lady has got some very screwed-up ideas."

"I'm sure you have the stats."

"Most Johns get the self-help routine."

He waited, let the J-word sink in. Drank another beer. Gauged the barometric pressure. Six-ounce glasses are easy to drink in one shot and in the Astor, people used them as punctuation. I didn't bite.

"Or how you can improve your self-esteem through sexual aberrance," he said.

"I have no clue what you're talking about."

"She doesn't come up with any of the stuff herself, you know. Steals it from other people. Like that thing about communicating with other dimensions through locative sexual experiences."

Inside my head a set of golf balls exploded.

Russell raised a closed fist at the waiter and turned it twice sideways. This was code for maximum load times the number of people at the table.

"Who are you talking about exactly?"

"Whoever," he said, and rubbed his chin with both hands.

Marianne vanquished her bra to reveal a set of freckled breasts and she reminded me of the character on an inane comedy show where misfits were stranded on a desert island, trapped by their own ineptitude.

"I have weird shit in my brain," I said.

"Drink up, guy. It'll take the edge off."

Ten glasses appeared on the table. We drank three each. The night was only going to go one way. Russell rocked back and forth on his chair and sang "Satisfaction," by the Rolling Stones, although that wasn't the tune the stripper was dancing to.

"I can't sit still," I said.

"I noticed."

"We have to move."

"I've got a few ideas."

"No jobs tonight."

"Just a small one."

"No chance."

"I'll get us a few downers," Russell said. "Pinks if you want."

Pinks were a popular diazepam used by the poolside set to curb married boredom or conduct half-hearted suicide attempts.

"My head is a neutrino."

"You can have them at cost."

"I need ten."

"You don't need ten."

"I must, under any circumstance, get laid," I said.

"Man, can't you think about anything else?"

"Like what?"

Another *Mein Kampf* lecture erupted on the horizon: power, blood and kited cheques.

"No political dissertations."

"Liberal pussy. Let's get some Jack Daniels and make plans. Relax. I only want to discuss."

Discuss? What could go wrong with that? Nonplussed. Under the bus. Besides, if my crotch touched the table one more time, I'd load my pants and Russell might not understand the gesture.

We stood and knocked a couple of beer glasses off the table. The breakage charge was fifty cents each, plus you were cut off, but General Wolfe was taking on the proportions of a huge undersea creature, so time to leave.

The 'DA had dried us out like peanuts, and the Astor had only a single clerk at the off-sales, who counted out change with a prosthetic hand.

"This is going to take forever," Russell said.

An inebriated customer up front made forever worse. He ruffled out bills at belt level through a drunken stupor. Russell's eyes flashed down to the cash just as they bumped shoulders. The line wasn't moving. The music was too loud. Life too short.

"Buddy, I'm next in line," he said.

"Whatever, buddy," Russell said.

Buddy wore a jacket that said Mike's Martial Arts on the chest.

"I'm next," he said.

"Of course, sir."

"Not you and your faggot friend."

"You're facing the wrong way, sir." Russell had never used the word "sir" before and certainly not twice in a row, so this wasn't a good omen. "The lineup is in the other direction, sir, and we don't want any trouble."

"Fucking rights," the man said. "And don't call me sir."

Russell picked a mug off the service trolley and swung it into Buddy's jaw. The glass exploded. The man dropped. Russell bent over, tucked the man's wallet into his jacket and took my arm.

"Walk out," he said. "Don't look back. Talk baseball."

We made our way through the tables and theorized the tenth inning of major league ball. Outside, the mist swallowed up the sounds of traffic. The second we hit Kingsway, Russell accelerated through the jungle of rain-soaked condominiums.

"Did you see his face when the glass broke?" Russell said. "Slow-mo action, man. I loved the white bits. You could see the veins. What a moron."

He tossed the wallet on the dash. "That'll cover our expenses."

Images of Marianne still embedded my brain. I imagined her strangling me on stage with a garter belt while Azy graded the performance.

"You look uptight, dude."

"I am uptight."

"How about something to steady the nerves?"

"Roger that."

"I've got a gun," Russell said.

He beat the red light with one palm on the wheel. Half a century earlier, the strip had been the parade ground for the king-to-be, and city hall had decked the route with new sidewalks and Edwardian lampposts. Now the road was just a thicket of used-car lots, hair salons and hookers looking forlorn in front of Chinese all-nighters.

"It's a chrome-plated Colt forty-five revolver," he said.

"I doubt it."

"From the US Civil War."

"They didn't have chrome then."

"Nickel, then. We can pop a couple of rounds, play some billiards, then if you want a girl, what the heck, I can probably arrange that too. Then we can prepare. Remember Madame Gauthier from grade nine French? Preparer, Monsieur Russell, preparer. I flunked."

I remembered only a long-legged woman with pastel scarves who corrected my conjugation with her crimson lips pursed tightly together.

"For God's sake," Russell said. "Keep your hands off your crotch. The cops will stop us."

Rollo Watch was a factory deep in the spleen of industrial Burnaby. Surrounded by creosote railway yards, the two-storey, featureless building could have housed blue cheese or iridium. Russell used an umbrella to lower a fire escape, and I got the VIP entrance.

Certainly, this was Russell's type of palace: unfinished floors, five by ten slate billiard table, a Panasonic amplifier and a liquor cabinet filled with Crown Royal. He plugged Rod Stewart into the eight track and a ceramic Neptune statue with trident gurgled into life.

"It just doesn't get any better than this," he said.

"Who owns this?"

He shrugged. Legal ownership wasn't in Russell's vocabulary. "Rollo Watch, I guess."

"They let you in?"

"I do work for the manager. In return, I am guaranteed facility use any time outside office hours. This is where I bring clients, do deals, sign contracts, form alliances. Go ahead, grab a CR, dude."

Russell teed up the red balls and chalked his cue. No doubt this was his game, so I filled two glasses with rye. The room exploded in a clatter of red balls.

"What kind of services?"

"Supply and services, I guess you'd say."

"You get him dope."

"Amongst other things."

"Is there a future in that?"

"I understand the principal of empire." Russell potted the pink and reset it with care on the table. When he missed the red, his teeth ground together, and he swung a portrait of Dean Martin aside. The wall safe opened and once the Colt was in his hand, I knew immediately how accidental shootings occurred.

"Put that away," I said.

"Don't be a pussy."

I bent over the table and the cue ball blurred. Russell stroked the barrel of the Colt while whispering profit margins to the hammer.

"I can't breathe with you fondling that thing behind me."

"Relax, man."

"Russell, it's loaded."

"What good is an unloaded gun?" he said, and then, finally, "In the candy bowl, on the television."

Three SweeTarts, two Black Cat bubble gums and a single oblong pill. Russell wasn't much for discretion.

"Just one?"

"That's all you need."

"I should probably freebase it."

"Don't even think that. You middle-class dudes want to freebase everything. Well, you can't. Cocaine is alkaline. Pinks aren't. You'll give yourself cancer, man."

Russell chalked his cue for the third time. Rod Stewart played "Maggie May."

"You know he was a fag," Russell said.

"I didn't know that."

I sunk a green and the game was no longer funny.

"What do you think of them?" he said.

"Who?"

"Fags."

"I don't have feelings that way," I said.

"In sort of a wishy-washy, noncommittal, steadfast way?"

"If you get rich, will you still work for her?"

"For whom?"

"Who else?"

"I don't form those attachments. That's your problem. Everything is a love affair for you. Too much college poetry. Too much Melba toast. Pretty soon you'll be doing errands for her, buying groceries, picking up lingerie. Then you'll write her haikus and want waterfront property together."

I looked for a place to do chin-ups. "You and I should enter the marathon this year."

"You're insane." He switched off the light and the moon stretched our figures across the pool table. "You see that Chinese store a hundred yards south?"

At the far end of the block, a stucco building lingered from prewar days. Above the transom, a giant round Coca-Cola sign shaped like a bottle cap glimmered in the light. Further explanation was unnecessary. Ring the Gong was a childhood ritual. All corner stores had huge metal Coke circles over the door. All children threw stones at them. All harried Asian shop owners ran outside wielding sticks to protect their property. Such were our sins.

"You're going to shoot somebody through the head."

"Who, dude? Who? It's two o'clock in the morning and we are in the middle of an industrial desert. There is not a living creature within eight hundred light years."

I checked my watch. Had two hours really passed? Was the bottle of CR really empty? Two more pipettes lay broken on the pool table. Russell shoved the Colt out the window, held his breath and fired. A yellow flash leapt from the barrel, and in the distance, the shattering of a window, a windshield or maybe nothing at all.

"You missed," I said.

Russell peered into the darkness for evidence of a hit. There was none.

"You give it a go then."

The gun was heavier than I thought and colder, mechanical and impersonal but the chambers spun around like a live-fire roulette wheel.

"Aim high," he said.

"My parents had guns."

"Sure, they did."

The revolver breached sideways, erupted and sent a round through the Venetian blinds. A pigeon soared past in a cacophony of feathers. The bird struck the light fixture, shrieked banshee style and grey fuzz filtered down to the pool table.

"Kill it," Russell said. "Kill it."

Claws scratched an aluminum vent. Russell seized the Colt and fired into the ceiling. The slug ripped through the piping and shattered a brass spigot that sprayed water on the pool table. This unbearable racket blew out the spring coiled inside me since the Astor Hotel. After leaping off the billiard table corner pocket and catching the vent with one hand, I stuffed the bird in my mouth with the other. Blood shot over my face and feathers spun off the animal's neck. Was I eating the creature for nourishment or just ripping it to shreds as its tiny beating heart made a last palpation on my tongue?

Russell stood quietly in the corner. He looked older in his worn jeans and blue corduroy belt.

"Dude, you are a freaking alien," he said, which is what we all want to be called when it suits us.

ELEVEN

MISTRESS ALEXIS DUNWELL, also known as Dun, Dun-Well, Lady A, Lady Zed and Mistress Azy because she'd do everything in-between, answered the telephone with a voice as thorny as a Brillo-brush. For a woman who made her living through erotic discourse, her temperament rang of too much Nyquil. She rolled out a series of decrees with utter indifference. I almost hung up. Of course, I didn't hang up. Stuffed in my rear pocket was Russell's hard-earned proceeds of crime and I didn't plan on holding onto any of it for long.

"I need to see you again." That was the line I'd rehearsed many times. There had been a hundred variations. I'd thought about, "I need your company" but that seemed too formal. "I've got some cash" was too crass and "I've dreamed about you incessantly," which although true, was too needy.

"Who is this?" she said.

"It's me."

"Me who?"

It was like we had never spoken. A wooden toucan bird taunted me from my grandmother's kitchen counter.

"Give me your name or I'll hang up," she said.

"Me, Cirrus."

"Do I know you?"

"From Tuesday."

"Which Tuesday?"

"I'm Russell's friend."

"Fill me in," she said.

"You suffocated me."

"You and a thousand others." Somewhere a flat memory floated to the surface. "I'm about to go into session, so be brief."

"I want to see you again."

"Of course you do."

Being in the pro-Domme market is a little like selling black tar heroin to someone who admires Samuel Coleridge. There's not much salesmanship involved after the first deal. I gave her the exhaustive list.

"That can't be accomplished in one session," she said.

I paired the list down to a reasonable three requests.

"All right," she said. "But that incurs a substantially higher rate."

"How much higher?"

The receiver got frosty.

"Mistress does not negotiate rates on the phone," she said.

The notion that we had established a rapport since the last torture tryst evaporated. I apologized for my audacity over the silent line while she considered the options.

"If you are willing to undertake extracurricular duties for Mistress, perhaps we can come to a mutual agreement."

The process in police interviews or diplomatic circles is called reciprocity. Do someone a favour and they feel inclined to return the same. The accompanying technique is called exclusivity. Make someone feel more important than their station warrants and they are more than likely to say yes to something beneath it. I still wasn't sure which way the process was working.

"There is a pair of heels waiting for me at Bosco's Shoes," she said. "Pick them up, then come over at the agreed hour. Same door. No screw-ups."

Shoes in tow and seventy-eight dollars out, I arrived at the same door and was greeted with the same indifference. Azy vanished down the same dark hallway without saying hello and perched herself on the same throne in the parlour. I laid the shoes down by her throne and she inspected her Virginia Slim as though there was a defect in the shaft.

"Don't just leave them there, put them on my feet, you fool."

Knee-high stilettos with chrome heels took some putting. The leather was coarse and covered with a film of oil. With one of her arches perched on my shoulder, I laced up the first shoe.

"We won't be looking after your stated requests today." She took a file to her blue nail.

"We won't?"

"Mistress is going to give you a new skin instead." She drifted off and hummed. Her alabaster eyes lingered on the lamp, the ceiling strut and then an invisible point far beyond us both. "Like a cocoon. Then you'll hatch. Into a moth, maybe. And fly towards the fire. Moths always do that. Because, basically, they're stupid. They combust. I like that part. When I was a little girl my bastard father made me go camping. I hated camping. Alone in some godforsaken national park with nothing around but leaking tents and boring bugs. So, I'd fire up the Coleman lamp and wait for the moths. That white ball burned away. The satisfaction I got from hearing those tiny perfect popping sounds was intense. Soon everything to do with moths and lamps excited me. Even the smell of camphor was arousing. Put your money in the mail slot and get undressed."

A baseboard heater percolated in the corner of the room. Azy wiped a smudge of balm from her left lip and examined me with some disdain.

"Trim your pubes," she said. "And when November comes invest in a tanning salon. Mistress despises pale men."

She struck me with a closed fist at the nape of the neck, wound me up in a spider web of mountaineering straps and clipped everything together with a D-ring. A garage hook descended from the ceiling on a metal cable and then the cellar spun counter-clockwise. Boots, mirror, legs. Cage, hips, boots.

Azy rolled a trolley with surgical instruments into place. Some were medical: scalpel, a dental pick, the rib splitter. Others were foreign and not meant for human use: a sickle with filigreed teeth, a clamp with spider leg bits and a pair of blue embalming bottles. She hooked up a crescent needle to one of the tubes, then slipped on surgical gloves and admired herself in the mirror. She turned and checked her calves to make sure they were perfect. They were. Next, she checked her ass and tanned shoulders, but they were perfect too, so with nothing left to fix, she gathered up my scrotum in one gloved hand and squeezed. She hummed "Lili Marlene" and "Non, Je ne regrette rien" by Edith Piaf. She turned the embalming jar upside down on an IV rack. Fluid ran down the tubes. Azy scored a bull's eye in my sack with the surgical needle. My testes swelled up to beach ball proportions until they threatened to explode. A second needle followed and perhaps a third. I screamed. Azy laughed, and I believe that is the happiest I have ever seen her.

"I would advise not moving." She fumbled through her package of Slims. "Or twitching, or speaking, or breathing. I left my smokes upstairs. Or maybe there's none and I'll have to run out to the store. Maybe the store will be closed, and I'll have to drive down to the US to pick up some Winstons. Have fun."

I said, "Please," but that one word made my zeppelins vibrate.

She pitched the gloves into a trash can. Then she stuffed a pink gag into my mouth and walked out the door. The click of her shoes faded out of the cellar, down the hall, along the stairs, then were gone. All was quiet on the western front. There was nothing except for the pounding of blood in my temples and empty space in all directions. My errant night nurse had made a terrible error in dosage, then left for a smoke break. If any more fluid drained from the jar into my scrotum, I would either burst or drown. A minute passed and then three and I caved. As my balls swung in bovine proportions, I cursed and shouted. I yelled, "cunt," "whore," "fuck you," "tit-tart" and "Sandwich Island," but it didn't make any difference. Nobody came. Nobody answered. Nobody cared.

With the click of returning shoes, I figured the Victoria Cross was in order or at least simply a peaceful deflation. But the shoes were not Azy's. This was not her figure, her smell nor her breath. Whoever stood directly behind me clattered out of my vision every time I squirmed around. The bottle emptied out, fell over and smashed. There was static jazz, brittle claws scraping on the concrete and then the flash of a white blouse. A piranha poke of pain seared my crotch and saline sprayed through the air. Then the lights went back on.

"You scream too much," Azy said.

A puddle of brine had squirted out of my sack and mingled with blood on the floor. She screwed in a new light bulb and fretted over the shattered drip.

"Where did you go?"

"I was gone five seconds," she said.

"Who was in the room?"

She snatched a plastic bag from the bench, pulled it up over my head and sealed the air lock in place with duct tape. Then she pulled the last surgical needle out. My body went warm and erupted. Maybe she kissed me during the evulsion, but I'm not sure. Afterwards we sat in her living room and drank tea.

"Did you enjoy yourself?" she said.

Her living room was neat and unperturbed. The mantel was polished, the air smelled of lemon and bright autumn sunshine came through the picture window that overlooked the Fraser River. A plastic rose, a vase of polished pebbles. The house was perfectly manicured, utterly uninhabitable and I didn't have an answer.

"It's not about enjoyment anyway," she said.

"What is it about?"

"You'll catch on after a while."

"What was the end bit?" My bloodied balls had already matted to my underwear.

"It's called the release shot," she said. "When I pull the last pin out, you can't help yourself."

Azy smiled and poured some more tea. She was at her most satisfied right after a session, when her professional acumen had brought order to the universe.

"Who else was in the room?" I said.

"I told you. No one."

"There were shapes moving about. Wings. Claws."

"It's part of the asphyxia. Don't sweat it."

"Ever had any one die on you?"

"Close is part of the fun."

I set the tea on the coffee table. The brittle china tinkled against the spoon. My ankles were numb and whenever I straightened my back cartilage cracked in my shoulder.

"Who pulled the first pin out?"

"It pops out on its own after your balls swell. Remember to leave the antiseptic on for the day. Your body will absorb the water from your scrotum by nightfall."

Azy had done a good job patching me up. A ball of white gauze with hospital antiseptic had been cast dexterously around my nuts then secured with athletic tape.

"Being left alone is not fun," I said.

"Is that because of your parents?"

"Who told you about my parents?"

"Russell."

"This has nothing to do with my parents."

"Probably it does."

Nolo contendere here.

"Being alone doesn't work for me, sexually speaking."

"How long ago did your parents die?"

"Five years ago," I said.

"Okay, maybe it doesn't. Time to move on."

"Pardon?"

"You heard me. Move on. Forget them."

"They are my parents."

"So what?" She may as well have been discussing the frost-free requirements for durum wheat or tool usage at the end of the palaeolithic period.

"And they didn't necessarily die," I said.

"So, what did they do?"

"They just never came back."

She got up off the sofa and walked over to the fireplace. She had changed into an evening gown that was slit up the leg. Her thigh reflected light from the window. "Same thing."

"My father went missing in the summer and then my mother vanished sixteen months later."

"Did they ever find bodies?"

"There were no bodies."

"What did the police say?"

"They have theories."

"Cops," she said. She obviously didn't like them.

I saw Fielding leaning against our mountain ash tree, his herringbone jacket open in the morning mist, gazing over my father's cornfield with defeat clinging to his face.

"As soon as they figure out there's no charges, they lose interest," she said. "No promotions, no noteworthiness, no stats. If this were a speeding ticket, they would have produced results a long time ago."

"The file is still open."

"Must make you bitter."

"My counsellor told me not to harbour bitterness," I said.

"Your what?"

"Like a psychiatrist but they can't give drugs."

"Then what good are they?"

On the mantel grew a tiny cactus with a red flower. She pushed one of the thorns with the tip of her finger. "Do the cops have any suspects?"

"They aren't even sure there was a crime."

She forgot about the cactus, and her eyes drifted up to the chandelier in a ripple of interest. "I like SM crime novels. I like the idea of the guilty getting punished. I'll lend you some. Actually, I like it better when the innocent get punished and they make the novels into movies. Who was the cop?"

"Fielding."

She shrugged. "No clues at all?"

"Depends on your definition of clue."

Azy was slowing down. After she was done with the cactus, she lingered over the plastic flowers, rearranged the stems, then lit some incense.

"Notes," she said. "Drawings, messages."

"No."

"How close did you look?"

"I've looked so close ants became elephants. As time went by everything became a clue. Tools, spools. Eels, orange peels and bottles full of iodine wax."

"Russell mentioned you went a bit off the deep end."

"He did?"

"He said one day you stopped showing up to school."

Russell was an expert at taking in sundry facts and turning them out backwards.

"Do you know him well?"

"He does odd jobs for me," she said.

"What kind?"

"Where did you go after grade twelve?"

"My grandparents moved us here."

"Mm." Something about my family history was making sense. She toyed with a gold-plated lighter, then placed it on the mantel.

"Where are your parents?" I said.

"My mother is in Winnipeg, I think. My father, I don't know or care. He was a bastard."

"In what way?"

"Are there degrees of bastardness?"

"Harsh," I said.

"You never met him. You're lonely and want to make false ideals about father figures. It's a symptom of delusional mythos syndrome. I can pick it out a mile away. I meet a lot of lonely people. Loneliness is a self-perpetuating cycle that's not likeable. A lot of smart, handsome people who come through my door spend their time alone and can't figure out why. Once you see the big picture, the reasons become obvious. Loneliness produces bad karma. Bad karma reeks of desperation. Desperation produces loneliness. I bet you don't do well at nightclubs."

"Understatement."

"Mistress can help you out. It takes time and effort. But you must accept what you are. Good people destroy themselves because they can't accept the facts. Knew a woman who hanged herself in her laundry room because she couldn't accept her inclinations."

"Sounds tragic."

"Pathetic, actually. Wrapped a vacuum hose around her neck and jumped off the dryer. Probably didn't even come. I bet you read Henry Miller."

"Some."

"Well, stop," she said. "That's part of your childhood and your childhood is over. It's a waste of time and effort. Are you bi?"

"My psychiatrist wanted me to have blood tests, but I was never diagnosed."

"Not bipolar, you moron. Bisexual. Do you do it with men?"

A tea leaf got stuck down my throat and from my bangled balls, a trickle of saline ran down my thigh.

She snorted a laugh. "Why don't you meet a friend of mine?"

"Is he coming over?"

"Already here." Azy let her head roll over the back of the chair and listened for movement. "I never session alone. Don, come on down and meet Cirrus."

The stairwell creaked and Don stepped through the door from the study loft. He was a massive man in jeans and a Western shirt who spent a lot of time in the gym and posing for cigarette commercials. The classic gay cowboy deal, but I was betting no one made an issue of it. He shook my hand, and his palm was warm and dry with that I'll-be-screwing-you-someday-soon confidence.

"Hey," I said.

"You look surprised."

"I didn't know there were other people here."

"There's always other people here," Don said.

"Don is cool," Azy said. "Cool and hot if you see what I mean. He makes sure we all stay safe and keeps a stock of gauze and adhesive tape handy."

"I worked on an ambulance once." Don sat down on the puffed chair, flicked a gold lighter over twice and sized me up. "You sounded like you had a good time."

"Ethereal."

"Don't sweat it," Don said. "I've done plenty of screaming inside these walls."

He clasped his hands in a sentimental gesture. The telephone rang and an answering machine clicked over. Azy stood up.

"Amuse him for a while, will you Don?"

Clearly, our world no longer interested her. Don watched her legs flit away, maybe for posterity, maybe for propriety, but soon enough, he reoriented my way. Don was ultimately a sexual predator, but an eminently likeable one.

"This place is like those old Hammer horror movies," he said. "Ingrid Pitt, dig her? Christopher Lee? Don't worry. You'll fit fine. We all start somewhere."

"You started here?"

"The Saint James Cross, downstairs. Yellow cedar. With a different Domme, but that's a different story. I'm a carpenter by trade."

He slipped a bag of peanuts from his vest pocket and offered me a shake. "I spend a lot of time here. The lifestyle gig works for me. I make her stuff. Stand six for new clients. Play a few role scenes when required. It's a good niche. Screen calls. I do US cigarette ads filmed here on account of the dollar."

"You listened to my call?"

"Soon it will be an answering machine," he said. "I hate them. Some clients won't leave their particulars. Azy's lost regulars, but hey, soon no one will speak in person. Just messages ad nauseam. Some guy was sucking my dick last week, and he said one day all phones will look like this. Ha. No point in fighting it. Like computers. In twenty years, the only sex will be electronic. Do you dig computers?"

I pictured two yellow pie creatures flogging each other on a tiny blue screen as they bounced back and forth between ping-pong paddles.

"I like Super 8," I said.

"A romantic, I know. The smell of the reel. The flickering of happiness. You probably think Alfred Purdy is cool. When I was young, I used to sniff the porno film before I threaded it into my dad's projector. I think it made me high. Then I'd struggle to jerk off before my parents came from the grocery store. Eventually I got caught with my pants down, so to speak. Gay porn too. They blew their cork on that one and threw the projector out. Guess that kind of ruined the nostalgia angle. That's the thing with computers. You can flick them on and off at will and never get busted. The reproduction is better than Super 8. The signals will be impossible to regulate. Everyone will have one in their house. You won't have to develop company or go to a theatre. People will produce porn in their own studios and ship it to consumers in Hong Kong. They dig rodeo porn. No middle-man costs. Profit margin will be unfathomable. We just have to keep the SPCA out."

Don nodded, stretched his jaw sideways an inch and changed the subject. "You work out?"

"Here and there. A little boxing."

"You're trim-tab dude, but don't worry. I don't sneak a peek unless I'm called. Besides, extraterrestrial stuff is not for me. Which gym do you use?"

"The community centre at Burnaby Lake."

He waved me off. "That's for housewives. You ought to try Atlas. Lot of hard-on bods there. Guys and girls. If you're into them. I can get you a membership for half-price."

"Cool," I said. I hated that word. Sometimes there's no place else for a conversation to go except to cool: Hey, man. I made your sister: cool. I swiped your calculus answers: cool. Everyone thinks you're a bug. My embalmed crotch needed rubbing.

"Relax," Don said. "The people who want intimacy the most are the ones who get nervous around strangers. Me too. Back when I was in school, everybody sat around watching basketball and not saying anything important. They'd talk sports. About hat tricks or Guy Lafleur, Alex Rodriguez or slam dunking. Then the girls would come in and they'd talk fashion. No one mentioned Nietzsche, or Klimt. Especially not Masoch or perversions, and even at that age I'd racked up a few. Those were painful years. I liked rodeo sports. I broke horses. Used to ride near Pincher Creek. But hey, you can't help what you are and pretty soon people get wise. Southern Alberta was not a place you want to be openly gay."

Don gazed off into nostalgic space that no doubt included chaps, rolling tobacco and covert meets by the Old Man River.

"What are you into besides the pins?" His cock had to be huge, his chest hairy and he didn't have a fey bone in his body. Basically, the kind of man you would tell everything and never speak to your old friends again.

"That's weird stuff man," he said. "But hey, no problem. I like that. Someone who's honest and tells you where they're at and doesn't bullshit you. You get a lot of bullshitters around here. That they've been flogged a thousand times or taken a twelve-inch phallus for forty days and forty nights. Then they're nowhere on a date. There's nothing wrong with saying 'I can't do that,' although Azy says you can take a lot and stay hard."

A sheet of red gauze sifted out of my trouser leg.

"You spoke Latin in the dungeon," he said.

"I can't remember."

"You rambled through the amo-amas-amat shit like a pro. I did Latin when I went to Catholic school. Worst two years of my life. Odd talents like languages are a plus around here for projects. Being able to take certain kinds of punishments without edit cuts is great. There's always a place for way-out acts. You mention Carl Jung. I'm into Jung too. We need people who work on the edge and have artistic flare. Most of the clients who pass through here are either afraid, stupid or crazy. They don't work out. They won't cross the line. Our projects are more visceral than run-of-the-mill porn. Porn is for children. The future of our species is collective consciousness and the best way of creating that consciousness is through SM. There's also a whack of money to be made."

Don leaned back in the chair and withdrew a package of Marlboros from his vest pocket. Azy strolled back in the room.

"I've got a seven o'clock," she said. "Can we make dinner for five instead?"

"Sure," Don said.

"It's the Major." She reminisced. "He likes to be tied up to the post in the basement and then be executed by firing squad. I've got a paintball gun. He's the real deal but getting on in years. One day he'll keel over with angina."

"I thought you were done with him," Don said.

Azy shrugged. She walked over to a Monet print, straightened the frame, then stared at me, waiting.

"I'd better get going," I said.

I walked across the hardwood floor towards the kitchen door. "Erotic Terrors of the Third Reich" was the coffee-table hardback on display. Garish photos of Gestapo bad girls performing eviscerations, executions and embalmings were out for visitors to peruse, although the colour photos of men being garrotted were probably staged.

Azy ran a finger over a string of pearls around her neck. "I'm having a party on the first of the month. Come along. Get to know the crowd. They're cool people. You'll have to attend at least two more private sessions first, though. Just to learn the ropes. I'm going to give you this so I can get hold of you when I have need."

She tossed me a black plastic box the size of a card deck. There were a couple of red lights and a small green screen.

"What is it?"

"It's hooked up to the phone system. You wear it on your belt. Any time I want you, I dial its number and I'll expect you to be here within the hour."

For well over a minute Azy stared into her datebook without uttering a word, then appeared surprised I was still present. "Don will show you out," she said.

TWELVE

MAYBE FIELDING WAS the last person I should have taken my mother's boots to. His conclusions would be calculated, patient, based on logic and the sensible world, and that wasn't for me. I imagined him on Sunday afternoons tending to his boyhood hobby: model Messerschmitt reconstruction and replaying the Battle of Britain with the same conclusion history always had taught.

"Lad, come on in." He held open the basement door of the detachment, the one behind the juniper bush where the civilian world never ventured.

The bowels of police stations smell of concrete, cleaning fluid and misery, and this one was no exception. There was a colour poster of a cartoon policeman on the wall that said "Treat Everyone with Respect" and another with a worried housewife in a red apron: "Do you know where my daughter is tonight?" From the floor above came the muffled cry of someone demanding a lawyer.

"Always willing to lend a hand when I can," he said.

The speech he gave me over the phone about the value of contaminated evidence was obviously over. Now I was getting the "we're all in this together" routine. He asked about my grandmother and if termites and ants were the same genus. We stopped at a door marked 4B, and as he fished through his ring of keys for the appropriate fit, I got the rundown on his new bifocal prescription. The keys flipped over one by one, either to emphasize the importance of his station or that his liking for Irish malt during the Suez Crisis made the bifocals come early.

"Now, where did these boots come from again?"

Different lab from last time. A long narrow room with a metal table, cutting tools and vice grips. Kind of what you'd expect to see in an industrial ed class.

"The constable brought them back."

"And she was in uniform?"

"I rode in the police car."

He walked through the lab rattling the keys. "We do everything here. Bag specimens, repair instruments, separate evidence. Quaint, but I call it home."

"Do bodies come here?"

"This is the industrial side of investigations."

Fielding motioned to a chair that was conveniently placed by a small desk. I sat with the boots on my lap. Cavernous skinny ankles, clawed toes and pyrethrum stench. This wasn't going to go well.

"How have you been?" He polished a magnifying glass with a cloth.

"Good enough."

"You look pale."

"Late night with friends."

"Friends," he said. He worked at a stain that was reluctant to leave, but I could see his eyes flit up to catch my every move. "I'm glad to see that you're making friends here. Vancouver is a lonely place. Loneliness is bad for young men. Been there. Done that. In the air force. I was stationed in Khartoum after the war."

"What's in Khartoum?"

"Nothing. Absolutely nothing."

"What did you do?"

"Standing patrols. Not much action after 'forty-five. I read. Hemingway, Orwell. Hesse. Did water colours: palms trees, sand, goats, sand. Also, sand. You get the idea. Some flying, but mostly recon."

"Have a girl?"

"*Es ist verboten*. Muslim culture and infidels off limits. You?"

"I'm not sure what my status is right now."

"Hard species to figure," he said. "What's her name, the new one?"

"Alexis."

"Often?"

"Off and on."

"Alexis. Sounds European."

"I'm not sure what she is."

"Keep a photo?"

"No."

"Ask them for a photo," he said. "For your wallet. That clears the issue up pretty quick. If they give you a photo, you're in. Blonde or brunette?"

"Blonde. Very."

Fielding stopped polishing. He gazed at the ceiling. Perhaps there were constellations present. Cassiopeia, Virgo or Orion the Hunter. "Where does this friend of yours live?"

"South slope."

"Not the very blonde Alexis who lives off Clarke?"

My heart pumped one last shot of blood through the silence of the room, then died. Something was still amiss on the northeast corner of Fielding's Zeiss lens, but he accepted the flaw with a shrug and slipped it back onto the mount.

"You know an Alex?" I said.

"Your vehicle was checked down there the other day."

"Why?"

"No clue," he shrugged.

"What is going on?"

"Take it easy, lad. Your vehicle was checked on a purely routine basis along with a hundred others in this city that day. The door was ajar. You weren't around. One of our good constables locked it for you. Then, of course, he filed a check-up slip on the event."

"Check-up slip?"

"An intelligence report on a slip of paper."

"How did you find out?"

"Through my job description," he said. "I read all the check-ups each morning. From Matsqui to Maillardville. Missing persons cases are built on them. Never can tell what a random check will reveal. We have a new computer system. A plate gets run; it goes into the machine. I have a list of names and if they match, a little pink light goes on."

"My Alex doesn't live anywhere near the mosque."

"You seem jumpy."

"Up all night," I said. And the night before. And the night before that too.

"With this lady?"

"No, a girl named Sal. Utterly platonic. She works in a museum. A fellow named Don. Cowboy. And an old friend from school, Russell."

That stone went down to a sunless sea.

"From school in Abbotsford?"

"We live close by now."

"What's his last name?"

"Can't remember."

Fielding bit the inside of his mouth and stepped to the table. He made a sweep of the surface with his cloth. "How's your brother?"

"Still an apprentice superstar social worker."

"Russell," he said. He scratched his throat. "Russell, Russell, Russell. Why does Russell from Abbotsford ring a bell? Ah well. It will come to me. But anyway, our new intel system. Brilliant. Everyone is feeding information to everybody else, eating it up. Like radio waves or syrup. I suppose you could say we're one big ant hive, communicating data through the modern touch of copper neurons."

"Super," I said.

The steam pipes on the ceiling, robust and unmovable, gave Fielding comfort. The argon light had an annoying hum that was giving me an epileptic fit.

"Anyway," he said. "Let's take a closer look at your exhibit here. We've got this new kind of all-spectrum light that shows up any criminal interference. Very sensitive. Made in Japan, wouldn't you know?"

I rolled the newspaper on the table. Fielding didn't seem to notice the smell. He flipped on the magnifying light. Everything under the bulb fluoresced into dirty yellows and sullen greens, and my hands appeared badly contaminated.

"Lad," he said with his eye on the light control. "The first thing I've got to tell you is that we must keep our channels open. Without communication, there's nothing. We are a team working towards a common goal. I'll take a look at what you've got, but this is what we call tertiary evidence. I don't know where these boots have come from. It is not sterile as our colleagues in forensics would say."

Fielding snapped on a pair of blue surgical gloves, then selected scissors from a cabinet. There was apparently a specific set of scissors for each chore. With the blades poised on the string, Fielding paused.

"Hobbes?" he said.

"What?"

"Is your pal Russell Hobbes?"

"Could be."

This was not good news. "What are you doing with the likes of him?"

"From elementary school. He's okay now."

"Not really," Fielding said.

"What's wrong with him?"

"Dodgy. Definitely dodgy."

"Define dodgy."

"Murky. Of questionable character. Find a new pal."

"Does he have a criminal record?"

"Not yet."

"Not yet could be any of us," I said.

"But more than likely him."

"He's one of the few people who talks to me."

"About what?" The detective leaned back against the counter, his solid middle-aged frame secure in its mass, his years of experience and decades of intuition coming into play to lead the conversation to one irrefutable conclusion.

"Genealogical lineage."

"He doesn't strike me as the academic type."

"He's read *Mein Kampf*," I said.

"Lord."

"*His* parents ditched him too."

"All I'm saying, lad, is you lay down with dogs, you get fleas."

"Can we look at the boots now?"

I pushed the package towards him. Fielding cut the string. The paper unfurrowed. He stared down at the goods as if he were staring down a deep well, waiting for a stone to hit the bottom. Then he pulled my parent's evidence box and thumbed through reports, witness statements, and stencil mimeographs before producing a photograph. He held the print at arm's length and compared it to the boot. The eyelets, the knotting of the laces, even the wear pattern on the rear of the heel, all identical, unabridged and not in police custody.

"Recognize them?" I said.

"Mm." I knew he wasn't going to say anymore. He spread his palms on the table. A small tick moved his cheek. His grey eyes were transfixed, delving back into the portfolio of memory to secure something he did not like one bit.

"She brought them back after Ms. Downs's place."

"Downs's place." He slipped the boots from the newspaper and ran his gloved fingers over the laces. His eyes moved back and forth between the photograph and the real thing, then he used the magnifying glass to examine the wear.

"Can we cut them open?" I said.

"Why?"

"To get a look inside."

"What exactly will this tell us?"

"Trust me."

A desperate line, for sure. Try it sometime in a make-or-break situation, when you're not sure what breaking it will mean and when the person on the other end probably does not trust you anyway.

When the spectrum bulb moved over the leather, the surface changed from black to mauve, and migraine squiggles moved around the arch. Fielding swabbed the gusset and put the sample in a vial of clear fluid. The fluid turned blue. A scratchy public address announcement echoed though the halls in a language only police care to understand, and Fielding cut through the calf with a rotor blade.

By the time the blade dug through the leather, strands of black fur fouled the motor completely. But this was not a man who admitted defeat, and so Fielding secured the toe with vice grips and resorted to a table saw. With the tongue peeled back like a gutted whale, the insides of my mother's history were exposed: ankle canal, two inches wide. Carpal ball: slits for not five, but six toes, and when Fielding turned the boot upside down, a horde of weevils emerged, well fed from the crystallized flesh that smelled of Chanel No. 5.

I threw up in Fielding's wastepaper basket. I threw up on a fingerprint pad and a broken credit card reader. Finally, I threw up into the brown vase that held my grandmother's papyrus grass as I walked through the front door.

My grandmother always forgave me, drank her first glass of sherry at four p.m. sharp and would never have less than two books on the go at any given time. She liked doing the classics alongside something pulpy. That week it had been *The Rise and the Fall of the Third Reich*, by William Shirer, and *Delta of Venus*, by Anaïs Nin. I drained the vomit from the vase into the geranium bed and figured I could give her a shot of sherry and she wouldn't notice the difference. I'd ask her about her books, Modernism versus Post-Modernism or Virginia Woolf's take on the lure of the stiletto. Then, if I wanted to get anywhere near the truth, a little morphine would come in handy.

GM sat on the rocking chair with her head rising and falling each time she turned a page.

"What were you doing with my vase?" she asked.

"Grandmom, do you prefer Nin or Shirer?"

She held one book in each hand and her eyes flicked back and forth between the two covers. "In one, people die without pleasure, in the other, they take pleasure in dying."

A tired clock in the kitchen worked its way to the top of the hour, the giant hands emphasizing the treachery of time or the stillness of the moment.

"How about a sherry?" I asked.

"It's seven minutes to four."

"Why not have one now?"

"If I have one at seven minutes to today it will be quarter to tomorrow and then two-thirty and soon, I'll be drinking in the morning."

"I do it all the time."

"I know."

"Is Nin a translation?"

"They all are and this one is coy."

My grandmother thought Anaïs Nin was coy. "As compared to what?"

"The others I have read. Coquettishness is a destructive force in any narrative. I dislike the terms 'bowels' and 'loins.' Perhaps my own prejudice, I thought at first, so I asked a sample size of people on the bus what their opinions were, and they concurred. Surprising the calibre of answers one can get on public transport."

"You asked people on the bus about bowels and loins?"

"I wasn't going to walk to the cemetery alone. It's Thursday."

Yes, Thursday it was. The cemetery ritual was the same every time; it rained, the water came off the firs, GM cried, and then we would walk away in small broken pieces, so how could I forget?

"I was out with Fielding."

"What did he want?"

Grandmom folded a red ribbon into the pages of her book. Herr Hitler would have to wait.

"He wanted to look at the boots," I said.

"You took him your mother's boots?"

"Turns out they weren't ordinary boots."

Outside the window the robins in the ash tree fought over berries, and no doubt my grandmother contemplated the evil of Goebbels and Goering, or how a nation of ordinary people would let such an extraordinary thing occur.

"The insides were filled with divots. There were six toes and room for claws."

"Then they were hardly your mother's."

"They were the ones from our house."

"Then they must have been brought from another house."

"They were in Mom's box."

Grandmother put down her book and lifted her bifocals from her nose. "Well, I checked your mother's feet many times and I can attest she did not have six toes."

"Are you sure?"

"Don't you think an extra set of metacarpals is something a mother would notice?"

Maybe.

"Did your mother have six toes?"

I couldn't recall.

"Well, Cirrus. Did she?"

"I remember Saturday nights," I said. "Dad wore suits and Mom wore mini-skirts with black boots. I remember you chastising her about the spurs."

"Your mother had many boots," she said.

"We cut these open."

"But why?"

"The ankle was two inches thick."

A girl on a bicycle rode down the crumpled asphalt of Clinton Street and my grandmother looked very old.

"We have exhausted this topic, Cirrus. They were not your mother's boots. You always get the logic of these events backwards. The boots were modified after she used them or a different set all together. A hundred different explanations are possible, but you always seem to cling to the most irrational. You think you've found a new clue, an idea, a new hope. But there is nothing new. There is only the past and you must let it go. It is a trick that politicians and door-to-door salesmen use. They tell you they have something new when in fact it's the same snake oil. Answer me, Cirrus. You have seen your mother in bare feet, haven't you? Of course, you have. And did she have six toes?"

Grandmother waited for an answer with her hand resting on the outcome of the Nuremburg trials. Every time I saw her, she appeared more a person of the past, a rearguard of an ancient legion left behind to fade away.

"Were my mother and father sexual deviants?" I asked.

"And neither were they communists or criminals."

"Swingers?"

"Pardon?"

"Spouse swappers," I said.

Grandmom shut off the reading light above the chair. Her complexion dampened into melancholia. There were already three glasses of Okanagan Port by the decanter. One for me, one for her and, of course, one for her departed spouse who would pop in for a few when I neglected to get her to the cemetery. Her face went from white to green, her eyes yellowed and the room smelled of burnt toast. In seconds her whole body was cold and then her throat expanded. On the floor, I swept the inside of her jaw, but no, nothing there save a stream of white bubbles issuing from her throat. The nail polish odour made me think diabetes, but then she started to vibrate, and I thought epilepsy.

A shot of sherry wasn't going to fix this. Froth slipped out of her eyelids. Some bubbles were delicate, breaking off her lip and floating upwards. Others were dense and formed a cocoon around her chin. The more I shook her, the faster the bubbles spread. The ambulance should have been the obvious call, but this was out of their realm, so I bound her to the chair with tie down straps and called my brother.

"Grandmom is having a spell," I said.

"What kind of a spell?" Stan said.

The television was on in the backroom. A documentary on Latin American insurgents coping with Catholic oppression.

"She's spewing bubbles."

"What kind of bubbles?"

"White ones."

"Like when she eats tapioca?"

"Like, right now."

"It's the asthma," he said. "Give her a shot of the puffer."

"It's not asthma."

"Maybe it's Alzheimer's. Spittle is one of the symptoms. She's locked herself in the bathroom again, hasn't she?"

"I've got her buckled up in the rocker."

"You've what?" he said.

"She's gone stiff."

"Is she conscious?"

"She's shaking."

"Call EMS," he said.

"We can't do that."

"Why not?"

"You know why," I said.

Now was not the time to be beating around the bush, so naturally my brother was going to do that. I was waiting for the inevitable epitaph of wisdom: "The key to winning is maintaining poise under duress." Or, "Some men are above sorrow, others beneath it, the best are courageous when inside it."

"Is her health care not paid up?" Stan said.

"I've no clue."

"Cirrus, that's your job to know. Call the ambulance."

"She doesn't want one."

"It doesn't matter what she wants. If she's unconscious, you've got to call."

"The spit is encasing her," I said.

"What are you getting at?"

"You know what I am getting at, Stan. That stench is coming off her. And she's making grotesque humming noises. It's so bad the room is vibrating."

"Cirrus, are you loaded? Jesus, you're stoned out of your mind, aren't you?"

I objected, but my credentials were not good. Neither was my track record, history of employment or curriculum of reason.

"Listen to me," he said. "I am going to hang up the phone. You are going to call the ambulance. Dial nine-one-one. Do not hesitate. When I call back, I expect them to be there. If they are not, I will call them and I will also call the police."

That I did not want. Not at any cost. The entire house constituted one massive on-view seizure. My description of GM's condition to the dispatcher must have been succinct. The ambulance was on the front lawn within four minutes. Red lights, white lights, flashing lights. Great, no blue lights. The neighbours came out.

The attendants were puzzled by a woman laying rigid on the rocking chair covered with spittle but set to work on her, attaching electrodes and saline bags. They wiped away the froth and plugged an IV into her arm. When the heart screen failed to get any reading, they became worried.

"Does she have a monitor?" one asked.

"A what?"

"She's breathing, but her pulse has gone silent."

"Which means?"

"What kind of medication is she on?"

"None," I said.

"Are you sure?"

I shrugged. Apart from the opium, T3s and massive quantities of sherry I had been feeding her, none I could think of.

"What are all those bubbles?"

"Can you check the medicine cabinet for us?"

In the end, I consented, but did no such thing. I riffled through every drawer in her room searching for a datebook. She had owned many simple black hardbacks secured with tiny padlocks. The notations might have consisted of philosophic musings, her contacts, private and professional, the living and the dead but hopefully one that would contain Gwendolyn's number. After inflicting damage on a porcelain banana and on pre-Confederation teaspoons collected by my grandfather I found the books in the bottom drawer, but the pages had been ripped out. More than ripped, they were mulched beyond recognition. They also shared the same odour as my grandmother, that confused fragrance of mothballs, cow parsnip seed and medical ointment that had dried in a cellar for decades. I gave up and went back into the living room.

My grandmother sat up in the chair and the colour had returned to her face. She looked fit. The bubbles had subsided to a white film, which she wiped away with a handkerchief, and her hair was perfectly in place.

"I think we're all right," the attendant said.

"You're kidding me."

"Blood sugar fine, pulse okay, heart rhythm on target but faint."

"You said she had none."

"Maybe we misread."

"Oh that," GM did up the buttons on her collar. "I've had that for years. I nearly drowned myself in Lake Athabasca when I was seven. Submerged for six minutes in ice water and everyone thought I was a goner. Ever since then, I've run into problems with doctors. They have a hard time finding my pulse. Didn't my grandson tell you about that? Cirrus, I was telling this fine attendant that we went through the same thing in 1967 at Expo, and all the French doctors got in a fuss. They gave me a silver wrist bracelet to wear, but of course I have misplaced it. I've told you about that, Cirrus."

The attendant stared at me and waited for an explanation.

"What about the bubbles?" I said.

"We're not sure."

"Not sure?"

They began putting their tools back in their kit with an aura of unconfirmed success.

"My heart is as solid as a horse," GM said. "Just faint. I fell asleep and my grandson could not detect any vitals, so he called you. Please put it on your records so we don't have to go through this embarrassment again."

"When was the last time?" the attendant said.

"November 11, 1977. We had other things on our plate, so the ambulance didn't come. They seem to have a cycle of about five years. At my age, I don't worry about it too much."

"What time do you think it is now?" he said.

"Forty-three minutes after four. You see, I do not lose track of time. My senses are perfectly intact. I remember everything. I hear everything, see everything. Go on, ask me a question. Ask me a square root question. I'm quite good at those."

He got out a calculator. "One thousand seven hundred and six."

"Forty-one."

"Amazing."

"Ask me a logic question."

"Do you want to go into the hospital as a precaution?"

"Absolutely not. I have work to do, and I do not consent."

The medic stared at me again. Somehow this was working out to be my fault.

I walked them to the door. A gaggle of blackflies collected on the mail slot. At a distance they looked like quivering molasses.

"Well?"

"Old people have fits," he said. "They don't have them diagnosed because they're old, and they go on. We can't force her to do anything. Medically there's nothing wrong with her."

"She was stiff as a board."

"She cracked when we got her off the chair that you'd tied her to. There's a condition with Gangliosides which produces iron-like strength in the muscles, but it's more common with young people."

"Can you do tests?"

"While you were out of the room your grandmother gave us the lowdown on the family situation."

"And?"

"Maybe you should get some sleep."

The phone rang. That would be Stan.

THIRTEEN

THE STORY APPEARED insignificantly on page D3 of the *Vancouver Sun*. Sometime during the late hours of Thursday night or the early minutes of Friday morning, a four-door coupe came to a stop outside the driveway of a middle-class home on Forty-Ninth Avenue near Cooke Street. Three masked assailants wearing black shirts and gloves proceeded to the side of the house and forced entry through the door using a pry bar. Once inside the detached split-level home, the intruders bound, gagged and assaulted the homeowners for a period of over one hour and fifteen minutes. Both victims, apparently married and in their forties, were not expecting any company and had no previous history with police. The assault was of a particularly gruesome nature. First the assailants stripped the couple naked and bound their hands and feet with duct tape. They then inflicted over one hundred and fifty lash marks, abrasions and cuts with flexible hose weapons to various parts of the thighs and genitals. Before leaving the assailants urinated on the couple, then put plastic bags over their heads which were secured with shoelaces. The homeowners were only able to survive the ordeal by chewing their way through the plastic and sitting upright to breathe. A small amount of prescription morphine, Valium and cannabis resin was stolen from the medicine cabinet, but no cash or electronics were taken.

If not for the watchful eye of an insomniac neighbour, the two most probably would have died. Although their initial injuries were not life-threatening, the attending emergency physician stressed that in a time of trauma the human body requires up to four times the amount of oxygen than at rest. That the couple got enough air through the small holes in the bags constituted a miracle. The neighbour, who wished to remain anonymous and would not answer his door for *Sun* reporters, was a paraplegic Korean War veteran who witnessed the entire drama through his vintage Zeiss binoculars. So far, the victims are not cooperating with police, and I can't say I blame them.

In the sexual underground of the middle class, everyone has their secrets, and clandestine is the way most want their lives to stay. Whether these unfortunates were truly victims of a brutal B&E or perhaps a complex sex game gone wrong was hard to say. But after only a few visits with Azy, I knew that it could be either. It could have also been a case of domination politics gone bad, and figuring out what subspecies of the hive that may have come from wasn't too difficult to discern.

In the Mistress's kingdom, six layers of civil servants dwelled within her catacombs struggling for satisfaction, release and, most of all, expiation. The first were the One-Offs, pronounced *Wunnofz*, and treated for basically what they were, the bottom of the bent barrel. These fleeting creatures were those who either believed what they were going to get was straight sex with a woman in a leather suit, or else they didn't have a clue what they were getting into. Many were long-time consumers of porn and lived their entire erotic existence in movie theatres and on dirty Super 8 loops. Face-to-face human interaction wasn't their forte, but by accident, mistake or too many

Big Bear Beers, the One-Offs showed up at Domme's door. Inevitably they left, bruised, humbled and sorely disappointed.

One-Offs came in all shapes, sizes and genders. Men did it on dares. Transsexuals were often confused. Women showed up from time to time wanting a lesbian experience. "Lesbians are the most tiring," Azy said to me. She dropped a green olive into a vodka martini and considered the frost on the glass. "They want to waltz in, talk down to *Chatelaine* and pay out in lavender soap."

Many One-Offs were fakes. Freelance journalists wanting to get the inside scoop on the BDSM scene and sell a story. Erotic photographers trying to make a commissioned pitch. About once a year, a vice cop tried to worm their way in as a One-Off, but the mistress, no greenhorn at judging heat, would shut them down before they collected any real evidence. "You can spot vice a mile away," she said. "When real customers come calling, they are looking for the erotic, no matter how misguided their expectations might be and it shows. The edge of their breath, the way their voice trembles. The guilt. But a cop has none of that. His aura is flat, two-dimensional, and you can smell insincerity on him like rotting meat. Sometimes, I'll have one over and string them along for several hours, playing card tricks or reading their fortunes until they get tired and leave having to fill out a dozen empty forms for their staff sergeant."

One-Offs all had two things in common. First, they were deluded. They fantasized about being flogged or tortured in Japanese concentration camps or erotically drowned in doomed submarines, but when the event was actually dramatized, it didn't turn them on. Like being in the army or trying to become a novelist, the idea was more enticing than the real thing. The second thing was that once they walked out Azy's door, they'd never be seen again. That was fine with her. She kept the money. They constituted up to a third of her clientele. But One-Offs came with certain risks. They could be bad publicity. They were often assholes, misogynists or con men who slipped by the telephone interview and would have to be coddled, threatened or ejected to avoid trouble. One-Offs never got anything too heavy, and there was little chance of them being damaged, let alone permanently hurt. They were never the victims of accidents.

Next came the Clients. Not Johns, mind you. Never refer to a Client as a John. Referring to a Client as a John was like a cop referring to a human source as a rat. Mostly of the professional class and relatively discreet, the Client comprised the bulk of Mistress Azy's business, time and focus. She kept charts, logbooks and photos. Off the top of her head, she could identify by name thirty Clients and that was without going to her secret black book. On the average, the Clients came once a month and paid between one hundred and fifty and three hundred dollars for services depending upon the complexity of the event. Do the math. Revenue Canada didn't get a cut.

The Client wanted detachment, precision and above all else, anonymity. Anonymity was the baseline of any dominatrix's enterprise. She sold not only a service but also a professional guarantee. Everything about a real Domme was blue chip. They were discreet, reliable and covert. If you passed one on the street while you were shopping, you'd see an attractive woman in a blue pinstripe suit and think banker, maybe financial consultant or civil law. While prostitutes had warrants and escorts couldn't keep their mouths shut, the pro-Domme peddled her silence to the Client. In turn, the Client gave not only money but indifference. The true Client wouldn't fall in love with their mistress, send her roses or worry about her glaucoma. The Client didn't want to be loved. They didn't discuss their personal lives. They always had money. No chance of accidents here, either.

The third class were the Courtesans. No Domme stayed in business for long if they didn't have a civil service or at least like-minded people forming their inner cabinet. They were often referred to as knights, bishops and ladies, and although the nomenclature was fugitive, everybody knew their role. These were the elite who may once have been Clients or friends but no longer paid for the Domme's company. Not up front, anyway. The Courtesans attended parties at the Domme's house, took her to plays, the symphony or dinner, even on vacations. Cancun was popular. Some were tradesmen, others, merchants (usually fetish ware) and a few artists. They were architects, musicians, glamour models or even neighbouring Dommes. When one Domme was visiting another, she often referred to her host as "Auntie," which was a sign of professional deference. Whatever their slot, all the aristocracy offered homage, service and witty conversation to their monarch. In return they got a social circle. Introductions. References and status. Lots of kink. And relatively free risk.

Three smaller classes existed within this sexual underground and although the Domme wouldn't admit it, from here most of her troubles came. These gnatty and ephemeral players eked out an existence at the periphery of the Mistress's kingdom but never managed to completely disappear. They were the Agents, Pets and Collared Slaves.

Agents were the subclass beneath the Courtesans. Frequently of lower intellect and poor interpersonal skills, they provided the services that the aristocracy wouldn't, basically, the muscle and steady supply of drugs for the Domme. A Courtesan wasn't about to get in a bar brawl with a bad customer or wait around on Granville Street to score a bag of weed. In return, Agents got minor fees or scraps of affection from the Domme, but they didn't session with her and weren't invited to parties. Although essential, they were a bit of a dirty secret. Nobody liked talking about Agents much.

The Collared Slave was a high-paying troubled Client who wanted all the Domme's attention and paid for it through the nose. Basically, they were a needy bunch. Typically, their sessions included conducting menial household chores or being locked in a chastity device during a party. They also got to go shopping with the Domme or have lunch with her if there was nothing else on. The problem with Collared Slave's was that they carried a lot of baggage, usually, a bad divorce or a wretched childhood. Collared Slaves liked to be at the feet of their Mistress during the entire party or sent on special errands like refilling her wine glass and answering the door. They thought they had status, which they didn't, and got jealous if another Client got too much attention. Azy once told me she made eighteen hundred dollars from a CS in a single month while his wife was on vacation. Then he disappeared.

Pets were a tragic anomaly in the hive. Confused individuals of either gender, the Pet had formed a conventional sexual attachment to the Mistress, and for whatever reasons the Mistress returned the fancy, usually because the Pet was gorgeous. Either male athletes with huge cocks or beautiful bisexual female centrefolds with enormous but crushable egos, their purpose was simple and entirely sexual. The Domme screwed them. They paid no money, weren't that bright and didn't last. Like a supernova in its last glorious moment, the Pet flitted around the party thinking they were the centre of the universe because they got what nobody else had. But they were wrong. The moment passed. The Domme tired. Then she simply made up an excuse, believable or not and cut them loose. Banished, gone and forgotten. It was a sad sight watching a Pet flaunt around at midnight, knowing that come morning she would be as present as yesterday's rain.

There was one more group worth mentioning, although they hardly formed a class. These were the Exiles, and their predicament was self-explanatory. They came from any of the above classes and had caused enough problems to get themselves permanently deported. *Excommunicado capienda*, as the Catholics might say. The reasons were many: mental breakdown, drug addiction, legal issues, malice or stupidity. The end result was the same. They were dismissed. Their attempted trespass was one of the few instances that a Domme might turn to the police, but more often the Agent looked after the trouble promptly. That wasn't pretty. The beatings were severe and done far enough away from the Domme's house that no evidentiary link could be substantiated.

I'd been thinking about what class I fell into exactly one day when I called Azy for a session with the last one hundred and fifty dollars I'd scrounged from a savings bond that had matured. Pearson was PM at its printing, so I relished getting the cash.

"Sorry, can't make it," she said.

"You can't?"

"I'm getting ready for a party on Saturday night." There was a horrible silence on the phone and then she said, "You are invited. Be here at eight. Don't be tardy. I can't stand tardy people. Come to the front door this time. Bring a costume."

The road outside Azy's was dark and slicked with rainbow stains, that time of the year when the water flushed everything into the gutter with lukewarm indifference. Damp leaves clung to the pavement and the street lamps held cream mist around their bulbs. In front of Azy's house, a red pickup truck squealed away in a patch of rubber and struck a trash can.

Audra, the perpetually dishevelled roommate and au pair pervette, answered the door but left the chain on. Her dark Latin eyes were filled with disdain, and they lingered on me for a full minute before she finally unbolted the lock.

"Interno," she said.

The front foyer was an off pink and the rounded archway well cracked, a tidy suburban home that had seen its prime in 1955. High ceiling, hardwood floor. Puffed sofas and tiled kitchen. Immaculately clean, as if nobody lived there between sessions.

"I don't know your name," I said to her.

"So what?" she said.

A dozen people hung out in the living room. Maybe another dozen in the kitchen. Hard to tell, they were clustered together, buzzing and whispering. Many of them looked like fishing lures decked out in chrome buckles, buckskin hides and brass spikes. Set by set, alien eyes flitted across me, passed judgment, then moved on.

"Where's Azy?" I said.

"Getting dressed."

"Aud," a woman said from the down the hall.

The roommate sighed and bowed her head around the corner while they spoke.

"Yes, it is," Audra said. "No, he doesn't."

"Find him something, would you?"

Audra sighed. Existence was an effort for her. She motioned me down the hall to a spare bedroom, the kind of place your aunt might keep for guests: ancient bed, a patterned quilt and a six-foot dresser. The air smelled of plaster.

"You must own leathers," she said.

"Sorry."

"Yeah, yeah." She opened the doors and ran her hand over a dozen hangers that sagged with Lycra gear and plastic skirts. After sizing me up, she clicked her tongue, then picked out a leather harness with crotchless shorts and tossed them on the bed.

"Do this," she said.

The harness was pure psycho ward stuff. Buckles, clasps and pitons salvaged from the Byzantine Empire. I had not a clue where to start.

"Take off your clothes." She dusted off a pair of Roman sandals and tossed them at me too. "Put your hands above your head. Well, go on. I see this always."

I pulled off my clothes and Audra leaned back against the cupboard door, folding her arms and sucking on her lip.

"In love for Jesus," she said through her thick accent. "You must shave your balls."

"Whatever," I said.

"No, now."

She opened a sewing kit and pulled out a pair of blue surgical gloves. Then she found an electric razor and plugged it in. The teeth made a horrid gravel contortion as if rocks were working through the blades.

"Hold up your sack," she said. "Don't think I'm going to do this touching for you too."

She got down on her haunches and went to work on my crotch marine corps–style. The hair fell onto the floor, and she muttered in Spanish.

"Too much pubic." She put the razor in my pants. "Too much. Too much. Take this home for Jesus, love. Make good use of it."

Then she kicked a three-legged stool out of the cupboard, stood on it and fingered me to raise my arms. The harness slid over my shoulders and the buckles were cold. Audra spun me around and did up the snaps. There were twenty-two all together and she worked with the speed of a sweat-shop worker.

"This is all I wear?" I said.

"You're a slut," she shrugged. "You wear nothing."

Back in the living room, the air was heavy with cherry incense that did a poor job of concealing the hash. Hash was the SM drug of choice in '81. Turkish hash. Everyone wanted to get stoned on Turkish hash and come hard. Really hard. All night. Excess was still in. Big white eyes. Small pupils. White teeth. Faces crusted with want and hideous bongo music playing on the stereo. One girl with a face painted like a puppet turned a lava lamp on above the television and shot me a sour glance. Either I was looking too hard or not hard enough. Where to start was a problem. Not with her, anyway. I stood in the corner with a glass of vodka punch. A fraternity leader on campus had once lectured me on the do's and don't s of attending cool parties. "When you hit a soircc," he said, "plunge. Start at one end of the room and work your way across. If you haven't had any success by the time you get to the far side, leave."

I plunged at the nearest couple. She was a buxom woman with a tight green sequin. He was a thin man with a red goatee and a Viking style leather vest. Both about forty. His slight nose made me think I'd seen him before. They were already sizing me up by the time I got close enough to speak.

"Hey," I said.

"Hey," he said back.

"You must be Azy's new boy," she said.

"Boy?"

She held out her hand, gazed once at my face and then down at my balls. She looked like the type of woman who would work at a brokerage on Granville Street and shook hands to gauge character. Her name was Rachael, and her husband was Tim. Tim had the defiant civil servant air about him, like he knew a code you never would and would make you pay extra on your income tax for it.

"Cool to meet you," I said.

"Very cool," he said.

"Great party."

"Wait until the play starts. Are you high yet?"

"High?"

"Did you get hash?" he said.

"Not yet."

"You should."

"Why?"

"You seem nervous." Tim let his eyes drift down to my dick. He fondled a metal broach on his lapel that was shaped like a salamander.

"It's cold in here," I said.

"You'll probably want to score before the scenes start."

"Hash freaks me out."

"I know but if it gets you hard, who cares?"

"Some people can get it up without hash," his wife said.

"Intensification is the apex of my love." Tim was either struggling to find a word that escaped him or else doing an audition for Lear at Stratford.

"I thought Azy hated intoxicants," I said.

Tim laughed. "Virtue looks best at a distance. That's at sessions, darling. Parties, totally different story."

"Dope turns everything into bug sex for me."

"That's not really a turn-on," Tim said.

"Then I get paranoid."

"Oh, great."

"Cannabis makes many people decidedly antisocial," she said.

"Well, we don't want that," he said. "How about a popper instead?"

"Go easy," Rachael said.

"I know it gets bigger," Tim said.

"Maybe he's not into it right now," she said.

"Now is all that matters. Now is it. Remember Andy Warhol."

"Try talking to him first," she said like I wasn't there.

"Yes, of course," he said. "We're architects. Are you into architecture?"

"Art Deco and Arthur Erickson."

"Okay," he said. "Whatever. How about petroleum?"

I wanted Azy to make me lick Rachael's shoe, not talk supply and demand. She had shiny knees, long manicured nails, and I pictured her sprouting wings and digging them into my rib cage.

"What about it?" I said.

"It's going to be a buck a litre soon."

"And?"

"And all hell is going to break loose."

"Over gas?"

"Totally a right-wing deal." Tim had a slightly effeminate manner when he got pissed off, and the petrol matter clearly pissed him off.

His wrist snapped around in sharp angular circles, and I still couldn't place where I'd seen him before. My guess was he had relevance to my parents' case. Maybe he designed their house.

"You're not a righty, are you?" he said. "Because righties don't get along here. Unless you're a fascist. Fascism is a different thing. It's sexual. It's in. But conservatism will be the end of us. That's always the way. Think Rome. Think Pinochet. Gas rationing is where it starts. Then comes the panic and the interest rates rise, finally the scapegoating and the vice crackdown. Do you read Wilde? That's Oscar. Whenever a society panics, they always take it out on sexual promiscuity. Witches, homosexuals, pornography and liberals. Do you know there's already a provincial bill criminalizing transgenderism?"

"He gets carried away," Rachael said.

"I'm confronting the facts," Tim said.

"I don't want to criminalize anything," I said.

"Fabulous. Integrity is a real turn-on for me."

"Tim," Rachael said, "everything is."

"I know, I know. How is your dance card looking tonight by the way?"

"He might be collared, Tim."

"He's not collared. Is that a slave collar he's got on? Is that a slave collar you've got on?"

"Ask Azy," she said.

"She's stingy with her subs," he said. "She gives out collars to everybody and expects a feudal lordship. I mean it's her party, but we are all free agents here. All free souls. This is an autonomous collective. Are you collared, yea or nay?"

"My husband is too forward with new people." Rachael adjusted my jock strap with her blue fingernails. "He gets himself into trouble all the time. He'll get dragged up and accost his victims in public libraries at the most inconvenient times. Especially after a few tokes."

"No accosting," Tim said. "Integrating. Social expansion is a founding pillar of our nation's wealth. No Domme tells me what to do. Now how about that hash?"

He held out a chunk of black resin between his thumb and forefinger. Even the ritual of hash smoking was an aphrodisiac. The ceremony of watching the toke go in. The *oh* moment when the dope reduces all thought to sexual obsession.

Azy barked a command from the back room with Tim's named tacked on the end. He wobbled to attention, stuffed the hash in his pocket and left.

"Later," Rachael said.

I bumped into Puppet Girl again and suffered a hard crack of déjà vu. The white paint, the small eyes. Fluttering, all bird-like and fragile. Couldn't place her. She hated me but I didn't know why. UBC coed, probably. A midterm I was supposed to have written on Monday flashed through my mind. The actual subject escaped me. I could not have cared less.

When a chunk of metal drops in a box of compasses, all the needles swing in the same direction, and that's what happened when Azy walked into the room. Her face, laden with makeup, displayed no trace of emotion. The heels put her at over six feet and the rubber suit looked wet. She walked from guest to guest and thanked them each for coming by either shaking their hands, allowing them to kneel or slapping them on the face.

A blue puffed stool towered over every other piece of furniture in the room, and that was where she went. She surveyed her kingdom. She snapped her fingers, and a thin Hispanic man with rippling abdominal muscles slithered out of a cupboard. His skin was slicked with oil. He wound his lizard body around the legs of Azy's stool as if his bones possessed not an ounce of calcium. Our good Mistress reduced a Slim to a stick of white ash while feigning boredom. The lizard man opened his mouth and accepted her hot cargo. Sizzle, wince, satisfaction. The crowd dutifully applauded, and Rachael put her hand on my ass.

After the opening act, the Courtesans discussed the day's events: the coming recession, the tactics of the police state and the evil of clear-cut logging. Soon the tide became twinged with the perverse. The kind of tortures that the Right Wing would inflict on the Kinky during the Reformation (being forced to read Bertrand Russell for erotic pleasure, have intercourse with ex-opposition leader Robert Stanfield or have the insertion of anti-erection devices by bovine-looking nuns.) Then, of course, the kinds of retribution that the Bent would inflict upon their Oppressors once the liberation was complete (hot waxing, being gibbet-strung on planks made from those clear-cut logs, or castration completed telepathically from a Kremlin-like lab in Ottawa). When Azy heard a torture that she particularly enjoyed, she summoned the minstrel forward and had him dole out extra details to the audience. A few canned, others legitimately spontaneous. An elderly man with a great deal of makeup and a few war medals pinned to his chest was particularly pompous.

"Personally, I envisage a hexapedal attack," he said. "Swarming the bastions of Normandy and embalming our foe in a lugubrious fluid that would stop their very hearts from beating."

"It's all about the war for you, isn't it, Major?" Azy said.

"My dear Mistress, all pleasure comes from war."

The old veteran got smug. He put a gin and tonic to his white moustache and nodded like he'd just drew up the plans for D-Day all on his own.

"And speaking of pleasure," Azy said, and let her voice hang.

Everyone knew what that meant. Everyone knew when the Mistress grew bored with academics she'd say, "And speaking of that," or "Since we're on this line of thought," and the talking was done. That meant we'd move downstairs.

Downstairs was decked with red lights, pots of incense, cages, crosses and shackles that had been set up by the Courtesans on schedule. Azy didn't waste any time. She cuffed me up and forced me to my knees with her stiletto. After issuing a couple of decrees in Italian, she located an elk-hide flogger. All I saw was the shadow of tails coming down on my back. When she paused for a breather, Don secured me to a set of ceiling hooks and hoisted me off the ground. The audience liked that part. Medieval drama. A lot of screaming. Maybe there was a chance my shoulders would pop, but who cared?

Some people are into flogging and others aren't. Most people watch a few rounds to get warmed up for their own scene. The important thing about a scene is to be in one. Embrace the pain. Moan a lot, even if it doesn't hurt. Roll your eyes if it does. Loll out your tongue. Try and touch your Top, but don't ever succeed. That's a no-no. Above all, keep your member hard. There's nothing worse than watching an SM party where people look like they'd rather be doing a crossword. For Azy, indifference was unforgivable. Any sign of nonchalance was greeted with astringent pain or complete dismissal. There's a scene in a 1960s comedy where Raquel Welch flogs a bunch of men on a slave ship. Like that, except no laughing matter. The only thing worse than indifference was levity. Attempts at humour were considered a personal insult and usually ended up with the SAM (smart-aleck-bottom) being reduced to a snivelling mess. Don't think there was any sort of logic to these responses. Sometimes, not giving into her cruelty was bad news. I hadn't called Yellow and wasn't begging for mercy. The more she hit me, the harder I got. She went from the elk hide to the nine-tails and then starting using an implement with metal burrs. In a few minutes she had broken out in a sweat.

"Get the hooks," she said to Don.

Don looked surprised but he never argued with calls. The grapplings were ugly looking creatures, as if they'd come off a fishing boat. Azy plunged them into a jar of alcohol in a half-assed attempt to make them sterile, then pushed the barbs through my pecs. The skin popped and violent images flashed through me: a crimson volcano, a breaking glass skull. Don heaved on the block and tackle. I ascended, spinning towards the ceiling with chunks of my flesh stretched into triangles.

A Vaudeville hatch in the ceiling, which would have been a trap door on the main floor, opened above me. Puppet Girl stood, arms crossed. Her white face radiated contempt as she mouthed a chorus of obscenities. Then she pulled up her skirt, spread her legs and let fly with a stream of piss. She must have been drinking straight out of the garden hose all night long because the cascade just kept coming. Gallons of the stuff, Niagara Falls style, and finally I couldn't hold back anymore. I screamed and rationalized my existence as a biologic creature and Rachael said, "Oh, my."

I spun around limp for another rotation, then realized the show was over. The once-mesmerized crowd was deserting us for the dungeon show where a young girl was being coated with flaming lacquer. I fell earthward and my shoulder blade hit the ground. Azy grabbed me by the hair. The makeup around her eyes had run. She was clearly pissed off.

"Don't ever ruin my scene again," she said. "Do not, do not ever, under any circumstances, shoot off without my permission."

Azy lit up a menthol, took one drag, then bounced the cigarette off my chest. Lizard man crawled over and licked up the smouldering butt with his tongue.

Back in the kitchen, Don was drinking rye and Coke and listening to Charlie Parker on the stereo.

"How are you, bud?" he said.

"Not good, I guess."

"Don't sweat it." He went to slap me on the back but then stopped. My skin resembled sandpaper. "That has to hurt."

"Good times."

"Just out of curiosity, do you not bleed?"

"Was I supposed to?"

"I was getting the hydrogen peroxide ready. To tell you the truth, I'm glad you came when you did. I'd hate to see you maimed because the Mistress has a bad hair day."

"How was that scene supposed to end?"

"What happened when you rehearsed?"

"We didn't."

Don gazed into his rye. "She'll get over it," he said.

He put disinfectant on my back, and I found a shot of Scotch. Puppet Girl leaned against the wall with her arms still crossed.

"Thanks for the shower," I said.

She stared at me with stupid hate. Mesolithic people plastered their faces up when they got ready for war. Even through the mud disguises, you could make out the anger.

I tried again. "Merci beaucoup. Gracias."

"You screwed up," she said.

The voice rang a bell. The features fell into place. I recalled a bored clerk sitting behind an insect terrarium.

"Sal?"

She cut me off. "Rule one. Don't call me Sal, here."

"What should I call you?"

"Carmen."

"Carmen?"

"From the opera."

"Which opera?"

"Don't bring up the museum, either."

"Is that rule two?"

"It's basic protocol."

"What protocol?"

"Common courtesy and fundamental etiquette. No blabbing. No outing. No private eye–shit. I'm not talking about your parents, am I?"

"Okay, Carmen of the opera who doesn't have an outside life, thanks for the golden shower."

"You just screwed up a beautiful instance of human realization supremely."

What a frail jaw she had. The kind of jaw that narrowed into a scrawny isthmus of flesh and wound up in a Neville Chamberlain speech. What you'd expect a chicken to give birth to.

"I screwed up, I've been told."

"Don't be surprised if you never get another party invitation."

"Who are you to say?"

"One who's been coming here for longer than you have and has a much higher place in this hierarchy."

"Why are you being such a bitch?"

"Because you are a prick," she said "A self-centred, egotistical, landed, middle-class, arrogant prick. You waltz into the museum any time you want and talk down to me. You treat me like a box of Cracker Jacks, then you say you'll drop around on a certain day and you don't bother. You bait me with coy promises because you think I'm lonely and stupid and I should cater to your every whim or desert my peers to suck your dick. Then you vanish for months and show up when I'm having lunch, making stupid jokes about my clitoris. A subject that you obviously have no tactical knowledge of. Coyness is the most pathetic form of narcissism. It's your whole life attitude, Cirrus."

What the fuck, Florence Nightingale.

"I'm sorry if I offended you," I said.

"I think you're too arrogant to mean that."

She was right. I didn't mean it. Not at all. I imagined Scooby-Doo pissing on her face and Don screwing her in the ear, and then I imagined a giant termite ripping her tiny potato chip tits apart inch by inch and spitting them into the termite turd bin of life.

"You have really nice-tasting urine," I said.

"Get me a glass of wine." She held up her plastic cup. "Riesling."

On the way down to get Sal her wine I passed by a mature woman who perched herself on a chair and examined her figure in a full-length mirror. She watched herself smoke. She sucked in luxuriously, then let the white tar slip out between her yellowed teeth, one of which had a gold filling. Her eyes fixated on the reflection, perhaps telling herself that she was still beautiful or had been once. Occasionally, she glanced towards the hall to see if anyone was noticing. I remember how petrified her body was, like the sphinx staring out across the desert sands, unmoved by the wind or sun, staying exactly the same age for the next ten thousand years and then finally, after a few minutes, her thighs moved together, she grimaced and gasped and then she ground out her cigarette, got up and walked out of the room, and I never saw her again.

FOURTEEN

IN THE MORNING I woke stiff and lacerated. By any standards of modern warfare, it had been a rough evening. The puncture marks on my chest had gone blue and dissolved to the size of buttonholes, and my joints ached. Tim had talked me into hash and cognac. There had been amyl nitrate and another flogging session too. I'd done public penance for my misdeeds, which involved Sal wielding a sterling silver dildo. My front tooth was chipped. I had a non-sterile nipple piercing. Later, in the near dawn darkness of Azy's basement, a lonely woman lay her head against my shoulder. I turned in comfort, but the figure morphed into a six-foot vespid that closed around my naked body.

At 0633 hours, my grandmother was still sleeping and for a very stupid reason I decided to head gymside for the early morning sparring class. The Kingsway Boxing Club was near the Knight Street intersection and at one time or another had been a vegetable store, a fishing tackle shop and an outpost for the Wisdom Church of South Sudan. The Jamaican coach, Kim Kimball, from Kingston, was a championship boxer, big on early morning workouts, and he despised anyone who was late. "If you want to box for Canada," he'd bark, "you will be up before the sun. This country wasn't built on people who slept in."

Inside, everything was dirt-brown and smelled of canvas. People were already skipping. A sign above the door, painted in blood-red ink, proclaimed Be True to Yourself. Show Respect. Destroy Your Foe.

The change room reeked of old gym wear, and I sat beneath a poster of Muhammad Ali. On the far side of the room a group of men wrapped their hands up in adhesive rolls and looked surly. This was all part of the mystique that the coach fostered. Everyone had to go through these bullfighting rituals and pretend that they were low class, breaking out of the slums and hungry for victory. By the time I got out to the bags I wanted to pound someone, all right. I imagined the pompous war vet from Azy's party taking a right cross so hard it blew open his jaw.

"Woody, Woody, goddamnit," the coach called from the other side of the gym, and I knew the holiday was over.

Kimball stormed across the floor wearing his red track suit sewn with maple leaves and a sweatband that smelled of Bengay liniment.

"What the hell are you doing here?" he said. His face was black and he was always stack-blown angry, in a Jamaican sort of way. "Goddam, man. What are you doing in my gym?"

"I want to box."

"You want to box." He raised his hands and glanced around to the waiting audience. "You hear that everybody? Woody-Puddy wants to box. My God. Clear the room. Clean the mats. Call immigration. The white boy has intention. You want to box, my ass."

Kimball ripped his towel off his shoulder and threw it on the floor. Then he put his hands on his hips, and his face went a lot redder than it needed to be.

"Where have you been?" he said.

"At school."

"At school, my tiddy. You haven't been here for three weeks. Does school go twenty-four hours a day? No. But boxing does. You think you can walk in off the street and expect to suit up, lazy George Foreman, and make a million dollars. Coach Kim Kimball spends four years working you up from a bullied teenager to an athlete, and you disrespect him? Remember who took you in when your grandparents brought you around. Remember who raised you up from the dirt of Abbotsford. You must work. You must suffer. You must suffer for Canada if you want to box. Every single day you must be in the gym to stay strong."

"I have been working out."

"You are a liar. A liar and a hypocrite. Wood-man, you are on the road to ruination. I know. I know the slums of defeat and I know the poverty of failure, and that is what your attitude says. You haven't been working out, you have been wanking off. You wanking off, Woody?"

"Not me, coach."

"And women and drinking too. That's what you've been doing. I can see it in your slumped posture."

"No girls," I said. Which was sort of true, but he didn't need to know.

"Oh, liar," he said. "Liar from hell. Let me see your lean."

Lean was Kimball slang for the hard-edged, mean motherfucker, poverty-stricken undernourished-gut-now-living-in-Canada look. The coach reached over and yarded off my robe. He could get away with this kind of thing because the stupid kids dug it and well, he was Jamaican. Every member of the club got a red robe when they'd done a hundred rounds in the ring. I suppose he expected to see fifteen extra pounds of flab or maybe knocked knees from too much fornicating. What he saw horrified him. My body was gnarled with the muscle fibres taking on a rippled-cod coldness.

"What is this?"

"Told you," I said.

"You lifting weights, Woodrow? I told you, no weights. Weights slow you down. Weights for beach bums, not boxers."

"Okay, a few weights, coach."

"Quit. You got one queer build, boy. You on steroids?"

"What are steroids?"

"Horse medicine. From university. Poison. Communist stuff. Holy shit, what is this gash in your chest? Are you on her-o-in, Wood-man? Heroin? Smack, sugar, junky-runk dope? My God, are you a drug addict, Mr. Know-It-All-White-Guy? a drug addict?"

"No drugs," I said.

"You are soul-fillet-hit."

"Fishing accident, KK. Look, I just want to box, okay? That's all. I'll try and come more often. Promise."

"You work on the bag for one hour, then maybe I'll let you shadow box."

"I don't want to shadow box."

"Oh, no. You want to leap in the ring and win a world championship. You want to fly to Panama City and take on Roberto Durán? Tell you what, Wooden-Puddin," Coach Kimball mused. He put one finger to his square jaw and pondered a Caribbean breeze. "You get in the ring and go three minutes with me, and I let you box. Otherwise, you beg for forgiveness and do three Pasta Points."

Pasta Points were a way that Kim Kimball had of embarrassing wayward boxers and essentially earning free labour from his constituents in these hardening economic times. A Pasta Point usually entailed one hour of a menial chore like cleaning the latrines or painting the gym.

"I'm in," I said.

"Uh huh," he said. "Don't worry. I won't hurt you. Much."

Kimball had one of his minions lace up his gloves, and then the lad jumped in the ring touting a Round 1 placard and danced around like a fairy on a summer picnic. The coach was a skilled boxer and there was no way to beat him straight up. Basically, he wanted to tire me out, to show everyone what bad shape I was in. If it looked like I was going the three minutes, he'd start pummelling me until I got cocky and took a shot at him. Then he'd deck me.

The bucktoothed youth who'd been assigned the unenviable task of gloving me up treated me like a leper. He kept shaking his head while he did up the laces and said, "You are one stupid son of a bitch."

Inside the ring, if I got hit, I got hit. That's what cosmetic surgeons were for. I had been pissed on, flogged and electrocuted by a harem of gorgeous extraterrestrials, so sixteen ounces of cotton wasn't anything to worry about.

The white floodlights flicked on, Kimball slipped under the ropes and then my eyes went out of focus. Or rather they came into focus. Perfect focus. The entire gym clear and sharp. Instead of the old, mean Kim Kimball's black face and white eyes, there were layers of red and purple vibrating off the spectrum. Hash flashback, I thought. Great. Trip out, get pummelled, then go psycho. Strangely, I could read the small print on the Liston versus Clay poster that hung on the far wall. Two youths mumbled boxing ethics in the change room. The smell of Aqua Velva wafted off the coach's neck. Kimball danced out and threw a couple of jabs. The wavelength of his face pitched infrared. Micro-air currents rolled off his jaw. From deep in his past rose the stench of street fights in the shitholes of Jamaica. He threw combinations. I ducked. Nothing hurt. The radio in the office blared the Rolling Stones, and on the street a trolley bus ran off its electrical wires. Kimball came in again and this time he meant it, he punched me hard and split my lip.

"You had enough, boy?" he said.

"Nice try," I said. You can't say the words "nice try" with a petroleum-based mouthguard without sounding derogatory in a racial way.

Kimball's muscles quivered. He went to the ribs and the gut. Green oil had collected on my abs that stunk of muskeg. His gloves slipped off. He pounded on. The air spat from his mouth with each blow, and then I realized that coach Kim Kimball was trying to knock me out.

"Enough yet, boy, enough?" A mouthguard flew across the ring.

I'm not sure what happened next, but Kimball was right. I had endured enough. The whole exercise was degrading, not very productive and keeping me from life's more important activities. Like drinking and screwing. I pounced mid-air, mouth wide open, kangaroo kamikaze style. Kimball's bulging neck muscles were the obvious target. In an instant they filled up three hundred and twenty degrees of my vision. His thyroid exploded in a nova of red, and I spat a flap of flesh skyward. Both off us fell through the ropes and collided in the spectator chairs.

"Christ, Christ," he screamed.

The homeboys tried to pull me off, but I was on top of their shoulders, back up in the ring, then hanging from the suspended canvas light.

"The white boy is mad."

Chances were, I could make the rafter if I tried.

"Get out of my gym, savage, get out."

No need to be told more than once. I hated the place. The stinking laundry, the old No-Pests strips and besides that, KK's mangled throat was bleeding egregiously. A long trail of frothy red blood followed me out onto the sidewalk, across the street and behind the 7-Eleven. Although my membership had been paid up until the end of the year, there was little chance I'd be going back. This all looked deeply suspicious, a poor lost white boy running down Kingsway in morning rush hour, his hands still laced with yellow boxing gloves and his jaw soaked in the blood of the legendary Jamaican head coach and successful Caribbean immigrant, Kim Kimball.

By the time I got home, I was badly worked up and badly needed another session. Everything led to another session. The crack of a hawthorne branch, the texture of glazed glass, or the jangle of brass jewellery. Statistically, there was no escape. All roads led to Rome. And Rome demanded cash. Lots of it. And cash meant work. I liked to call it work. Russell preferred the term "art form," which I thought was a bit fruity, but I could see his angle. Perfection itself. Most criminals aren't perfect or artists at all. In fact, they're woefully incompetent. Our national police service reports that for every ten burglars who commit more than one break and enter, nine are caught. Basically, criminals are losers. Why? They break the cardinal rules of good housekeeping; they repeat their *modus operandi* ad nauseam, they involve too many middlemen, they blab and they hoard a plethora of culpable goods that offer no return.

Russell understood the principles of theft aesthetics. He never went back to the same place twice. He didn't specialize in one genre of product, and he always had a buyer: a certain neighbour who needed one hundred and forty diamond-bit petroleum drills, another associate who could move fifty bottles of morphine, or a lost uncle to restore an original Robert Bateman. "Never take an article there isn't a ready-made market for," he said to me once as we drove away from the Zeus Zirconium Shop with five fillets of precious metals that were usable in either cruise missiles or cutlery moulding. "Never hang onto the product longer than you have to and never get greedy." For the high-end transactions, Russell didn't even demand payment up front. Once, we merely deposited a Zhou Dynasty vase repossessed from Garbey's Gifts through the window of a Kerrisdale home and drove away. "They'll pay," Russell said as he waited for the red light on Forty-first Street. "In the end, they know they have to."

A typical evening with Russell went as such. October 11, 1981, 0133 hours: the pair, referring to themselves now as "the Artists" were charged with gaining access to Essondale Addiction Services, a privately run psychiatric ward in a bedroom suburb of the Lower Mainland. The plan was to penetrate the low-level security facility and make off with an experimental antipsychotic medication that could only be got with a Solicitor General's note. Which, of course, our client did not have. The clinic was an experiment in privatization that the provincial government was undertaking with wild abandon, so I felt no moral qualms about the venture.

Tactically, the mission was a pushover. The windows were unsealed. There were no bars. The lone security guard was sixty years past prime, and the nurse was in the cafeteria watching *Late Night*. Russell and I donned our service uniforms, stuck a ladder and a half dozen mops in the back of his truck and drove through the back garden. I climbed the ivy brick wall, then lowered a harness down for my non-mountaineering partner. "Dude, you creep me out with that lizard shit," was all he said when he clambered over the sill. Inside we located the petty cash box and netted six hundred fifty dollars. The prescription cupboard was exactly where we figured in the head nurse's section, and the lock cut easily with bolt snips. Fifteen hundred dollars' worth of the essential medication waited on the top shelf, and within four minutes we were done. We even had time to replace the lock so entry might remain undetected in the morning. I wanted to swipe a pair of lace underwear located at the bedside of a slumbering patient, but Russell thought this unprofessional. We used thirty dollars to buy a bottle of Glenlivet, then delivered the aripiprazole prototype to a warehouse in Port Coquitlam for a premium of eight hundred sweet ones. The drug was discontinued the following year after a number of clinical fatalities.

Day jobs became inevitable, and the first time Russell got me on a steady pay-off he feigned disgruntlement over my session time. With a tin of Heidelberg tucked between his legs, he blew the stop sign on Buller and whacked the Hawaiian dancer hanging from the rear-view.

"You stay up too late."

"You're upset," I said.

"You're unreliable."

"Just give me the tactical forecast."

"The problem is market imbalance."

"What's that got to do with it?"

"Earth to Woodenhead, supply and demand equals everything."

Russell pitched his beer out the window and made a sudden jag towards an orange tabby cat on the roadside.

"Fricking animals." He surveyed the line of warehouses that were his professional domain. "I'll give you the lowdown on the economic structure of our existence, but this is all classified top secret. No blabbing to girlfriends, grandmothers or priests. The issue is this: let's say we were to break into said place."

"Said place?"

"And let's say from said place we were to steal said tools, say, power drills. What would we do with these power tools to turn them into said cash? They might be nice power drills, but to us, they are meaningless. Unless you want to pursue carpentry and you don't seem the type. I know what you are thinking. Why can't we take them to a pawn shop? Could do. Used to be able to. But those days are past. Not only are pawn shops asking for photo ID now, but most power tools have a serial number on them that the boss keeps track of. When you take a power tool to a pawn shop, they enter the number into a database, like in science fiction, and if that number matches the one the cops keep, you are busted. The market for industrials is glutted and that limits our options."

"To what?"

Russell stopped the truck under a chestnut tree and gazed across the soccer pitch where a dozen girls played field hockey.

"Doing many jobs for low return or taking on big ticket jobs which require special equipment is risky. Too much like real work. Don't like it. No, the inevitable conclusion one comes to is that merchandise is not the future and cash is."

"You're suggesting we start sticking up banks?"

"You watch too much television. Everyone who sticks up banks gets caught. I am talking about money from sources who won't even notice the loss. Who wouldn't even care. Safe, quick and much more moral, but of course that involves doing what you've said you won't do."

Russell leaned back in the driver's seat and pulled out another Heidelberg. The beer was still warm and when he popped the cap, foam spat over his dashboard again. The green-skirted girls on the field chased after a black ball.

"I like it when they hug each other," he said.

The house was actually a home. A collection of retirement homes off Marine Drive built in mock Tudor fashion that had survived the zoning officer's purview. The development sat in the bilge of the Fraser River and was subject to frequent flooding; a half-constructed dyke surrounded the village.

"They look fine from the outside but inside they're dumps," Russell said. "Everyone is old. They all live together in this commune-like affair. Creepy, really. They share colostomy bags. The place is going bankrupt, so everyone is moving their cash around. None of them believe in banks. Half of them teeter on the edge, so prepare yourself."

The target house was number 79, a two-storey infill with white stucco and fake cedar beams. After knocking and announcing our presence with a fake company name, a total lack of response from the house suggested something already amiss. Russell turned the doorknob. I slipped a nail file into the chamber and the weight of tumblers fell into place.

Inside, the air was stale. No lights. Cooked meats on the counter, old linen beside the sofa and a thousand years of memories decaying anaerobically in drawers. In this curtain-drawn world, the sky was perpetually dark. Shawls, cuckoo clocks, sacks of Montreal peppermints. TV guides stacked up to waist height in domestic fiords. Russell went to the hutch. He always started at the bottom drawer and worked his way up. At the kitchen sink I summarized all the places my grandmother might hide cash: the radio, the envelope bracket, the plant pots, coffee cups with plastic lids and a porcelain golden retriever with a baying blue mouth. This was not a rip and pull. We were not looting. We were reappropriating. No Victrolas. No power tools or silverwear. Non-fungible merchandise only, please. We had time. We had a cover story. We stuck to it.

Russell and I spoke infrequently on the job. We communicated through a series of glances, shakes and hand signs. Given enough time we could have done the Governor General's house just to secure the Robin Hood angle. In the spare bedroom, more drawn drapes, more boxes of old clothes and more mothballs. Our homeowner had used enough naphthalene to render the atmosphere unbreathable, so we pushed through to the master bedroom. The inner sanctum was bathed in beige light. The smell was not good. An image of tiny dead kittens beneath our front steps flashed from my past. In the centre of the king-size mattress a white-haired, crinkled face gazed to the ceiling with eyes glazed open. The woman appeared to be asking why.

A great deal of grease coagulated in her nostril. I watched our host's figure, uncertain if I wanted to see the chest rise and fall or not. On the dresser beside her was a two-six of Bombay gin, a handwritten copy of Shelley's *Ode to the West Wind* and a small vial marked Paregoric. Russell stepped over an ancient pair of stained nylons to the bedside cabinet. Beneath a row of socks, inside a postal sachet waited a geologic deposit of twenties. A mile deep of green. Russell nodded. Bull's eye, old bean, and we were gone.

Outside the sun was bright. Blue jays fluttered from tree to tree, unaware of the fate that awaited them with the bulldozer.

"We'll have to wash our clothes with carbolic soap." Russell smelled his cuff.

"Do you think she was dead?"

"Who knows?"

"Maybe it's better if she was."

"In fact," he said. "Turf your clothes out. Forget the carbolic."

Occasionally, we saw our handiwork in print. Russell cut out the Crime Beat section from the Vancouver *Province* on Monday morning and handed me a copy. Kind of like being published, but in an unauthorized biographical sort of way. "Sometime between 0130 and 0615 hours on 1981-10-15, culprit or culprits unknown gained access to Burnaby Welders Ltd, 5195 Finch Ave, by bending a metal reinforced doorway. Once inside, the culprits made their way to the clerical room where they pried open the cash box and acquired $450.00 in small bills. One precision circuit detector valued at $985.60 is also missing. A large deposit of folic acid found at the points of entry will be submitted to the Identification Unit for analysis."

"Folic acid?" Russell said.

Once I had the money, reason evaporated. I called Azy, and no matter how much she asked, I went. And each time, she seemed to ask more. I often wondered where the threshold was. If there were a magic amount where I would say no to having my mouth stuffed with a neoprene golf ball or air supply cut short with an Armani necktie, I hadn't reached it. Even dialling the numbers became foreplay. A typical exchange went like this:

"Good afternoon, Mistress."

"Good afternoon, slut."

"May I serve you today, Mistress?"

"You may, slut, although this might be your last time."

"Why might that be, Mistress?"

"Because I am going to murder you, slave. Sting you to death. Reduce you to a struggling mass of puss inside a doomed cocoon."

"I am enticed, Mistress."

"You are a drone, bitch."

"When may I come, Mistress?"

"You may never come, whore. But you will be present at my hive two o'clock post-meridian time. And this time you will also bring a dozen sterling silver Queen Mary dinner forks, one night pass for the Keg restaurant, fifty Tylenol Number Fours and your regular tribute."

The good Mistress often got carried away with the death and dispersal narrative. "I might strangle you slowly with a Banyan vine, whore, or stuff you down a drain in a sewage trough with a cattle prod or perhaps let boiling tungsten seep around your dick and leave the remains in a heap of Miocene gravel out in the Skagit Valley while I have a pedicure. That is not for you to decide."

Tungsten boiling at eleven hundred degrees might not really seep around genitalia, and the alluvial layers in the Skagit were Holocene, not Miocene, but was she truly insane? Would she really kill me? And if so, how? Sure, she got carried away with the plastic bag routine, but *c'est la guerre*. Trepidation was not a value Sir John A. founded our great nation on, and so cash in hand, I drove down Forty-First wondering how life could possibly get any better.

Every so often, my brother phoned to check on my welfare and my affair posed some dilemma. If I said to him, "Stan, I've met this beautiful woman who I'm having the greatest sex with," the reply would be, "Whom, Cirrus, it's with whom." Stan usually called at four o'clock on Sunday.

"What's wrong?" he said.

"Nothing's wrong," I said.

"Are you sick or stoned?"

"Stan, it's three fifty-seven. I don't start drinking for another three minutes."

"You are hungover, aren't you?"

"Drank two light beer last night."

Drinking light beer, any kind of light beer, was considered an abomination in '81, and the notion that a Canadian brewing company dared produce a light beer legally was considered treasonous.

"Light beer?"

"I was on a date."

"With who?"

"Whom Stan. It's with whom."

"Whatever. You met a girl?"

"If it will appease your socialist sense of equilibrium I'll go out and date a guy next week."

"Knock it off," he said. "Where did you meet her?"

"An independent business seminar."

"You don't go to those."

"Our lab class was doing a specimen extraction in the Venue. She was lecturing. The Fraser Institute. You know that one Stan. They save your tax money from perdition. She is an ex-biologist. I asked her out."

"Who paid?"

"I did, Stan."

"With what?"

"I took the extension with Environment Canada."

Lie, but Stan took the bait with begrudging caution.

"We went for a workout. She's thinking about starting up a gym franchise. With our Nordic influence here, people will pay big dollars to work out at gyms."

"Like the Y?"

"The Y is Neanderthal. This is where people pay to do exercises in a big bright room with tons of sunlight on chrome machines and wear latex pants while they seal real-estate deals. Huge in LA already, and she has a draft concept plan for here. Know what that is? That is when a charted accountant puts a viability stamp on it."

"How many times have you gone out?"

"Maybe a dozen."

"Is she psycho?"

"I'm taking her to meet GM. Because of her Presbyterian background, family meetings are a big deal."

"Then, um, sort of, big brother, what exactly does she want to do with you?"

"We talk bugs. *Actias luna*."

"Who?"

"Moths, Stan. She's also, what's the euphemism, nightly active herself."

"You said that. She owns a gym."

"No, vibrant," I said. "You know, exuberant."

A gorgeous, puzzled silence ensued at the other end of the line.

"She did the Spa King Mud Test."

Spa King was the Scandinavian, Jurassic predecessor to modern gyms. The Mud Test was a medieval torture device that suburban women subjected themselves to get a contour of their figure and fat content. The process involved being dipped in mud, having electrodes taped to your tits and being able to come up with four hundred dollars to be assigned a "mud value analysis," which was expressed numerically in the perfect notation of one hundred, one fifty and one ten.

"She did the mud test?"

"I watched."

"What did she score?"

"One oh three, one forty-seven and one oh nine."

"You are shitting me."

"Ask her."

"When?" he said.

Best not to push the actual date part too much. Did Queen Isabella want an exact date for the return of the Santa Maria? Did Tecumseh expect promises to be kept? Of course not. I left the details to his slender imagination and pictured Mandy beating a mountain of mashed potatoes into indifferent pulp.

"She hasn't asked you for any money, has she?"

"Why do you ask that?"

"This sounds too good to be true," Stan said. "Spa King."

"She quotes Adam Smith so I am going to enjoy this while I can."

"Don't be too promiscuous," Stan said. "There's nasty stuff going around."

"That's what penicillin is for."

"This stuff doesn't get cured with penicillin," he said. "People are dying."

"In Prince George, maybe. Can't you for once say, hey Cirrus, sounds fabulous? Have a good time and poke her once for me."

"Have a good time, big brother," Stan said, but didn't bother with the last part.

FIFTEEN

ON SUNDAY AFTERNOONS, my grandmother went shopping. She never said what we were shopping for or how long it would take, only that it needed to be done. Often, we roamed supermarkets with crates of rutabagas or kiwis, only to abandon them hours later in frozen foods. She loved malls: their asphalt perimeters and crustacean bulwarks, the light coming through roofs and the entombed butterflies in plastic domes, the notion that one could walk for miles indoors, not get wet and choose between kettles, kippers, dandelion spray and dentures. After the shopping was done, she'd usually have another request, like the science centre, botanical gardens or the zoo. Then came the menial chores: garden shed cleaning, insecticide application and wind chime maintenance. In my more charitable moments, I put it down to senility. In less benevolent times I'd say she was trying to keep me busy. So when Fielding called at quarter after twelve, I was more than obliging.

"Do you have a moment, lad?" he said.

"Many."

"If you're busy, I can call back."

"I'm unscheduled."

"Just tertiary things," he said.

"How can effects of my parents' be tertiary?"

"I've not said your parents yet."

Fielding never lied to me. I don't think he possessed the ability. Being a cop, lying was something you only did to criminals, and I didn't yet fall in that category. Not to say he didn't present portions of the truth, bits of the truth, modified orders of the truth, subspecies of the truth and bureaucratic slants of the truth, but I think to him, this was pretty much the same as The Truth. I asked him once, "Did you ever lie to Internal Affairs?"

"Not a chance," he said. He hated Internal Affairs intensely. "If they ask you, Did you hit your arrest, say to them, 'Hit him? Did I ever.' Then list the reasons why you did. Nations weren't built on apologies."

"I'm free," I said. Or was then, anyway. A faint ghost of my grandmother picked up a paper bag and shuffled sadly down the hall.

"Not at the office."

"Why not?"

"Tenor."

Tenor. You know the game is off-kilter when your opposite talks about tenor. Like when someone says, don't worry, it's free. Or, do you trust me? Sure, you're okay to drive.

"Where?"

"How about the Wey Diner. Fabulous wonton. Informal. Say fourteen twenty-five hours?"

Fourteen twenty-five hours. Now that was informal. Cordova and Main was an informal section of Chinatown next to skid row. Battered bricks, used car lots and a lot of sewer grates that weren't on the city's cleaning list. Also, trash cans from Seattle, condoms by the crate, plastic bags containing cardamom and stacks of bronze dragons leaning against shop doorways. The cafés attempted a sense of derelict propriety proclaiming that they had the same cook since 1957 or had served the community since 1922. Mahjong cellars, millipedes and morphine. Was this really where my parents came for Cantonese duck or where my mother ventured to buy rattan birdcages, and the strange Yixing pipes that simply couldn't be used for tobacco alone?

The Wey fit right in. A long narrow café with a row of red booths on one side and a linoleum counter on the other. The air was heavy with soy vapour, and Asian men sat at the counter smoking unfiltered cigarettes. Fielding waited for me at the rear booth with a copy of the *Daily Worker* in his hands and a toothpick in his mouth. He never changed. Moustache, tweed jacket and black oxfords. His fedora had made a rebirth.

"Let's go." He stood up before I had a chance to sit.

"Why?"

"They're out of wonton here."

How the Wey could be out of wonton was an unbelievable proposition, but Fielding tucked the newspaper under his arm and walked me through a kitchen of steaming chickens with no one noticing.

"You look pale, lad," he said.

"Studying late."

"How's your pal Russell these days?"

"No clue."

"Alex?"

"Haven't seen her."

"Read a story about her the other day," he said. "In the *Vancouver Sun*, no less."

A long blast of cooling steam shot out of an air duct and the alley was filled with the scent of fish roe.

"What's up?"

"Come along, lad."

We walked around the corner to number two forty East Cordova, and I figured what else could be up at the Vancouver Coroner's office?

"Why didn't you tell me this?"

"Protocol," he said.

"What protocol?"

"The protocol which says if I told you over the phone what we had, you would have told someone else. And that would have been a breach. You wouldn't have made it here anyway. You would have taken an R&R break, blown a lid, drank a quart of Johnnie Walker and not have made it until tomorrow afternoon, and we don't have that long."

"Why not?"

"They're decaying."

Two forty East Cordova was not a nice place. Probably never had been. Sort of a famous place, though. The autopsy of Errol Flynn was conducted here along with the dismembered victims of the Milkshake Murders and the pair of bloodied swaddles from the Babes in the Woods tragedy. Most of the bodies from the Second Narrows Bridge collapse were rendered here too, and my father had wor the iron engineering ring from that great 1958 fubar the week he disappeared.

Inside, the light was slightly green and there wasn't going to be loads of conversation. But a lot of paperwork. A lot of drawers and stamps and steno sheets completed in triplicate pink. Fielding signed a registry before a half-asleep commissioner, and we walked down a long hallway beside a row of gurneys that were being prepared for storage. His Blakeys clicked on the floor and at the telephone booth, he consulted his notebook.

"I expected it to be busier," I said.

"The action has moved to VGH."

"Action?"

"The active autopsies."

"What do you keep here?"

"The others." A brass-shelled light hung from the ceiling on a long cord. Fielding held the rim. I honestly think he had a fondness for the place.

"I don't like the new police buildings," he said. "New buildings of any kind, really. My accountant has a new office in Metrotown. Plastic palm trees. False ceilings. Don't like it. No sense of permanence. I guess you might say they make me feel lonely. Couldn't do business there. Teal walls. Swedish chairs. No thanks. I'd much rather pass my time in a solid place like this that you know will be around tomorrow. A place where people respect what they do, and you'll get a fair shot regardless of your disposition."

He slipped his key through the lock in the door, and I finally got the morgue I was waiting for. A little bit like the nave of a church except odd tools hung from the wall and there were a lot of sinks equipped with hoses. Half a dozen chrome tables, and one had a canvas sheet over the top.

"I don't have to tell you," Fielding said, "that nothing here today goes outside this room."

The constant hiss of air escaping a valve kept the room from being silent. Fielding donned his rubber gloves, then split an evidence box plastered with biohazard seals. The haul: a hacksaw, five large drills bits, a pair of manacles that were badly rusted and a bag of conical shards that could have been bone.

"We found quite a few of these," he said. "Clustered together in a midden. We've got lab tests being done, but as you can imagine, ones like this go to the bottom of the forensic priority list and it may be years before we get answers. There's not an offence attached to this file, and the Solicitor General gets stingy when it comes to fishing trips. Our boys had a few pecks at the tools, for what that is worth. Hard metal. Perhaps an alloy. The small pieces are organic materials, but beyond that, your guess is as good as mine."

My first guess was shark teeth. They were about the right size and shape, but a closer examination revealed they were made not of calcium, but of fibre and sinew. A voice in the back of my head recited kingdom, phylum, class, order, family, genus, species, and already the beast I imagined was out of the realm of possibility.

"*Aegypti*," I said.

"Which is?"

"Mosquito."

"Rather large for a mosquito tooth, don't you think, and here I thought they only had suckers."

"Where were they found?"

"With them." His head tilted towards the table and his lips curled together. Perhaps he had stayed up the previous night practising. "I hesitated to tell you anything about this. Probably a totally separate affair. Didn't want to complicate the issue. These findings didn't even start as a police investigation. They were brought in by the Geologic Survey of all people, which is why they are here and not up at VGH. And yet, who am I to say? I'm a detective, not a scientist. A detective exploring all channels in a missing persons case and although I'm tempted to write this off, a little voice in the back of my head said, *give him a shot, Fielding, show the young man. He deserves that.* And indeed, you do. You are a young man of substantial potential in the worst of circumstances, so I owe you at least this. Far better than time kept in the wrong company. You see, lad, your name has come up. It keeps coming up. Again and again. And that's not a good place to be. Nothing grand, nothing exotic. Only petty, seemingly unrelated, mundane blips. Now I can understand how a young man in your position would get lost out there. You want what most young men want: sex, power, fame but most of all meaning. More than anything else our species demands meaning. We will do the most extraneous things to have the smallest amount of meaning attached to our lives, and my job here is to make sure neither of us comes up empty-handed."

Layer by layer, the mist rose from the field of my father's farm, from the edges of the river, from the stubble of winter willows and from frost on barn doors. The mist moved around the birch branches and settled in deep country ditches where, maybe once, a pair of insignificant corpses had calcified, waiting to become either part of my history or simply part of the precipitation cycle where they would be washed out to sea.

Fielding tossed me a pair of the black gloves and then moved what must have been a puke bucket to the centre of the room with his foot. He pointed at two gas masks that hung beside the door, just in case, I suppose, and then he pulled back the sheet.

"That's two of them," he said.

The two creatures were naked, black, burnt, sleek and greased. Entangled in each other's charred limbs with grasshopper-crushed skulls and crenulated gills that ran the length of their throats. The lips had peeled back to expose triangular teeth, and the nostrils widened into craters. Perhaps the couple had been deep-fried in napalm or embalmed in peat. Perhaps they had just performed the greatest Cretaceous kink session known to our earth and then frazzled at the point of ecstasy, or maybe this is how they had looked in life. For one of the smallest seconds, I thought they might be my parents but not even my parents had been so astonishing.

"They are so beautiful," I said.

"Pardon?"

"So utterly perfect."

Fielding stopped with his foot on the bucket.

"I'm just not seeing that part of it, lad."

Mummification had reduced the muscle structure to rope. Bile had exuded from their orifices, then congealed around the genitals, so a socialist might say they had already done it; a liberal, that they were about to; and a conservative, that they ought never.

"Are they petrified?" I asked.

"This is nothing prehistoric. The tests may be awhile coming back. But we're talking years, not millennia."

The mastodon size of the male's member caught my eye.

"It's pierced," Fielding said. "As if it matters."

Many, many times pierced. Through the shaft of the organ, then coiling around the testicles like a spring ready to receive FM signals from a therapist light years away. Maybe Fielding had been too embarrassed to bring up the particulars of the female cadaver, but she was pierced as well: in the nipples, eyebrows, labia, throat, and ears. The wounds had cauterized in a curious way, primitively and perhaps not so nicely.

"Were they tortured?" I asked.

"Does anything on them look in any way familiar to you?"

I leaned over the woman's carcass; the smell of linseed filled my nostrils. Some cuts were old, other new, all done in successive layers to form a recognizable pattern.

"They resemble the tattoos my parents had."

"Aye, lad," he said. "Yes. They do."

The shadow of a nurse flitted past a pane of translucent glass. A long while passed. Fielding waited, then finally handed over one of the gas masks. The air was becoming ripe and the filters on the sides of the mask fluttered as Fielding breathed.

"What is your theory?"

"My theory?" His eyes fixated on the pair, unmoving as if he had been studying their plight for weeks. "They are poor unfortunates who had an unfortunate end and no proper burial."

"Will they go to the museum?"

"Museum, lad? I don't quite follow you."

"Surely creatures like this have to be kept."

"Of course, they'll be kept. But human beings don't go to a museum. That's not the way our system works."

"You think they're human?"

"Of course, they're human."

I lifted the blackened arm. Between his elbow and ribs was a thick flap of flesh, an embryonic wing, a stunt gimmick like skydivers from the 1950s used to wear, and under his chin the set of black gills were plugged with river silt.

"They have wings," I said.

"Flaps, anyway."

"What about the gills?"

"One sees many strange anomalies in the forensic world. May be a matter of scientific conjecture what the neck appendages actually are, but I would bet genetic deformities, not gills."

Fielding's mask moved at the jaw. He was sticking his tongue into his teeth, rolling over the possibilities. Deciding which ones were admissible. And then it was over. We stood in a room that was bright and painted; there was air freshener and bright piñata birds dangling from the ceiling, a radio that played piped music. Just the kind of place you'd take a child when you wanted them to forget a tragic occurrence. Fielding washed his hands with antibacterial soap and suggested I do the same.

"That's not anything a young man should look at," he said. "But there was no choice. Eventually this will get to the newspapers. Everything does. Then you might think I was hiding something, which is untrue. Six years ago, a middle-class man and woman disappeared without a trace. Their bodies were never found. There were no clues. No reason, no rhyme. No charges were ever laid. After, their son set out on an understandable but obdurate quest to find them, and along the way, turned over various bizarre objects to police and made several dubious acquaintances. Much later, the police came across a different deceased couple, entombed and embalmed, who were the product of a dysfunctional life which ended in a dysfunctional death. Perhaps biogenetically deficient people who had been living up valley generations ago under the most forlorn conditions. They got caught in a mudslide or were buried in a massive bog. Probably chronic drug users and didn't know what hit them. Nothing to do with the original missing couple, but the police officer and the son have a pact to share all their information, so this sort of thing doesn't happen again and here we are."

"Doesn't that tell you there's a direct connection?"

"No."

"The tools went from my father to those corpses."

"You have the chronology backwards. The tools originated at the site then spread out from there. Into contemporary nomenclature. Your father's and many others."

"Can I see them again?"

"They're put away." He pulled out a pair of post-mortem cigars from his vest pocket. "The air rots them."

"What happened to your hat?"

"I must have put it aside," he said.

And then I stepped out into the tragedy of Cordova Street with the sun in my eyes and the blackened carcasses still in my head. The pruned voluptuous skin, the entanglement of limbs: even Fielding, leaning back with his professional sense of detachment must have experienced a twinge of emotion. I was due at the zoo in twenty minutes but worse, had not enough money for Azy after. The zoo was the last place I wanted to go. The animals stank, the popcorn produced dysentery and the walkways were stuffed with middle-aged loners befriending squirrels. This abode of losers would shanghai anyone into their club who dared linger too long.

Stanley Park was, in fact, the most melancholy respite on earth, producing more suicides per acre than any other place in the nation. Only this morning, Francis Anne Dewer, forty-one, was found deceased by Lost Lagoon with self-inflicted gunshot wounds. Last week, Jonathan Harvey Milton, sixty-six, was disinterred from the Hollow Tree, dehydrated with hemlock poisoning. In April, the partial remains of a Japanese tourist along with his wallet were discovered by zoo officials in the polar bear pen. Hapan Harakio, twenty-nine, had climbed the fifteen-foot fence and never came out. And as a matter of historical interest, the first internal combustion motor to be parked in the urban retreat, on September 27, 1921, also turned out to be its first suicide, a monoxide asphyxia.

My grandmother sat on the slatted bench beside the monkey cage ignoring the ugly creatures that taunted her from above. She wore her drab brown coat and gazed out over the Vancouver Yacht Club as if one of the boats were hers but she had forgotten which one.

"Cirrus?" she said.

There was no one else it could have been. She had no friends, no relatives in town and no workmates. A howler monkey leapt from bar to bar in his titanic outdoor prison.

"Where have you been?"

"With a friend," I said. Or friends, depending on how you counted.

My grandmother stood, pressed out the creases of her coat and held out her arm for me to take. With elbows locked, we made our way through a thicket of spent geraniums. The insane scream of peacocks punctuated the air.

"Is she a decent girl?" she asked.

"Define decent."

"Hard-working."

"She works a lot," I said.

"Large corporation?"

"Proprietorship."

"Hobbies?"

"Drama, costume making, leather works."

"Horses?"

From a passing transistor radio, the last permissible vestiges of disco music lost themselves in a tangle of columnar bushes.

"None."

"Then what is the leather for?"

"Long story."

"Are you in love with her?" my grandmother asked.

"It's not that kind of arrangement."

"Then what kind of relationship is it?"

"One of necessity."

"Does she want money?"

"Don't they all?"

"Don't be a chauvinist," she said. "Is she after your family attributes?"

"No. Am I passing this test?"

"I get a bad feeling," she said. "When you come home late. The combination of fear and excitement. That smell comes home with you, and I sense something disingenuous about the woman."

"You haven't met her," I said.

My grandmother pursed her lips and we walked to the pay booth. The city had upgraded it into a glass kiosk with pink kangaroos embossed on the side.

"Her chatter sticks to you like laughter on grade schoolers. Some of her acquaintances seem all right. Most of them don't wash enough. The architect and his wife, not a bad sort, but rather entitled. I feel sorry for the young girl who hangs around out of necessity. She seems to be quite lonely. The one who you see separately, Rosco."

"Russell?"

"Be all right if he had a father figure to set him straight."

"You haven't met any of these people."

Grandmothers always wore red lipstick that flaked too much when they knew they were right and you were wrong. Then they would smile, and the lipstick would crack to prove the point. "Do you know practising witchcraft is no longer illegal but practising false witchcraft is?" she said.

"You've lost me."

"She has hurt you already, hasn't she?"

"That's a matter of perspective."

"It's no excuse for cruelty."

"I give up."

"Then it is agreed," she said. "You won't see her or have anything to do with her or her kind anymore. You may speak with that war veteran friend or help her other associates with their rodeos but that is all. Please have Roscoe over for a sherry sometime. Is it much farther to the panda exhibit?"

"We can cut through the insect display."

"I don't want to cut through the insect display."

Maybe out of charity, maybe out of spite, I led her by the arm inside. The insect display was a huge tower of plaster shaped to resemble an African termite mound. The idea was to have the public exposed to the daily business and tribulations of exoskeletal animals through a series of glass walls and plastic portals.

A beekeeper in a white plastic suit stepped out of a service door. He waved a smoke can around in figure eights. The smoke reminded me of Azy's Virginia Slims. My grandmother put a finger to the glass. A crimson winged creature fluttered to the pane.

"I used to come here with your grandfather," she said. "Although I wasn't as much a fan. He watched them for hours. We did everything together. The cinema. The zoo. We read together. We walked together."

She let her hand slide down the glass. Behind a net, a cluster of monarch butterflies swirled around a tropical branch in a veil of black and yellow.

"There's something I need to tell you," I said.

"I miss him so much it hurts me every day, every hour and every beat of my heart."

The orange flutter of wings followed her index finger as she moved it through a hole in the net.

"I wasn't with my girlfriend this afternoon," I said.

"With whom, then?"

"With Fielding."

"Whatever for?"

"He showed me a pair of corpses."

Grandmother's face ossified. The display plaque before her read *Danus plexippus*. "But not those of your mother and father."

"Maybe trapped in a peat flood years ago."

"A tragic but common event after the First World War."

"They wore the same trinkets as mom and dad."

"I'll lend you an anthropology text," she said. "Trinkets are everywhere. Deltas shift. At the end of the ice age, it was far up the valley. Peat forms with the submergence of muskeg material into an aerobic environment that prohibits decomposition. During the Great War people suffered from influenza. They died in their cabins, in their gardens or on the roadside. They sank into bogs by the dozen along with their dogs, cats and tools. I'm surprised that the police haven't found more."

"Did you find any?"

"A US Confederate soldier from the Carolinas. Not a bad-looking fellow. Uniform still intact. Shoelaces done up. That was in our garden near Agassiz. Did you know that peat bogs can produce a yellow mist during autumn mornings? The gas causes anything from vomiting to hallucinations. I'll give you references."

My grandmother snapped shut the twin pearl clasps on her purse. The stick insects in the nearest pen were the same kind that hapless Sal kept in her museum. One of them dropped from the branch and crawled towards us. His relatives followed and soon there sat a dozen at the lip of the glass, staring into my grandmother's face.

"The question you should be asking yourself," she said, "is why a policeman would take you to see a pair of podzolized embalmed unfortunates? Water runs downhill. Prostitutes want money. Let's leave. My arthritis hurts."

"These creatures weren't human."

"He likely suspects the same fate shall befall you if you stay on your present course."

"They had wings."

"They did not have wings."

"They expanded like an accordion."

"Are you intoxicated?"

"No." But I was sweating badly and confused. Probably from too much amyl nitrate or arousal the evening before. "I touched them."

"That was foolish of you."

"I liked it."

"That is untrue."

"I was aroused."

"Stop."

She let her hand rest on the white latticed collar that separated her throat from the buttons of her bodice and gazed into the hornet display. Dozens of creatures with thin torsos and stingers as long as their abdomens pulsated on the other side of the glass, their shiny black abdomens bobbing up and down in pre-attack pose. My grandmother tucked her purse under her arm and turned to leave. I held her wrist.

"Let go of me," she said.

"I've seen bodies like that before at our old house."

"That is not possible."

"I've had sex with them."

"Cirrus, you are clearly intoxicated."

With one matriarchal shake of the wrist, she broke free of my grasp and smashed the portal on the wasp display. The black-coated insects squeezed through the crack and flew straight for her neck. She backed up over a mop and cascaded through the glass, which split into a thousand shards. Throughout the fake hive, insects exploded in anger. They emerged through heat vents and air shafts, crawled out of honeycombs and cracks. Yellow jackets, clay diggers, spindle-legged daubers and crystal-winged bees launched their attack from the ground and thickened the air with shimmering bodies. They converged as one grey tornado, then dropped like an anvil until my grandmother became a sea of pulsating insect tar. They stung her over and over, as if they despised her completely, utterly and passionately. They were in her ears, up her nose, on her eyes and in her mouth. She chewed them up and spat them out, but they turned around and crawled back in.

I dragged my grandmother by the shoulders over the broken glass and through the door. A panicked worker sprayed us with a fire extinguisher, but the bugs didn't care. They followed us down the dingy tunnel out into the sun and they darkened that too. The only thought crossing my mind was that parties that weekend were likely out.

On the far side of the walkway stood two penguins on a diving board, watching us with heads cocked in curiosity. I did not know if my grandmother could swim or if she even liked penguins, but that hardly mattered. A dedicated green hornet was pumping her eyelid full of formic acid, and so I rolled the two of us over the pond edge and we fell. We struck fishy water. The bubbles were cold. Noise vanished and a penguin sailed past upside down. My grandmother lost her false teeth, but at last, the insects began to drown. When we broke the surface, the wail of an ambulance drew near. I recall the ambulance attendant cutting off our clothes and examining our punctured bodies with incredulity.

SIXTEEN

OUR SITUATION WASN'T looking good. Not good at all. The physician went over the particulars of my grandmother's case and the medical facts were getting too septic to deny. She was to be hospitalized for three days. At least. Plasma injections, blood transfusions. Anticoagulants. But strangely no antihistamines. None. The stings hadn't festered in a way that was usual in humans. In fact, they hadn't festered at all. The good doctor stared at the test results and then at me. Like I would know. Hundreds of stings reduced to mere pinpricks on her aged flesh and then vanished. He was worried. The malicious bugs had done more damage pulling vital juices out than they had pumping their own poison in, he concluded. Unbelievable. Well, what she needed was rest and intravenous fluids. An issue with her blood type. He droned on. I contemplated my next session with Mistress Azy. Her spurs. Her bullet bra. Her lips opening in a cauldron of cigarette smoke. The sincerity of my satisfaction would be intense.

"She was stung over three hundred times," the doctor said. He raised his voice a little as if I wasn't paying enough attention.

All across the nation, the insides of emergency rooms had been transformed from wartime white to pastoral green. Concentration was impossible. The office was a pale olive colour, and piped-in elevator music played a bland rehash of an old ABBA song.

"And should not be disturbed for at least twelve hours," he finished.

How then, was I supposed to ask her for money? The good doctor obviously did not understand the dynamics of my hormonal situation and had failed to explain the most salient question of the day: Why was my grandmother still alive? A fluke of nature. Non-poisonous bees. A miracle drug trial she had been on for years unknown to the rest of us. Maybe extraterrestrials. I pondered my next move. Bring up the past? Mull over my own case studies? Do nothing? Probably. Indecision can be a great ally.

"There were a lot of them," I said.

"And they swarmed only the two of you?"

Understatement, but true. Their black bodies had descended out of the biblical sky in locust fashion and saturated my grandmother's frantic body while no one else in the zoo had suffered so much as a scratch. The doctor pivoted a pen across his lower lip.

"Unlucky, for sure," I said.

"That's over fifteen milligrams of apitoxin."

"Melittin?"

"You are familiar with it?"

"I studied bugs in school."

He leaned against the wall and checked the tip of his pen. "Then I'm sure you'd understand what an unbelievable occurrence this is."

"Fifteen milligrams. Hard to believe."

"We did tests."

He seemed proud of himself. He had a white coat, doctors still wore them in the eighties, a yellow pen and a set of glasses which were too big for his face, the type of man who accepted the decline of deference in our culture with grace.

"That much poison must have taken a while to pump into her," he said.

"Just the time it took to drag her to the penguin pool."

"I'm surprised she didn't go into anaphylactic shock. Especially at her age."

"She's getting on."

"Did she ever work with bees?"

"Not that I know of."

"Did she have allergies as a child?"

"I wasn't born."

He pulled his glasses off his face and swung them around his finger. "How many times did you get stung?"

Outside the door, the admitting nurse glanced up from her papers at the triage desk. She was a handsome woman with an officious set of eyebrows. No doubt she was trying out for the women's triathlon team and would probably make the cut. I imagined her showing up at Azy's in cycling Lycra.

"Dozens," I said.

"Where?"

"Everywhere."

The doctor reached out and lifted my arm. He rolled it over, searching for a sting location but found none. Then he used his flashlight on my pupils. He thought for a long while. I didn't like it.

"I just don't see any."

Which was true. There were none to be seen. Punctures, pinpricks and incisions, but hardly any redness and no swelling.

"Do you mind," he said. "If we take a blood sample from one of your bites before it vanishes all together?"

"Why?"

"I'm wondering if your family genetics provides an immunity to these toxins."

I imagined the nurse sticking a needle into my flesh and then revulsing with whatever the results might show.

"Our religion forbids that," I said.

"Really?"

"Abstain from pollutants, things strangled and samples of your sin," I made the last part up.

And then the good doctor shrugged, stood up and turned towards his green hallway. He had other patients to tend to, a young man who had crashed his motorcycle into a light standard, a woman with meningitis and an infant who would need a new tongue after licking a toaster.

The nurse bit into a depressor.

At home, I sat in the living room watching a red mountain ash-leaf spin to the ground while I awaited the oncoming judgment. The phone rang.

"Hey, Cirrus."

"Hey, Stan," I said.

"What's new?"

"Not much."

"What do you mean, not much?"

"Well, not a lot anyway."

"Why didn't you call me?" he said.

"I was about to."

"Grandmom called from the hospital."

"I guess that's why your line was busy," I said.

A cauldron of pressurized steam built up on the far end of the line, so I held the receiver as far away from my ear as possible.

"Grandmom called from the hospital and said she had been attacked by a swarm of bees, so she's taking life-saving plasma in the emergency ward."

"Vespid wasps, actually Stan. Totally different genus. And she's out of emergency. A few quarts of plasma and she'll be fine."

"What in the name of good God happened?"

Stan was angry. I could understand that. I could empathize. He was at the wrong end of the intelligence cycle. With no raw data, the situational viscosity was ambiguous. Basically, he wanted clarification.

"Tactically speaking, Grandmom was stung repeatedly by many different genera of Hymenoptera from the insect display at the public zoo. This was a highly unusual event as insects never swarm with those not in their own hive, let alone their own species. We took her to the hospital for precautionary reasons. She is all right."

"All right?" he said. "She was bitten a thousand times."

"Three hundred."

"Whatever. Three hundred. What did they give her?"

"Blood. Anticoagulants. Fluids. She lost a lot of fluids."

"What other medicine?"

"None that I know of."

"Why not?"

"There was a complicated medical explanation for that. I didn't follow. I was stressed."

"Jesus," Stan said. His palm struck his head repeatedly. "How many stitches?"

Here I could be precise. "Thirty-six. Two dozen of what they call red sutures and one dozen of the blue variety, which I guess are the temporary kind. She doesn't appear to have any nerve damage and there are no broken bones."

"How did she fall through this sheet of glass again?"

"Remember the insect terrarium? You went there in grade six. She fell over a mop and crashed through the exhibit. There should have been a handrail. I think we've got a civil suit here for sure. The insects understandably got upset and attacked. I pulled her to the penguin pond and the ambulance came. C'est tout."

"To the penguin pond?"

"Into the pond, actually. There was only one option. The bastards swarmed, Stan. We needed to get under fast. Wasps can't swim. Nothing is infected. The birds didn't mind."

"How did she fall backwards into an exhibit?" he said.

"She's old, Stan. She tripped."

Stan sucked in air and held it for a second. Then he let it explode in a small puff of exasperation. Strange how we develop these annoying little habits so early in life.

"Did you get stung?' he said.

"Many times."

"Where?"

"Mostly on my dick."

"Probably a blessing."

"The doctor said to use calamine lotion." I unzipped my fly and yarded out my cratered balls. Rouge blisters with green peripheries that were recovering with remarkable speed. If the tiny pinpricks scabbed over by morning, I could probably make a functional appearance at Azy's Mid-Month Party on Saturday night. "Everything is under control. She'll be out in three days. Don't sweat it."

"I am sweating it, Cirrus. This is serious. She could have died. You could have died. I checked those animals in the encyclopedia. They kill people."

"It was a freak accident," I said. "Could happen to anybody."

"I know, big brother, but it always seems to happen to you."

"This wasn't my fault."

"I'm not saying this was but Jesus, Cirrus. Either Grandmom gets bit by insects, or she passes out after one of your sherry-fuelled cosmological discussions. You fall through the roof of a taxidermy store. You OD on MDA. Your penis gets stuck in a milk bottle. You lose your transcripts from school and get put on academic probation. How is school anyway?"

Good question. I had no clue. I was pretty sure I showed up for one of my midterms, but it was such an insignificant part of my life that he may as well have asked me what colour the campus meter maid's uniform had been. Actually, that would have been more significant.

"I've been reinstated," I said. "There's no trouble."

"Is there trouble with anything else?"

"No."

"Are you sure?"

"Of course, I'm sure," I said, and then, "Why do you ask?"

Of all the things a close relative can do, the dramatic, painful pause is the most cliché.

"We had an interesting visitor the other day," he said.

"Visitor?"

"Mm," Stan said, and I could see him proselytizing, leaning back in his Ikea chair and propping his tan Hush Puppies up on the stone coffee table. He had all the prerequisites for a man who would one day be deputy minister. "I would call it more of an encounter. Outside of Vanderhoof. We got stopped by the police."

"What is a Vanderhoof?"

"A small town near Prince George."

"Sounds horrible. Were you speeding?"

"Not speeding. Not anything. The police followed us for ten kilometres, then stopped us at ten thirty-two in the morning and took my particulars. Then at nine minutes after eleven they were still on the phone, with us pulled over. Mandy had an orthopedic session. Which she missed. The good constable came back to the car and asked Mandy and I all kinds of questions. Strange questions. Bizarre questions. Quite frankly, we were flabbergasted. Then they asked if they could search the car. I didn't mind. Hell, I had nothing to hide. I asked them what they were looking for, perhaps I could help. They said something about artifacts and right away I thought, oh God, when is the last time Cirrus drove this car? Long time ago. Anyway, another car pulled up and a civilian, a woman who insisted she was not with an enforcement agency, got out and they took, and get this, a swab from the trunk of the car and put it in a plastic jar. A swab, can you believe it? And so I said, 'Are we under quarantine?' And they said, 'No,' and came up with a rather unbelievable story about anthropologic remains and when exactly was the last time I had seen you? And I said, 'Is this swab for criminal or health reasons,' to which there was no precise answer, and it's not like I'm closed to the bureaucratic needs of our nation, but why is it, big brother, why is it that whenever bad things happen your name is always attached?"

"Me?"

"Yes, you. And so, they let us go without much of an explanation. Mandy and I went home. A few hours later a different Mountie and a different civilian came around to the house. They were quite pleasant. We had tea. She was from Trois-Rivières. They asked a lot of questions and finally said that an isty-bitsy red flag had come up when they ran our licence plate, and then of course the topic drifted back to you again. Where you were, what you were doing, who your friends were and, of course, what were you doing with Mom and Dad's file, to which I replied, 'God only knows.'"

"They needed a warrant to go through your trunk," I said.

"Well, they didn't have one."

"Why did you put up with that repressive right-wing crap?"

Far down the electromagnetic spectrum of patience, my social-working brother was summoning his last strands of strength. I could see him rocking back and forth on that patent leather chair, wanting, wanting so badly to smash the phone into a thousand pieces but instead calling on his mentors Gandhi, Mother Mary Teresa and, of course, Tommy Douglas to make him a better person and not do anything that would diminish his professional aura.

"Because I wanted to help," he said. "Whether or not they needed a warrant was not relevant to me. I wanted to know what is going on and still do. Please tell me now, Do you have bubonic plague or are you selling child prostitutes?"

"Get a grip, Stan."

"That is why we are talking, because one of us has one last teetered grip on reality and that person is me. Your grandmother has been attacked by wasps, you spend half your time loaded and the police were quizzing me on your sex life. These were serious people, Cirrus, and they didn't need to point a gun in my face to convey the fact this was a substantive issue for them."

"What did they want to know about my sex life?"

"If you had a girlfriend."

"If" being the operative word.

"Fielding has made a breakthrough," I said.

"Who?"

"Detective Fielding. Mom and Dad's case."

"Oh, Cirrus, give it up."

"I'm not giving anything up."

"This is not fucking funny anymore."

I had made Stan say fuck.

"He showed me a pair of corpses, Stan."

"What?"

"Not Mom and Dad," I said. "But maybe related. Definitely not human."

"What, wait. Slow down. He showed you what where?"

"In the morgue. Creatures."

"What kind of creatures?"

"Hard to say. Dead ones. Winged, blackened and well, it looked as if they'd been screwing."

"I'm lost." His pitch slipped up a semi-tone. "If they weren't human, what were they and who was screwing?"

"That's all I can tell you, Stan. It's true, over the past few months I've messed up a little. I've made questionable liaisons. I've gone into the grey area of civil litigation concerning evidence retention. *Mea culpa.* The result is blowback. Hence your visitors. Have you read Gouzenko's memoirs? You should. They are doing security checks on me in case, well you know, in case."

"In case what?"

I let the silence linger on the line so Stan could filter through his tiny, straight Progressive Conservative consciousness what was transpiring on the other side of the kaleidoscope.

"In case the truth gets out," I said.

"Have you taken LSD today?"

"No."

"I'm coming down," he said.

"Whatever for?"

"To straighten the world out. It is clearly no longer spinning. I've got accumulated time they won't pay out, so I'm driving down Monday."

"Where are you going to stay?"

"Where do you think? At my grandmother's house."

"Here?"

"Yes, big brother, there. Don't worry, I'll sleep downstairs. If there's anything there that shouldn't be, and I mean of the indictable variety, perhaps you could move it along before I arrive."

Stan hung up and I tasted razor blades. I remembered my little brother as a chubby, red-faced baby who pissed himself incessantly and followed me around the house with a rotten Hudson's Bay comforter stuffed in his mouth and bits of saliva-balled cotton rolling down his jaw. I remembered him bawling his eyes out the day the police told him that his mother was lost and laughing when I told him a stegosaurus lived in the tool shed. That little brother was gone forever, lost in the mist of the Fraser Valley. Now he was an officious, narrow-minded twat that I didn't want back in my house, my city or my life. A bee buzzed on my lap. I swatted at my belt. But this was no bee at all. This was Azy's plastic paging cube. The letters on the front display said CALL ME.

SEVENTEEN

ARCHAMBAULT'S RISTORANTE ITALIEN was, of course, an Italian restaurant on Commercial Drive, expensive and one of Azy's favourites. She had wanted clam pasta with fettuccini and parmesan. They didn't have any, so she had to settle for the clam tortellini. The blue librarian suit constituted daily battle dress. Her blouse revealed her freckles. Her displeasure was already in the open.

"When I was growing up," she said, "all we ever had was Red River cereal. My father was gone and my mother usually hungover. Now I eat pasta for breakfast."

"How do you make it?"

"I don't. The house girl makes it with a champagne cocktail."

This was her nature. When Azy wanted something, someone else fetched it. A set of shoes with brass buckles, a burgundy corset she had read about in *Vanity Fair*, a parrot from Costa Rica. The ideas sprouted like azaleas in her head, and the lieutenant of the day was charged with picking up the tab.

Although I had never been to Italy, the inside of the restaurant seemed too Italian to me. Dark wood, a lot of dusty wine bottles and plenty of wicker. Waiters with greasy black hair and bow ties still brooded about Mussolini's finer hours.

Two things on the wine list became apparent. First, Russell and I would have to do another job quickly if I was to keep my girlfriend in a fashion to which she was accustomed and second, although perpetually in a state of sexual fixation, Azy wasn't all that interested in actual sex: intercourse, coitus, copulation, coupling, banging, screwing, fucking, diddling, doing. Not with me anyway. On the far side of the table sat the perfect goddess: gorgeous, erotic, bent and utterly untouchable. An entity who gained immense sexual satisfaction from choking a young sub into hypoxia but blasé about administering CPR. If I were a collared slave, then sex wasn't an option anyway. That wasn't natural. Clients paid the money. Slaves took the beatings. Pets did the dirty. No idea who held that position. Don maybe. Even if he was gay. Perhaps because he was gay. That would be rather up her alley, forcing a gay man into the one place he didn't want to be. But he'd been around for too long. Possibly the architect and his wife, a status symbol for sure. Wide open California ranchers with white linoleum and chrome taps. But they were too reasonable. The house girl was too wretched, Sal too obvious. Maybe a romantic unknown whom I hadn't met. No one in the household mentioned that area of Azy's life. Especially not Azy. She never crooned about the stickiness of courtly love or taking long walks on the beach. Erotic pleasure was never resolved with affection. Azy climaxed in a burning of the Reichstag dimension that had nothing to do with intimacy.

"Make sure the tortellini comes with an oyster sauce," she said. "And stop squirming around on that chair."

"I was stung by wasps."

"How?"

"By taking my grandmother to the zoo."

"Why were you doing that?"

"I'm asking myself the same question right now."

She paused. Her stone face was absolutely symmetric. "Where were you stung, exactly?"

"Everywhere."

She consulted her date book, did an algebraic equation involving bodies, desire and numbers and got worried. "Are you going to do the party in one piece? I mean in one functioning, presentable piece."

"I can make it," I said.

"Gangrenous cocks aren't a glamorous item and I need you to be gorgeous for the show."

"I'll use calamine."

"Fix it." She tucked her book away. "Or I'll get a stand-in."

"A stand-in?"

She shrugged. Stand-in, of course. She checked her hair in the reflection of the smoky glass mirror. "Describe it to me in detail. The creeping and stinging part. Try not to bore me."

So, I told her that my skin was stung black as tar. That their sandpaper wings cluttered my nose and throat. That my flesh turned to a bubbling cesspool of lava, moving, boiling, corrupting. That wasps sting out of malice. That sometimes they lay their eggs in the body of their paralyzed prey until the young wasps hatch inside the victim and eat it alive.

"Like it." She bit down on her pearl necklace.

"I thought I was going to die."

"So why didn't you?"

"We made it to the penguin pool."

"Pity." She paused and did what she always did; she looked for the erotic angle that meant another session was to be slotted in her calendar. "Just the same, I think there's something here to work with. I'd like to do a stinging scene. Had a client once who wanted to be stung and injected with collagen. Naturally, I was happy to oblige him, but I don't think we ever got the scene to maximum potential. One day he stopped coming back. Too bad because I had a costume he'd spent over a thousand dollars on. Made from an experimental polymer. Only produced by one company in North America. On Beresford Street."

"What happened to him?"

"God knows. Clients. Unreliable most of them. You know them for years, then one day they vanish. Like a kitchen utensil. He'd take me out to dinner, the opera. He had money. No personality or real interest in long-term relationships. Perfect. Then one day he never showed up again. I would have forgot about him immediately except he'd got me a time-share in Maui that is good until the end of the century."

The waiter came by. Tuxedo. Black bow tie. He had a large handlebar moustache and might really have been Italian.

"Yes?" he said.

Azy stared up at him. There was a brief flicker between their eyes. He put a bottle of Montalcino down on the table and I realized we had not asked for any wine.

"The lady would like oyster sauce with the tortellini," I said.

"But sir, it comes with clam sauce."

"Put some on anyway."

"She will not like it," he said.

"She knows what she wants."

The waiter stayed silent. Perhaps Triste was on his mind. Then Azy lifted her chin. She put a finger to her jaw, indicating he might have been good-looking in an offensive way and he vanished.

"You've been here before," I said.

"He's probably having his period. Italian men are like that."

"Tell me he's not waiting at your party."

"Your wasp story made me sentimental. How about a cocooning scene? I like to see my victims paralyzed and suspended so they can't breathe. Spinning, suffering, begging." Azy put her shoe between my thighs. "Pick up that polymer for me. It's transparent, so everyone will see the horror on your face when you fail to break free from your chrysalid. Saran Wrap is too flimsy, and rubber too gauche."

She lit a Slim. She hummed "Lili Marlene." The negotiation was complete. No matter that there was only one place on earth that produced this product. Nor that they were going to use it on the upcoming space shuttle mission. Or that it ran about two hundred dollars a square foot. Those details were my problem.

"Who's going to be there this round?" I said.

"Everybody who's anybody. Lots of exciting people. People who are into heavy. Counts, lawyers, sheiks. I'll need you for a couple of scenes. Versatility is a must. Drink lots of fluids. Take uppers. Talk to Don. He can give you stuff that will keep your dick hard."

"I don't have that problem."

"You don't know what we're going to do to you."

"Made it through last time."

"That was child's play," she said. "Besides, I'm not talking about breaking anything physically. Any fool can do that. I want your existential hole. That's my real line. I could have broken you with pain on the first date. Taken a pair of welding pliers to your nuts. Would have been the last anyone saw of you. No, what really turns me on is breaking a man spiritually. Forcing them to do what they are opposed to. Not just sexually, but genetically. Then make them believe they enjoy the privilege. Don't start with your university crap. If I listen to another Margaret Mead lecture, I will puke."

"What's Don's weak spot?"

"That's obvious."

"The architects?"

"They say they love each other so much. But in fact, their marriage is a mess. They've been to all kinds of fruity counselling and Gaya Love-Ins on Salt Spring Island. They said they had no desire to hurt any sentient being. I changed that. Inside a month I had them flogging everything that moved and branding each other to the point of scars. Absolute savagery. No doubt they'll be involved in a murder-suicide one day. It's beautiful."

"Sal?"

"Sal is a silly loser who wants to believe that she's an underachiever. Thought I could make her a Domme one day, but now I don't know. Maybe I should force her because it will break her heart when she finds out how lonely the job really is."

She pushed a wad of smoke between her pearl teeth. The crevasses in her lips were so angry a man would fall in and never be seen again. She hummed an old war song, then halfway through the refrain she slipped into a Christmas carol.

"Where did you learn that song?" I asked.

"I don't know it's a song."

"Do you know the words?"

"No," she said. "I just hum."

"But you changed songs."

"So what?"

"You were humming 'Lili Marlene,' then you switched to 'Rudolph the Red-Nosed Reindeer.'"

"I was imagining stinging you to death."

"Who taught you those songs back to back?"

"Nobody taught me. I just mix them up. People do that all the time. When you're being beat you quote Nietzsche and then Groucho Marx. I don't quiz you on that."

Old history chapters needed to be reviewed. "My father sung those together."

"Oh?" she said.

"What are the chances?"

"Of what?"

"Of you singing the same songs in exactly that order."

"Quite high," she said. "I do it all the time. Mix up songs. Who doesn't? I do it when my mind wanders or when I'm getting a little bored."

"Did you ever meet my father?"

Azy sat back in the chair. This was Hollywood come true. "I'm told that kind of thing runs in families."

I told her his name. She shrugged. How often did people use their real names with her?

"What did he like to do?"

"No clue."

"Not much to go on there."

I fumbled for my wallet. My fingers got thick. SIN card, driver's licence, gym pass, then finally the muddled family photo. Azy turned the Polaroid around with a little finger. Her left eye screwed up trying to focus. There was only half interest.

"If I showed you a grainy photo from ten years ago of a face you met across the street, would you recognize them?" She picked up the photo by the edges and spun it sideways. "Is that your mother too?"

"Maybe you saw the two of them together."

She didn't bother to look again. "Honestly, Cirrus, I couldn't tell you. I see many people. Many hundreds of people. Over the years, probably thousands. Dozens of couples wanting millions of combinations. Most of them came once and went. Occasionally, one or two left me sports cars or diamonds. Those I might recall. You think I can remember every face that walks through my dungeon? What if I did? What would that prove to you? Would it satisfy this notion of guilt you possess?"

"It could be valuable information for my case officer."

"Case officer?"

"The one who tends my parents' file."

"Listen to me." She snubbed her cigarette out. When a beautiful woman gets angry it's an ugly sight. "And listen to me carefully. I don't know or care about what happened to your parents. I don't want to know. It's none of my business. Me, I'm the only business I care about, and right now you belong to me. I don't want to get mixed up with case officers, and I don't want my stable boys associating with that side of the law. That's instant excommunication as far as I'm concerned. I need safe, devoted servants who know what they're doing and who stay off the deep end. I've had enough flakes who think they're involved in General de Gaulle's assassination or the resurrection of extinct birds. You worry about one thing when you're with me and that one thing is keeping me happy. You understand?"

"Loud and clear," I said.

"Because if you don't, I'll find another who will."

"I read you."

"Get down on your knees."

"Here?"

"Of course, here, you bitch."

On the far side of the mostly deserted restaurant, a grandfather clock clicked over the seconds in the way you'd think it did in Milano circa 1933, ochre, loud and in the warm fuzzy sun, rather stately.

"Did you hear me?" she said. "Do it. Do you think I keep you around for your scintillating conversation? Get down there on your knees and lick my shoe."

And so, I did. In the south vestibule of Archambault's Ristorante Italien, at the corner of Commercial Drive and Grandview, I got down and licked her patent black leather Gucci shoe. For my stupidity and passion and youth and to tell you the truth, I rather liked it. People often ask, What is the attraction of being beneath a woman's foot? The shape? The smooth waxy skin, the glistening instep, the shame? I could smell the dust on the floor, the grand cedar of the table, the wet ferns that roosted in clay pots on the windowsill. Out the window, smog that drifted down from the dry patches of Mount Seymour through Tamarac and onto the Japanese cherries clustered along the boulevard. People like to say Vancouver is a messy city, a reckless city, neither Mediterranean nor temperate in the autumn with its amber grass, worn fences and women striding off curbs in white hot pants, but Vancouver is the perfect city to lick a woman's foot in public. The ideal city for debasement in full view. I got down on my pitiful knees, pulled off her shoe and stuck her foot far down my throat until I gagged. Her toenails were blue, like Neptune, and I choked them down until the spit frothed out and dribbled onto the rug that was worn down by heels, maybe hers. Her favourite phrase during these sessions was "choke on it, whore, choke on it," and she pronounced the word "whore" like we wanted to believe Russians would say it: "horre."

An old man in a brown suit with red tie and white hair shot out from the booth kitty corner to us and his face exploded in steam.

"For God's sake," he said. "Stop this."

Azy leaned back and smoked. "Why?"

"This is obscene," he said.

"Pull your dick out," Azy said to me. Her finger lingered on her crotch and so I obliged. The idiot was robust and blue, bloodied despite all the insecticidal attacks, and I rode his keel on Azy's sapphire ankle until the Sputnik was set to launch. The waiter free-fell in at terminal velocity.

"You cannot do this," he said. "This is too much. This time you have gone too far."

Azy threw a glass of Montalcino in my face.

"Get this pig off me," she said.

Surely one more thrust and I'd be done.

"Too, too far," Alberto said. He seized my shoulder and made a feeble slapping attempt.

"Call the cops." Azy lifted her leg so the calf muscle flexed Aphrodite.

"Much too far."

I didn't know if his real name was Alberto or if he was really Italian. The angrier he got the more of his accent he lost. Perhaps he was only hired because he looked Italian. I didn't know either if Azy was truly upset or if this was just another scene. She'd probably bill me for it, then ask for a tax receipt. Unknown too, was the truth about El Salvador, the end of the Cold War or the categorization of the newly discovered disease Kaposi sarcoma. What I did know for sure was that Alberto had a new kind of wireless phone the size of a lunch box, which he yarded from his coat pocket. He began frantically punching numbers into the panel. Chances were, he was calling the police. Azy leaned back and furrowed another Slim. She appeared halfway between boredom and indignation, perhaps the way someone would look if they finally found a dirty passage in the midst of an Ayn Rand novel.

Remember the creepy person in high school who was voted the most likely to be charged with indecent exposure? Or the barrister who despite her position was photographed having sex with both a judge and defence counsel at the same time? The neighbour who got caught with his pants down on John Patrol or the innocent only-in-mind dental hygienist who went to Los Angeles seeking a part in a Tennessee Williams' play and ended up in guess what kind of VHS tapes now distributed in her hometown? The fact of the matter is, it could happen to any of us, right? And so, realizing the stagnation of irony, the tenure of tactics and the reality of police response time, I got up and left.

EIGHTEEN

RUSSELL PULLED HIS truck to the curb at Broadway and Commercial. When I had called him on the phone, he'd told me he was only a few blocks away, but twenty minutes later, he was still geographically honing in. He wore a dirty Montreal Canadiens jersey, which I prayed was stolen because the thought of the Russell team cheering en français frightened me horribly.

"What is going on?" he said.

"Just drive." The truck seat was cluttered with wire cutters, screwdrivers, large-sized tins of Molson Fifty and a ripped *Penthouse* magazine, Cynthia Peterson as your cover girl.

"Is there someone I should be avoiding?" he said.

"The police at this moment."

"Why?"

"Sticky wicket in Italian."

Russell popped a Fifty, sucked foam and pulled an abrupt left down East Tenth.

"That's handy intel to have. The cops want you. Great."

"Domestic situation."

After the panic shed, Russell found the predicament amusing. "Punched her lights out, I hope."

"Why would I do that?"

"Contrary to what the fembots would have you think," he said, "they want you to be boss. Even the so-called Dommes. Women can't stand weak-kneed dweebs and that is almost your category right now."

Russell got debriefed on the moment of exposure, the lost Montalcino and 911 call. He drove, as always, with one palm on the wheel where his universe was divided into two halves: things that mattered and things that didn't. A woman with pink shorts crossed against the light and Russell lifted his beer to her indifferent smile.

"Don't tell me," he said. "This isn't the first time. Last time she sealed you nude in a bus depot locker. The time before that it was the emergency ward with a catheter up your dick whining to the triage nurse. That's a favourite. Or maybe the old guy pissing in your mouth at the French consulate. Please God, please tell me, not door number three."

Russell reached into the glovebox and pulled out a new pair of tempered Japanese bolt cutters that produced *over 5,000 lbs of Asian tiger pressure with each touch!* with receipt still attached, so I presumed he had paid for them. "I got you this, buddy. Happy fucking birthday."

The Rolling Stones played "Start Me Up" on AM radio, then, a news flash: "Brewers' union may strike. Prime minister may prorogue. Charles and Diana may marry."

"I don't care who you screw," he said. "Or if you ruin your life and destroy your mind. Or if she cuts your dick off and she will do that given time. What I care about is my business partner getting busted for unworthy causes."

"Don't you get carried away sometimes?"

"No."

"Let's not bring up your old ladies."

"Let's do that," he said. "I am into this dialogue. It is precisely because they are old ladies I fraternize with them. I tell them what to do. They comply. No complexities. At least I get a hotel. Or, correction, a suite. I'm not going to get canned for yarding my wanger at a family restaurant. And a foreign one at that. Italy. The war. They lost. Think about that. One dumb incident gets you cop-clobbered and I am in trouble."

"Why would you be in trouble?"

"Dude, deep wells have no staircases."

"I wouldn't tell them anything," I said.

"That is consoling, in theory. But in practice, a different story. The notion of you waiting to see a JP and spending nineteen hours in the slammer with a bunch of drunks who want to know how many cigarettes you have leaves me insecure with your academic theory."

"What could they possibly do?"

"They'd say, 'Tell us what you know about Russell and we'll spare the woman.'"

In the left lane, a Dodge Charger with chrome manifolds and dual exhaust sped past.

"Spare the woman?" I said.

"You heard me."

"Where do you get these lines from?"

"In tough spots, life comes down to the basics. Greed, lust, fear, cars, gasoline, power. Cops know that."

"They don't know who she is."

"They know everything," he said. "Listen, I'm tuning you in to the realities of conducting business in the latter half of the twentieth century. Why put yourself in this position? I bet you dropped a load of cash, and you didn't even get laid. I don't understand you people.

Why can't you ball like everybody else? I'm not questioning your patriotism, but you hang out with pretty screwed-up minds."

"They're cool people."

"Name one."

"Don," I said.

"Fagito, man. Do not let that cowboy saddle up behind you. He's not interested in the horse. Or the architect. Christ, him and his wife spend half their lives repainting their kitchen new degrees of taupe. How many shades of taupe can there be? That is a sickness. Could you trust any of those idiots in a bind? Then that so-called Major. What a pompous ass."

"He was in the war."

"The only war he has been in is with his hemorrhoids. That dick would not know the butt of a Lee Enfield from the butt of a young boy. And that housemaid of hers? Illegal immigrant from the Philippines. Wait 'til Immigration shows up. You'll find out who your real friends are. Keeping their company doesn't make good economic sense."

"And B&Es do?"

Russell pitched his Molson and flicked a Marlboro from his vest pocket, a move I'd seen him practice many times. The cab filled with tar.

"I've been wanting to talk about that," he said. "I guess now is the time. The answer is no. Now, I'm not putting down the fine work we've done. But the future needs true soldiers of fortune. We can't jeopardize everything for loser customers who don't understand what we're trying to accomplish. The B&Es were a stepping stone."

"To what, murder?"

"That never pays, either. You know the saying."

"What saying?" I said.

"There are more things in heaven than on earth."

"Please, stop."

Russell left the quote unsourced and held out a cake container. "Take a look," he said.

The Edwardian tin bore a faded pastoral scene from an uptight English flower garden, a Shetland pony standing by a rusted fence in Lancaster. Russell had stopped breathing.

Inside were a stack of dried papers. Crudely drawn sketches of muscular men and women in various iterations of fascist uniforms in rural settings: with horses, by barns, beside tractors. All striking Aryan poses on wheelbarrows or standing firm with rakes clenched in their fists and loads of loot stacked at their feet.

"See that scenario?" he said. "That is order. That is satisfaction." His fingers curled around the steering wheel. "Everybody working towards something. Everybody standing for something. The problem with this country is it stands for nothing. Everybody waits for everyone else to do the work. And when a real worker makes the slightest slip, the crowd bites his asshole off. I'm not going to be that. What I fear most is becoming nothing. So, you make a mistake or two along the way? Who cares? If the world had been left to cowards, we'd still be living in grass huts. Take fascists. People say, 'Oh, they were evil, they were bad.' All right, they screwed up once or twice. Who hasn't? I'm not talking about invading Caribbean countries or gassing people because they go to the wrong church. I'm talking about what matters to both of us. I'm saying, dude, you've got to have a dream."

Russell pursed his lips. The inside of his cab smelled of worn upholstery.

"You drew these?" I said.

His face tinged red, and he stared straight ahead through the windshield to a faraway goalpost.

"When the idea turns into a concept," I said, "maybe we can get a federal grant. Right now, let's head to Beresford Street. I need plastic wrap."

"Go to Safeway."

"Negative. It's got to be clear and hold hundreds of pounds."

"For what?" he said. "Jesus, don't tell me."

We turned past the Vancouver General, the old brick fortress dating from the 1920s where people went to die because there were a lot of Garry oaks on the lawn. A beautiful late summer day rolled across the city and beside an ancient burger stand, a giant plastic grandpa eating a sandwich winked at me in his white shirt and skinny tie.

Polyurethane aluminums have an amorous smell during production and the instant we hit Enviro Plastics I knew I was in love. Enviro concocted everything from industrial bubble foam to space lighting, but its major customers were US defence companies. The front door was locked, a security camera was in place and the cash register was dutifully open and empty in plain view of the window.

Outside the rear delivery door, Russell donned a pair of construction gloves and unrolled mat magnets from the back of his truck. SHEBOB'S INDUSTRIAL MOVING was our advertised cover and a set of plates that we clipped fore and aft actually did register to a moving company.

We used a plowman's dick to breach the entrance, sort of a wrecking bar with a spring-loaded release, which pried the lock from the frame. They were on all the lists of prohibited weapons and B&E paraphernalia, hence confiscatory on sight. Russell scrawled the address on the bottom line of a pink work order sheet and tucked it under the windshield wipers.

"Just in case," he said.

The baseline of our operation had to be speed. Fast, fast, fast. Balk at the plastic strips hanging from the rafters. Ignore the rows of tubing that glowed like the aurora. Go. Only the target product mattered.

"What do they use all this crap for?" Russell said.

"Subzero electrical conduction."

"That explains why there is no alarm."

Our experimental layer of sheeting was found inside a warehouse-size freezer. A clear wall separated an arctic environment from a tropical garden with, as the technical sign proclaimed, "only a nanometer of protective plastic." Banyan trees, banana bushes, pepper stems and hibiscus grew in pots without sun and without dirt, bombarded by full-spectrum lighting and nourished by spider web thin tubes.

Russell rolled a hibiscus leaf between his thumb and his finger. "Are you thinking what I'm thinking?"

"Probably not," I said.

"Earth to Woody. Tune in."

"To what?"

"The price of weed."

"Twelve hundred dollars a pound."

"Retail," he said. "Farm production cost is thirty dollars per."

"That's in Colombia."

"I'm a nationalist and patriot. Look at these lights."

I had grown weed behind my grandmother's hydrangeas last year and choked on the half-burnt podzolic roots. The cats ate it. The dogs pissed on it. Half a square bale wouldn't get a flea high.

"Homegrown stinks," I said.

"Don't you get it? Banyan trees, banana plants. Growing like weeds. This is perfect. You don't have to do B&Es. You don't have to cross borders. Just set the lights and plant the seeds."

"And where would this weed grow?"

"Your basement."

"My grandmother's basement?"

"She is in the hospital."

"For three days."

"Who says she'll still have her marbles when she gets out?"

"She reads Tolstoy."

"But soon she'll fall asleep in chapter one. You've studied electricity. You've studied amps and ohms. I know a half a dozen dedicated, suburban pushers. Hard-working plebes. Twenty lids a week easy. Sell them at ten. We keep nine. That's a hundred and sixty a week for the rest of our lives. Can you say Mazatlán?"

"I can't rip off my grandmother."

"We're not ripping her off. We're helping her up. We steal nothing. She's not being abducted. She's been included in the family enterprise. Use the profit to buy her slippers. Morally, this is the right thing to do."

"This is too long term."

"So was Rome," he said. "One fast rip-off from our technical suppliers here and we are set for life. The market says go. Importation is too risky. Too many middlemen. Too much organized crime. Bad for society. Weed grown under our lights is safe and pure. No Agent Orange, no customs receipts. We must corner this before college kids catch on. They'll get student loans to subsidize the fertilizer. That's socialism. This is the ground floor, Woody. To the victor go the spoils."

"The spoils?"

"Back the truck up," he said, his fingers still clutching the flowering hibiscus.

Later that night, when the darkness came and the last bits of pollen lifted off the chrysanthemums I couldn't help going to his house. At first I thought, *he's your partner, your accomplice and you shouldn't do this to him*, but Looking Fits do this to everybody in the end. And so, after midnight when the house was utterly silent, I found myself following the path of pheromonal guidance to his nest.

Or half-nest, actually. Russell lived in the basement suite of a duplex off Imperial Street, which had been blue collar during the fifties and slid down the social chaparral from there, a landscape of television antennas, motorless Plymouths parked in wet bramble fields and stucco hardware stores. The inside of the house smelled of potatoes. A grey plaid couch, a grey rocking chair and a poster of Led Zeppelin on the panelled walls. Items that were either stolen or waiting to be fenced: three vacuum cleaners, eight chrome-rimmed tires, four dozen ten-gallon aquarium tanks with (blue) pebble filler.

The bedroom was dank and reeked of my colleague's detritus: a large-framed bed with puffy comforters and a photograph of Miss April tacked above the headrest. Russell was not alone. This one was older than the last one. Worn but not weaselly, she owned the woman's salon off Kingsway and Imperial, a brown cedar building that smelled of aerosol and catered to the retired pastiche crowd. Her hair was dyed off-red, and the wedding band that had been removed from her finger was tucked into the pocket of the black slacks laying folded on the dresser. Russell was asleep. His face was blank, and I envied him. As if when he slept, curled in a slightly fetal position, he truly rested and thought of nothing but peace. His scrubby hair showed the first signs of receding.

In the bookcase waited layers of *Popular Mechanics*, *Penthouse*, *Hustler*, *Playboy*, then beneath, *Batman* comic books along with the *Avengers*, *Spiderman* and the *Incredible Hulk*, over three hundred originals in all. Russell wasn't big on history. His sole non-fiction text was in fact, *Mein Kampf*, battered and spat up. The edition had survived three beatings at the B'nai B'rith Centre and an onslaught of pencilled comments in the margins. There were also new editions of *Rommel: Desert Rat!* and *Nazi Nymphos!* Hard to class these as non-fiction and besides, their spines remained uncracked. In the international section, a dozen Italian war comics where our artist had drawn a maple leaf over the fasces and changed swords into hockey sticks. (Russell truly had an undiminished sense of patriotism in his id.) Sheets of tracing paper had been used over comics to stencil in the body forms of Aryan characters now performing good or at least constructive atrocities. There was an abundance of women milking dairy cows. Then came the freehand drawings, hundreds, if not thousands, of crude sketches with exaggerated attributes. Pigs, chickens, horses. Many, many horses. People too. Drawings of large men in tragic but heroic poses: on the deck of a sinking ship, planting flags on mountaintops, blistered battlefields and in one sketch, on a beach that might have been Normandy or Waikiki. Sailors in white, mechanics with bulging biceps, winking at transmissions.

The more recent sketches experienced a change in hue: there were no busty blondes or bristly brunettes, no women officers with high boots, actually, no women at all. Only men emerging from the comic embryos to load machine guns, start tractors or perhaps liberate chartered banks on the lunar surface. More farm animals. Boars with reins. Marijuana plants. Fields of marijuana plants. Nations of marijuana farms. A few of the heroes had manly bulges in their pants, and the handshakes between victorious army captains were a little more than chummy. One sketch of a woman had been crumpled up and stuffed into a sock. Uncrinkled, the paper revealed the likes of a plain woman in her thirties, and so I dug deeper into the stratigraphy of Russell's past, to a sketch of a woman standing by a blackboard, prim-like, out of the early sixties, and there were notes to a Miss Caraway, whom I remembered distantly from Abbotsford Elementary as a pale and thin woman who would probably remain a spinster forever and was despised by the more elite members of the faculty.

Dear Mrs. Caraway, Dear Miss Caraway, Dear Caroline, Dear C. I am out of school and over the age of eighteen now. Dear Caroline, I have always thought you were the most admirable of all teachers. Dear Carol, although you do not know me ... Dear Carol, I love you.

The notes never finished and down in the deepest recesses of the drawer was a simple photograph of a woman who had the slightest resemblance to Russell, and so I thought it was his mother except someone had drawn horns coming out of her head.

NINETEEN

YOU ONLY HAD to know Azy for a short while to realize that holding court was her favourite pastime. She liked it more than fast cars, plum wine, menthol cigarettes and genital sex, if she ever liked genital sex at all. The Mistress brought a stool from her dungeon and placed it in the centre of the living room when parties started. Perched atop her throne, she sat in seraphic silence and gazed over her subjects who waited in line for a moment of her cruelty. Her duties were many: giving thumbs up or down to SM scenes about to be played out, lending advice to other tops on business proceedings and allowing her stamen of aroused indifference to be the pillar of the evening's procession. Sort of a sexual manifest destiny. If other mistresses showed up, usually semi-pro Dommes whom she had tutored, they ought not perch themselves on a higher chair, speak in a more guttural voice or give contrary evidence on matters of scripture. She would tolerate her subordinates calling other tops "Madam," but never "Mistress," and permitted the most favoured protegés to refer to her as "Auntie."

Soirees like this sound like they would be a lot of fun, but in reality they were a lot of work. Everything had to be carefully considered and properly executed. Guests had to arrive when requested and leave when excused. Crosses constructed, floggers cleaned, needles sharpened. Liquor purchased and weed obtained. Except of course, Azy didn't do any of the actual work herself. That was the duty of underlings. The Mistress frequently made cool assessments of the arrangements in progress: "Make sure Ellen is scratched from the list if her acne isn't cleared up." Or, "Tell Richard imitation leather is not permitted."

Although there was always an official reason for the pre-soiree gathering — a new member to be considered, an important prop developed or an inaugural party to be planned — there was usually an ulterior motive, predictably a torpid, mundane and labour-intensive motive. A plumbing fixture needed to be installed, a pair of shoes fetched or the latest copy completed for her weekly contribution to the *Vancouver Singles Magazine*, where she headlined, though rarely wrote, the "Mistress Says" column.

"Mistress Says" was a ten-column inch advice feature that appeared weekly on page eighteen of the city's only swinging periodical, the *VSM*. Amidst the squalor of grainy black and white photos, coded adult personals and dubious professional services, the Mistress offered technical words of wisdom to those troubled enough to write in. (What to do when anal hooks get stuck? Is the proper term collar or dog collar? How should a slave address another slave in the playroom if only one Mistress is present?) The problem was, Azy didn't much like writing and appreciated research even less.

I got assigned the task of writing the column after foolishly bringing over my measly copy from the university press, *The Ubyssey*, to impress her. The editor at the time had dismissed me for being non-analytical and completely disrespectful of deadlines. No matter. Azy saw the angle and the recruitment was non-negotiable. She fielded the hot question of the week. I bustled off copy with the precise amount of sarcasm, scientific conjecture and authority. The column's byline, after all, proclaimed that the good Mistress had been a pro-Domme in Paris, London and Singapore and held two PhDs in the social sciences. When done, I would submit the draft for approval. I never got away with less than three rewrites. Too long, too short. Too pestiferous. *Ti definisci uno scrittore*? Often, I simply moved the paragraphs around and the verdict went from appalling to astounding instantly. The last duty was to get a printed *VSM* copy back to Azy so she could sit on her stool and read the prose while guests listened attentively.

With her literary fame secured for another week, the Mistress could focus her attention on party attire. "Dressing in leather is more than a way of life," she said. "It's a second skin that transforms the body into a totally new species of desire." Not that it had to be leather. Pinstripe suits, high-heeled shoes, rubber, PVC and metallic gloss would do. She wore librarian glasses from time to time although the actual lenses were fake.

Usually, the court events started at seven and progressed to a play party by eleven. But on the twelfth of October I was summoned at two in the afternoon. Probably not much happening but tedious housework, yet "COME QUICKLY" was a distressing tone for the mistress of ice. A strange series of images flashed through my mind. Kristallnacht, the shattering of glass, the burning of books. Azy's door swung open, and she vanished instantly down the hall.

"Don's in the living room," she said. The air was stale, the kitchen quiet.

Don leaned back on Azy's couch in his cowboy Gestapo attire: unbuttoned shirt, chaps, brush cut and muscle band around his bicep. He sipped a gin and tonic and watched the ceiling fan rotate.

"Where's Azy gone?" I said.

"Changing."

"Already?"

"You know her."

"And Sal?"

"Trussed up on the cross."

"What's the scene?"

Don shrugged. Outside, oak leaves around drab wartime bungalows were going red. "Yes, well. I guess I should probably fill you in on that," he said. "It's not actually a scene."

"What?"

"Bit of a disciplinary matter. Don't sweat it. She screwed up. She knows the rules."

His jaw crushed an ice cube, maybe attempting to grind out an explanation. Beneath his armour of leather was a muscular but aging body showing the first signs of nostalgia.

"Don't get me wrong," he said. "She could walk away anytime she wants. But to where? Look at it this way. This is one of the few times you're going to see Azy legitimately turned on. Have a drink. I'll give you advice. You're in pretty good stead here. The Mistress was impressed that you'd haul your wanger out in public, so I wouldn't do anything to threaten that status. It only takes a second for her to lose patience, or interest, if you get what I mean. Lap it up. This is the real thing."

"What did Sal do wrong?"

"That's not for me to say."

A young woman cried from downstairs. I wasn't sure if it were Sal or not. The voice didn't sound human.

"Looks like we're needed," Don stared at the lemon in his drink one last time, then put his gin away.

Downstairs, the air was dry and smelled of furnace lint. Don had talked about buying a humidifier, but he obviously hadn't got around to installation. The amber lamp was on, and Sal was arced tits up over the wooden cross, bathed in peach light. Except for her painted puppet face, she was nude and looked like a homeless cat.

Her stomach and thighs were covered with sweat, so she'd obviously been there a while. Azy stuck a cattle prod under Sal's butt and her hips shot up in a yellow flash.

"Get her upright," Azy said.

The first time I saw Don I had a pretty good idea I never wanted to see him angry, and then I knew why. His hulking frame yarded the cross into a vertical position with one obscene bench press and the post hit the floor. The cartilage in Sal's elbows cracked. Then he hooked the beam to a block and tackle and winched it off the ground. Sal hung there like a crucified whore, sagging and shedding drops of sweat earthward.

"I've had enough," she said.

"Shut up," Azy said.

In her own pathetic way Sal was almost erotic. Waifish and pasty, she'd make the ideal model for the village girl who was about to be lynched by the angry peasant mob or hanged for a murder she didn't commit. Then she saw me and moaned. She was broken, humiliated and I liked it a lot.

"Get me down," she said.

"Why?" Azy said.

"This is no game anymore."

Our good Mistress found the proposition amusing.

"That's fine, Don," she said. "Thank you. Cirrus and I will take it from here."

Don nodded and pulled off his leather gloves.

"Don't go, Don," Sal said. "Jesus, don't go."

Azy inspected her pack of Tekels and there were only two left. "You'll be back on the weekend, won't you?"

"I'll be back Saturday afternoon," he said.

"Say hello to the rodeo boys for me."

Don stuffed his leather gloves in my hand on the way out. "Break a leg, fella," he said.

For a few seconds Azy watched a spider make its way up the ceiling. She spoke to the little creature and her voice got breathy, the same guttural rubble that got Marlene Dietrich through most of life.

"Well," she said. "Looks like it's only the three of us now."

"Fuck off," Sal said.

"What should we do first?"

"Get me down."

"Take a good look at this poor little pathetic bitch, Cirrus. Step up close and tell me what you see."

Maybe Sal had been dieting for a few weeks because I couldn't recall her being that thin. Her lily pelvic bones stuck out at bad angles as if she'd just struggled through puberty. I ran my finger through the pool of sweat that collected in her navel. She spat on my face. Saliva rolled down my jaw.

"Slap her," Azy said.

Anybody can do this. Easier than most people know. What's essential is cupping the palm and the proper arc so the flesh resonates with the blow. Put a lot of sadistic ardour into the act and the satisfaction is immense. If your soul snarls up in a grotesque parody of the Loch Ness monster, you're on the right track.

Azy pulled a white sheet off the medical bench. Lined up in a row, begging for selection, were the usual suspects: the horse fuller, the metal splays, a tungsten bow and a host of smaller magnesium screws. Also prepared were more elaborate instruments, what might have been a vulva splitter for Venusians, a spider-shaped claw to open thoracic cavities and a handgun that shot electrified darts.

"I think you are familiar with these," Azy said.

Her unblinking eyes were on me, waiting for a weakness that I wasn't going to give.

"Naturally."

"Pick one."

The chrome knitting needle looked good. Azy dipped the instrument in a jar of blue gel. My school nurse had kept tongue depressors in a similar jar. Her name was Miss Pontifex and she had been in the war and served at Ortona. Azy put on a pair of surgical gloves, spruced Sal's nipple, then punctured her nib with the needle. Sal screamed and wouldn't stop.

"Red," Sal said. "Red, you crazy bitch, red."

I can't lie about what I heard. Or that I did nothing. Sal's eyes welled up with water. This was too good to stop. The way the needle wagged and spattered blood on the floor. The way her mouth kept moving even after the crying ended.

"The place is soundproof." Azy sat back on her throne. "We've tested it with this decibel meter from the city."

I've often wondered what she thought of at times like that, sitting back and smirking: trips to the Eiffel tower, her pension plan, Hemingway's real meaning or perhaps nothing at all.

"You can hear me," Sal said. "You can hear me. I called red."

"Pierce her nip," Azy said.

"Me?"

"Don't see anyone else here."

Penetration achieved forthwith. The popping sound reminded me of the wasps stinging Grandmom's face. Sal's eyes were jammed shut and the few words that scrambled out of her mouth sounded Polish.

"Put on a pair of gloves," Azy said. "Then take the jar from the table. The one with the yellow fluid. Pull out the sponge. Shove the sponge under her nose. Don't breathe any yourself."

Litre jar. Maybe amyl nitrate. Maybe amphetamines. I didn't know or care. I pushed my prisoner's jaw shut and rammed the sponge up a nostril. In her panic she sucked in, convulsed and pissed herself. The urine spiralled in a candy cane pattern around her thigh, then finally spread a yellow pool on the floor.

I reflected. Certainly there was a point when you knew it was all wrong, Mr. Speer. But you went on. You did it anyway. Yes, sir, I did. I can tell the court I did it with modernity and pride. Sal's stomach palpitated in little dog patters, which bothered me a bit, but everyone was having such a good time, at least in the dramatic sense.

"It must be like drowning," Azy said. "But I wouldn't know. I've never done that to myself. I often wonder why people do. The important thing is that it makes her horny. You can do anything to her."

A single finger flick indicated the next act. Calipers on deck. My task was to get the circuitry right. Magnesium clips were attached to electrical wires, the wires plugged into a green transformer. The transformer was connected to a diode. Industrial and dirty, this was Stalin-era technology at its best.

"I've been thinking this over for a long time." Azy got off her throne and rested a palm on Sal's forehead. "For a very long time, because we've been friends for years. I've grown quite fond of you, but we can't go on like this. It's not working anymore. Not for me, anyway. You think you're young and smart and can have whatever you want but life doesn't move that way. We have rules and you've broken them. You thought it cute to break the rules. You'd be Smart Alec Masochist, and that's all right at other parties but not here while you are serving me. So, we'll have to burn this bad practice, no pun intended, out of your mind. And there's no other way except through your body. I'm not much into Buddhist cleansing. I can feel you trembling, so, don't get me wrong. In any other circumstances we'd probably both enjoy this game. But this time around you must not."

"Don't do this," Sal said.

"I'm not going to do anything," Azy said. "Our good friend here, Cirrus, is going to perform the dirty. I'm going to watch."

Sal's panicked face rolled my way.

"Do not do this to me, Cirrus," she said. "I do not consent to this, understand? This is not a joke. I want to have children one day."

"How predictable," Azy said. "Play the motherhood card. Good thing you're not black, lesbian or Jewish. The speech would go on for hours."

I coated Sal's temple with a swab of fluid, then attached a set of sponges to her skin. Sal started praying. Really earnest prayers about the things she had done wrong, the people she had cheated and a curious segment about all the animals she should have loved, but didn't.

"Stick it up her cunt," Azy said.

Once inserted the horseshoe could not be dislodged. This instrument had been tailored to fit precisely. The good Mistress motioned. I flipped. Sal's spine split up in sparks and her muscles rippled. Her bladder ejected the rest of its cargo and the spray shot horizontally. The piss kept coming and coming. She must have consumed a swimming pool before the session.

"Here's the way it works." Azy pinched Sal's earlobe. "We'll turn the power up. As long as you keep your dirty little twat dry, nothing bad happens. But if you go wet, bad news. Cirrus turns the ohms into the red which will melt your fallopian tubes. You don't want that."

The transformer made a hummingbird noise.

"Get my purse," Azy said.

"Purse?" I said.

"You're buying me lunch."

"Where?"

She thought. "The Blue Boy has scampi today."

"What about her?"

"I don't know. What about her?"

The Blue Boy Hotel at the corner of Southeast Marine Drive and Fraser is named after the famous Gainsborough painting from 1770. A reproduction of the work hangs out front huge enough to scare away anyone with taste. He's an effeminate young lad with a bit of a paunch who I wouldn't have done under any degree of arousal. Azy liked the Blue Boy because the chance of clients coming here was slim and the restaurant manager owed her favours.

We got a patio seat and watched pulp barges roll up the river. Azy conducted a survey of the restaurant occupants and rated them for kink potential. Two college girls, three longshoremen and a middle-aged secretary.

"No, no and no," she concluded running through the patrons in order of appearance. "Dreams about it only, thinks about it then hates himself, not interested and just plain can't."

"You can tell?"

"Micro-air movements, maybe. Experience mostly. The girls too prissy. College women find kink a threat to their marketability. Longshoremen reek of common testosterone. And the steno, look how she crosses her legs. She punishes herself for wanting to be punished."

Punished. Right, that.

"Do you think Sal is all right?" I said.

She glanced at the menu and then at the river. "Oh, God. And yes, you. Horny and oversentimental. You played with her a couple of times and now you have all these lovey-dovey emotions. Sentimentality is the same thing as self-pity. It's a sickness I despise. You believe in traditional affection and that your parents always told the truth. Well, I've got news for you. They didn't. I don't romanticize weakness. I cure it. The only cure for sentimentality is arousal and that's what I teach. You can't tell me you didn't feel better after you'd finished with Sal. You had that tool stuffed so far inside her the other end came out her nose. They have the butternut scampi here on Wednesdays."

A tall man in his late sixties approached the table. White moustache, blue pinstripe suit. The kind of man who probably owned lakeside property and went to school at Oxford.

"Don't we know him?" I said.

Azy tossed matches into the ashtray. "Let's pretend not."

"Is that the Major?"

"Yes, that's him. He doesn't have his face on today. He's here to make trouble so say as little as possible."

The Major harpooned a leaf with his cane tip and examined the catch.

"Good afternoon, Alexis," he said.

"Do I know you?" she said.

"I'm sorry. Miss Dunwell, yes?"

"Whatever."

"Keeping well?"

"Until now."

"It's a beautiful autumn day."

"Smells of pulp."

"The backbone of our economic prosperity."

He was proud. Maybe he'd just published his memoirs.

"Not mine," she said.

"Too true. Mind if I sit down?"

"Actually, we were leaving."

True, the Major's face was badly barnacled, but it was unlike Azy to walk away from any kind of affront.

"But you just got here."

"The stench is a little rife."

"The price of an industrialized society," he said. "I was out for a long walk. Thinking about how things fall into place in the autumn. The seasons. The leaves. Unusual for the leaves to get such a beautiful brilliant colour here. The marine west coast climate dictates that they usually go yellow then brown. But this year, red and oranges. Directly related to the amount of sugar trapped in the stems. Common to continental climates. Exhilarating. And exhilaration triggers synaptic connections in our minds, leading to the most startling epiphanies. I've made quite a few of those lately."

"You have a point to this?" Azy said.

"Only that we need to chat."

"I've got company, as you can see."

The Major half-smiled. "Business or pleasure?"

"All pleasure. He's a friend. And a boxer."

"An athlete. I have seen. Never introduced in civilian circles."

Rule of Kink 23(1)(c): recognizing play partners for the first time openly in civilian circles without permission is discouraged. In business circles, it is forbidden. If everyone in the circle is bent, then asking for an introduction usually gets you one. Unnamed associates stay unnamed. Loose tongues get shunned.

"Colonel, this is Cirrus. He's a friend of mine from the university. Etymology."

"Fine pursuit." He appeared surprised. He touched the end of his white moustache. "But your host flatters me. I was not a colonel. Only a major."

"In the war?"

"Of course, in the war."

"Which regiment?"

"Highlanders," he said.

"Seaforth?" I was going to say, my father too, but this didn't seem like the time. Besides, the Major had a point he wanted to kick around.

"Perhaps your scholastic friend can help us out," he said.

"I'm sure he's not interested."

"No objections if I inquire?"

Azy shrugged.

"Cirrus. You've done calculus, haven't you?"

"One and Two. Diff equations."

"A mathematician," he said. "Just what we're looking for. One who can calculate the probability of existing in two different dimensions at once."

"I'm lost," I said.

"Me too," Azy said. "He can't help you."

"But he can. The civilian population of the world shouldn't decide our future."

"All the more reason not to do it now," she said.

The Major sat down and perched his hands on the curve of his stick. His grey eyes searched my person for a clue or weakness. "I can tell a lot about a man by getting near to him," he said. "By sensing their vibrations, their intent. Their deceit. What genus has sensory organs beneath the skull that distinguish prey from foe even in darkness?"

"*Corixa.*"

"The boy is truly outstanding, Mistress."

"Let's not put the theory to a test," Azy said.

"I sense a military background, also."

Only the father. Holland. Forty-five. Wounded twice. But that wasn't going to help me here.

"Is there anything else?" Azy asked.

"Have you seen Sal around?"

"No," Azy said.

"Are you sure?"

"Why wouldn't I be?"

"Have you seen her, Cirrus?"

Obvious Kink Party Protocol: no.

"I don't know a Sal," I said.

"Carmen?"

"No Carmens either."

His lips flinched. "I can't get hold of her."

"Maybe she doesn't want to talk to you," Azy said.

"We always tend specimens on Wednesdays."

Azy swatted at an annoying bottlenose fly on her sleeve. The Major examined the end of his cane, either for dog shit or to see if it would transform into a bayonet, and then he swung it around his arm.

"Take some advice," he said to me. "Stay away from this one. The last thing you would want your father knowing is that you keep her company."

"My father is dead," I said, and then I didn't like him much at all.

The Major's foggy eye narrowed. In a younger day, he might have lunged, but that day had passed, so he left the stage with damaged pride and the leaves of Southeast Marine Drive falling around him.

"What an asshole." Azy snapped a drink coaster on the table.

"Does he know where Sal is?"

"He's not a colonel or a major," she said. "He wasn't in the war at all. He was a pacifist during the forties. Hung out with Trudeau in Frogland, then got sent to prison because he wouldn't fight for his country. After, he started up this military fetish magazine and made a killing. Boys in Armour or some such crap. I'm not big on the military, but what he does is cowardly."

"Why do you hang out with him?"

"I don't," she said. There was an explanation on the way. "I take his ill-gotten money and reappropriate it. He's always had this dragonfly migration fetish that we replay over and over again. Whatever. For a while he was charming. Good at parties. Historical theatrics. His dick was enormous. Of course, his dick doesn't get hard anymore, so who cares? Now he's annoying and he's got to go. Go like a cat."

"I don't get it."

"Ex-Comune-a cat, O."

"Don't take his calls," I said.

"He'd still talk."

"What could he say?"

"Personal things. Classified stuff."

"Go to the police."

"Last I heard, they dragged you into an interview cell and beat the shit out of you."

"Who told you that?"

"You did. You had a belt around your neck and a cattle prod up your ass."

Phallic images blurred in the past. The waiter brought a package of Silver Slims, matches and a white rose. She picked them off the sterling silver platter and winced. "This is the kind of opportunity vice detectives get boners for. Let's go."

The dungeon smelled of dried urine. Sal bolted up like a mine rescue team had arrived when the lights went on. "Learn anything?" Azy secured the cuffs on Sal's wrist.

The prisoner opened her mouth but all that came out were strands of spit.

"I can't hear you," Azy said.

More spit.

"Hit the switch," she said.

I did and Sal bent up into a horseshoe of pain.

"Again," she said.

This time the poor girl twisted into a clove hitch and the sound was hard to identify, a magpie or crow, but the smell was not. Singed flesh. Not like a hair or scalp singe but the deep-inside-a-burning-wombat smell and I hated her. She was as Azy said, a poor, pathetic creature who needed damage to secure her character.

"Now stand up on the chair," she said. "Pull out your cock and piss on her."

Without considering a proper ground, I did as instructed, and when the stream hit the target, a yellow arc exploded off my zipper. Sal's body shook once with a chicken wire of light, then went slack.

"Idiot," Azy said to me. She slapped Sal's face a few times but there was no response. "Idiot, idiot, idiot. I told you to stop."

"You did not."

"Untie her."

I put my ear to Sal's chest. Too much ringing to hear anything. Azy tossed a glass of ice water into her face. Nothing.

"Maybe we'd better call an ambulance."

"Are you out of your mind?"

"Then what?"

"Get her out of here."

"Where?"

"I don't care where," she said. "Your place. The dump. That's up to you."

Azy sat on her throne and smoked. Then she pulled out her date book and flipped through the pages.

"Are you still here?" she said. "I have a five o'clock. Take responsibility for your actions and cut your losses. Take her to the clinic. Or take her home if you like. But a word to the wise. Don't screw her. You'll get VD. Her clothes are in the corner."

Inside my car, Sal slumped forward onto the dash and left a trail of spittle on the glovebox. Her clothes were ordinary. Black slacks with lint. A secondhand ski jacket. Exactly what you'd expect from someone who worked in a pet store. I secured her in the seat with the shoulder strap, then drove away. At the corner of Knight and Fifty-Seventh, my passenger moaned and wiped her face.

"Where do you want to go?" I said.

Sal's head lobbed back, and she rubbed her chin. She bit her lip. Her cosmos was one big cotton swab.

"Do you want to go to the hospital?" I said.

"No."

"Are you all right?"

"What does it look like?"

"I don't know. What does it look like?"

"Take me home," she said.

"I'll take you to the hospital."

"Do you plan on telling them everything when we roll up or would you dump me on the front steps?"

I considered the facts at hand. "Where's home?"

Home was Imperial and Kingsway. A stone's throw from my grandmother's house. Two blocks from my last B&E. Somehow, in the last four years I had never bumped into this creature on a bus, or grocery store or sidewalk. Of course, I never used the buses or went shopping, and with all her clothes on Sal wasn't the kind of girl who stood out in a crowd.

On never-ending Forty-First Avenue, a line of traffic lights and Ukrainian sausage houses brought time to a near standstill. "Does it still hurt?"

"My nipples are pierced, my clit is cut in two and I probably have radiation poisoning in my uterus. What do you think?" Her head fell against the window. Her eyes were a distant red, not watching the grey-panelled life of west Burnaby slide by.

"Isn't that what you wanted?"

"What do you want me to say?"

"The truth."

"Didn't you hear me call red?"

That I did. Either three or four times. In desperation, in anguish, in horrible gut-wrenching pain, I did.

"I didn't know that was your safe word."

"Of course, it's my safe word," she said. "It's everybody's safe word, you idiot. There's not a single person in this city that doesn't use red as a safe word. It's like a UN convention and you ignored it."

"I figured Azy would have stopped at the right time."

"She never stops."

"Then why do you keep going back?"

Sal put her palm to her cheek and gazed at me incredulously. I was then the most stupid person on the planet and we both knew it.

"I counted on you," she said. "I counted on you as a reasonable, compassionate individual in a free society to use common sense and you failed. Turn left."

The apartment block was exactly what I expected, a dull brown stucco building dropped in the middle of suburbia where only old-age pensioners dwelled. One of the walls was covered with ivy.

"Thanks for the ride," she said.

"I'll walk you up."

"No, you won't."

"Listen, I know you think I'm an asshole."

"You are."

"I promised Azy I'd get you in safely."

The hallway smelled of cabbage. The wallpaper was worn, and doors were brown with undersized knobs. She lived upstairs at number 202. Not much inside. A bachelor suite with a television, a beige sofa and an alcove for the bed. Crocheted tiger cubs hung on the wall.

"Do you want anything?" She hung up her coat.

"Scotch."

"I don't have any alcohol."

That one I hadn't heard before.

"There's tea." She was indifferent. She put a white kettle on the gas element, then went over and turned up the thermostat. A single click and the vents heaved. She sat on the sofa. I sat on the bed. She put a hand on her jacket.

"Do you ski?" I said.

"I wish."

Out on Imperial Avenue a steady stream of trucks flooded out between the apartments into the commercial district.

"Why do you live here?" I said.

"It's cheap."

"What do you do?"

"I go to work. I sleep." The kettle boiled. "Sugar?"

Sugar? I had no idea. The last time I had tea was with opium. Sal got up, winced and held her crotch.

"No sugar," I said. "What else do you do? You don't ski. Okay. Do you have any pets?"

"They're not allowed here."

Her bone china cups were enamelled with gold lambs.

"How long have you been seeing Azy?" I said.

Everything was far back in history. Most things got smaller. "Three years."

"How did you meet her?"

"Same way you did."

She glanced down at the worn carpet that once had held the pattern of a cat with a red bow around its neck. "I met her through *VSM*. I don't know why I should be telling you. I don't like you much. Truth is, I didn't have any friends. I didn't go to college. My parents are gone. I bought the magazine from a Chinese grocer and answered the advertisement. As a guy, you're lucky. You can go and meet people or go to a pro. For a woman it's harder. Not just the safety thing. Can you imagine for a second what's insinuated by answering an ad that costs money to get a reply? No woman should ever do that. But I did. I'd rather be thrown in jail than be found out for that."

She poured the tea and sat back down, bow-legged. The inside of her thigh was probably already festering.

"I met good people," she said. "Assholes too, but I have met a few who understood me, even liked me. Whether I had tits or money was irrelevant. They'd call me up on the phone. We'd go out. We'd laugh. Vancouver is still a small town. You get banished from one Domme's place and you have a reputation. A lot of Dommes won't do women. Going to male tops is stupid. Besides, as cruel as Azy is, the first time I asked her how much, I didn't have it. She said, 'Don't worry, just bring an offering.' After that I paid what I could afford and here we are."

"You don't pay?"

This could have been Sal's moment to light up a cigarette in satisfaction, but Sal did not smoke. She rearranged a crease in her slack.

She sniffled, then wiped the last bit of puppet makeup out of her eyes.

"You love her, don't you?" I said.

Sal did not answer. She stared out the window. A house sparrow lighted on the sill, found a few seeds that had been left on a wooden shelf, then got bored and flew away.

"You go to college. You have friends. You'll have a career. Russell says you're a boxer. I saw your stuff in *The Ubyssey*."

Sal sucked on Lipton tea and the room felt slightly damp.

"I'm sorry about what happened," I said.

"Don't lie," she said. "I can stand a lot of things out of people but lying isn't one. You aren't sorry. You don't feel guilty. You will go back, and I will go back, and everybody will go back because that's the way things are and that's the way they will always be."

TWENTY

WE ARE ALL lost in the desert. We are all alone. We meet company we shouldn't: Phoridae, *coriacea*, Blattodea, then find things we can't fix. Lineage. Tragic faults. Or Helen's High Coiffures, right across the street, where a legion of souls born in the nineteenth century had their hair stacked into cumulus curls before the climax of the recession.

"Are you hungover or what?" Russell sucked vinegar off his fries, then wiped the grease onto the sleeve of his bomber jacket. A red underground sign above us stated that we were in the Finest Fishery on the Fraser, and dogfish passing as cod proved the point.

"Sort of," I said, which was sort of true. I couldn't remember. I recalled the moon and the beating of flesh but couldn't recall the brand of intoxicant. I was hoping not airplane glue.

"You could have shared, dude."

"I've got a lot on my mind."

He leaned back in the plastic chair and used a napkin to dab his chin. "I bet. I bet. I just hope brain power well spent. You worry me, guy. You wander. You go AWOL. You forget plans. Given any thought to my proposition of the other day?"

"What day was that?"

The Beresford job all seemed so long ago. Now before us, a black and white television hung above the deep fryer. Pierre Trudeau in his gunslinger pose. He did well with the women and supposedly smoked pot. He said fuck you to the separatists. He said fuck you to the British and fuck you to the Americans. He said fuck you to, well, everybody and I respected him for that.

"Focus," Russell said.

"Do you know a Detective Fielding?"

Russell thought. Although he was pretending to be in deep contemplation, obviously he didn't have to think too far. "Maybe as a juvenile. I don't think he was a detective then."

"He is now."

"Super."

"He's worked my parents' case for years."

"The same guy who was in Abbotsford is now here?" he said.

"Bingo."

"Why is this too horrible to be true?"

"He took me to the morgue. He showed me bodies. Two mummified bodies. I knew right away they were the missing link to my mother and father. Male and female. Embracing. Very sexual. Except dead. With wings. Gills too. A cross between grasshopper and scorched sardine. The guy was hung like a horse and the chick had salami-thick nipples."

"Woody," Russ said. "You need help."

"That's why I'm talking to you."

"Try a shrink."

"I've tried."

"Are you sober?"

"Yes."

"Then we should fix that."

"Don't you want to know what happened to the corpses?"

"Not really," he said.

"Fielding slid them back in the cubbyhole without telling me the whole story."

"So what?"

"We have to go back."

"Dude, this is out of control. Let me make calls. I'm sorry about the shrink joke. That was out of line. What you need is intense social therapy, and that I can provide."

"I need to get back in that morgue."

"And what would you do back at this morgue?" he said. "Interview them? Give them mouth to mouth? If they are in the morgue, they are dead. That is what morgues are for."

I couldn't recall if I had slept the night before or ever. My elbow slipped, my skull struck the window and knocked a stuffed red snapper off the sill.

"Fielding strings you along," Russell said. "So you stay in his back pocket. When things get dull, he pulls a parlour trick. Two rubby-dubs who had the wrong formula for freebasing. He's a cop. And a creep. Put the two together and you have a PhD in creepery."

"I know what I saw."

"I don't get it, dude. What did you see?"

"Beings both insect and human."

"And what does that make you, a fruit fly? Jesus, Wood, I hate to be the bearer of bad news, but you must face facts. One, Fielding is recruiting you. He wants to turn you into an informant, a human source, a rat. And that makes me apprehensive if you can see my position. Two, buddy, your parents are dead, okay? I know it's tough, but it's true."

Outside, Vancouver stunk of the rain that had either just been or was about to come. Clogged eaves, slugs in curb cracks and oil drums in back alleys reducing themselves to rust. Russell unzipped his jacket with a manicured stroke and fished around in its inner pockets. Jackknife, linseed oil, three provincial violation tickets and a Ramses condom. He strolled to a pay phone, checked both shoulders and dropped a quarter into the slot.

I pondered the precise genre of tools I'd need to get into the morgue. Huge blocks of west coast granite built into a medieval fortress three storeys high. Crowbar, plowman's dick, jackhammer, all useless on this kind of campaign. Heavy artillery would be required.

Russell talked on the phone confidently. He laughed, he pontificated, he rolled his hands in generous circles expounding the evening's party favours that would arrive free of charge and be more ecumenical than ever. Dynamite was what I required. And a fuse. More precisely, C-4 and a timed detonator. I'd seen the August edition of *Soldier of Fortune* magazine. There was a mail-away address, but that would take months. Where could C-4 be got immediately? The naval base? A hardware store? A demolition shop? Maybe. Who demolished morgues? How about a wrecking company? My eyes flicked far down the street to a row of semi-commercial properties and a cluster of letters came into focus. Wren's Wrecking and Demolition. Established 1952.

Russell hung up the phone. He was uplifted. A waft of Irish Spring rolled off his shoulders. "Buddy, I've got us a date. Cindy and Cherice. Ten percent chance those are their real names but a hundred percent chance you'll get your rocks blown. Firm beyond belief and they go for hours. Also, I've landed us off-market quaaludes to ease your worried mind. But that's for after. For the main event, I've bagged the usual high-quality Russell Hobbes Herbals to elevate our ladies' interest. A bottle of CC from the jar shop and we'll be right as dodger. We can discuss the new locale for our hydroponics."

"Thanks, no."

"What, you want vanilla ice cream?"

"I need your help elsewhere."

He pushed his hair back and pitched an empty package of Export 'A's into the gutter. "That succubus has got you into necro-crap, hasn't she? She's turning you into a grave robber so one of her clients can play Jack the Ripper. Dude, this is sick."

The pay phone rang once, twice, three times. Russell stomped over and picked it up. Nothing came from the receiver except for a high-pitched buzz. Up in the grey sky a murder of crows circled the phone booth and screamed. Russell abandoned the line.

"Fielding is listening to us right now," he said. "When you break in, he'll bust you. And he'll want his pay. Just a little info. Just a small tip. Just who's who in the zoo. Your mistress, your comrade in arms. It's the oldest cop game in the book. Think about this from a business perspective. Commercial viability, nil. Chance of success, zero. Liability if caught, astronomical."

"I'll go alone," I said.

There was nothing left for me on the street corner save rainwater spilling out of a sewer drain and a dead robin beside the telephone staff. Russell punched a mailbox. I had a frothing desire to tear up the entire block looking for explosives. The red lettering on the door of Wren's Wrecking bloomed up in front of me proclaiming Office Hours 9 to 5, Monday to Friday except Wednesdays When We Are in the Field. In the field? Perfecto absolut, like the vodka. Only a second more and the wet concrete of suburban Burnaby would have slid away in a clatter of wings, but Russell grabbed my elbow.

"Knock it off, marathon boy," he said. "I give in. We'll go together. Let me breathe for Chrissake. I'll come along. This once. Because we are partners. But this job takes planning, right? Morgues are a Fort Knox. We'll have to figure the angles, conglomerate contingencies, et cetera. So, we need focus. We'll have a drink, a few babes. Then we'll move together, fortified and satisfied. You can't pull off this kind of operation uptight and horny. Confide in your partner. Here I have the experience. Here I have a legacy. You're befouled. You're twisted. You can't help your cause unless you help yourself first. And only the proper therapy is what I can provide, right? Say right, Woody. Say right."

"Whatever."

"Negative. Say right."

Right, Russell. Right. You were once again, as always, right.

Cindy and Cherice looked like sisters, but in fact weren't. Two lithe blondes with matching red and white sailor tops who hadn't had quite enough calcium in their diet as youths now perched themselves on the top floor of the Metro Towne Towers. MTT was the coolest place to be in Burnaby's bucolic suburbs. An *e* had originally been added to make the name more Anglo-Saxon, but it didn't stick. Metro Towne.

The inside of their apartment smelled of banana incense and all the puffed furniture was cream white. So was the shag carpet. Whatever C&C did, they did okay. They both smiled at the same time.

"Hey, babes," Russell said.

"Hey, Russie," they said, and laughed.

"Yeah, yeah," Russell said. He didn't like being called Russie. Cherice kissed him on the cheek, then made him take off his shoes. He surveyed the room and took in the framed oil painting.

"It's a Van Gogh," she said.

"Looks weird."

"He's got no ear now."

"How does he hear?"

They both laughed again. "It's Rent-an-Art. Last month we had Rembrandt."

"Incredibly cool," Russell said. "Ladies, this is my partner, Cirrus."

Cindy shook my hand. Her palm was soft. She gave complete eyeball contact while shaking, like all this was too fabulous to be true.

"You're a doll," she said.

Tapioca foyer, marble counter and sunken living room.

"You girls want a drinkola?" Russ said.

"Thought you weren't going to ask," Cindy said.

"I always ask my girls."

Cherice went to the coffee table that had been polished with scented cleaner and shut off the answering machine that already had a lot of red lights flashing.

"Do you mind if we square out first, Russie?" she said.

"You ladies do have all night, don't you?"

"All yours." Cindy held onto my middle finger.

"Super," Russ said. The two of them vanished into the bedroom.

"What are you into?" Cindy asked.

Petrified insects, Dr. Mengele torture scenes and being suffocated with One Hour Martinizing bags probably, but I figured this wasn't the venue to talk shop.

"Russ says you're in university."

"UBC."

"Must mean you're smart."

"Or not smart enough."

"I like you," she said.

We sat and the couch sank a foot. Russ and Cherice appeared flush with the success of their negotiations and looking like newlyweds. She punched a code into the elaborate locking system on the front door.

"Let's get down," Russell said from the kitchen counter. He uncapped a bottle of CC. "What do you want? I can make anything."

"Make me a Tom Collins," Cindy said.

"What the hell is that?" Russell said.

"It's a girl drink."

"I only make guy drinks."

"Okay, make Daiquiris."

"What is a Daiquiri?"

"With cognac and dry vermouth."

"Make four, Russie," Cherice said. "Then we can be guys together."

The girls rolled back in their seats. Russell gazed at a posted recipe, got ice cubes and splashed everything together in four glasses. When he served the drinks up, Cherice looped her arm over his shoulder.

"Here's to our new horticultural venture," he said.

"What kind of volume are we talking?" Cherice said.

"Can you say kilo-ton?"

"That'll be kilo-fun."

The twins loved Daiquiris, which they then referred to as Manhattans. They crossed legs and talked art deco.

"Did you see the PM on TV?"

"Who cares?" Russell said.

"He's hot," Cindy said.

"Why?" Russ said.

"He smokes pot."

"He's a fag."

"He is not," Cindy said.

"Would you vote for him?" I said.

"Who votes?" Russell said.

"You should vote," Cindy said.

"Yeah, you're supposed to pay taxes too," Russell said.

"Are you going to vote for him, Cir?"

I didn't have time to answer.

"We'll probably just screw him."

"For a fee," Cherise said.

"Get us another Manhattan, Russ."

Our hosts tuned in a music video on the television and started dancing. Cheerleaders filled a room full of soap and slid across a lubed sausage.

Russell dumped three ounces of rye into each glass and didn't care about what went in after that. "Dude, these are classy girls," he said to me. "They want to get to know you first. They want to have conversation and fun. Don't worry, you'll get it all. But don't ask for that kinky shit or start talking about dead parents or bugs. They're not into that."

We had a second Manhattan, then a third, and by the fourth the western sky scuttled red and the smog from Burrard Inlet bent spindles of glass highrises to the horizon.

"The sunset is very art deco." Cindy set a gold-plated hookah on the coffee table. In this elaborate ritual, one first unscrewed the copper-top Buddha, then poured Merlot into the neck. After the fluid chamber was sealed, the weed went into a bowl and the screen snapped into place, but I got lost on the mechanics of how the gases went through the red wine into the rattlesnake hose.

"Let's do balloon races," Cherice said.

The twins peeled their clothes off like it was standard operating procedure but left their white bobby socks on. Cherice summoned two pink balloons from beneath the lawn chair.

"Peel for us, bitches," Cindy said.

Russell peeled down to his underwear but wouldn't drop his drawers. The weed worked overtime in my head. I undid, dropped, and there was a split second of silence in the room.

"Dude," Russell said. "What the holy happened to your hair?"

Centre stage, two dark stars of culture collided at my expense.

"It's an in-thing," I said.

"Where, the prenatal room?"

"Don't tease him," Cindy said.

"He looks like a Ken doll."

"Everybody does that now," she said.

"Everybody does not."

"We do," Cindy said.

Cindy and Cherice bumped hips. Their hair was so blonde you couldn't tell.

"That's different," he said. "You guys are girls."

"Russell gets it. We're girls."

"Yeah, yeah. Let's race balls."

The race wasn't really a race. The game was more of a circus, and if there was a right way to play, I wasn't catching on. The rules involved drinking rye out of the bottle, getting the balloon to stick to your partner's cleavage, then moving under the telephone cord and back to the liquor table without using your hands. There was a penalty point for knocking the phone off its jack. At the end of each circuit, the team who was behind had to take a hit from the hookah and either Cindy or Cherice did a cheerleader dance. Russell was getting his rocks off but after five rounds he was beat.

"I know it's fluffy," Cindy said. "But Russie digs it."

"He's got a sentimental streak."

"You don't strike me as a fluffy guy."

"Nope."

"We'll do fine tonight."

Cherice sucked her Manhattan from Russell's lap. Russell's underwear was still firmly in place and seemingly that's the way things were going to stay. She kissed him and I couldn't figure the algebra because working women didn't kiss. Dommes didn't kiss. Girlfriends kissed, but that's not what this was. The music video ended. A hockey game came on. Russell's eyes drifted towards the blue line.

"Let's have a hit then," Cherice said.

"You mean a hit *plus*?" Russ said.

"Yeah, yeah."

Cindy pondered the chronology. "Now?" she said.

"Why not?"

"We can keep it up after a dozen hits," Russell said. "It's the SAS conditioning program we stick to."

Cindy shrugged. Russell set a brown lump of resin, which was "direct via diplomatic pouch from Cambodia," on the table and

Cherice pulled the battery from the smoke detector. "We don't pay eight hundred a month to smoke on the patio."

A roll of anticipation, licked lips, rubbed fingers and cajoled beads. Not bad pornography actually, two waifs suspended briefly between a rainforest condo and oblivion on a snakeskin hookah hose. Cherise pulled half of East Asia into her lungs. then CPR'ed the vapour down Russell's throat.

"They like each other," I said.

"They like something."

Cindy sucked up one last hit of opium and said, "Well, in Xanadu so did Kubla Khan, I guess."

"Coleridge?"

"When I'm alone."

She rubbed her face and poured half a glass of rye. Mixer no longer necessary. Russell's underwear was buttoned up. "Which is most of the fucking time. Look, it's your nickel. What do you want?"

"I promised Russell I wouldn't get into that."

"Screw Rus. He's a pig. He's out of it. They both are. Whisper it in my ear."

I leaned over and whispered.

"Don't you think that's kind of dangerous."

"That's kind of the point," I said.

"I don't know, Cir." She thought. "Hey listen. How about a shower? I give great golden showers. You'd like it."

She was really a sweet girl. This looked like we had a sweet deal. Cindy got up and fell over. A stuffed toy panda got its guts squashed. The squeeze box wailed.

"I dig shaved guys," she said. "God, Russell is a dork."

We went to the bathroom. The walls were pink. The mirror was huge. The mermaid tub was sunk into the foundation.

"Nice place," I said.

"It ought to be," she said, but didn't say why. She lit up a cigarette and fumbled around until the butt managed to fall into the toilet. We both stared at the unlit smoke.

"Get in the tub," she said.

Cindy wiped her nose, peeled off her socks and stepped in. Far above me, her hair fell over her face, and she seemed to be years older. She played with herself half-heartedly. Someone scored an overtime goal on TV. Cindy's fist curled around the shower handle and her lights went out. Spit eked out of her mouth. She mumbled about being back in nursing school and slid to her knees. When she collapsed on my chest, all she said was, "I don't like reading alone, either."

I rolled my tight-bodied colleague to the starboard deck. Her makeup smeared. I looked for a Kleenex. That was a mistake. No Kleenex to be found. Instead, Al Aauin Rouge, imported from Dakar and the date on the side of the tube read 1975. I pulled open the drawer: hair rollers, bobby pins, a package of orange-flavoured condoms and a *TV Guide*, all the prerequisites for life in the eighties. In her bedroom, or maybe Cherice's bedroom, were the photo albums. There were pictures of them naked together on a beach, naked on a boat, nude on the ski slope and in the back seat of a Mercedes Benz, also buff. There was a list of talent agencies and checklists for applicants willing to do the following: partial nude/ full nude/, soft core/hard core, /fetish/other—all, and there had been disagreement about the last category.

In the living room, a barely conscious Russell was spooning a less conscious Cherice, both oblivious to each other's presence in the forest of white shag.

"Russell." I got down and shook his shoulder. "We have work to do."

No response. Cherice belched. I pinched his collarbone.

"Who's the fruck?" he said and stuck his thumb in his mouth.

My jeans were on the couch, my shirt was in the kitchen. I couldn't find my shoes. I turned the doorknob. Nothing happened. I turned the brass counter-clockwise. Still locked in. The computer lockbox, which had been drilled into the door without managerial approval, lit up yellow letters. Door double safety–locked. Sign of the times. This was a fireproof steel-rimmed frame. For certain, if my Looking Fit went one step further I could yard the lock apart, but an opiated female voice called my name and so I went out on the balcony. The sapphire lights of Kingsway streamed westward through a chilled night. In the distance the urban core glowed inviting white. Down that cloistered archive of cement, glass, memories and exhaust was my morgue. In the bowels of that morgue were the bodies, the corpses of my ancestors and the bones of my faith.

The distance between Cindy's balcony and the one at suite 2124 was six feet. Two metres. Not far. Any grade-school long-jumper could do that. Sort of a long way down if you missed but I didn't plan on missing. A taxi stopped on the circular drive twenty floors below. The passengers got out ant-size with no clue what hung directly above them, and so I stood on the banister.

Leaping is a matter of faith, really. If you imagine yourself on the other side, you'll probably get there, and I did except with a pot full of chrysanthemums in my mouth and a silver steak fork embedded in my thumb. I knocked over a tricycle and struck a propane barbecue. The sliding glass door was open, and inside the air smelled of grandparents, slippers, housecoats, bottles of Metamucil. A glass of Pepsodent sat on the table, and down the hall there was a snoring peace, unaware of the horror that had crept into their home. In a moment, I was at the very spot three hundred feet below where I probably should have become another statistic for the suburban press.

Night is a surprise of light when you're young, the array of streetlamps, the arc of circuits. The first gas outlets came in 1887, with their quivering yellow glow, then later, the fluorescent and sodium bulbs, each one with its own frequency and texture. Like flowers, you can divide streetlamps into families: the argons, the neons and halogens. Subcategories too: filtered, nitrated and polarized. Each its own brothel of sweetness. Kingsway, my cathouse of candescence. I shimmied up the first pole with my fingers cutting deep into the painted metal, bathed in the light and scrambled on to the next.

Kingsway was a network of fabricated suns that cut through the concrete landscape towards the core. Virgin twinkles, spheres and silicon moons, all for my feasting pleasure. The sharp lemon of GE lamps sending erratic molecules off into patterns of epilepsy. The cool business hum of fluoride green and near white iodide. Noble gases reminding me of my Grade 3 teacher, Mrs. Harr, who stood through her lecture on synonyms, antonyms and homonyms with a yardstick rapping her skirt that the school board asked her to lower. At Main and Hastings came the mercury vapours, eking out their hazel affection in harvest, and the most beautiful realization was that no other creature like me had ever visited these bulbs.

Or at least hadn't until I broached the light on East Cordova. The bulb had been soiled with the stench of an interloper, smelled of wet ash, and the trail crept up the steps to the foyer of the coroner's office. I sobered up, cursed the burns on my hands and followed the stench of the intruder inside.

People think a morgue is a dull place, a quiet place and they may be well right about the first part, but it is anything but quiet at night. Popping, bloating, bleating. Liver walls collapsing and tendon joints eschewing their own limbs. Not to mention aural fluids cascading in waterfalls for those who have the ears to listen. At midnight, the shift changed over. Oxford shoes, white lab coats and necks soaked with perfume hurried back to the living, and I only had to think more centipede than wasp to gain entrance.

In the basement, chrome cases waited for their deceased cargo while FM filtered in from a freshly installed stereo system. I was surprised at the congestion. Perhaps Fielding had brought me in at a slow time or else this was the final outflow before the office closed permanently. Not all the bodies had been tucked in. Most waited patiently on trolleys covered only with a paper sheet. Folios were clipped to the gunnels, others had only plastic numbers. I recalled Fielding smoked a cigar that day and had waved me into the wash-up room with the burning tobacco wafting through his hair. I went through the record drawers looking for any mention of my colleagues. Hundreds of pages of pink and yellow sheets, autopsies, attributions, coroner's conclusions, police follow-ups, all flaked and aged but nothing of interest, and so I went straight to the tombs and opened the first cubbyhole.

The stall was occupied with the body of a young woman whose chart indicated she had fallen from a roof during an all-night party. In the next cubicle, an overweight Italian gone down from congestive heart failure. There were others, but they all looked so common, so plain and not at all what I had been hoping for.

There was no hint of where Fielding might have moved the bodies. And so, I'm sorry for what I did next, although I was in a rage, a prepubescent, self-centred, scorched earth tantrum rage, but I did it anyway. I yarded out the old man by the ankles and let him fall as a stump to the floor. His Gumby leg hit the cement and folded into his ass. He may as well have been made of rubber. The young woman fared no better. Her elbow struck the cupboard, then her head hit the floor. Putrescent juice burst from her ear, and I would have kicked her as one last piece of punctuation on her irrelevant life, but down the hall, a light flicked on.

A figure stood perfectly still with one finger on the switch. When she sang, I recognized the voice. Her shadow fluttered over the glazed lab window, a pair of pearl strap glasses, the hair in a hive and a bluster of birch leaves in tow. The white lab coat twirled around a corner, and I knew at once who went there, and Gwendolyn Sharpe was no night nurse.

She moved quickly. Only a flicker at the corner of my sight. By the fire extinguisher, up the stairs, clattering on the tile, and she was gone. I recalled a few things about Gwendolyn Sharpe. She liked leather gloves. She drove a Jaguar, careered in India and was friends with my grandparents during the war. Now she darted from hall to hall with a frame that moved as sparse as an aurora and a wake that cut sharp to the bone.

Outside on Cordova, I tried to keep up, but my game was off from the start. I tripped on a firehose. I lodged my foot in a sewer grate. Either I had become infected with a horrible morgue disease, quick-acting cholera, or else three hours on the tops of lampposts had made me torpid. Gwendolyn's scent lingered by the bus stop and then drew me down broken pavement under a railway trestle. I followed her up Arbutus Street where Japanese cherry trees held their last amber leaves and at the crest of the hill, in a neighbourhood stuffed with marble fountains, I threw up on a fire hydrant and knew at once that although Gwendolyn Sharpe could no longer be seen, she had always been watching, waiting, and would soon be close enough to touch.

TWENTY-ONE

I'M NOT SURE what Azy had against the Major. A rare skin disease, a predilection towards stuttering, or perhaps intermittent flatulence. Maybe he reminded her of her father, I didn't care. My orders were precise: to proceed down the alleys of South Vancouver, through the ever-growing tangle of hydro wires, burgeoning sports malls, failing bowling alleys and terminate his loquacity. For my effort I would be granted two free sessions and a permanent invite to monthly parties. How I was going to shut him up, or what precisely I might do when I found him remained unclear but shut him up I would. In fact, I had very little plan. Azy had left the details purposefully vague.

"Just fix it," she said.

Within days of her request, I had a road map of the Major's activities scrawled in a notebook along with diagrams, spreadsheets and probability parameters. The Major lived alone. He had a cat, an orange creature with a lame paw and acerbic breath. The house was far too neat for my liking. A split-level contemporary with dim light and polished fir smelling of Lemon Pledge. Rank sentimentality ruled the roost: Inuit statues, model planes and a legion of stuffed animals that he had no doubt collected from past safaris. The dining room table was bare and a sequin sofa from Tuscany was never sat in. He had a double bed from when his wife was alive. But that was long ago.

Now, he was alone, and his life appeared a mission dedicated to avoiding that fact. Each morning at seven forty-five he rose, showered with Irish Spring, combed his hair with a pearl handle brush, then sat down to a bowl of Red River cereal.

The average morning stay in the residence was twelve minutes. Anything longer left him lethargic. Easy to see why. The sallow reflection on the glass, the yellow walls, the crepe tablecloth, all of this had to be abandoned before the solitude turned his blood to ash.

Without hesitation, he ventured out the door, cane in hand and cap applied, regardless of the weather. He walked swiftly for a man of his age. Down Forty-Ninth, towards the great gardens of Granville Street where he stopped to smell the baskets of gardenias. He chatted with each of the storekeepers and was familiar with their daily affairs.

"Mr. Dalloway, how is your son's leg?"

"Hairline fracture."

"Hockey mishap, yes?"

"Goaltender."

"Theirs is a special burden."

Or, "Mrs. Bidden, how is the terrier?"

"Better," she said, and he would produce a Milk-Bone.

The Major returned home by ten, stored the groceries, then made sure the lights in the residence were out to reduce energy consumption. He flicked switches twice and often repeated the names of exotic rivers, the Zambezi, Iguacu or Po, while doing so. This nervous tick came to include explorers, or doomed ones anyway: Nansen, Cabot and Scott. Excluded from the equation was a single bulb in his study closet, which was left perpetually on.

Next, the Major ventured to the calendar and studied the mission statement for the day: Monday, record water levels at Vivian Creek; Tuesday, examine Albany Forest for pine beetle progress; Wednesday, nematode count. If his sexual needs were anything like his housekeeping habits, his sessions with Azy must have been unbearably dull.

Glass vials and sticky paper were a must on trapping expeditions. He was only interested in the rarest kind of catch, darner or emerald dragonflies, boatman bugs and orb weavers, and once they were glued to his pad, he placed them with tweezers into his vest pocket case. The field work was finished at noon, and he was home by one. Once embalmed, the specimens were mounted in his greenhouse, although ultimately, they must have been transferred to a secondary vault because with his moribund dedication the shed would have been filled in a week.

His academics were sloppy. He made no effort to categorize subjects according to genus or species and his note-taking often amounted to nothing more than sophomoric musings. Here's an example: "the Ordanatana is a sanguine but quick-witted species, that separated from the evolutionary chain early in the Carboniferous owing to its basic humours, melancholy blood, lust and hate, which brings me to the brink of enuresis." If there was a Nobel-worthy nomination in there, it had skipped the notice of the academy.

As the afternoon passed, the Major sat as many old men sit in their pachyderm graveyards, sifting through card decks, tins of shoe polish and sepia photographs, looking for a clue to life that would never be resurrected. Bouts of déjà vu left him calling out the names of dead friends. Hair rollers and clothes pegs then crushed beyond recognition when none of them answered.

By three o'clock the old soldier was withered. This was the nadir of the day for him as I'm sure it was for most people in his predicament. Three o'clock *post meridiem* time. Too early to call it quits and too late to start anything new. (Midday doldrums were hard on Sartre, Camus and Poe too.) In those few desperate minutes, the Major was on the verge of losing command. He quoted snippets of Oscar Wilde that were supposed to cheer him up but only made him feel worse. Inevitably, he ended in his chair staring at the cupboard door, listening to Mahler, slowly being drawn into its orbit like an asteroid to a dark moon.

At four, the grandfather clock chimed, and the good Major rose from his desk. With trepidation, he opened the cupboard door that revealed nothing but a bare cupboard. Devoid of shelves, drawers, sheets or books. The only object tacked to the centre wall was a two by three portrait of his dead wife kept ever illuminated by the one-hundred-watt bulb that had no switch, and he wept beneath its frame.

And then the pain was done. The stoic household silence swept away, Spartan regime dismissed, and the commissioned officer became William Spencer LeNobel, civilian and aged man of passion. The effect on his face was palpable. His eyes dried. His wrinkles smoothed. His lips and fingers moved in sanguine, almost fey flutters and by four-oh-five, he had his first gin and tonic in hand. Minutes later, he was in his easy boy chair listening to Wagner.

Slowly, like the seasons in Vancouver, the tenor of the afternoon changed. The way he pulled the spare flesh on his throat, the subtle downslide of magazines from *National Astronomer* to *Vogue*, from *Vogue* to *Argosy*, *True Detective* and finally the pin-ups of Irving Klaw.

If the Major had a second gin and tonic, the plans for the evening were cast in stone. This was the moment I liked best about the old man. Rubicon crossed, he'd rise, go to the telephone and use the eraser end of a pencil to dial the number which he had committed to memory.

"Hello," said the pleasant female voice on the other end of the phone line.

"Mistress Payne, how are you today?"

"I am well, Spencer. And yourself?"

"The air is damp and so my arthritis has acted up."

"I'm sorry to hear about the arthritis," she said.

"It comes with age."

"We are only as old as we feel."

"And the reason for my call, madam."

A delicate silence waited on the line for six gorgeous seconds.

"Age, Spencer?" she said.

"Loneliness, madam. Sequestered and abandoned solitude."

"And how do we fix such an ancient anthropologic malady?"

"I know it is late," he said, and the second melodramatic pause lasted into eternity.

"Is seven fine, Spencer?"

"Seven is perfect."

And then he hung up. The deal was completed in a few short, stilted sentences that would not have negotiated a junior high school student a spot at the prom. At precisely 1845 hours Spencer changed into his blue pinstripe suit and started his vehicle in the garage, a 1971 Chev Impala which was in such impeccable shape I could only conclude the vehicle was kept garage-bound since his wife's passing. After drinking in the rain-soaked elms, he popped a breath mint and drove down the alleyway towards Kerr Road, where a mistress who was not Mistress Azy put a fitting end to his disconsolate day.

Strategy therefore dictated the best time to call the Major would be right before three o'clock, at the pit of his despair. Cruel, I know, but both beauticians and battalion leaders must be Machiavellians. At that opportunity, I would catch the scorpion with his skin half shed and dispatch him quickly. Perhaps, he would collapse in a sullied mass of pity on the floor and suffer an aneurysm.

Moving closer to his house, I thought of my parents. And it was all bad. My mother wandering away from the playground in her chiffon dress, leaving me alone on the jungle gym. My father shutting the furnace pilot light off before vanishing on a weekend fishing trip. By the time I got to the corner of Forty-Ninth and Arbutus, I yearned for the fear that would rip across the Major's face as his existence imploded.

He sat where he always sat, in his stained-wood study, wearing his loafer suit with a brass pocket watch stuffed into the vest. He had one hand on his globe and the other on a copy of *Hamlet*, with his index finger following what I'm sure he thought was a racy passage. Beside him lay tubes of embalming glue. He didn't notice my presence until the lock on the study door clicked.

"Who's there?" His vision was worse than I thought.

"Who do you think?"

He recognized the voice. He stood with his familiar fingertips-on-the-table gesture.

"Ah, my boy," he said.

My boy, lad, young man, son. Traits of a generation never die. Raze his kind to the earth and salt the ground they walked on.

"That's me," I said.

"What on earth are you doing in here?"

"Use your imagination."

The Major glanced down at the chessboard and his stupid face reddened.

"Well," he said with salamander satisfaction. "Welcome. Come in. I couldn't recall we had an appointment."

"Phoning ahead would ruin the surprise."

His eyes moved across my torso.

"Surprise can be exciting," he said. "Think of El Alamein. Of Hastings. Of Theognis and Cyrnus."

"And here I am."

"I had no idea you were so inclined."

"You were mistaken."

"Forgive me," he said. "I thought you were simply Azy's houseboy and often they don't have independent yearnings."

"I've been promoted."

"Commissioned. Of course. A gin, then." He walked over to the decanter on his mahogany desk. "If I had known, I could have made preparations. Have you seen my cellar? No, of course you haven't. I have such an interesting cellar with many, many unusual friends. We can play. All of us. Together. I'll give you the tour. So many new species of pleasure to explore."

The clock slipped over. The cat slid off the chair. Outside the window a blister beetle bobbled against the pane, its red legs chipping the cedar sill, and then I blew my stack.

"I haven't come here for that, you cocksucking socialist faggot," I said.

Those words slipped out before my sound editor had a chance to veto the banality. The Major pinched the flaccid skin around his Adam's apple. He was legitimately disappointed.

"I should have guessed." He pushed the decanter away. His eyes fell floorward and he slipped one hand into the pocket of his suit. "Every time a young man uses the words 'faggot' and 'socialist' in the same sentence it means he has limited imagination or is acting at the behest of another."

A single push and the door behind me closed. Besides jumping through the window or locking himself in the closet, there was nowhere for him to run. Tactically, the game was already over. Scenarios of Azy's affection blossomed on the horizon.

Without alarm, Spencer tucked a felt marker into Hamlet's swansong scene. "I wondered how long it would be before the next of her brutes came along."

"Now you know."

"Well, turn around and march out. I don't take to threats and don't respond to blackmail. I fought my way across Europe so libertines like yourself could have a reasonable life."

"D-Day is over, princess."

"I understand bravado, but you're going about it the wrong way. If you don't want gin, I have Scotch and prime Canadian whisky. We can have a chat about our shared interests and common ancestry."

"We don't share anything except an address off Clarke Drive and I'm not interested in your liquor."

"No, you're probably blasted out of your mind already. She did mention you had a practice of sniffing, snorting and smoking anything you could get your hands on. What did she tell you?" He glanced up at the clock: eleven minutes to three. "That I raped her? Or perhaps that I went to the police? How about that I was a spy for the Internal Revenue Service or another dominatrix? That last one always infuriates the less confident of her serfs."

"Fuck you."

"You read a lot, I see."

The best I could do was regurgitate Azy's conspiratorial concerns with additional cursives. The Major became petulant.

"I have shrapnel in my hip," he said. "I can't see more than thirty feet and I gave up my commission decades ago. What possible threat could I pose to anybody? I hope you didn't break much getting in. Not the glazed window, anyway. That came all the way from the Transvaal."

"I came in through the heat vent," I said.

He put a finger to his jaw, mulled the facts over, and then his eyes darted about the room to the telephone.

"Don't even try," I said.

"I was going to get a tonic." He reached for the seltzer bottle. The beautiful, old, clear kind that had the carbon dioxide pump and gold trigger.

"You don't drink for another ten minutes. You spend this time bottling blowflies and butchering Shakespeare. Then you go to your closet, get down on your knees and have a good cry."

His worn wedding band clinked against the spout of the bottle. "You sadden me. But don't worry. I have no intention of going anywhere. You want to extract useless information from me through medieval means, so go ahead. I'll tell you whatever you want to know. Probably a few things you don't. Then take what you like. It's par for the course with your kind. The last of her thugs wanted cigarettes. Can you believe that, cigarettes? I don't suppose Azy told you what happened to them, has she? The only thing I ask is that you don't destroy my specimens. They're vital. They have a lot of memories attached, and despite your malice I suspect you have a sentimental streak. I'll show them to you if you like."

"Sorry, not interested."

"Of course not. The cold-hearted mercenary knows only conquest. You do fancy yourself a mercenary, don't you? Crimea, Rhodesia, Sierra Leone. Perhaps not. You obviously don't have enough martial background to appreciate that. My next guess would be the private detective. Hard-boiled Chandler type. No, too common. I'm betting you hold yourself in near religious esteem: a Teutonic Knight. Grails, virgins, vestibules. We'll see how far the nobility extends after you're done. Once your type gets worked into a frenzy the reptilian brain takes over. Did you know the reptilian part of our brain is over three hundred million years old? The only part older than that would be the arthropodic centre. From the first time I saw you, I knew you were her worker bee. Her drone. Beware the autumn, little drone. You don't seem to have any special talents and you certainly don't come from any kind of family, so your days in the hive are done. If you don't mind me asking, what did your father do? Or did you not have one?"

The Major waited patiently and hummed a few bars of "Sentimental Journey." On the wall behind him hung a chalkboard filled with black and white photos: Spencer in uniform in the Belgian Congo, Spencer in Cyprus by a dam project, Spencer in Honduras over a ballot box.

"Leave my parents out of this."

"Have they disappeared into thin air? Walked out on you? More than likely fabricated. The number of Azy's disciples who can't account for their past is overwhelming."

In the second of my rage that caused distraction, the Major sprayed me in the face with seltzer, seltzer that had been laced with ammonia. I tripped over the globe stand and he lunged for the closet. The door locked. I yarded the knob from the wood in a fit of splinters, but the good Major was gone.

The cellar hatch lay open. My head struck a lamp hanging off a cord. After a dozen steps, there was green light and the bottom of an entombed swimming pool, the black swimming lines still painted on worn concrete. Porpoise tiles, curved edges, chlorine vents and chrome rails leading to the nouveau riche vanity that had been popular in the sixties amongst Vancouver's jet-setters, then transformed into an aquamarine bomb shelter during the Cold War. Paeonia roots broke through the rafters. The air was thick with borax. A construction table ran the length of the basin. Dozens of leather-working scalpels, canvas clippers, sewing machines, darning needles and embalming beakers lined up in production mode. Then came the shoes. Many, many shoes. Thigh boots, silk boots, leather boots, boots with spurred cuffs. Strips of tanned leather hides, ankle forms, arch supporters, a hundred wooden heels and countless mesh-wire feet.

A stuffed ferret stood on its hind legs and raised one paw in arrogance. A crocodile hide was stretched over the toe of an anvil. The skin had been cured with arsenic.

"Do you not yet see?" the Major said.

"Where are you?"

"Surely you must understand by now."

"You own the taxidermy shop."

"Everybody needs a hobby."

I walked over to the iron arch mould. "And you make boots for Azy."

"I'll make them for anybody." The Major stood in the corner of his studio with his white hair still in place, the buttons on his tailored suit still done up, his oxford shoes still polished. He reached up to the darkness, pulled on a cord and the swimming pool turned bomb shelter–zoo lit up in stage light. An embalmed carcass of a giant grasshopper with a wingspan of a Cessna floated above us and I kept thinking: Gwendolyn Sharpe, Gwendolyn Sharpe, insects, boots, Gwendolyn Sharpe.

The distance between us closed quickly, and this time there would be no miscalculation, no furlough, no mercy. My exoskeletal creature took over and I struck him in the face with a right cross, and I struck him in the chin with an upper cut, and then my hands riveted around his throat. Brave as he might have been, a wounded sixty-nine-year-old veteran with bits of shrapnel still embedded in his hip stood no chance against the monstrosity of youth.

For vice, I seized a tube of glue off the table and stuffed the nozzle up his nose until the white foam came out his mouth. It bothered me that he didn't panic. I wanted to see that dreadful look of a gazelle being taken down on the savannah. But all I saw in his eyes was the reflection of my father walking away between the elm branches, never looking back, and then nothing but contempt.

The good Major had, of course, been right. I didn't stop there. I ripped his prize trophies limb from limb. The bighorn Sheep, Kenyan jackal and Meller's mongoose, all shredded and shorn. I pulled the antlers off a stuffed white tail and chewed on the pulpy nose until the black base dissolved between my teeth, and then I snapped the spine of a beaver, stomped out the eyes of a woodland bison and then I went to work upstairs. I overturned his desk and broke his globe. There were chestnuts in the centre. I dishevelled his books, the volumes of Keats and Shakespeare, Kant and Wordsworth and then stuffed his chess set into the oven and set the dial to four seventy-five. The sentimental blow, the one that would hurt most, I saved for last. Into his sacrosanct cupboard I went and ripped the photo of his wife off the wall. She was a homely woman, white blouse with dark hair, staring into the camera with horse eyes and a sad, black bow tie.

I broke the glass frame across my knee and a bundle of her photos and letters flooded over my feet, handwritten notes from the war, the Depression, a UN mission in Nicosia and a photograph — a black and white snapshot of the Major, his wife and a woman wearing short pants who looked frighteningly familiar, standing by a bungalow, and then there was simply nothing left to break.

By the time I got back to Azy's street, the sun had set. Houses glowed with Halloween lights. On her back porch, I realized my flesh was cold, dried-perch scaly. Every time I closed my eyes, an image of the Major flashed before me: the Major with his hands over his face, the Major sprawled on the floor holding his hip. His broken cane, his ripped shoelaces.

Azy came out wearing a black dress with the sides slit to the hip. Her hair was done up in a bouffant and she sported a frosted martini.

"Where the hell have you been?" she said.

"Where do you think?"

She put down the glass on the stove. "That was this afternoon. It's now after nine."

"Why didn't you tell me he wasn't human?"

"That's why he needed a pounding." She flicked her Slim into the sink. "But you need not be all day there. Recall, we have a show tonight."

Not really. There might have been an agreement in principle, but she couldn't complain about running overtime on a job that she herself had commissioned.

"You could have told me what he kept in his basement," I said.

"If anyone asks, I know nothing. You know nothing. You smell."

Not, "Are you all right?" Or, "Are you hurt?" Or, "Thank you." Just, "you smell." Once she had established the deed was done, she picked up her glass again and thought of the future, or at least the evening ahead.

"What's on your face?"

I wiped my cheek. The froth stuck to my palm. As a youngster I could recall balls of pith being left by cicadae in the tall stalks during baseball season.

"Get in the shower," she said. "Then have Don lube you down. And don't, for God's sake, go downstairs yet."

She turned away, her black shoes leaving tiny scuffs on the kitchen floor. She had on new cologne. Sort of a fascist soft sell. In the shower, the hot water scalded my skin and washed away dirt, blood and wisps of short white hair. When the room was filled with steam, Don came in wearing nothing but his chaps.

"You're not scoring any points, you know," he said and handed me a towel.

"Following orders."

He held up one hand. "All I know is the Countess is downstairs and she's waiting."

"Countess?"

"She's Russian."

"Really?"

"Eastern European, anyway."

"A real countess?"

"Get dry. Azy only sucks up to power or money."

I got out of the shower and the muscles in my back tightened.

"Are you on steroids?" Don said.

"Everybody wants to know."

"Well, you look cut and she's going to like that. She digs it when hard men get broken. Steroids or not, you'd better keep it up all night."

"No problem."

"All right, little doggie. Let's get to it."

Don lathered his hands up with Nitro-Glo and rubbed me down, sort of a cross between tanning solution and industrial grease. Nitro made the skin smooth and golden and reflected the lights in a cheesy Latin stain. Popular with muscle builders and porn stars. Then Cowboy Don handcuffed my wrists and put a halter over my head. The tangle of leather and chrome was a hybrid of horse bridle and space station. A rubber bit went in my mouth, the studded collar went around my neck and reins grew out of my jowls like antennae. Everybody had their hobbies.

In the parlour, Azy pandered to a woman in a black suit and an Arab man who stood around trying to look like a bodyguard. The Countess was stone-cold stunning. She actually did look Russian, aloof and Tsarist, the kind that wouldn't have any problem gunning down a thousand kulaks for fun.

Don pushed me to my knees, and I went into the regular head-bowing mistress routine. She had exceptional calves, as they all do, and she caught me looking, which we all must, and she liked the attention distantly as they can't help. Her ice pick stare was preordained and my turgidity expected as well.

"Da," she said.

Azy came over and whispered in my ear. "She wants a show. You are going to give her one. Do exactly as you are told. No improvs, no deviations and do not say a word."

That meant basically I was going to be a prop. Props don't talk. They don't voice opinions or have desires. Props exist solely for the pleasure of their user. It didn't take a chartered accountant to figure out where the economic dynamics for this night lay. The Countess wanted to watch a scene deep from the repression of her Slavic past. No negotiation. This was her dime and I had it coming.

Azy produced two tungsten pins that resembled tuning forks and punctured my chest with them. My muscles bled and the blood trickled down to my groin.

The Russian sat back and snorted. Her bodyguard got her a lime for her soda. Then Azy came over and touched the forks with a wooden stick until they hummed. A beautiful oboe pitch emanated from my pecs and when they vibrated my whole skeleton rattled along. I screamed. The Russian smiled. She rolled her pearls. When they were finished their martinis the Russian nodded and Azy stood up.

"Just kill him," she said to Don.

Don looked pretty proud of himself, got down on his knees and launched my prostate into orbit. I made a lot of groaning noises, then Don twisted the halter behind my neck garrote style and the Russian liked this a lot. She leaned forward in her throne and let the air slip out of her mouth about Treblinka, glasnost and the dirtier bits of *War and Peace*. My vision went grey around the edges and bubbles sparkled in my head. The Russian pressed close to me and said, "Fuck him, little whore, fuck him," which was sort of backwards, but I got the message anyway.

TWENTY-TWO

AZY WANTED ME back the next day because she said I required the demented, the deviant and draconian. This could have been code that the session would be extremely rough, or a new kitchen faucet needed installing. Hard to tell. She had spoken quickly into the telephone with sharp-edged consonants blasting down the line. The alliteration worried me too. Although the Mistress had always maintained that she despised intoxicants, the evidence au contraire was mounting. Her mood swings had been atrocious, and at the last party her pupils had been nothing but ink dots.

"When?" I said.

"Now."

There was traffic in the background of the receiver and the sounds of people laughing, murmuring and probably drinking.

"I'll be there in ten minutes," she said.

Ten minutes dominatrix time translates to an hour and a half for the rest of the universe. I lingered hoodlum style outside her back gate kicking at rocks, hovering over bushes, and tinkering with birdhouses. Anything to look like I wasn't about to commit a break and enter, which given any other circumstances I probably would have. This was prime B&E country, and the temptation was great. One could pick out the feasible targets in a second. Middle-class bungalows left to ruin decades after stucco went out of style, scant mortise locks on the doors and simple night latches on the sheds. Easy pickings, really. Quarters and dimes left in cups on windowsills as teasers. Portable stereos unplugged on workbenches. Everything ripe for resale. Forgotten rings, necklaces, discarded amber, emeralds, garnets and yes, of course, a garter hanging on an indoor sycamore tree. I was truly tempted, just for sport, to pull off a quickie before my Mistress touched down. But here I would need a cover story and I had no props. Russell's truck with a trade sign would be good, a ladder even better. A skateboard would have been handy, but then I remembered that nobody over the age of fourteen would be caught dead there, so implausible at best. The bottom line was that twenty-one-year-old men didn't hang around in back alleys except if they were up to no good or waiting for a dominatrix.

A 1967 Beaumont pulled around the corner. Bottle-nosed and reckless, the whale made a hard right into the neighbour's automatically controlled garage door. The taillight vanished into darkness and the bumper struck a garbage bin. Just as the driver cursed an inattentive spouse, I gave grace to the gods of bachelorhood. Better you than me, I thought.

"That's you, track star." Azy stood in the main door swinging a set of car keys around her finger. "I don't carry groceries."

The inside of the garage smelled of lawn mower and grass.

"I didn't know this was yours."

"The neighbour is a dull man and hasn't been right since his wife died."

In the trunk were two bags of party favours, a box of shoes along with a case of champagne and fifty feet of hemp rope that had probably been purchased at the shipping yard. Obviously, we weren't going to make two trips.

"You were hot with the Countess," she said. "But don't let it go to your head. You're the kind of toy everyone forgets instantly."

Pretty fair compliment, I guessed. In 1981, being told you were hot was actually better than being hot and porn stars were more popular than presidents. We walked through the gate that had been carefully crafted with roosters etched into the cedar.

"Too bad your dick isn't bigger. Apparently, they're working on surgical enlargements in Copenhagen."

"Denmark?"

"The surgery is illegal here." She contemplated a situation that clearly was unjust.

"Because why?"

"Is everything deniable on that other issue?"

"We went over that."

Her face was blank. Azy didn't like being corrected on business minutes but this time she wasn't sure.

"At the party," I said.

"Nobody cares about a little shit like that anyway, and without us he has no one to talk to."

"He has another mistress."

Yet one more thing wrong with the world at large. She threw her cigarette into the neighbour's bird bath.

"Who?"

"He didn't say."

"You didn't find out?"

"He wasn't coherent in the end."

"I should have given you a camcorder," she said. "It's like Super 8 only there's no reels. They're the future in porn. Speaking of that, there's a new artifact I'm dying to try. It shoots fifty thousand volts. They are being used in South America on political dissidents. You pull the trigger and darts fly out on cables. They puncture the skin, complete the circuit and voila, instant muscle paralysis."

True, an op-ed in the *Christian Science Monitor* claimed that Pinochet had been the most prolific offender for years, but what worried me more was that Azy's pupils darted from left to right with hypersonic speed. At that point, I formed the opinion that she was either crazy, loaded out of her mind or drunk with vengeance and this might not be the best time for a rough session.

"I'll pass on the less than lethal routine," I said.

"I'll put a plastic bag over your head."

We can't help the way we are. Fish swim. Birds fly. I made a second of hesitation, which for Azy was as good as written consent. She stuck her key in the door.

"Don't worry," she said. "Everything will be fine."

But as soon as the door swung open, I knew everything wasn't fine. A thick compost stench hung in the air. Azy babbled on about hemlock garrotes and wanted to know what my collar size was.

A tin of sugar had been spilled on the stove. Crescent tongue marks on the counter. Grey spittle on the fridge. The curtain on the living room rustled once as if whoever had committed the intrusion had just left.

"Where's Audra?" I said.

Azy dropped the keys into a cherry bowl. Her eyes narrowed.

"Hair stylist."

"Don?"

"Another rodeo."

I recovered the baseball bat from the broom closet. After flying over a dozen missions with Russell, I knew exactly what to look for: points of entry, scrape marks, direction of travel. Yet, none present here. There was no ransacking, no usual macro-trauma associated insults with thuggish B&Es. Not even the micro disturbances discernible only by experts: scuffs, heel cirques or smear prints on sills. The dried pampas grass remained in its vase, the Magritte still hung perfectly in the hall. The unwelcome had been, dropped their pheromones and left.

Downstairs was a different story. Couch overturned. Light bulbs shattered. The furniture fabric ripped into long strips. Spitballs hung from the ceiling and everywhere phlegm coloured the walls. Azy pulled a handkerchief. The dungeon was worse off: hobby horse crushed, wooden cross chewed, ropes frayed, cuffs twisted, half-inch metal shackles bent and contorted, the corners whitened with fatigue.

"Don," she screamed, even though we both knew he wasn't there. She kicked the St. Andrew's cross that had been cleft in half. Then she punched a hole through the lampshade.

"I thought you said you took care of this," she said.

"I took care of that."

"Obviously not well enough."

Not the time to argue inductive fallacies. Or quote Shakespeare on the best safety laying in fear. Azy was pissed enough to rip a pack of Tekels in two and smack her own temple.

"Suppose they come back for more?" she said.

"More what?"

She checked the postal slot where clients dropped their cash, then sprinted upstairs. I surveyed the damage from my haunches. It really was fabulous work. The perpetrators had been thorough, methodical and utterly vindictive. Not a single erotic implement remained undamaged. Elk-hide floggers pulverized, chrome needles twisted into pretzels and clamps etched with acid, rendering them useless. What impressed me was the sheer brutality necessary to bend iron cuffs. Hundreds of pounds per square inch. Jackhammers, wrecking bars or electric vice grips might be likely candidates. But no, this wasn't the work of a machine, but of an animal, and the air in Mistress Alexis Dunwell's dungeon got very dirty indeed.

The leather straps not ripped but gnawed. The fabric not scissored but mulched. Everything was fluid drenched and smelled of an orangutan cage. So, gnawed, mulched, digested and spat up. Azy came back in the room. Her perm was coming out.

"They didn't take money," she said. "There's still four and change in the chute."

I did a quick calculation: four hundred fifty times three sessions in two days. Eighty thousand a year. Plus tips.

"Does Audra have a key?" I said.

"Audra doesn't have anything."

"Who could make a copy?"

"Nobody."

"There's no forced entry."

"Then they came down the frickin chimney." Her face hardened into bottom-line calculations. She counted off debts, missed appointments and promotional options.

"What's the stink?" she said.

"Animal excretion."

"What kind of animal?"

"Do you have any infestations?"

Azy sorted through all the possibilities and she kept coming back to the same one.

"It's him," she said.

"He can barely lift his cane."

"Then it's one of his stupid psychic friends."

"What psychic friends?"

"Mind readers. Whatever. The one who finds children. He keeps fucked-up company. You're going to have to get on this one right away. And look into that Copenhagen thing while you're at it."

Copenhagen, clairvoyance, Cache Creek, and all the charnel house memories from my life on Clinton Street now led to one dismal conclusion: I was not going to end up the hero, the discoverer or even the apologist and so, in the end, I met Fielding at the cemetery.

Not my first choice. I wanted a pub. I needed a pint, but he said no, out in the open where all was quiet, and this was his nickel. Forest Lawn was the median point between our two worlds, and

I ended up standing over my grandfather's grave thinking there weren't many coincidences any more. A lot of famous people got buried at Forest Lawn: Aberhart, a premier from Alberta; Victoria Cross winners from both wars; a few local rock stars that had died ignominious deaths.

Fielding came over the hill in a bluster of wind, his black raincoat billowing, his brimmed fedora bending. Here was a man who always underdressed by half a degree and looked comfortable in that element of camouflage. He stopped at the crematorium and smelled a bundle of chrysanthemums that had grown from a mortar crack, like he had all the time in the world. Then came to my side, rolled a toothpick in his mouth and read the name on the disc at his feet.

"The good ones always go too soon," he said.

"My grandmother still talks to him."

"My mother did that too."

"I wonder if it would do any good if they answered."

"Don't go there, lad," he said. "Keep the living busy. Walks, theatre, ferry trips. Stops the monologue. Coming to the cemetery helps. Psychologists call it realization. Do you bring her here often?"

The dead, the dead, always the dead. My life for the past six years had been consumed by the hungry dead. The stone for my grandfather was a brass saucer with his name and no dates, but still more than my parents had. On the fence at the edge of the cemetery, there was a sign that read NO HUNTING.

"She's ill," I said.

"Serious?"

"I guess."

He checked his watch. Gold strap, black face. "Keep the house dry. Moisture is a magic carpet for bacteria."

Fielding rattled the change in his pockets.

"Do you like hot dogs?" he said.

"The last time I had a hot dog was Grade 2."

"In Grade 2 I watched the Depression arrive. But we still ate hot dogs. Coping mechanism, I suppose. There's a stand near the crematorium. Bratwurst pepperoni. The vendor is Greek. He sells them in Central Park after the semi-pro games, then makes his way to sell the leftovers to cemetery staff."

After only a dozen steps, strings of peppered smoke drifted through the hedge. The hot dog vendor waited patiently in a white chef's suit beside his barbecue. Each time he flipped a sausage a yellow flash leapt from the grill.

"Is he waiting for us?"

"Lad, I must tell you. Over the years, I've met a lot of people for hot dogs. Never in the same place twice. But I always know where the stand is going to be. So maybe I've blown my cover, but what the hell, honesty is the best policy. Go ahead and tell me what's on your mind."

"My friend's house was broken into."

He shrugged. "Did she call the police?"

"No."

"Why not?"

"She's paranoid."

"Strange how those two always seem to go together," he said.

I couldn't decide if Fielding had aged, or if he already knew what I was going to tell him. Or if he would give me the same standard lines about morality and missing people as last time, as every time, as the first time, but what the hell, speak, you ancient beast. "There was a lot of money in the house," I said. "They didn't bother to take a dime."

"Is this your friend down off Clarke Drive?"

"The place was badly worked over."

"Youths, probably," he said.

"Too sophisticated for that."

"Ah." His dour smile summed up everything a policeman would think about those who didn't call the police after a crime.

"What's your theory?"

"Not my case."

"Whose would it be, if it were reported?"

"Depends. B&E. Unless other arrangements were made."

Arrangements. Maybe I'd wait a bit. Maybe we could walk. If I waited long enough, perhaps Fielding would give.

"So, the vandalism," he said, finally.

"No televisions or stereos. Only personal things."

"Perhaps not youths then. Although these days the courts are forgiving of that activity. But no. No, lad, it's likely the perpetrator knew the victim, and probably intimately."

"Can't see it," I said.

"When a thief breaks into a rich house, they steal gems and cash. When they break into a drug addict's house, they want drugs. But if they break in, steal nothing and only piss on the pillows, well, that is a statement. Once I investigated an art museum theft. The culprit wanted a Tom Thomson. Which was strange, because in the same room, there was platinum. There were diamonds. He lowered himself via a set of elastic ropes through the glass skylight into the main floor. Unfortunately, on the way down he slit open his scapula. Pulled his bleeding body past three Ming vases valued at thirty thousand dollars to get to his target."

"What happened to him?"

"Died."

"Wasn't there blood on the painting?" I said.

"*Algonquin Park* will never know the difference." Fielding owned a piece of history the rest of us never would. "My guess is a buyer pre-offered him cash. Now, there's a small chance your perpetrator was a slum-ridden lunatic who picked the place at random. But what are the odds of that? We're a city of a million people now."

"The damage was vindictive."

"Suitor. Spurned lover. Estranged spouse."

"She doesn't have any of those."

"Extremist political affiliations." He rolled his hand over. There was an angle I was obviously not seeing.

"No interest in politics."

"Well then. She's an innocent and this is totally random. In which case we shall never know."

"That's not very satisfying."

"No, Big Guy. It's not. But I'd still bet donuts to dollars she has since had contact with the person who has committed the offence."

"She says no," I said.

Fielding stared up at the queer October sky and a red-tailed hawk circled the lawn, then lighted on a mausoleum eave. "Then she's lying to you, lad."

The Greek vendor was a poorly shaven man with a thick moustache and a lot of hair on the back of his hands. He leaned against his barbecue cart and never let go of the spatula. The bratwurst, salami and liverwurst were almost sold out. "Ethnic holiday," he said. "People are hungry after tending to their dead."

There were two quarter-pound chipolatas left on the rack. Fielding pointed with a gesture that meant everything on them and pulled out two fifty-cent pieces. The vendor dished up the dogs. They soaked the buns with fat instantly.

"The house was covered with fluid," I said.

"Blood?"

"No."

"Semen then. Culprits like to leave their mark."

"There was gallons of the stuff."

"They save it up," he said. "In jars. Not only with men. I did one case where the perpetrator smeared her monthly on the mirror."

He bit into the dog and a bubble of fat slithered down his chin.

"I don't think this was from a human being," I said.

"What kind of animal do you suspect?"

"What were those things in the morgue?"

"Descendants of freaks who smoked too much Ganga and raised an incestuous family in the wild. They were born with maladaptations and eked out a living by pilfering rural garbage. Hardly human, and that hurts me to say that. But if you've worked enough files where you find jaws agape, ribs showing and lungs extruding it challenges your boundaries. Found a coal miner who had been dead for years. He had learned how to make a crude form of MDA. Assembled all his chemicals in a shaft and then one day they exploded. Completely embalmed in nitrate phosphorus. Down there for a decade before we found him. No one notices them missing. No one cares. I only wanted to show you what happens when life goes astray. You're young. You're entitled. You never see it. But I see it all the time. The outcast, the bizarre. Those who were exiled from birth, and I don't want you ending like that."

"Were those my parents in the morgue?"

"Lad, those people are nowhere near your parents. And I don't concede you believe that. Do you know what I think? I think you are using the loss of your parents as an excuse for utter licence, which is not liberty, and from your strategic position, definitely unwise. I know you came for advice, so I'll give some to you. Starting macro. Cut down on the drinking. Climb a mountain or join the army instead. Lay off the weed. Take up painting. Landscapes, none of this Pablo Picasso garbage, and don't linger over Marxist poets. They all end up killing themselves. Try flying. I know a colleague who can get you well cued for the air force if you're inclined. Stay away from opportunistic company. They may seem like fun, but in the end, they'll destroy you and rub their heels in the ashes of your conscience."

Fielding overdid the metaphors, but he was a hard fuck to not like. I stuffed the dog in my mouth and the gristle hurt my molar. The salt, the grease and the chewy bits of what may have been hoof slid down my throat. The fog was covering all of the south slope, turning tree tops into dim pinpricks of green.

"Eat regular meals too," he said. "Listen, lad, I won't be the one to take you off to arrest processing when the hammer comes down. That will be another detective. Probably in robbery or vice but I'll come and visit you in jail. Not to bail you out, mind. And not to say I told you so, but to make sure you're all right. Your survival is important to me. For sentimental reasons. Remember this, jail is not fun, there's no women, no drugs and you would miss your parents even more than you miss them now."

TWENTY-THREE

IN THE END, all our fathers disappear. They leave. They go. They vanish behind an elm, between two trailers, onto a tram or at a fork in the forest trail. Into old age. Unpensioned. Uninterred and for the most part, utterly fragmented. At first, they are half gone, shadowed in wars that were not fought for the reasons we believed. And suddenly they are gone completely, dissolved in myths built on rules we did not understand. But we keep looking. We never give up. We search with compasses and maps. With binoculars and microscopes, forensics and sextants. Equations and theories. On top of mountains, at the bottoms of lakes. In temples, in whispers, in the darkest of homes, in the cruellest of winters and the autumn of lies. We look everywhere, except for right in front of us, right at that very moment.

Even Russell J. Hobbes, who leaned back on the box of his newly painted Dodge truck, beneath the wilted berries of a mountain ash, had, at least that very moment. He had his toothpick, his Marlboro cigarette and his wide-belted jeans. Remaining suspended in time was his primary objective, always twenty-one, never weeping for what had slipped through his fingers and always believing the summers in Vancouver were endless.

The Dodge had been pimped out Deep South style. Rodeo red paint job, chrome exhaust manifolds that extended vertically from the cab and a Black Sabbath emblem enmeshed permanently in the grill.

"Hot, isn't it?" he said.

I skipped judgment.

"Thought we'd go for a ride," he said. "Discuss business terms." He flicked his smouldering tobacco into the dried grass and watched the sparks spread blade by blade towards the rail ties.

"Not at my house."

"Relax," he said. "We'll tackle the geographic details over dinner."

"I don't have any money."

"Dude, how is that possible? Wait, don't tell me."

"I spent it on prescriptions for my grandmother."

"That is such horseshit."

Which was mostly true. Ninety-six percent, anyway. I had put down four dollars and thirty-eight cents towards a prescription for T3s the doctor had written for Grandmom and consumed at least half for myself, but inevitably, the other one hundred and sixty dollars had been invested elsewhere.

We drove through the opaque landscape of afternoon Burnaby. Ashen oak, railway lines of tar and scarabs in the sunlight. Worn upholstery. Flat warehouses smelling of fennel and backyards dotted with terriers and parakeet cages. Maybe the last day of warmth before the the Gulf of Alaska rains moved in to drench the city with the annual cycle of fog.

On the roadside, Russell spotted two high school girls wearing striped sailor tops and history's last recorded pairs of hot pants. They had books tucked under their double Ds and one of them applied lipstick. Russ raked a quick swivel on the steering wheel and the Dodge lurched sideways in a spray of gravel. He blew the girls a kiss. They gave him back the finger.

"Don't bother," I said.

"Cheer up, dude. I wasn't going to kill them."

"A hit and run is not flattery."

"Are you on your period? You look like a kid who's had his dog put down. No wait. Cat. You're way more of a cat kind of person. Me, I hate them. Once I gave my sister's cat airplane glue and watched it fall off furniture all day."

"You had a sister?"

"That was a long time ago," he said.

A long time ago Russell had been an awkward child, like everybody else. I remembered him sprawling down the halls of our elementary school with his hair exploding and his fists striking walls, doors or any human face that happened to be inconveniently placed. There were fragments of his past that stuck out like sharp rocks, a penknife used for threats, a dead raccoon found beneath his desk. He once spat on a teacher, but there were also vast periods of time when he was simply not there. He played no instruments or sports, was not once in the school theatre. I remembered him only for his lost and violent ways, and no one had ever known if he had a sister, or even parents, and it would never have occurred to anyone to ask.

"Do you have any normal relationships?" I said.

"I know this customs guy. He gets confiscated military gear from Chile. I trade them for Rompies. That is normal. You spend too much time worrying over useless stuff. Our future is doable, Woody, as I shall now demonstrate."

Fascist governments. Temperate rainforests. How the two of us wound up together was starting to look like natural selection. We hurtled down a dirt road along the banks of the mighty Fraser River uncomfortably proximal to our Tuesday job at the geriatric home. Dykes, farms, old barns, a scene straight out of Jongkind. Russell shifted gears. Most certainly we were not really going anywhere, but just getting smaller and smaller.

"I have a date," I said.

"Did I hear you right?"

"I'm telling you where my priorities are." I flipped through a copy of *Hustler* that was stuffed into the glovebox. Beside the August edition were a stack of business cards that read Russell Hobbes, Publisher; Russell M. Hobbes, Member of Parliament; Russell P. Hobbes, PhD; and a new one, Russell T. Hobbes, Esq., Horticultural Entrepreneur.

"Genius, don't you think?" he said.

In the centre of a pumpkin patch, gourds exploded under our tires and sent yellow strands spattering across the earth. There were cornstalks and hay bales that had been abandoned for years and I wasn't liking the imagery one bit: rustic seclusion, bucolic philosophy and an emasculated sense of the future that reeked of river water. To the left, the Cambie Street Bridge unloaded a stream of commuters from a hard day's work so they could go home to die. Upslope, a new legion of suburban lots were having swimming pools pre-dug into their municipal contract. Either way, this was the drowned land. This was the swamp land. Russell stopped at a fence and pointed at the New Jerusalem: a silo, a corral and red barn with a half roof collapsed.

"Have we taken up farming?"

"Not farming, dude. Get the gate."

I got out of the truck and went to the lock, an iron sway bar with an embroidered latch. Maybe before the war someone had thought they were going to get rich raising pigs. Dumped in the boggy field were crates of expired explosives, so someone had thought they were going to get rich doing that too.

Russell parked the Dodge by a barn. A stray chicken moulted in a culvert and down the road a sheep did Wagner. Basically, the animals were in bad shape. A skinny cow, a lame duck. The field stunk of rotting squash.

"This is so farming," I said.

"Horticulture, buddy. Horticulture. There is a difference. Farming is for fags."

"What do you know about horticulture?"

"I know weed sells for twelve-eighty a pound." Russell lit up and leaned over an oil drum. "Think about it. All this land. All this seclusion. All this market availability. Remember the high-tech lights, guy? Your grandmother is excused from jury duty."

"The plan doesn't sound very exact."

"When they built the railway, did they know where exactly it was going? No, they didn't. They put down the tracks, pointed them and the next thing they knew they had a country."

"They guessed the Pacific Ocean."

"The only liquid Macdonald could find came in twenty-six-ounce bottles. But the point is, Woody, he took a chance. He gambled. He won. We can too."

Suddenly the night was late. My head pounded. The thought of duck soup was revolting. There was an infection starting in my ribs where two nights previous, persons unknown had perforated me with a set of Nubian bone pins. I picked straw off the hood of a rusted Massey Ferguson.

"Triple negative on a rural career," I said. "I've got school to finish."

"Dude, I hate to break it to you, but you have not been to classes in three weeks. Last time you talked about school was when we were whacked on weed. You listed all the midterms you said you were going to write telepathically. Even I didn't buy that. You are what they call a grade A dropout. Besides, school is a dead end. How often do you get laid there?"

"Nobody gets laid on a farm either. People go crazy and then they go missing."

"No more trips down memory lane," Russell said. "Nobody is going missing. Here, we are masters of our own fate. Weed, 'DA, acquired goods. Girls, if you like. I'm not ruling anything out. We could start a newspaper: *The Daily Worker with Horse*. We could have a beer hall. A Putsch. Give history lectures. There is one electric meter on this entire local for a hundred outlets, if you get my meaning hydroponically. We could issue passports. Freedom, equality, fraternity, blah, blah, blah, but we need the farming front basics. That's where you come in. Silos, tractors, you know that stuff."

A squabble of fowl broke out from the loft and a crippled mallard plummeted into a water trough. In my mind, a horrid image of my mother catching her bikini strap in our old backhoe flashed on. She had turned her suntanned chest and waited pensively while the neighbour crossed the field to lend a helping hand.

"I hope you're not too attached to this plan," I said.

"I've already made the initial investment."

"What kind of investment?"

"I've bought a horse."

"You'll kill it," I said.

Russell took a carrot from a slop bag and went to the fence. He whistled. Then he called a few names; he obviously hadn't named the creature yet, and from the guts of the barn came the sound of a plodding, ancient animal. A pint-sized Shetland, probably a reject from a children's carnival, limped to the fence and showed its ugly teeth. One of its eyes had gone milky white.

"Beauty, isn't she?"

"It's a he, Russ."

Russell stuck the carrot between his lips, then leaned across the fence. The horse stubbed its hoof on a stone and gummed the carrot out of its master's mouth.

"Please, stop," I said.

"Why are you so negative?"

"Because I'm going."

"Going where?" he said. "I am the one who is trying to show you the straight and narrow and all you give me is disrespect."

A sad collection of chickens ate seed out of a milk flat. Beside the crate was a stack of burlap sacks and blocks of ice. Inside the sacks were a variety of skinned animal carcasses: chickens, ducks, maybe coyote or possum, which confirmed the obvious, that my arch criminal associate was now a player in the underground poultry market.

"This stinks."

"Stay away from that bitch," he said. "She's absolutely psycho."

Russell stuffed a carrot into his mouth. He was hurt and I liked that part. His shoulders got half a size smaller, and I should have boxed his face black and blue like when I first met him by his truck with Azy.

"You should know. You're her janitor, Hobbes."

"Yeah, well. At least I don't beg nutty bitches to choke me to death."

"I guess we'll leave that to Miss Carmine and the Sailor Boy Sissies."

Russell let the carrot slip away. The horse didn't bother to pick it up. He stroked the animal's mane. His chin crumpled like a dried prune.

"Don't come around anymore," I said.

And then I turned and walked out across the Brussels sprout field and made my way back towards the argon lights of Marine Drive.

I got home angry. No surprise there, I'd been doing that for five years. But this time I knew I had only myself to blame. Break a few vases. Snap a few picture frames. Complain about the hardship I endured as a child and curse my kindergarten aid. Russell J. Hobbes, psychopath, petty thief, bully, stranger and ultimate lowlife had made me feel something no other human being could: guilty, and I hated him for it. Lie down with dogs, as Fielding would have said.

I opened the basement door and wondered where my half-medicated grandmother was. The furnace creaked over. Stan's ancient bicycle gathered dust under the stairs. My skin itched. My scalp hurt and calcified blotches broke out on my arms. Looking Fit on the way for sure. ETA about seven minutes at best. Upstairs, a rancid smell of floral juice lingered in the hallway, and a sickly-sweet layer of pustule piss was smeared across a Toni Onley painting my GM wanted to believe was genuine.

Her bedroom door was ajar. The inside looked murky and the odour emanating from the dark was septic.

"GM, are you in there?" I said.

No answer. I knocked twice.

"I need to talk to you, Grandmom."

Still nothing, but there was truly scant reason why she would want to talk to me. In the past few months, I had got her stung by wasps, swiped her medicine, mixed too many lies with the truth and used her basement as a stolen property depository. I pushed the door half an inch. The silence made me wonder if I could remember CPR. This was one of my greatest fears coming home: finding her cold in bed, gums blackened, eyeballs dried, and having to put my mouth on her black pit knowing the cause was hopeless, cruel and totally unnecessary. Why could she not disappear neatly as my mother and father had done? To be honest, that dream wasn't the worst one. The worst was that I would come home and find her copulating with a giant scorpion, his red tail flashing back and forth as the two of them writhed in arthropod pleasure.

"Grandmom, if you are here kick the bedpost twice," I said. "If you're not, don't bother. Something has died in there. Not you, I hope."

An October breeze moved through the bedroom window and brushed the drapes. A faint buzz drifted through the night. The streetlamp cast a wedge of light across the bed and revealed only two pillows, a flowered comforter and her polished hutch decorated with a framed photo of Granddad. He was holding a glass of JWB, looking pleasantly pissed.

Although the comforter was flat, the stench emanating from the linen was undeniable. I waited for the closet door to open. Perhaps she passed out with a double dose of Nyquil while trying on new shoes. In the window I saw a dank reflection of a creature that was not at all likeable. Handsome, perhaps, determined sometimes, but also cold, waxy and utterly inhuman. A high collared Jekyll and Hyde driven totally by desire and a tight selfish mouth that spoke often to company not of his own species.

Time to find a drink, a dram, a draught, a woman in latex, anything, any place but here, and the comforter cackled. Then rippled. When the quivering sounded too much like laughter, I ripped back the covers. A million flying ants pulsated on the sheet, buzzing, chattering, squirming, waiting, plotting. The tiny yellow caplets bubbled in their satisfied *I told you so* tirade and then the winged beasts exploded from the bed. They spread out tornado style, vindictive and guttural, bringing with them the ugliest memories from my past: a bolero gone bad when my father broke the Mixmaster; my mother with a migraine, choking the cat, then pitching it into the sink; a forlorn couple staring in silence at each other over a forgotten anniversary dinner. The creatures twisted around the room and bounced off the window. They turned through the curtains and blew past the venetian blinds. Finally, the crystalloid wings struck a high-pitched Bach as they bounced off the ceiling, and they were up my nose and they were in my ears and down my pants too. Most were no bigger than a pebble with serrated jaws looking for anything sentimental to feast upon.

Grandmom's sheets were soaked with mucus; old come stain, bottom of the barrel hotel slime cack, except thicker; a sticky resin with traces of blood branching out in fractal ice formation. Enmeshed in the waxy mud were my grandmother's slippers, her watch and ankle bracelet. In the centre of the mattress lay a sunken outline where her body should have been, and had I possessed the decency to check on her welfare in the past three days, I would have noticed there too a hospital bracelet with her name and admitting number embossed upon the side.

I backed out of the room, wiped the bugs from my face and stuffed my grandmother's sweater under the door. There was no trace of my GM anywhere in the house and no signs of a struggle, no breached entrances, no broken windows, no ripped purses, nothing. The household totally lacked any indication of human intrusion, and over the course of the last few months, I had become an expert at identifying those.

A few of the creatures that had made it out of the bedroom attached themselves to the light bulb in the pantry or were trying to figure the intricacies of our vacuum bag. The clock above the fruit cupboard said nine fifty-four. Grandmom was never out past nine-fifteen. Groceries were completed at seven-thirty. She was home from the library avec Tolstoy, Cohen and Richler by eight-twenty.

All her medication was in place and accounted for including the evening dose, so either she had OD'd, or forgotten to administer or was simply gone. The most prudent plan was to start combing the back alleys. They all looked the same at night: cedar fences, dented garbage cans, bramble bushes and stray transmission lines. You didn't have to be senile to get lost in this suburban mess. Problem was, Azy's party started at ten, ten-fifteen if you were fashionable, ten-thirty if you were brave because the doors were locked promptly at eleven. I had thirty-five minutes to form a plan, then make the eight-mile drive to Kerr Road on half a gallon of gas. The phone rang.

"Who is this?" I said.

"This is Stan."

"Stan who?"

"Which Stan were you expecting?"

"I was hoping for GM."

"Why?"

"Can't find her."

"What do you mean you can't find her?"

"No big deal. She's just not here."

"Where did she go?"

"No clue," I said. "Bingo, maybe?"

"She doesn't play bingo, Cirrus."

"Canasta?"

"How could you lose your own grandmother?" he said.

"I did not lose her."

"She's right out of the hospital. Your job was to look after her."

"She's feeling much, much better."

"What's going on down there?"

"Nothing," I said.

"What's that noise?" Stan said.

"The house is slightly infested. Don't sweat it, Stan. It's nothing a good exterminator can't handle."

Stan breathed a deep mature sigh. Just another problem for him to solve. Just another Dunkirk to plan. Another Armageddon to avoid. I could hear him opening his black day-timer and adding this latest catastrophe to his list.

"Where are you?" I said.

"Driving west on the Trans-Canada Highway."

"Why?"

"We talked about this."

"Not on my calendar, Stan. Must be a different brother."

"Cirrus," he said. "Did you just visit a brewery?"

"When are you arriving?"

"We're in a garage," he said. "The car is broken."

"Your car is brand new."

"The radiator is plugged with bugs."

"What kind?"

"I have no clue, Cirrus. You are the expert. Besides, they are bug mulch now."

I thought a burst of hail might have swept over the roof, or perhaps a volley of automatic gunfire had erupted on Clinton Street, but in reality, it was only my pulse breaking the two hundred mark.

"They swarmed the car," Stan said. "Mindy got stung."

"Is she all right?"

"The doc gave her Benadryl."

I wanted badly to say *screw you, Stan! You are on acid, aren't you? You were drunk and you crashed the car and now you're trying to blame it on me.* But I knew that was even less likely than clay diggers in his carburetor.

"Let's start working on a plan to get Grandma back," he said. "Go to the pharmacy and the late-night shopping markets. She can't have gone far."

"I'll take care of Grandmom. I think you should put off your arrival for a while."

"No chance, big brother. I need to bail us all out from whatever mess you have got us into."

"I think under the circumstances, that not coming here would be the best bail. I can fix this situation. This will be fine. Things will work out, like when Mom and Dad were here."

"What?" A sequestered silence stuck in the line. "Don't romanticize crap, Cirrus. This is long distance."

"I am not romanticizing anything."

"Mom was a slut and Dad was a nasty drunk."

"I'm not listening to this."

"Then be useful," he said. "Get in your car and come get us in Hope. We'll all look for Grandmom together."

"I am not driving to Hope."

"Are you too loaded to find the car keys?"

"I'm going out to look for her by myself."

"As if," Stan said.

I slammed down the phone, smashed it over the fridge and then got in the car and drove westward. Halfway through the intersection of Forty-First and Kerr, the first Fit hit home. There was the typical preamble — a strong sense of melancholy, the ability to remember minute details from the past and a feeling of displacement as if my body was a salty outline in a shallow sea. Then the centre line went fuzzy, but the rest of the world became absolutely clear: lost twigs, lunar cycles, blue auras, backgammon boards, stripes of grease, oyster shells, the reason for desire itself and most poignantly, the route to Gwendolyn Sharpe's home.

Although I'd never been there, all I had to do was keep the car pointed intuitively and make a conscious effort to not make the turn down to Azy's place. Of course, just thinking about not going to Azy's place made my thoughts drift that way, and on top of the lamppost, dead ahead, an owl landed, white and luminous. Except of course, this was no owl at all, being nine feet high, exoskeletal and bending the city fixture earthward with its weight.

The creature lifted its barnacle head and waited for the perfect ambush moment, when the car was at the point of no return. And at one hundred and five kilometres an hour, that point came quickly. The beast swept down, and the mystery of whether insects could scream was solved once and for all. Its cry spread out across the city, past my old farmhouse and into the Fraser Canyon where my brother lay stranded with his pathetic girlfriend and scrubby dog. Glass shattered. Claws punctured the windshield. The car jumped the boulevard, plowed through a bush and struck a municipal tamarack tree. Steam shot out of the radiator and my 1976 Buick Skyhawk was destroyed with a little less than two hundred and thirty thousand miles on the clock. Oddly, the vehicle had been spun counter-clockwise at the last second, avoiding a direct hit on the trunk, which would have propelled me promptly through the windshield in my usual unbelted state. Although the dash and speedometer were shattered, I suffered not so much as a cut. A total enigma, really. Remaining abundantly clear however, was the reality that the night air was already filled with police sirens and I wasn't going to find Gwendolyn Sharpe that evening. She had already found me. The only sane thing left to do was abandon the Buick and spend my last few hours of freedom where it really mattered.

In later years, I'd interpret the smell for what it was, but as I stood on Azy's porch, battery acid appeared a likely candidate. From inside the house came the faint sound of bass and the din of party conversation gone wrong: arguments over pressure points, asphyxiation limits and the correct adjectives for slave humiliation. When you go looking for your parents, be careful where you go. The search will always take you to places you don't want to be.

The Mistress opened the door and she looked different from the last party, desultory, agitated and bored. Her hair was tinted red and twisted in stray tangles on her head. She smoked a cigarette that was burnt down to the filter and her pupils were black dots.

"You're late," she said. A sullen woman in a rubber coat strode through the rear foyer, leaving the upstairs utterly empty. The only remains of any action were a dozen spent beer bottles, a knocked-over pretzel tray and an undecipherable stain on the floor.

"I crashed."

"Don't when I've got clients to appease."

Azy's costume was new, a cross between praetorian guard and praying mantis. Metallic scales clung to her torso and her thighs were slicked with Nitro-Glo. I recalled watching a Super 8 reel where the good Mistress choked a Filipino boy blue between those muscular limbs and left him motionless on her Persian rug, smeared with oil.

"Get me a drink," she said.

I went to the bar. The air reeked of hemp. Obviously, the rules on intoxicants were loosening up. Half the lights were turned down.

One of them had been smashed out. A plastic pumpkin cast an orange hue on the wall. A holiday I had worshipped since childhood had utterly escaped my consciousness.

In the kitchen I met Audra, or at least observed her. Azy's house girl had been bound and gagged to a wooden rack by the sink. The knots keeping her limbs in place were so tight her skin turned grey and the ball that had been stuffed into her mouth had the word SLUT etched into the rubber. I'd like to say she was nude, but there wasn't a lot of skin left to be seen. The greater part of her body was covered in sealant wax. Only her dark bush of pubic hair lay exposed. A tub of pink paraffin steamed on the counter. Another ladle would have entombed her completely, which meant pore suffocation, but she didn't seem to care. She gazed up to the ceiling stoically, figuring whatever happened here was probably better than at the other end of an immigration hearing.

Audra was slow at realizing she was no longer alone. One eye drifted aft in sadness, wet with tears, but she couldn't utter a word with the gag down her throat. Azy entered, picked up the ladle and studied the concave bowl intently.

"I understand slavery." She flicked her ash into the sink. "I know why it has existed for centuries and why it will continue to exist always. It has nothing to do with economics. The Romans, the Goths, the Mandarins, they all knew. A culture that embraces slavery is strong. Slaves are weak. They are incapable of comprehending pleasure on their own. The slave enjoys servitude because they will never know loss and so it goes on. She's still a virgin. Can you believe that? It's a custom they have in Pango Pango or wherever she came from. No intercourse and no pubic hair shaving. I can't stand humans who won't shave. They're like mastodons."

Azy made a Jackson Pollock squiggle of wax on the woman's breast. Audra shut her eyes and endured.

"Where have you been?" she said.

I didn't bother to answer. She wouldn't have listened.

"You missed a good show." Her voice attempted enthusiasm, but her minuscule dark pupils didn't flinch. "Don't worry. We'll have another. You're the star. Wash first. You're covered with that horrible film again."

Then she picked up the entire pot of wax with both hands and dumped it onto Audra's torso. The wax spattered on my shoes and trousers. The girl's jaw quivered as if she were repeating an ancient prayer. Azy smoked. The wax hardened.

"What happened to everyone?" I said.

"I had to weed out the fakirs."

"The who?"

"The last thing we need is the UN here."

Azy put her finger under my chin. She smiled an unfriendly smile. "But now you're here, I don't have to worry. Do I?"

Of course not, Mistress. No worries at all, Mistress. I was there. I was hers. Azy used her manicured fingernails to get beneath the hardened wax on Audra's crotch. Then she ripped everything back and Audra choked on spit. The hair stuck to the wax like a thousand dried earthworms on a hot sidewalk.

"Do you want the vinegar?" she said to her racked roommate.

Audra cried and shook her head.

"Get it," she said to me.

A two-six jug of household vinegar waited on the counter. I recalled my mother standing on a chair scrubbing the kitchen window, humming "Somewhere Over the Rainbow" with a vinegar bottle like this one.

"Don't give it to me," Azy said. "Dump it on her."

I waited a second. I figured in a moment she'd move onto something else: napalm, bamboo shoots, sulfuric acid or else settle for reminiscing on the aesthetics of de Sade, but she watched me. The insect creature spread its bony wings and I dumped away. The screaming was pure joy and when done, Azy leaned forward and kissed me on the mouth. The empty bottle rattled on the floor.

"Let's go downstairs," she said.

The good mistress sat up on the counter and put one hand on Audra's forehead. A minute passed and her eyes wandered towards the door. Outside, a thousand moths circled the hanging porch lantern.

"Are we waiting for someone?" I asked.

"I suppose."

"Sal?"

"God, no."

"Are you all right?"

"I'm fabulous."

"You look lost."

"No more than you," she said and had a good point.

She turned and walked out onto the porch. I went downstairs to the parlour. Don was watching gay porn on the television with a younger man in a cowboy hat who was getting up to leave.

"What's up?"

"Azy's in a mood," Don said.

"Has Sal disappeared?"

"No point in getting sentimental."

The youth adjusted his hat brim and tightened the buckle on his pants. "Party's over," he said. He bumped past me with a petulant gesture and went up the stairs.

"Azy's deep-fried her housemaid," I said.

Don shrugged. "I think someone may have slipped her MDA."

"That should turn her on."

Don gave me the once over. "Look bud, sit down and have a beer. I'd play it cool tonight."

"I don't want to play it cool."

"Really man, I don't want to see you lose your nuts."

The stairs creaked. The wainscotting rippled. On the far side of the room Azy crossed one slicked leg in front of the other and I didn't care about my nuts. People have asked me why humans do this sort of thing, abide so much, suffer so greatly, take so many foolish chances, and the truth of the matter is, before the dark glass of desire only the truly living know the pain of absolute free will.

Rachael and Tim leaned against the door frame. A threesome looked good. Tim could drag out in his best Mae West imitation and the amused mistress would tie his dick into a pretzel. Azy slithered up to Rachael and squeezed her ass.

"How do you feel about hive play?" she said.

"Pardon?"

"Insect sex."

Azy's lips parted into a predatory pout that was obscene and lethal. Hallucinatory bongo music played in the background. Rachael disengaged her ass from Azy's hand and studied the bubbles in her gin fizz.

"Negative on the six-legged stuff," Rachael said.

"What's your issue?'

"No one is into it anymore, Alex."

"Cirrus is."

"I'll leave that up to him," Rachael said. "Things have gone a little sour for us tonight."

"How about hub-bub here?"

Tim checked his watch, swiss with aluminum dials.

"He's not into it either," she said.

"Can he not speak?"

"It's late," Tim said.

"Fucking princess," Azy said.

She turned my way. Her breath smelled of apples. Her fingers clattered around my collar, undid my buttons and then there was that beautiful Titanic feeling of sinking down to the cold floor again.

Tim raised his tired eyes, shot me a warning glance and then said to his wife, "Do you want to split?"

"Yeah," she said. "Let's go."

"Hang around," I said. Good friends were always fun to have. The more the merrier. Besides with Tim in play there was always an air of Greek tragedy in the making.

Tim gave my torso a winsome glance. "Watch yourself, guy," he said. He took his wife by the hand, and they glided up the stairs. A yellow dress bounced off the back of her tanned ankle.

Azy sucked in a breath and twisted a set of clamps. Leaving without permission was a cardinal sin. The crow's feet around her eyes flexed. She flipped on the winch motor and whispered poetic threats in my ear. Always nice to hear, but a lot didn't make any sense: tambourines, tangerines, how many men had loved her, what her cruellest month was and how awfully fond she was of me, which wasn't exactly true, so that should have been my first clue. There were others. The odour of fructose. The buzzing of wings. How sloppy her knots were. Her nose twitching. Then everything around me vibrating, the fault lines in the ceiling, the pressure bars in the air, the cobwebs strung as spandrels in space, but I ignored all of that. Just like I ignored the clove hitches around my neck, the locked D-ring in the rafter and the brambles in my scrotum. When the winch lifted me skyward, my shoulder blades touched and cartilage snapped, but I missed that also, because the available oxygen left in the cosmos shrank faster than Saturday night cocaine. This was only her warm-up act and already she was sweating. Usually Azy liked the tension, the crescendo, the tease, but with me spinning above the rug, that had all been forgotten. She got into a flogging routine way too fast and there was a lot of wraparound. After she beat my ribs with horsehair, wire brushes and nettle fern, she ripped the brambles from my crotch with duct tape which split open my perennial divide. The blood on the floor didn't seem to faze her. Perhaps it was not mine. In the corner she found the plastic wrap that Russell and I had swiped from the warehouse. The texture appealed to her. She pushed her tongue into the plastic, licked, and her eyes fluttered shut. Finally, she cut off a long strip with a scalpel and wound the translucent bandage around my knees, my chest and my neck. My flesh moistened and rivulets of sweat collected under the plastic. In half a minute, I was soaked, but all Azy could do was to bite her lip and push back her hair.

"You look like someone waiting to become something," she said.

At the winch box, she collected a half-inch rope and bit down on the coil. Her heel skidded on the floor. Either she, the earth or the shoes were too high. Then she slung the rope through an eyelet, made a slip knot and plunged the hemp over my head. Any other time I would have been keen, but Azy mentioned her father a couple of times and the plot got very unsexy. She used the words "bastard," "prick," "whore," and "irascible charlatan," and with that algebra, the discourse of the evening plunged to the density of a blackhole.

"Ease up," Don said. He came around the corner holding a tin of Molson and sat wearily on the couch.

Azy wasn't listening. Her nose screwed up Brillo-brush stiff and she stuck a finger between the hemp and my throat. Not much room there. That part she liked also. She chewed her lip. Bits of red gloss spat out of her mouth. Then she toyed with the shackle winch and decided when would be the most erotic moment to let the slack go.

"I don't think it makes any difference to you" — she studied her knuckles for the longest time, almost as if she had forgotten who they belonged to — "if your parents are dead or alive, or if you are either. Your kind makes me sick, and they always have. You and your sycophantic friends. Running secret societies to purge the world of anything that frightens them. Well, I frighten them. They send you along to work for them and you end up working for me. Don't get me wrong. I appreciate the irony. But you're like all the rest. I use you for your squalid egos and then I let you down."

She ground her cigarette into my chest. The stench of tarry burnt flesh filled my lungs.

"Red," I said.

"That is the one word life never says."

She slapped me, then spat on my face. This failed to fix the problem, so she unhooked the chain from the back of the harness, and I wasn't much better off than a tightrope walker with a noose around his neck. The plastic held her attention. She pulled a sheet between her hands and watched the ceiling light reflect crescents of white through the thin surface. I had one last chance to breathe in before she vacuum-wrapped my head up like a Tupperware container. The drumbeat that was my heart accelerated and the room became a translucent, airless bowl. Don put down his drink and stood up.

"I said, knock it off, Azy."

His hulking frame moved across the room, too slow for my liking, with his sad tired face doing what it had done too many times before.

Azy spun around, reached for the stun gun and pointed the barrel straight at centre mass. The weapon made a popping noise and bits of confetti flew out in a cannon burst. Two darts snaked across the room in a millisecond, punctured Don's chest and blew his arms back. He tumbled over the sofa, taking out the loaded cocktail table. Azy kept squeezing the trigger until he buckled up twice and went limp.

Then the room was silent. She gazed down at her victim as if he were a potted plant. A cluster of the paper chips had stuck to her arm. She wiped the sweat from her lips and then went over and picked up one of the spilled drinks. After sucking out what was mostly ice and carpet fur, she stood in front of me and plumbed the swizzle stick into my balls.

"Now we can get back to business," she said.

Her face was creased in a fashion I had never noticed before, long crevasses of the past that cut across her forehead. The jade L'Oréal base I had spent a hundred dollars on wasn't helping. No pupils. No skin tone. Basically, she looked half dead.

When her eyes drifted off in different directions, I couldn't tell what she was looking at or if she cared. I had already tried begging and knew that wasn't going to accomplish much, so the best I could do was pull an Audra and endure. Besides, with a sheet of plastic creeping down my throat there wasn't going to be much noise coming out. Azy let the shackles drop and the hemp cut in deep. The world bounced once, hard, the Klimt on the wall rattled and a fire alarm blew steam through my ears.

All the world was grey. Fuzzy and undersea-like. The curtains rustled. The lampshade fell over and for once, I felt fortunate that I had an exoskeletal neck structure. A hum crept out of the baseboards and coagulated in a flurry of shadows. At first the swarm settled on the fire hearth, then on the mantle. Onto the St. James's cross and over dolomite ashtrays. Then they darted from perch to perch and grew larger. Azy finally noticed them and stopped to stir her drink.

"Get lost," she said as if addressing an unwanted servant. She gazed up at the ceiling. Nothing. Behind the cross, gone too. The shapes always moving just out of her vision. She swore, picked up the photo of a slave from years past and pitched it across the room. Then maybe she just forgot. The fan on the ceiling flipped over and she used the breeze to cool her face. All the props were in place. The show could go on. We would all be famous once more. She spat the cherry out of the piña colada, then tossed the glass onto the carpet.

At that point, I understood a lot of things. The pleasure of not knowing how life might turn out. The foolishness of fractions. The half-truth of scripture. This glory of living in the absolute moment no matter how much one's soul might seek salvation from the past. So as Madam Alexis Dunwell's canting mouth opened into a black pit of pleasure, it came as no surprise that the horde of shadows, which had been flirting about her room, coalesced and swept down upon her perch.

No surprise either, that the room cut itself into a thousand cathedral images and I could see down each corridor. Into each escape route. Go forward, my servants, stripped and naked and see into that black heart of the beast. My shoulders expanded until ropes frayed and wavelengths of light deepened off both ends of the spectrum. From my broken cocoon, I saw Azy laying sprawled on the carpet covered in pith. With her arms splayed and nails broken she was ordinary, almost plain. But everything seems plain with calcified flesh, coruscated limbs and wings beating in the opportunity of morning. There was the wall, the stairs and I was in the kitchen, smelling the sink and the melted wax and watching a wide-eyed housekeeper staring at a creature she could not believe was real, and then I was out on the porch, through the fir boughs and down the alley towards both the lost, the found, the living and the dead.

Martin West was born in Victoria and spent his youth working and living in the Canadian west. His previous novel, *Long Ride Yellow*, won the 2018 ReLit Award for Fiction. He was previously a ReLit nominee in the short fiction category in 2016 for his collection *Cretacea and Other Stories from the Badlands* (recipient of a Gold IPPY award). The title story, "Cretacea," was a finalist for the Journey Prize, and his story "Miss Charlotte" appeared in the 2017 edition of Best Canadian Stories. Martin currently lives in Calgary, Alberta.